WARRIORS

TIGERHEART'S
SHADOW

DAWN OF THE CLANS

Book One: *The Sun Trail*
Book Two: *Thunder Rising*
Book Three: *The First Battle*
Book Four: *The Blazing Star*
Book Five: *A Forest Divided*
Book Six: *Path of Stars*

A VISION OF SHADOWS

Book One: *The Apprentice's Quest*
Book Two: *Thunder and Shadow*
Book Three: *Shattered Sky*
Book Four: *Darkest Night*

EXPLORE THE **WARRIORS** WORLD

Warriors Super Edition: Firestar's Quest
Warriors Super Edition: Bluestar's Prophecy
Warriors Super Edition: SkyClan's Destiny
Warriors Super Edition: Crookedstar's Promise
Warriors Super Edition: Yellowfang's Secret
Warriors Super Edition: Tallstar's Revenge
Warriors Super Edition: Bramblestar's Storm
Warriors Super Edition: Moth Flight's Vision
Warriors Super Edition: Hawkwing's Journey
Warriors Field Guide: Secrets of the Clans
Warriors: Cats of the Clans
Warriors: Code of the Clans
Warriors: Battles of the Clans
Warriors: Enter the Clans
Warriors: The Ultimate Guide

Warriors: The Untold Stories
Warriors: Tales from the Clans
Warriors: Shadows of the Clans
Warriors: Legends of the Clans

MANGA

The Lost Warrior

Warrior's Refuge

Warrior's Return

The Rise of Scourge

Tigerstar and Sasha #1: Into the Woods

Tigerstar and Sasha #2: Escape from the Forest

Tigerstar and Sasha #3: Return to the Clans

Ravenpaw's Path #1: Shattered Peace

Ravenpaw's Path #2: A Clan in Need

Ravenpaw's Path #3: The Heart of a Warrior

SkyClan and the Stranger #1: The Rescue

SkyClan and the Stranger #2: Beyond the Code

SkyClan and the Stranger #3: After the Flood

NOVELLAS

Hollyleaf's Story

Mistystar's Omen

Cloudstar's Journey

Tigerclaw's Fury

Leafpool's Wish

Mapleshade's Vengeance

Goosefeather's Curse

Ravenpaw's Farewell

Spottedleaf's Heart

Pinestar's Choice

Thunderstar's Echo

SURVIVORS

THE GATHERING DARKNESS

Survivors: Tales from the Packs

NOVELLAS

BRAVELANDS

WARRIORS
SUPER EDITION

TIGERHEART'S SHADOW

ERIN HUNTER

HARPER
An Imprint of HarperCollinsPublishers

Special thanks to Kate Cary

Tigerheart's Shadow
Copyright © 2017 by Working Partners Limited
Series created by Working Partners Limited
Map art © 2017 by Dave Stevenson
Interior art © 2017 by Owen Richardson
All rights reserved. Printed in the United States of America.

Library of Congress Control Number: 2017943577
ISBN 978-0-06-246772-0 (trade bdg.)
ISBN 978-0-06-246773-7 (lib. bdg.)

17 18 19 20 21   CG/LSCH   10 9 8 7 6 5 4 3 2 1
❖
First Edition

ALLEGIANCES

SHADOWCLAN

LEADER   ROWANSTAR—ginger tom

DEPUTY   TIGERHEART—dark brown tabby tom

MEDICINE CAT   PUDDLESHINE—brown tom with white splotches

WARRIORS   (toms and she-cats without kits)

TAWNYPELT—tortoiseshell she-cat with green eyes
APPRENTICE, SNAKEPAW (honey-colored tabby she-cat)

JUNIPERCLAW—black tom
APPRENTICE, WHORLPAW (gray-and-white tom)

STRIKESTONE—brown tabby tom

STONEWING—white tom

GRASSHEART—pale brown tabby she-cat

SCORCHFUR—dark gray tom with slashed ears
APPRENTICE, FLOWERPAW (silver she-cat)

QUEENS   (she-cats expecting or nursing kits)

SNOWBIRD—pure white she-cat with green eyes (mother to Gullkit, a white she-kit; Conekit, a white-and-gray tom; and Frondkit, a gray tabby she-kit)

ELDERS   (former warriors and queens, now retired)

OAKFUR—small brown tom

RATSCAR—scarred, skinny dark brown tom

THUNDERCLAN

LEADER   **BRAMBLESTAR**—dark brown tabby tom with amber eyes

DEPUTY   **SQUIRRELFLIGHT**—dark ginger she-cat with green eyes and one white paw

MEDICINE CATS   **LEAFPOOL**—light brown tabby she-cat with amber eyes, white paws and chest

JAYFEATHER—gray tabby tom with blind blue eyes

ALDERHEART—dark ginger tom with amber eyes

WARRIORS   **BRACKENFUR**—golden-brown tabby tom

CLOUDTAIL—long-haired white tom with blue eyes

BRIGHTHEART—white she-cat with ginger patches

THORNCLAW—golden-brown tabby tom

WHITEWING—white she-cat with green eyes

BIRCHFALL—light brown tabby tom

BERRYNOSE—cream-colored tom with a stump for a tail

MOUSEWHISKER—gray-and-white tom

POPPYFROST—pale tortoiseshell-and-white she-cat

LIONBLAZE—golden tabby tom with amber eyes

ROSEPETAL—dark cream she-cat

BRIARLIGHT—dark brown she-cat, paralyzed in her hindquarters

LILYHEART—small, dark tabby she-cat with white patches, and blue eyes

BUMBLESTRIPE—very pale gray tom with black stripes

IVYPOOL—silver-and-white tabby she-cat with dark blue eyes

APPRENTICE, TWIGPAW (gray she-cat with green eyes)

DOVEWING—pale gray she-cat with green eyes

CHERRYFALL—ginger she-cat

MOLEWHISKER—brown-and-cream tom

SNOWBUSH—white, fluffy tom

AMBERMOON—pale ginger she-cat

DEWNOSE—gray-and-white tom

STORMCLOUD—gray tabby tom

HOLLYTUFT—black she-cat

FERNSONG—yellow tabby tom

SORRELSTRIPE—dark brown she-cat

LEAFSHADE—tortoiseshell she-cat

LARKSONG—black tom

HONEYFUR—white she-cat with yellow splotches

SPARKPELT—orange tabby she-cat

QUEENS

DAISY—cream long-furred cat from the horseplace

CINDERHEART—gray tabby she-cat

BLOSSOMFALL—tortoiseshell-and-white she-cat with petal-shaped white patches (mother to Stemkit, a white-and-orange tom-kit; Eaglekit, a ginger she-kit; Plumkit, a black-and-ginger she-kit; and Shellkit, a white she-kit)

ELDERS	**GRAYSTRIPE**—long-haired gray tom
	MILLIE—striped silver tabby she-cat with blue eyes

WINDCLAN

LEADER	**HARESTAR**—brown-and-white tom
DEPUTY	**CROWFEATHER**—dark gray tom **APPRENTICE, FERNPAW** (gray tabby she-cat)
MEDICINE CAT	**KESTRELFLIGHT**—mottled gray tom with white splotches like kestrel feathers
WARRIORS	**BREEZEPELT**—black tom with amber eyes
	NIGHTCLOUD—black she-cat **APPRENTICE, BRINDLEPAW** (mottled brown she-cat)
	GORSETAIL—very pale gray-and-white she-cat with blue eyes
	LEAFTAIL—dark tabby tom with amber eyes
	EMBERFOOT—gray tom with two dark paws **APPRENTICE, SMOKEPAW** (gray she-cat)
	LARKWING—pale brown tabby she-cat
	SEDGEWHISKER—light brown tabby she-cat
	SLIGHTFOOT—black tom with white flash on his chest
	OATCLAW—pale brown tabby tom
	FEATHERPELT—gray tabby she-cat

HOOTWHISKER—dark gray tom

HEATHERTAIL—light brown tabby she-cat with blue eyes

ELDERS   **WHITETAIL**—small white she-cat

RIVERCLAN

LEADER   **MISTYSTAR**—gray she-cat with blue eyes

DEPUTY   **REEDWHISKER**—black tom

MEDICINE CATS   **MOTHWING**—dappled golden she-cat

WILLOWSHINE—gray tabby she-cat

WARRIORS   **MINTFUR**—light gray tabby tom
APPRENTICE, SOFTPAW (gray she-cat)

DUSKFUR—brown tabby she-cat
APPRENTICE, DAPPLEPAW (gray-and-white tom)

MINNOWTAIL—dark gray she-cat
APPRENTICE, BREEZEPAW (brown-and-white she-cat)

MALLOWNOSE—light brown tabby tom

BEETLEWHISKER—brown-and-white tabby tom
APPRENTICE, HAREPAW (white tom)

CURLFEATHER—pale brown she-cat

PODLIGHT—gray-and-white tom

HERONWING—dark gray-and-black tom

SHIMMERPELT—silver she-cat
APPRENTICE, NIGHTPAW (dark gray she-cat with blue eyes)

LIZARDTAIL—light brown tom

HAVENPELT—black-and-white she-cat

SNEEZECLOUD—gray-and-white tom

BRACKENPELT—tortoiseshell she-cat
APPRENTICE, GORSEPAW (white tom with gray ears)

JAYCLAW—gray tom

OWLNOSE—brown tabby tom

ICEWING—white she-cat with blue eyes

ELDERS   **MOSSPELT**—tortoiseshell-and-white she-cat

SKYCLAN

LEADER   **LEAFSTAR**—brown-and-cream tabby she-cat with amber eyes

DEPUTY   **HAWKWING**—dark gray tom with yellow eyes

WARRIORS   **SPARROWPELT**—dark brown tabby tom

MACGYVER—black-and-white tom
APPRENTICE, DEWPAW (sturdy gray tom)

PLUMWILLOW—dark gray she-cat

SAGENOSE—pale gray tom

HARRYBROOK—gray tom

BLOSSOMHEART—ginger-and-white she-cat
APPRENTICE, FINPAW (brown tom)

SANDYNOSE—stocky light brown tom with ginger legs

RABBITLEAP—brown tom
APPRENTICE, VIOLETPAW (black and white she-cat with yellow eyes)

BELLALEAF—pale orange she-cat with green eyes

    APPRENTICE, REEDPAW (small tabby she-cat)

QUEENS

TINYCLOUD—small white she-cat (mother to Quailkit, a tom with crow-black ears; Pigeonkit, a gray-and-white she-kit; and Sunnykit, a ginger she-kit)

ELDERS

FALLOWFERN—pale brown she-cat who has lost her hearing

TWOLEG NEST
GREENLEAF TWOLEGPLACE
TWOLEG PATH
TWOLEG PATH
CLEARING
SHADOWCLAN CAMP
SKYCLAN CAMP
HALFBRIDGE
SMALL THUNDERPATH
GREENLEAF TWOLEGPLACE
HALFBRIDGE
CAT VIEW
ISLAND
STREAM
RIVERCLAN CAMP
HORSEPLACE

MOONPOOL

ABANDONED
TWOLEG NEST

OLD THUNDERPATH

THUNDERCLAN
CAMP

ANCIENT OAK

LAKE

WINDCLAN
CAMP

BROKEN
HALFBRIDGE

TWOLEGPLACE

THUNDERPATH

KEY
To The
CLANS

THUNDERCLAN

RIVERCLAN

SHADOWCLAN

WINDCLAN

SKYCLAN

STARCLAN

NORTH

HAREVIEW
CAMPSITE

SANCTUARY
COTTAGE

SADLER WOODS

LITTLEPINE ROAD

LITTLEPINE
SAILING
CENTER

TWOLEG VI

LITTLEPINE
ISLAND

RIVER ALBA

WHITECHURCH ROAD

KNIGHT'S
COPSE

PROLOGUE
❧

The black tom had had this dream before. It was a dream of a forest, one that he had never visited in his waking life, and whose silence was unnerving to a cat who had grown up surrounded by Thunderpaths. As the dream took shape around him, he felt pine needles beneath his paws, and musty scents filled his nose. A thick bramble wall enclosed the clearing he stood in. It was swollen here and there by dens that seemed to have been woven into it. Cats squeezed in and out of them. Some crossed the clearing; some stopped to talk to one another; others padded eagerly toward a pile of prey at the far end, sometimes walking right by the black tom as if they didn't see him.

Because they didn't. He wasn't really there.

He'd seen these same cats each time he visited the dream, and he was learning to recognize their pelts. Now a brown tom with white splotches and light blue eyes carried a bundle of fragrant-smelling leaves toward one of the dens. A skinny old tom slid out to greet him. "I'm glad you've come." The old cat nudged him inside. "He's been coughing all night."

At the other side of the clearing, a tortoiseshell she-cat murmured anxiously to a large ginger tom. A pure white

1

she-cat watched, her pelt ruffled. Behind them, three young cats shifted their paws uneasily.

The dreaming tom pricked his ears. *These cats have never been this worried in their lives . . . and they don't know what to do.*

Anxiety was fluttering in his belly. Why did he dream of this place? What did it mean? As he wondered this, the forest blurred around him. The ground seemed to shift beneath his paws; then suddenly it fell away, and he swirled into darkness.

Stars spun around him until, with a jolt, he felt solid ground beneath his paws again. Soft green meadows rolled away from him on every side. Above him, a wide blue sky stretched to the distant horizon.

More cats. The dreaming tom blinked as he saw ranks of cats lined before him, their pelts sparkling with starlight and their eyes flashing eagerly. They were staring straight at him. His belly tightened with alarm. "How . . . how can you *see* me?"

A black she-cat stepped forward and dipped her head. Her fur was sleek, her frame well-muscled, as though she'd never known the hardships of hunger or cold. "Don't be frightened," she told him softly. "We mean you no harm."

A broad-shouldered dark tabby tom joined her. "We need you to do something for us."

"What can *I* do?" The dreaming tom stared at her. "I'm not like you cats. . . ."

"You take care of those around you, don't you?" the black she-cat asked.

"I do what I can to ease their illness and heal their wounds."

The she-cat blinked slowly. "A cat who cares for others is

special to us," she mewed. "That is why we chose you to be our messenger."

"Strangers will come to your home," the broad-shouldered tabby chimed in. "They will need your help, just as we need it."

Puzzled, the dreaming tom frowned. "And you need me to give them a message?"

"Not exactly," the black cat meowed quickly. "But let these strangers guide your paws."

The dreaming tom's gaze drifted past the she-cat to the starry cats gathered behind her. Their eyes were fixed on him, burning with need. He backed away, his heart quickening. Why had they chosen *him*? "I don't understand."

"Please!" The black she-cat's mew was tinged with fear. "If you don't help . . ." Then her voice trailed away, and the vision of the starry cats and meadows began to dissolve into darkness. In its place the dreaming tom saw the forest clearing once more. But the bramble walls were torn, the dens ripped open. The tortoiseshell she-cat lay at the head of the clearing, blood oozing from wounds scarring her pelt. The three young cats he'd seen stumbled past. One collapsed, a gash showing across his belly. The old tom lay panting beside shredded branches. A brown cat was sitting nearby, so thin that his bones showed though his thin pelt. His pale blue eyes stared desolately at the fallen cats as though he were frozen to stone by their suffering.

With a jolt, the dreaming tom woke. The first thing he felt was the weight of the small tom-kit sleeping in the curve of his belly. He lifted his head and blinked into the darkness, his heart pounding. The kit whimpered and twitched, clearly having a dream of his own.

He wondered, just for a moment, if it was a similar dream.

"Rest, little one." The tom leaned down and soothed the kit with a soft lap of his tongue. His dream lingered, unsettling him. *If you don't help* . . . The black she-cat's frightened words stuck in his mind. He tried to tell himself it was just a meaningless voice in his head. And yet he couldn't shake the feeling that it was important. . . . He'd dreamed of the brambled clearing before, but his dream had never shifted to the dark place of starry cats. He wondered if it meant something. As the kit quieted and relaxed once more into deep sleep, the tom stared into the shadowy night. *Dreams are just dreams.* He tried to dismiss it. But this dream had felt too real to be ignored.

Chapter 1

Worry pricked at Tigerheart's paws as he bounded between the pines, moving so fast he barely caught their scent.

I have to reach Dovewing. . . .

He leaped over ragged roots, his tail slapping against tree trunks and his legs battering the long grass. His pelt prickled with anticipation, and his belly fur tingled with nerves.

He always grew tense when he got too far away from ShadowClan. It was still struggling to rebuild itself in the aftermath of the rogue leader Darktail's meddling—first tempting away its younger members, then challenging Rowanstar for the leadership. ShadowClan had turned on its leader and chosen to follow the rogue. Rowanstar, Tawnypelt, and Tigerheart had abandoned the camp to Darktail and his "Kin," and Darktail had proved himself even more brutal and vicious than Tigerheart could ever have imagined. Many ShadowClan cats had died or gone missing. Then RiverClan suffered as Darktail took his war to them. Eventually, all of the Clans joined together in fighting back, but even now, Tigerheart could not let himself relax. He was constantly worried that danger was out there somewhere.

Today, though, his biggest worry was that Dovewing wouldn't wait for him.

He skidded down the slippery rise and jumped a ditch. The sun was starting to sink.

I miss her. I got too used to seeing her every day, he admitted to himself.

When Darktail's rogues had driven them from their Clan, Tigerheart, Rowanstar, and Tawnypelt had sought sanctuary with ThunderClan. Living beside Dovewing every day, he'd felt the love he'd once tried to leave behind flaring anew. At first she'd kept her distance, but he knew that her old feelings had been stirred, just as his had been. And when they were sent on a quest to find Twigpaw, they grew closer than they'd ever been.

After ShadowClan had reclaimed its old territory, they'd made an agreement to meet—whenever they could—in the dappled glade on SkyClan land, just beyond the place where the ShadowClan and ThunderClan borders touched.

Tigerheart knew he was being disloyal to his Clan. He had told Rowanstar that he was going to patrol the border, and instead he was meeting Dovewing. The lie still felt sour on his tongue. Dishonesty was the last thing his Clan needed right now. Rowanstar had lost confidence in his leadership, and with so few cats, the whole Clan was stretched to its limit just keeping up hunting patrols and border patrols, let alone fortifying the camp against harsh leaf-bare weather. Food was scarce, and the shattered dens were still not ready for the first snow. Rowanstar needed his support now more than ever.

Tigerheart had been trying his best to restore his Clan's

confidence by backing up his father's decisions and setting an example for his Clanmates, as their deputy. But the strain of such responsibility was tiring. Being with Dovewing let him forget his troubles for a while. With her, there was no need to carry the weight of his Clan. He could let the burden slip from his shoulders and simply be himself. Once he reached her, the anxious tingling in his paws would disappear.

Ears pricked, he rounded a bramble patch and crossed a stretch of withered ferns. His heart quickened as he imagined Dovewing scanning the forest, hoping to catch a glimpse of him. A purr rumbled in his throat. He was nearly there, the misty forest air slicking his pelt. *Please still be waiting!*

He raced up the slope to where the trees thinned. Ahead, sunshine seeped through the mist and lit the sheltered glade. Beyond the bracken he saw pale gray fur. His heart soared. *Dovewing.* Two days apart had been too long. He crashed through the damp undergrowth and scrambled to a halt beside her.

Her eyes flashed with relief. "You came." Dovewing thrust her muzzle into his neck fur. She was trembling, and he thought he could hear a note of worry in her mew.

She was silent so long, apprehension spiked through Tigerheart's fur. "Did some cat find out about us?"

"No." Dovewing's ears twitched nervously.

"What is it, then?" Tigerheart stared at her blankly. What could be so bad that she couldn't find the words? "Something's wrong. I can tell. . . ." *Have you stopped loving me?* He braced himself.

"I'm expecting kits."

Kits? Shock numbed him. "Mine?" He wasn't thinking straight.

"Of course yours!" Fury flared in Dovewing's eyes. She lifted a paw to bat at his muzzle.

He barely felt it. He was too shocked by what she'd said. *Kits . . . our kits!*

He took a deep breath to gather himself—the last thing Dovewing needed was him gawking at thin air.

"That was a dumb thing to say. I'm sorry. You just . . . took me by surprise." Then the tingling of joy he'd been starting to feel began to fade. "Have you told Ivypool?" Dovewing had always been close to her sister.

"Ivypool barely talks to me these days. I think she suspects I'm seeing you." She stared at the ground, her eyes full of sadness. Alarm rippled through Tigerheart's pelt, and his breath quickened. How could they hide their relationship now? What would this secret do to ShadowClan? It was already so fragile. Cats were bound to take sides in a scandal like this. And the fallout might destroy the uneasy peace that had passed for unity since the rogues had left.

He saw the expectation in Dovewing's gaze shrink to disappointment as he stared at her wordlessly. His thoughts were spinning, but he had no idea what to say.

She looked away. "This makes things so much harder, doesn't it?"

Tigerheart shook his head. Having kits with Dovewing was something he'd dreamed of, and yet . . . "It's bad timing, Dovewing. Our warriors are losing respect for Rowanstar.

And they keep looking at me, like I'm supposed to take his place."

"Is that what you want?" Dovewing stared at him with wide eyes.

Tigerheart shifted his paws, trying to find the right words. "ShadowClan is weaker than it's ever been. They need a leader they can believe in."

Dovewing inhaled sharply. "And that leader has to be *you*?"

"I don't know." Tigerheart stared at the grass beneath his feet. "I'm trying to support Rowanstar, but that might not be enough."

"What about me?" Dovewing's mew caught in her throat. "What about *us*?"

Tigerheart felt his heart breaking. *There* must *be an us. I've struggled too long without you* . . . "I love you, Dovewing. I will *always* love you. We can sort this out, I promise."

Raising his head, he cleared away the choking thoughts of Clanmates and responsibility and gazed at Dovewing. He could see her belly growing already and imagined the tiny kits inside. A purr broke from his throat. *Our kits.* He weaved around her, letting his purr throb through his whole body and hers. "Our kits will be beautiful and brave. They will grow into fine warriors."

As he spoke, hope flickered in his chest. Perhaps this was meant to be—perhaps these new kits would help restore ShadowClan to its former strength. "You can join Shadow-Clan *with* me. We could be together. There would be no more hiding or lying, and we could bring up our kits in the same

Clan." It seemed the perfect solution. His belly tingled with apprehension, but he hoped that she would be excited about raising their *shared* kin in the pine forest. It might take her a little while to get used to ShadowClan's ways, but she'd be so well cared for, he knew she could be happy there.

He knew *they* could be happy there.

His thoughts were tumbling so fast over one another, he hardly felt her freeze. Only when he pressed his muzzle against her cheek did he realize that she'd become as stiff as stone.

"I can't do that." She stared at the ground, defeat heavy in her gaze.

"I know it will be hard, but Dovewing, it might be the best thing for the kits." Tigerheart tried to catch her eye. "The best thing for *us.*" *And for ShadowClan.*

Slowly she lifted her gaze. Fear shimmered in her eyes. "I wish I could believe that," she began haltingly. "But . . . I've been having dreams."

"Dreams?" Tigerheart struggled to understand. Dovewing wasn't a medicine cat. She'd lost her special powers moons ago when the Dark Forest had been beaten. "All cats have dreams."

"Not like these." Dovewing's gaze glittered unnervingly. Whatever she was about to say, she believed strongly. "These dreams mean something. I can *feel* it."

Tigerheart's pelt prickled with alarm. "Are they . . . *bad* dreams?"

"I dream of the ThunderClan nursery. I'm alone in the camp, and I'm watching the nursery from the clearing. Something feels wrong, so I go to look inside." The fur along her spine lifted as she remembered. "It's empty. The nests are old and tattered, and shadows are creeping from the corners. They swallow the floor and the nests. I run outside, but the shadows follow. They reach through the entrance like dark flames and lick the walls, growing darker and stronger until the whole nursery is lost in blackness."

As she spoke, Tigerheart felt like he could see everything she described, so clearly. He had to shake his head to chase the images out of his head. "It's just a dream," he told her, not sure if he believed it himself.

Dovewing drew away. "But it's not!" Her mew was taut with fear. "I have it again and again, and every time I do, I wake up filled with dread because I know it's a sign."

Tigerheart blinked at her. The fear in her eyes was real, but he tried to tell himself it was just because she'd been worrying about this by herself for so long. She could share the worry with him now. "Have you asked Jayfeather or Alderheart about it?"

"How could I?" Dovewing lashed her tail. "They might guess." She glared down at her swelling flanks. "I've been expecting for a moon and it's starting to show. They may have already guessed I'm expecting kits. Telling them I'm having dreams about the nursery will just confirm it!"

Tigerheart tried to make his voice sound bright . "If a medicine cat believes that nursery dreams are normal, perhaps they are."

"Not like this!" Dovewing hissed.

"Well, you could ask them if they've had any signs from

StarClan." Tigerheart was starting to feel exasperated. Why was Dovewing so sure her dreams were special? "Maybe they've had a sign that will explain your dream. They're medicine cats, after all. You aren't."

"I don't need a medicine cat to explain my dream!" Dovewing's eyes flashed with frustration. "I *know* what it means. It means our kits mustn't be born in ThunderClan!"

Tigerheart fluffed out his pelt eagerly. "So . . . maybe you're meant to join ShadowClan! That's great. I know you'll be happy with us. Don't worry about any cat's reaction, either. No cat has time right now to get mad at having a ThunderClan cat in camp. And if we bring new kits, new life, to Shadow-Clan, then every cat will be happy, because we'll be making ShadowClan stronger."

"No." Dovewing glowered at him. "I'm not raising our kits in ShadowClan. Believe me, I've thought about that, and I know it's what you want, but . . . That's not what's right for us either." Tigerheart forced his pelt to smooth. *Neither Thunder-Clan nor ShadowClan?* What, then, was she thinking about?

Dovewing's mew was firm. "We have to leave the Clans."

Stunned, Tigerheart stared at her wordlessly. *Leave the Clans?*

"We *have* to." Dovewing dug her paws into the earth. "I've dreamed where we should go. A huge Twolegplace with nests that reach into the sky. I saw a roof there with sharp points that stick up into the sky like gorse spines. We must find that den. Our kits will be safe there."

Tigerheart's pelt bristled with anger. "This is nonsense!" He met her gaze. "Why would our kits be safer in a strange

Twolegplace? How can we raise them away from their Clans? Our Clans are what keep us all safe!"

Dovewing narrowed her eyes. "The Clans are a mess! So many cats have died fighting for territory lately, who's to say there will even *be* Clans a few moons from now?"

"So you want us to run away?" Tigerheart could hardly believe this was happening. "You want to abandon your Clanmates? You want to bring up our kits so they never know their kin or the warrior code?"

"No!" Desperation sharpened Dovewing's mew. "I don't *want* any of this! I just know we must go. The dreams come every night. I don't just see them; I *feel* them. If I ignore what they tell me, I fear that something terrible will happen to our kits!"

Tigerheart turned in an anxious circle, his thoughts fighting one another.

"This isn't a choice for me." Dovewing's mew hardened. "It's what I must do."

Tigerheart felt sick. "I can't just leave."

Dovewing's eyes were stricken with panic. Tigerheart looked away. His forepaws twitched, as if ready to walk with her as far away from here as she wanted to go. But his hindquarters felt heavy, like they wanted to pin him to the ground so that he could never leave ShadowClan. He yearned to be with her, but he was afraid to abandon his father when things were so terrible. It made him feel like his body might be torn in two.

"Tigerheart!" She sounded anxious.

He felt her breath on his cheek and forced himself to look at her.

"I don't want to do this without you, Tigerheart!" Her mew was shaky. "I need you."

"*ShadowClan* needs me," Tigerheart mewed desperately. "Rowanstar can't lead without my help. You're right—Shadow-Clan's a mess. If I leave, it may not survive."

"Then stay!" Dovewing's green eyes flashed with rage. "If your Clan is more important to you than your kits, stay with them. I'm going." She backed away from him, grief twisting her face. "My Clan can look after itself. I'm protecting my kits."

"Dovewing!" Desperation spiked Tigerheart's pelt. "We'll be better able to protect our kits if we stay with our Clans."

She held his gaze. "I'm leaving in three days. If you want to leave with me, meet me here. If not, I . . ." Her tail bushed, and she looked at the ground briefly. Whatever she had to tell him next seemed hard for her to say. "I will go without you."

Then she turned and pushed her way through the under-growth.

Tigerheart stared after her, his heart beating so loudly in his ears that it drowned the sound of birdsong. A gust of wind sent the mist swirling among the trees and rocked their branches. He felt dizzy. Dovewing had given him an impossible choice. She needed him. His unborn kits needed him. But so did ShadowClan. *Who needs me the most?*

CHAPTER 2

❧

Can I leave? Should I stay?

Two days had passed since Dovewing's ultimatum, and still Tigerheart's thoughts chased around his head like kittens trying to catch their own tails. He had one more day to make up his mind, but the right decision felt like a piece of prey he just could not catch. *What am I going to do?*

"Tigerheart?" Grassheart's mew shook him from his thoughts.

He turned his gaze distractedly toward her and found the pale brown tabby blinking at him. "We're supposed to be hunting, right?" Irritation edged her mew.

"Yes." Tigerheart shook out his pelt. "Sorry. I was thinking about something else."

"Think later. Our Clanmates are hungry." Grassheart sniffed and cast her sharp gaze around the forest. "We need to take something back to the fresh-kill pile. Have you noticed the way Ratscar's ribs are sticking through his pelt?"

Guilt dropped like another stone in Tigerheart's belly. His Clanmates were hungry. Dovewing was expecting kits. His father was struggling to regain the respect of their Clan. He should be able to fix everything, but he couldn't even focus on catching prey.

Snowbird's white pelt showed between the withering ferns a few tail-lengths away. The she-cat was sniffing the pine-strewn earth. "I think I've picked up a rabbit trail."

Grassheart hurried to her side. "How fresh is it?"

"Fresh enough." Snowbird began to creep away from the ferns, her tail-tip twitching with excitement. As Grassheart shadowed her, Tigerheart glanced toward the SkyClan border. He could smell their scent where it marked the pines at the top of the rise. Had he made the right decision when he suggested SkyClan should take some of ShadowClan's land? There might be more prey if they had more space to hunt. And yet how could they spare the cats needed to cover so much territory? He flicked his tail. It *had* been the right thing to do. SkyClan needed a home. And after all the problems the Clans had had with the rogues, maybe StarClan would look favorably on cats who spread kindness where there had been fear and mistrust. He just wished his Clanmates thought the same. But Scorchfur, Snowbird, and Stonewing had made it clear that they were not going to pretend they were content to give up land to another Clan. Tigerheart closed his eyes as fresh worries crowded his thoughts.

Above him, thrushes sounded like they were having their own arguments over territory. A cold wind rustled the branches. Grassheart and Snowbird were out of sight now, tracking the rabbit. As Tigerheart turned to follow them, paw steps thrummed at the top of the rise.

"Hey, Tigerheart!" Sandynose stood at the SkyClan border, Rabbitleap beside him. Their pelts were ruffled and their eyes bright. Sandynose's flanks heaved. "The squirrels in this forest are fast!" He glanced at the trunk of the pine beside him. A tail bobbed upward and disappeared among the branches.

Rabbitleap dipped his head politely to Tigerheart. "I hope you're having better luck than us."

"Not yet," Tigerheart mewed heavily. Did luck have anything to do with it? Perhaps if he were a better warrior, he'd be able to feed his Clan single-pawed. If he were a better son, Rowanstar wouldn't be so overwhelmed by leadership. If he were a better mate—

Small paws thumped the ground.

Grassheart's urgent mew sounded through the trees. "Prey!"

Tigerheart stiffened as a rabbit raced past him, shooting up the rise so fast he didn't have time to untangle himself from his thoughts and give chase. It hared across the border, a tail-length from Sandynose.

The SkyClan tom ran after it. Pelt bristling with excitement, Rabbitleap raced after him.

Tigerheart froze. He'd let prey fall into another Clan's paws.

"You mouse-brain!" Grassheart thundered to a halt beside him. "Why didn't you catch it?"

Snowbird caught up to them, eyes sparking with anger. "We drove it straight toward you!" She shot a look at Grassheart. "I thought Rowanstar was the unreliable one."

"Like father, like son," Grassheart snorted crossly.

"That's not fair!" Tigerheart shot back. "Rowanstar could outhunt any of you, and I was distracted—"

He realized the two she-cats had stopped listening. They were looking up the deserted slope. Their noses twitched.

"I smell SkyClan." Snowbird curled her lip at Tigerheart. "Is that what distracted you? Were there SkyClan cats here?"

"I was talking to Sandynose and Rabbitleap," Tigerheart confessed. He wished that was all that had been distracting him.

Grassheart frowned as she stared at the churned pine needles where the rabbit had scrambled to the top of the slope. "And you let our prey run right into their paws," she growled.

Irritation rippled beneath Tigerheart's pelt. He'd had enough of trying to persuade his Clanmates that having Sky-Clan as neighbors would make them safer, not weaker. He was tired of making excuses for Rowanstar. He was tired of chasing prey that preferred other Clans' land. *Maybe I should leave with Dovewing!* Dovewing made him happy. She needed him, and so did their kits. And he loved her.

Pine needles swished at the top of the rise. Sandynose and Rabbitleap appeared at the border. The fat rabbit Tigerheart had missed was dangling from Sandynose's jaws.

Snowbird hissed, her eyes glittering with fury. "Have you come to gloat with *our* prey?"

Sandynose tossed the dead rabbit down the slope. "We came to return it." He glared haughtily at the white she-cat.

Snowbird bristled. "We don't need you to hunt for us!"

Tigerheart caught her eye, warning her to be quiet. When a Clan was hungry, pride was sometimes worth swallowing.

Grassheart padded toward the rabbit and glanced back at Snowbird. "Ratscar will be grateful for the meal."

Snowbird narrowed her eyes. Tigerheart looked at her expectantly. Surely she could smell the warmth of its blood? Wasn't she hungry enough to accept SkyClan's kindness? Tigerheart's belly ached with hunger. He hadn't eaten since sunhigh yesterday.

Grassheart turned her gaze to him. "We should take it."

Tigerheart nodded. "It would have been our catch if I'd been quicker."

As Snowbird growled under her breath, Grassheart dipped her head to Sandynose and Rabbitleap. "It was kind of you to return the prey."

Sandynose bowed stiffly and turned away. Wordlessly, the SkyClan warriors padded from the border.

Snowbird sniffed. "They're almost as smug as Thunder-Clan."

"They were being generous," Grassheart pointed out.

Tigerheart's pelt prickled hotly. Another Clan had killed prey that he should have caught. He tried to ignore his shame. At least this was a chance to persuade Snowbird that giving SkyClan their land had been a good idea. "We're lucky to have such honorable warriors close by."

Snowbird headed back toward the ferns, her tail twitching. "Only you could see luck in losing half our territory," she grumbled.

Grassheart rolled her eyes at him. "She'll be fine once she sees Ratscar eating this." She scooped up the rabbit and headed toward home.

Tigerheart scanned the clearing as he led Grassheart and Snowbird into camp. "Where's Ratscar?" he called to Whorlpaw, who was sharing tongues with Flowerpaw at the edge. There was no sign of the skinny elder.

Whorlpaw looked up. "He's doing border patrol with Juniperclaw."

Tigerheart blinked. Elders weren't supposed to go on border patrol.

Scorchfur was at the fresh-kill pile. "I offered to take his place, but he said there were so few cats in ShadowClan now, he should help." His gaze flicked to the rabbit Grassheart was carrying. "Nice catch." He looked hopefully at Snowbird. "Any more where that came from?"

"We'll go out again soon," Tigerheart promised. He glanced at Rowanstar and Tawnypelt at the head of the clearing. They were talking, their pelts prickling anxiously. Shouldn't they be leading a hunting patrol? Talking wasn't going to save the Clan.

The bramble entrance rustled. Tigerheart turned, surprised to see Juniperclaw leading Willowshine and Alderheart into the camp. He pricked his ears. It was strange to have the ThunderClan medicine cat here, even stranger to see RiverClan's. Mistystar had been determined to restore her Clan's strength and had decided, after the last Gathering, that she should close its borders. So why was Willowshine roaming outside her territory?

Ratscar followed them in, his mangy old pelt rippling with unease.

Tigerheart sat down in the shadow of the rock and watched the two medicine cats approach Rowanstar. They looked worried. Did they bring news from StarClan? Perhaps they'd had a vision as ominous as Dovewing's dreams. Perhaps Alderheart had noticed that she was expecting kits. He searched the ThunderClan tom's gaze, looking for a sign that Alderheart knew more than he should, but Alderheart was staring at Rowanstar as Willowshine spoke.

"I've had a vision. We need to find a cat with an extra claw," she told the ShadowClan leader. "It's the only way to fend off the coming storm."

"Do you know any cats with six toes?" Alderheart leaned forward, his gaze fixing more intently on Rowanstar.

No visions of shadows swallowing the ThunderClan nursery. No hint that Dovewing was expecting kits. Tigerheart's thoughts drifted. *Should I be relieved?* If the medicine cats hadn't shared Dovewing's dream, maybe she *was* wrong. This new prophecy about a six-toed cat might be enough to show her that her dream was just a dream. If it was something more, then StarClan would have shared it with the medicine cats, not just her.

Scorchfur's sharp mew hooked him from his thoughts. "How can we send out a search party? We have barely enough cats to patrol our borders."

Rowanstar dipped his head in agreement. "The SkyClan border can't be left unguarded."

Anxiety pricked Tigerheart's belly. How could he leave a Clan that didn't even have enough cats for a search party? *There must be some way to persuade Dovewing to stay.* He pictured meeting her at sunset tomorrow. What could he say to make her see that they would be safer raising kits with their Clans, beside the lake? And yet he couldn't shake the worry that maybe she was right: Darktail had nearly destroyed them. Perhaps the Clans were no longer strong enough to protect their kits.

An angry hiss jerked him from his thoughts. Scorchfur and Tawnypelt were facing each other, eyes blazing with fury.

"Why do you think we chose a rogue over Rowanstar?" Scorchfur snarled. "He was a weak leader then; he's a weak leader now."

Tawnypelt's fur bushed. Spitting, she sliced her claws across her Clanmate's muzzle.

Tigerheart froze. What was happening? Why was his Clan fighting *itself*? As he watched, Scorchfur swung his claws at Tawnypelt's face.

Tawnypelt ducked away, yowling with pain.

Her eye! Panic sparked Tigerheart into action. With a yowl, he threw himself between the fighting cats. He shoved Scorchfur away from Tawnypelt and shielded her, hissing.

Rowanstar stared, his gaze stricken with shock.

Tigerheart turned to face Tawnypelt. "Are you okay?" He gasped at the blood welling beside his mother's eye. He felt fur brush his flank as Puddleshine slid in beside him and gently eased him out of the way.

What in StarClan had they been fighting about? Dazed with shock, Tigerheart turned. Alderheart and Willowshine were hurrying out of camp. Scorchfur had backed to the edge of the clearing.

Rowanstar stared at the dark gray tom with undisguised contempt. "How can we trust a Clanmate who turns on his own so easily?"

Scorchfur glared back at him. "How can we trust a leader who gives up on his Clan at the first sign of threat?"

Tigerheart's gaze flitted from the two toms back to his mother. Puddleshine was quickly lapping the blood beside her eye. "It's only a flesh wound," he reassured her. "Your vision won't be harmed."

Relief swept Tigerheart as Puddleshine led Tawnypelt toward the medicine den. He could hardly believe that one Clanmate had tried to blind another. Nothing could be further from the warrior code. He'd known tensions had been running high, but how had it come to this? *I should have stopped it.* If his thoughts hadn't been wrapped up in Dovewing, he might have prevented his Clanmates turning on one another. *Instead I was worrying about whether I should leave my Clan.* Guilt choked him. He pictured Dovewing, waiting, frightened and alone, carrying their kits. Love seemed to tear his heart into two; the pain left him breathless.

"Tigerheart." Puddleshine was padding toward him, Rowanstar at his heels.

"Is Tawnypelt all right?" Tigerheart met his gaze anxiously.

Puddleshine nodded. "She's in my den. I put herbs on the wound. She's resting. But I must speak with you and your father."

Tigerheart frowned. "Why?"

The medicine cat's gaze moved from father to son, dark with warning. "There's something I must share with both of you."

CHAPTER 3

Tigerheart glanced uneasily around the camp. Was there time to talk with Puddleshine? The fight between Scorchfur and Tawny-pelt must have shocked the Clan. Perhaps they should be reassuring their Clanmates instead.

"Snakepaw." Strikestone waved the apprentice closer with a flick of his tail. "Come with me. We're going hunting." He was clearly trying to divert her attention from her mentor Tawny-pelt's injury, and the tensions within the Clan.

The honey-brown tabby she-cat looked at him eagerly. "Can Whorlpaw and Flowerpaw come?"

Strikestone turned to their mentors, Juniperclaw and Scorchfur. "We can hunt together. The fresh-kill pile needs filling, and the youngsters can practice hunting in groups." He eyed Scorchfur warily, as though worried the dark gray tom was still enraged enough to claw at his Clanmates' eyes.

But Scorchfur dipped his head and grunted. "Okay." He beckoned Whorlpaw toward the entrance with a flick of his muzzle, then padded after him as he headed into the forest. Flowerpaw and Snakepaw exchanged glances, then followed, Juniperclaw at their heels, Strikestone just behind him.

Tigerheart stepped toward the brown tabby tom. "Thank you," he purred.

Strikestone dipped his head. "Don't mention it," he said, before joining the others on their way out of camp.

Tigerheart watched them go, enjoying the feeling of his anxiety draining away. It was good to see the warriors working together to diffuse the tension and keep the apprentices busy. Rowanstar hadn't even seemed to notice. He was staring at Puddleshine. "What do you want to tell us?"

As Puddleshine lifted his chin, Tigerheart remembered suddenly how young the medicine cat was. In the moons since he'd earned his medicine-cat name, the young tom had seen so much. They all had. It was easy to forget that Puddleshine had been trained by Leafpool from kit to full medicine cat in little more than a moon. And yet Tigerheart trusted him now as much as he'd once trusted Littlecloud. He could see earnestness in the young tom's pale blue eyes as Puddleshine began to speak.

"I had a vision this morning. I was watching the camp as it woke. The rising sun cut through the branches and sent long shadows over our Clanmates as they climbed out of their dens and began to move around the clearing. As I watched them padding in and out of the shadows, the sun seemed to strengthen. I could see it beyond the forest, growing fiery, and, as it did, the shadows in the camp became longer, darker—"

"Are you sure this was a vision?" Rowanstar looked puzzled. "It sounds like any other sunrise."

Puddleshine gave a slow nod. "The sun shone *intensely*," he breathed. "As though, at any moment, the whole forest might catch fire. And the shadows were so dark, it looked as though night had cut swaths through the camp. Between the shadows, the sunlight was blinding. Not like dawn light. It was so bright, I had to turn away." He stopped, shifted his paws. "Then, suddenly, the sun dimmed. It faded beyond the trees and became so weak that it seemed to melt into the pale dawn sky. As it did, the shadows faded. The fierce stripes that had marked the clearing dissolved until no trace of shadow was left in camp. For a moment, the whole forest was awash in sunlight so soft that it was impossible to distinguish between light and shade."

"The shadows disappeared." Tigerheart breathed the words. He could barely imagine it. The camp had always been shaped by shadow. Even at sunhigh, the pines and brambles marked the clearing with patches of darkness.

Puddleshine blinked at him. "Without shadows, what is ShadowClan?"

Tigerheart knew the stories the other Clans told of ShadowClan—how darkness molded their hearts, how they thrived on the power they found in shadow where other Clans would wither. Of course, they were just nursery tales, told to frighten kits, but wasn't there some truth in those stories? To be a ShadowClan cat was to grow up in the enclosing gloom of the forest, to feel hidden and protected by it, to learn to move within it and use its cover for stealth. "But you said when the vision started, the sun was strong."

Puddleshine nodded. "And the shadows were strong."

Rowanstar flicked his tail. "But shadows are *always* strongest when the sun is strongest. We've always known that."

Puddleshine stared at him. "The vision was sent to remind us that when the sun is strong, the shadows are strong."

Tigerheart's pelt pricked ominously. "And when the sun fades, the shadows fade."

Puddleshine's ears twitched nervously. "In the vision, the shadows *disappeared*."

Tigerheart swallowed. Was Puddleshine trying to tell them that ShadowClan was going to disappear?

"But how can we control the sun?" Rowanstar looked confused.

Puddleshine dropped his gaze. "Perhaps we don't have to. I think the sun represented something else," he murmured.

Rowanstar stared at him, his pelt prickling irritably. "What could it possibly represent?"

You. Tigerheart stared at his father. How could he fail to understand? *The sun represents you.* His throat tightened. If Rowanstar was weak, then ShadowClan would disappear. Wasn't that what was happening already? He pictured Scorchfur's claw flashing toward Tawnypelt's eye. The Clan was crumbling. *You have to be strong.* The words dried on his tongue. How could he accuse his father of being weak in front of their Clanmates? It would crush him.

He looked hopefully at Puddleshine. Perhaps *he* was going to warn Rowanstar.

"So?" Rowanstar glanced impatiently at Puddleshine. "Tell me what the sun represents. You're the medicine cat. You're meant to know these things."

Tigerheart's chest tightened. *Tell him.*

Puddleshine glanced apologetically at Rowanstar. "We are being warned that ShadowClan may disappear."

Tell him that he's the sun! Perhaps Puddleshine didn't realize what the vision meant. Or perhaps he believed that warning Rowanstar he was weak might weaken him further. Tigerheart tried to read Puddleshine's gaze, but he saw only worry.

"What should we *do*?" Rowanstar flicked his tail.

Tigerheart looked his father in the eye. "We must stay strong," he meowed. "As strong as the sun."

Rowanstar just looked at him. Tigerheart stared back, waiting for the ginger tom's eyes to light up with understanding.

But Rowanstar looked as confused as the other cats. Tigerheart wondered if maybe he should say something to his father. . . .

But won't that make him look weak, if he needs his deputy to explain a vision to him?

He turned away, feeling sick. Tomorrow, Dovewing was expecting him to leave the forest with her. But how could he abandon his Clan now, when they needed him most? Rowanstar clearly needed support. If Tigerheart left now, then the shadows would fade. ShadowClan would disappear.

But Dovewing was willing to make her journey alone if she had to. He had to stop her. Once he'd made sure that Rowanstar and ShadowClan were strong again, then they could journey wherever she wanted to go.

He ran across the clearing, anxiety fizzing in his pelt. He

headed for the entrance and ducked through the bramble tunnel. The damp leaf-fall air seeped into his fur as he headed for the ThunderClan border. He felt cold. The ground felt chilly beneath his paws. He had to talk to someone. He had to save his Clan. He had to save Dovewing.

As he neared the border and ThunderClan scents began to drift between the trees, he slowed. The fear that gripped him spiraled into panic. *What am I doing?* He couldn't reveal their secret about the kits! If Dovewing's Clan rejected her, she'd never forgive him. She had a plan. He couldn't ruin it by betraying her.

He stopped. But what if Dovewing told a Clanmate about the kits herself? What if she felt close enough to another cat to confide her fears?

Ivypool! Of course! The sisters had been close until recently. Dovewing had complained that her sister hardly spoke to her now. She must miss having Ivypool to confide in. *If I can mend their relationship, Dovewing might tell Ivypool everything.* Tigerheart lifted his head eagerly. *And then Ivypool could persuade her to stay.*

Tigerheart snatched desperately at the hope. He broke into a run. He had to find Ivypool and speak to her!

Tigerheart crouched beside the ThunderClan border until sunset. When there was still no sign of Ivypool, he crossed it. Slinking through the shadows, his mouth open to taste for scents, he crept across ThunderClan land. What if she was patrolling the far side? Could he wait outside the camp until he saw her return and catch her attention?

Anxiety fluttered in his belly. He shouldn't be on Thunder-Clan territory. But he had to see Ivypool.

Suddenly her scent touched his nose. It was fresh. His heart soared. *StarClan must be guiding us!* He scanned the shadowy forest. Twilight was sinking fast into night. He widened his eyes, trying to glimpse her pelt, and heard paws scuff the ground beyond a stand of bracken. He caught a scent that tasted like Dovewing's—a little harsher, but familiar. Taking a risk, he whispered into the shadows. "Ivypool."

He heard a sudden movement. Some cat had turned quickly. Fur brushed the bracken stems. They trembled in front of him as Ivypool pushed her way out.

"Tigerheart?" Hostility gleamed in her gaze. "What are you doing here?"

"I have to talk to you."

"To me?" She curled her lip. "Are you sure you're not looking for Dovewing?"

"I'm sure."

Ivypool growled at him. "Twigpaw saw you and my sister meeting near the border. You know that's against the warrior code, right? You could get her into big trouble."

Tigerheart stared into her burning gaze. Urgency writhed like captured prey in his chest. "I love her, Ivypool, and she loves me. But she needs you."

Ivypool narrowed her eyes. "Is that why you're here? To tell me that you're in love, so everything's okay?" Her mew dripped with contempt.

"She says you're shutting her out," Tigerheart urged. "I

know you're angry with her. But she needs someone to confide in."

"You mean she needs me to approve of what she's doing so she doesn't feel so guilty!" Anger sharpened Ivypool's mew.

"Don't you care about her?" Tigerheart pleaded.

Ivypool's pelt bushed. "How dare you?" she spat. "Of course I care about her. And if *you* cared about her, you'd leave her alone."

"I can't." Helplessness swamped Tigerheart. He wanted to blurt out the truth—that Dovewing was expecting kits. He wanted the truth to fix everything. He wanted Ivypool to forgive Dovewing and reassure her that raising her kits in the Clans would be great. But he knew the truth might make things worse. And telling the truth should be Dovewing's choice, not his.

"Ivypool." He gazed at her desperately. "Just talk to her. Please."

"I will." Ivypool whirled away with a snarl. "Once she's stopped seeing you." Her silver tail lashing, she pushed her way through the bracken and disappeared into darkness.

Tigerheart watched her go, his chest tightening with panic. Ivypool had been his last, desperate hope at persuading Dovewing, and now that hope had died. Dovewing only had him. *I don't want to do this without you, Tigerheart. I need you.* He pictured her wide, stricken gaze, and his heart ached.

He curled his claws into the earth. Rowanstar was Shadow-Clan's leader; he was responsible for the Clan. *It's not my duty to hold the Clan together.* Tigerheart headed for the border. *I've carried that burden for too long.* He pictured Scorchfur's snarling face as he attacked Tawnypelt. He remembered the treachery of the apprentices who'd brought the rogues into the Clan. *Let them hold themselves together.* Bitterness rose in his throat. *Or tear themselves apart.* Determination pulsed through him as he padded through the deepening night. *My responsibility is to Dovewing and my kits.*

I love you, Dovewing, and I won't let you down.

CHAPTER 4

Tigerheart could taste rain on the wind. Thick clouds darkened the sky above the pines, casting the forest into gloom. *Not good traveling weather.* His chest tightened as he thought about meeting Dovewing. Sunhigh had passed long ago. He must leave soon. She'd be waiting.

He reached up and tucked a stray tendril into the bramble wall of the ShadowClan nursery. Rowanstar had given orders that all the dens be repaired and strengthened. Rain was coming, and he wanted the Clan to be warm and dry in their nests. Grassheart and Strikestone were working on the warriors' den. Flowerpaw, Snakepaw, and Whorlpaw poked wads of moss into the holes in side of their own den, while Tawnypelt and Snowbird wove extra brambles into the walls of the elders' den.

Tigerheart's throat tightened. Could he really leave? This was the only life he'd known. Sadness jabbed at his heart. He might never see these cats again. He'd be leaving the forest to live in a *Twolegplace*! His pelt prickled nervously.

Around him, his Clanmates were working together, following Rowanstar's orders without question. He pushed his doubts away. *Dovewing needs me more than they do.*

Rowanstar was padding around the camp, inspecting the work. He nodded approvingly as he passed Whorlpaw, slowing to point out a gap near the bottom of the wall that still needed filling. Whorlpaw dipped his head to the Shadow-Clan leader and quickly reached for another wad of moss to plug it. Tigerheart's chest ached with hope. The Clan would be fine without him.

"Tigerheart!" Rowanstar was crossing the clearing.

Tigerheart tensed. What did Rowanstar want? He glanced at the darkening treetops. He'd been hoping to slip away soon. Keeping his fur smooth, he tugged two strands of bramble closer together before dropping onto all four paws to face his father. "Yes?"

"Take out a hunting party." Rowanstar had stopped beside the fresh-kill pile. A thrush and a vole were all that was left from the morning's catch.

Tigerheart relaxed. *Perfect. I can slip away easily while I'm in the forest.*

"Take Grassheart, Snowbird, Juniperclaw, and Scorchfur." Rowanstar's green gaze scanned the camp.

Tigerheart followed it. Where *were* Juniperclaw and Scorchfur? Hadn't they been helping Grassheart and Strikestone fix up the warriors' den? Perhaps they were outside camp, fetching bracken to weave into the den walls. "I'll find them," he told Rowanstar. He beckoned Grassheart and Snowbird with his tail as he headed for the camp entrance.

He ducked outside and stopped a few tail-lengths from the

camp. Opening his mouth, he let the musky scents of leaf-fall bathe his tongue. He could taste the fresh scent of his missing Clanmates, but in the misty air it was hard to tell which way they'd headed.

Grassheart stopped beside him.

"Can you tell which way Scorchfur and Juniperclaw went?" he asked her.

"Don't worry," she mewed quickly. "We can hunt without them."

It'll be easier for me to slip away from a bigger patrol. Tigerheart looked at the pale brown she-cat and saw her pelt prickling self-consciously. "Do you know where they are?"

"Who? Me?" Grassheart glanced at Snowbird as the white she-cat reached them. Guilt flashed between them. "They were helping with the dens last time I saw."

Tigerheart pricked his ears. Grassheart and Snowbird were hiding something. "What's going on?"

Snowbird shot Grassheart a warning look.

Grassheart flicked her tail. "We promised we wouldn't tell," she mewed apologetically.

"Promised who?"

"Scorchfur and Juniperclaw." Grassheart dropped her gaze.

"What are they doing?" Tigerheart thrust his muzzle closer, his pelt rippling with foreboding.

"They're . . . on their way to join SkyClan."

Join SkyClan? Tigerheart could hardly believe his ears. The shock that his Clanmates could be so disloyal was undercut by guilt, and a thought so selfish it made him feel sick. *ShadowClan's supposed to be losing one warrior today, not three.* "When?"

"Now." Grassheart didn't look at him.

"But they hate SkyClan." Scorchfur and Juniperclaw had always made it clear that they disliked having SkyClan anywhere near ShadowClan's territory.

"They said they wanted to be part of a real Clan." Grassheart shifted her paws.

Snowbird stepped forward. "It's not just that they're unhappy here," she mewed. "Scorchfur was really upset that he nearly blinded Tawnypelt. He's scared what will happen if he stays in ShadowClan."

Tigerheart blinked at her. "Scared of his own Clanmates?"

Grassheart shifted her paws. "Scared he might lose his temper again, or that Tawnypelt and Rowanstar might want revenge."

"But we're *Clanmates!*" Tigerheart blinked in disbelief. "We take care of one another!"

"Juniperclaw says that ShadowClan cats have forgotten what loyalty means," Snowbird mewed.

Tigerheart's hackles lifted. "But Juniperclaw left his Clan to join the rogues!" How dare he accuse his Clanmates of disloyalty when he'd been one of the first to betray them? Anger pulsed beneath Tigerheart's pelt. He pushed it away. This was no time for recriminations. ShadowClan was already dwindling. How could *he* leave if they lost two strong warriors like Scorchfur and Juniperclaw? Puddleshine's warning would come true; ShadowClan would disappear completely. "I have to stop them." He bounded toward the SkyClan border.

Pine needles swished behind him as Snowbird and Grass-heart gave chase.

"Go and hunt!" He waved them away with a lashing tail. "I'll take care of this." He wanted to sort this out as quickly as possible. Nightfall was closing in. He had to persuade Scorch-fur and Juniperclaw to return to ShadowClan, and then slip away and meet Dovewing before she left without him.

I'm a snake-heart. He ignored the voice ringing in his head. *I'm only going to persuade them to stay so that I can leave.*

No. He was doing the best he could, for Dovewing *and* his Clan. With him gone, ShadowClan would need Scorchfur and Juniperclaw more than ever.

Heart pounding, he raced between the trees. He could smell Scorchfur's scent trail now. Juniperclaw's was beside it. He followed it easily over the ditches and to the rise that lifted to the SkyClan border. As he neared the bottom, he glimpsed their pelts slipping around a stretch of brambles. "Stop!" His yowl rang through the damp forest. He saw them stop and pulled up as their faces turned toward him. "Let me talk to you!"

He climbed the slope, fixing them with an urgent glare. "Grassheart told me you're planning to join SkyClan."

They looked at each other, then padded toward him. Their gazes were distrustful.

"Please don't go." He stopped in front of them, panting.

Scorchfur narrowed his eyes. "Why not?"

"You're ShadowClan!" Tigerheart stared at him imploringly. "You can't just forget that. It's where you were born and raised. You think like ShadowClan cats; you hunt like ShadowClan cats; you fight like ShadowClan cats. You don't even know what SkyClan is like! You'll never feel you really belong there."

Juniperclaw glanced nervously at Scorchfur. "Maybe he's right."

Scorchfur frowned. "ShadowClan isn't the Clan it used to be. SkyClan might be better. We can teach them some useful skills."

"'Teach them some useful skills'?" Tigerheart fought to keep his claws sheathed. "If SkyClan learns how we fight and hunt, think how easy it would be for them to defeat us." He turned his gaze on Juniperclaw desperately. "They might take over the whole forest. You don't want that, do you?"

Juniperclaw's eyes widened with alarm. "I hadn't thought of that." He looked anxiously at Scorchfur.

Scorchfur snorted. "I thought you said SkyClan cats were our friends."

"Friends can have a falling-out." Tigerheart leaned closer. "What if there was a border skirmish with ShadowClan? Could you fight against us for SkyClan?"

Scorchfur's pelt prickled uneasily. "ShadowClan won't be fighting any battles for a while. We're hardly a Clan anymore."

We won't be if you leave. Tigerheart scrabbled for another reason for the warriors to stay. "If you join SkyClan, you'll probably have to retrain. Like Twigpaw did. She'd already passed her ThunderClan warrior assessment when she joined, and she's *still* training to be a SkyClan warrior."

Juniperclaw pricked his ears. "You don't think they'd make me a 'paw, do you?"

Tigerheart shrugged, trying to appear calm even as he felt each moment slip away like escaping prey. Time was passing. He had to get to Dovewing. "They might, once they found out that *rogues* gave you your warrior name." He was bluffing, but he could sense Juniperclaw wavering.

"You're just trying to scare us," Scorchfur grunted.

"Even if they don't make you 'paws, do you think they're going to treat you with respect?" Tigerheart countered.

Scorchfur met his gaze challengingly. "After I fought with Tawnypelt, why would ShadowClan treat me with respect?" He sounded angry, but the anger was clearly directed at himself. "I wish I'd never gone for her eye. It was a fox-hearted move. But I was so mad."

"I should have intervened earlier," Tigerheart admitted.

"*Rowanstar* should have intervened earlier," Juniperclaw remarked pointedly.

"And he would, if it happened again," Tigerheart promised. "It just took him by surprise. It took us all by surprise." He tried to think of something more to say. He could feel they were relenting. Just a few words more. Perhaps it was best just to admit the truth. "We need you. ShadowClan is in trouble, and without you we may not survive. You're both great warriors, and I know we can all put our differences aside and work together as a Clan again. We survived Darktail. We survived the Dark Forest. We can survive this. We just have to try." He didn't hide the desperation pulsing in his chest. If he was going to leave, he had to make them stay.

Scorchfur's ears twitched. "Okay." He glanced toward the border. "I'll stay."

"Me too." Juniperclaw sounded relieved.

Joy washed Tigerheart's pelt like a soothing wind. His chest expanded as he turned toward camp and began to lead the way through the forest. He just had to get them halfway there—far enough that they wouldn't change their minds—and then he could make an excuse and go to Dovewing. "You won't regret it."

"I'm still worried about Rowanstar." Scorchfur fell in beside him. "When he first became leader, he seemed so strong. But now, whenever we face trouble, he doesn't know what to do."

"He reunited the Clan after Darktail, didn't he?" Tigerheart reminded him. "That took strength."

Scorchfur huffed. "He didn't reunite all the cats. Some of our Clanmates are still missing."

"Didn't they die?" Juniperclaw murmured darkly.

"Why did we never find their bodies?" Scorchfur argued.

Juniperclaw shot his denmate an anxious look. "Do you think some of ShadowClan is still roaming beyond the forest?"

"Of course not." Tigerheart meowed quickly. "Why would any warrior stay away from their Clan?" As he spoke, the words felt like thorns on his tongue. *I'm about to leave my Clan.* Guilt seemed to freeze his heart until it stung. *This is different,* he told himself. He focused on the trail ahead. Soon he'd be with Dovewing. Then he wouldn't have to think about

ShadowClan anymore. *No more guilt.*

Bracken rustled at the edge of a ditch. *Prey?* Tigerheart pricked his ears. Scorchfur turned, his gray fur twitching excitedly. Juniperclaw tasted the air.

"Is it a rabbit?" As Tigerheart spoke, he saw Juniperclaw's eager gaze sharpen into horror. A rank stench rolled across the ditch. It wasn't prey. As Tigerheart tried to recognize the smell, he glimpsed black-and-white fur through the bracken. A roar sounded as a cruel snout thrust out.

Badger!

The great creature scrambled clumsily over the ditch and lunged at them, its beady black eyes glittering wildly. What was a badger doing here? No Clan had reported a set near their territory!

Tigerheart, numb with surprise, recoiled as its fetid breath bathed his muzzle. The badger turned. Its rump knocked Tigerheart into the ditch. As he scrabbled breathlessly to his paws, the badger snapped at Juniperclaw. Juniperclaw screeched with pain. The badger had the black tom's paw in its mouth. Pelt bushing, Tigerheart leaped onto the badger's back, dug his claws in hard, and bit down on the back of the creature's thick neck.

Releasing Juniperclaw, the badger spun heavily beneath him. It lifted its snout and glanced over its shoulder at Tigerheart. Rage sparked in its eyes. With a growl, it threw itself onto its side and rolled. Tigerheart squawked as the badger's weight fell on top of him. "Get its belly!" he puffed at Scorchfur. But the gray tom had already flung himself, claws slashing, at the badger's exposed underside. With a roar, the badger's limbs closed around Scorchfur.

It heaved itself upright. Tigerheart still clung to its back. Scorchfur wailed, trapped beneath it, his muzzle dangerously exposed to the badger's snarling jaws.

Juniperclaw slashed at its nose. The badger threw its head up, howling with pain as claws sliced its snout. Tigerheart thrust his muzzle forward and snapped at one of the badger's ears, sinking his teeth into the leathery flesh. The badger jerked as though hit by lightning. Rearing, it threw Tigerheart from its back with a desperate howl of pain.

Tigerheart hit a tree with a thump that sent the forest spinning around him. His head cracked against the bark with such force that for a moment he thought his skull had split. White pain flared behind his eyes. Tree roots jabbed his ribs as he dropped like dead prey. Dazed, he glimpsed a flash of black-and-white fur at the edge of his vision. He felt the ground shake.

"Tigerheart!"

He heard Juniperclaw's panicked cry and felt a tug of loyalty. His Clanmates were in danger. Blindly he staggered to his paws and shook out his fur. Juniperclaw and Scorchfur were dodging around the badger, lashing out in turns at its hefty flanks. The badger spun and snapped at them, its eyes frenzied.

Struggling from his stupor, Tigerheart smelled its fetid stench once more and felt heat pulsing from its pelt. This badger was sick. He could hear it wheezing. Was this why it was foraging so far from its home? Had its denmates driven it away?

The badger staggered as Scorchfur struggled from beneath it and leaped, quick as a squirrel, to Juniperclaw's side. The black tom's paw was oozing blood where the badger had bit it, but he was still standing. The warriors faced the badger as it eyed them murderously.

"It's sick!" Tigerheart yowled, ignoring the throbbing behind his eyes. "We can win if we work together!" He scrambled past the flailing badger and slid between his Clanmates. They lined up beside him and faced the stinking creature, ears flat. Tigerheart dug his claws into the earth. Juniperclaw bared his teeth. Scorchfur lowered his head, eyes like slits. Slowly, they crept forward, hissing together like snakes.

Confusion glistened suddenly in the badger's eyes, and it froze. The heat from its stinking fur rolled over Tigerheart. For a moment he remembered the stench of Puddleshine's medicine den when yellowcough had gripped the Clan.

Scorchfur lifted his head and snarled menacingly.

Confusion turned to fear in the badger's fevered gaze. With a grunt, it backed away. *It knows it's beaten.* Triumph surged in Tigerheart's chest as the badger turned and lumbered heavily in the opposite direction. It stumbled into the ditch and floundered there for a moment.

"Let's give it some scars to take away," Scorchfur growled.

Tigerheart blocked him with a paw. "It's already sick," he meowed. "Let it go. We can send out a patrol later to check that it's left our land for good." *Actually, you can send out a patrol,* he thought. *I won't be here.*

The badger hauled itself from the ditch and shambled through the bracken, disappearing into the shadowy pines.

Tigerheart looked at the sky and realized with a jolt how late it was. Sunset had passed and left the forest in darkness. *Dovewing!* She might be gone already! The thumping in his head made him wince. He flicked his tail toward Juniperclaw. "How's your paw?"

Juniperclaw was licking his wound gingerly. Pain sparked in his eyes as he met Tigerheart's gaze. "No bones broken, but the wound's deep."

"Get him to the medicine den," Tigerheart ordered Scorchfur. "Tell Puddleshine the badger was sick. The bite might be infected."

Scorchfur blinked at him. "Aren't you coming with us?"

"There's something I need to do." Tigerheart turned and leaped the ditch, heading toward the meeting place. He had to do it now. Before Dovewing left. Before he lost his nerve.

Juniperclaw looked puzzled. "I thought you hit your head."

"It was nothing." Tigerheart's head was throbbing, but he tried to ignore it.

"Will you be gone long?" Scorchfur called after him.

Tigerheart didn't answer. He didn't even look back. He didn't want to see the Clanmates he was leaving. He didn't want to think about them. But he could feel their surprised gazes burning his pelt.

I don't care. He had to reach Dovewing before she left. Panic drove him faster through the forest. He scrambled around brambles, fighting the dizziness that swayed him one way and then the other. He leaped fallen trees clumsily. He'd done one last deed for ShadowClan before he left. *But did it cost me the one cat I love best?* He thought of Dovewing's green eyes, her gentle wisdom, her open heart that loved without limit. She'd said she would leave at sunset and, as darkness enfolded the forest, he knew that it was long past. His heart beat in his throat as he raced on. *I'm coming! You're the most important cat in my life. . . . I can't lose you.*

Please, Dovewing . . . wait for me, just a little bit longer.

CHAPTER 5

When he reached it, the glade stood in shadow, empty. He stared, at first in disbelief and then with awful certainty. A breeze whisked through the trees, and shriveled leaves fluttered to the ground. *She left without me.* Grief seared his heart. Above him, thick cloud hid the moon. Rain began to fall, pattering lightly on the canopy. It grew heavier, and as Tigerheart stared bereft at the deserted clearing, drops began to seep through the thick pine branches and splash onto his pelt.

He stood numbly, the ache in his head growing sharper. He could feel heat behind one ear where his head had struck the tree.

What do I do? Confusion seemed to weave his thoughts into knots. His paws led him forward. He opened his mouth, instinctively tasting the damp air for Dovewing's scent. It hung in the glade, so fresh that his heart leaped. He could catch up with her. She must have waited a while.

He lowered his head and followed her scent trail like a fox. It skirted the boundary between SkyClan and Shadow-Clan before cutting straight through ShadowClan territory. *She's heading for the Thunderpath.* He knew the Twoleg route that divided the forest and the marsh, which lay beyond Clan boundaries.

Does she know where she's going? Through the throbbing in his head, he tried to remember what she'd told him about her dream. *A huge Twolegplace with nests that reach into the sky. I saw a roof there with sharp points that stick up into the sky like gorse spines. We must find that den. Our kits will be safe there.*

Did she know where this huge Twolegplace was? He'd never heard any of the Clan cats speak of it. Perhaps Dovewing hoped that the Thunderpath would lead her to it.

Pain pressed above his eyes, dulling his thoughts. *I just have to follow her scent,* he thought numbly. He padded on, letting his paws and Dovewing's scent guide him while he fought the pounding in his head. The rain grew heavier, thundering onto the canopy, and when he finally reached the forest's edge, he walked out into a downpour that drenched his pelt and half-blinded him.

Monsters growled on the Thunderpath ahead, lighting the thick rain with their burning eyes. Their paws threw up spray. Tigerheart hung back. The Thunderpath was jammed with a stream of monsters thicker than he'd ever seen. Were the Twolegs migrating? Their monsters streamed after one another like geese heading south for the winter, leaving no gap to cross. Tigerheart stopped a few tail-lengths from the edge, out of reach of the filthy spray. His head spun as he stared at the stampeding monsters. Had Dovewing found a way between their rolling paws? He tried to glimpse a gap, but the speeding monsters made him dizzy, whipping past him one after another. Rain pounded his pelt, streaming into his eyes. Blinking rapidly, his head aching, he sank to his belly and watched the passing monsters helplessly. *Dovewing. Why didn't you wait?* His heart seemed to crack open with loss and frustration. They should be facing this together. Why hadn't he met her in time? The night darkened around him; the burning lights from the monsters blurred. Their growling faded as his thoughts jumbled and he collapsed into unconsciousness.

He dreamed. Puddleshine stood beside him as the sun rose over the ShadowClan camp. Tigerheart knew at once that he was in the medicine cat's vision. The sun burned beyond the trees, casting black shadows in stripes across the clearing. Juniperclaw, Tawnypelt, Snowbird, and Whorlpaw padded from their dens. Grassheart yawned in the middle of the clearing and stretched as a dark shadow fell across her glossy pelt. Rowanstar moved beside the rock near his den, his eyes flashing in the dawn light. Tigerheart blinked in the fierce sunshine as it sliced between the trees, half-blinded until suddenly the sun began to fade.

"Puddleshine." Tigerheart called to the medicine cat watching from the edge of the clearing, but the brown tom didn't seem to hear him. His gaze was fixed on the clearing as the sun dissolved into the pale blue sky and the shadows evaporated like mist.

I'm seeing what he saw. Tigerheart knew where this dream had carried him and watched intently. He glanced toward his father. Would the ShadowClan leader fade with the shadows? Rowanstar blinked beside the rock, his gaze blank as though unaware of the changing light. Then, suddenly, the sun brightened once more. Tigerheart jerked his nose toward it. *Puddleshine didn't mention this part of his vision.* He narrowed his eyes as the sun reddened and intensified until it looked like flame burning at the edge of the forest. The shadows in camp darkened once more, reaching across the clearing, casting his Clanmates into gloom. Then Tigerheart saw himself standing at the edge of the clearing, his outline carved from darkness by brilliant sunshine. His pelt shimmered in the fierce light. The shadow he cast was long and black, far darker than any other in camp, while across the clearing Rowanstar dissolved into milky light.

"When the sun is strong, the shadows are strong."

As Puddleshine's mew rang across the clearing, Tigerheart felt cold. A chill gripped him and he struggled awake. Rain was seeping through his fur. He blinked open his eyes, Puddleshine's words ringing in his ears. *When the sun is strong . . .*

He sat up. The rain was still falling. Weak dawn light filtered through the gray clouds. The Thunderpath lay empty, the marsh stretching into a haze of rain beyond. He felt groggy, his head still aching. He shivered with cold and fluffed out his pelt. *When the sun is strong.* Puddleshine's words buzzed in his ears like a bothersome fly. Unease tugged in Tigerheart's belly. The dream meant something. He could sense it. *The sun.* Tigerheart stiffened. *The* son! *When the* son *is strong, the shadows are strong!* Understanding burst like starlight in his thoughts. Rowanstar wasn't the sun that would make ShadowClan strong. Only the *son* could save ShadowClan from disappearing. *The son is the sun!*

His headache faded. Energy fizzed beneath his pelt. He had to get back to his Clan. He was the one who could save them! He headed away from the Thunderpath and hurried into the forest. Why hadn't he realized earlier?

As he crossed the wet forest floor, the sound of rain pounding the branches above him, guilt jabbed at his belly.

Dovewing. The thought pricked his heart. *I'm sorry.* His Clan needed him too much. And if Dovewing had truly needed him, she would have waited. . . .

She had to understand—his whole Clan was at stake.

He reached the ditches and crossed them, his belly feeling more hollow with every leap. Grief tugged at his heart. *I have to save them.* As he saw the bramble wall of the camp looming ahead of him, Tigerheart lifted his chin. Dovewing would have to take care of herself for now, and their kits. He ignored the shame that clawed in his belly. If ShadowClan was to survive, he needed to be here.

CHAPTER 6

In the days since Dovewing had left, the rain hadn't let up. Tigerheart trudged through it now, following Stonewing, Juniperclaw, and Whorlpaw home from a hunt. The swelling behind his ear had eased since Puddleshine had treated it with nettles soaked in rainwater. His headache had lingered for a day but was gone now.

Tigerheart held a soggy sparrow between his jaws. The others carried prey too. Whorlpaw was clearly proud of the young rabbit he'd caught and walked with his tail high, despite the rain dripping from the trees and the earth squelching beneath his paws.

It had been a good hunt. The patrol had worked well together. Tigerheart felt hope flicker in his chest each time Juniperclaw called out to Stonewing to warn him of prey heading his way. And whenever Whorlpaw dipped his head respectfully as Juniperclaw gently adjusted his hunting crouch or showed him which part of a bracken stalk held prey-scent even when it rained, Tigerheart had dared to believe that ShadowClan would grow stronger and more united with time. Perhaps it didn't matter if Rowanstar wasn't a strong leader.

Perhaps it was enough that Tigerheart was there to support them. Meanwhile, hunting and patrolling would bring the Clan together. Training their young to be great warriors would remind them of what it was to be loyal and brave. In a few seasons, the rogues would be forgotten and ShadowClan would thrive once more.

But where would Dovewing and his kits be by then? The thought pricked Tigerheart's chest. Would she come back once she felt their kits would be safe with the Clans? If not, perhaps he could find a way to join her as soon as he felt that ShadowClan's future was secure.

He dared not think about the dangers waiting beyond the Clan borders. *She's a warrior.* The thought comforted him. She'd survived the battle with the Dark Forest. And the rogues. But what if she *wasn't* all right? He pushed the thought away, fear slicing his belly so sharply he winced. Was his Clan really worth endangering his mate and kits for? Frustration itched beneath his pelt. Why did he have to make such a choice? It wasn't fair.

Juniperclaw halted as he reached the camp entrance. Stonewing and Whorlpaw stopped beside him. He dropped his prey and sniffed the air suspiciously. "ThunderClan cats have been here." He looked at Tigerheart. "I wonder what they wanted."

A fresh chill crept through Tigerheart's damp pelt. He could guess what they had wanted. Especially when he tasted the air and smelled Ivypool's scent. They'd be looking for Dovewing. Of course her sister would come here. His fur prickled nervously. Had she said anything to Rowanstar about the secret meetings?

"Tigerheart!" Tawnypelt called through the entrance. "You're back." She hurried out of camp and quickly nosed Tigerheart away from the patrol.

Stonewing called to her. "What did ThunderClan want?"

"One of their warriors is missing." Tawnypelt glanced at the white tom and flicked her tail nonchalantly. "It's their problem, not ours, but they wondered if we'd seen her."

Juniperclaw narrowed his eyes. "I hope Rowanstar didn't let us get drawn into ThunderClan's problems."

"Of course he didn't," Tawnypelt answered sharply.

"We've got enough of our own," Juniperclaw grouched. "First it's prophecies about coming storms, then it's six-toed cats, then missing warriors. ThunderClan is always coming to us with some problem. I hope Rowanstar was firm with them."

Irritation flared beneath Tigerheart's pelt. "Of course he was firm," he mewed curtly. "Why wouldn't he be?"

Stonewing dropped his thrush. "He's not exactly decisive these days."

"How dare you?" Tigerheart glowered at the tom. His gaze flashed to Juniperclaw. "You weren't here when ThunderClan came. You don't know what was said. Don't assume Rowanstar let any cat push him around. You have to trust him!" His hackles lifted. "He's our *leader*." He glared at Juniperclaw and Stonewing until they dropped their gazes.

Whorlpaw shifted his paws uneasily. "Which warrior is missing?"

"Dovewing." Tawnypelt's mew was even.

Whorlpaw's eyes widened. "Perhaps the sick badger got her."

"Nonsense." Tawnypelt flicked her tail impatiently. "We sent out a patrol to check that the badger was gone, remember? There's been no scent of it on our land since the rain started."

"Perhaps it went onto ThunderClan's territory," Whorlpaw persisted.

"If she was attacked by a badger on their territory, they'd know about it," Juniperclaw pointed out.

Tigerheart shifted his weight self-consciously. He was the only cat who knew the truth. He dropped his gaze. Ivypool must be beside herself with worry. ThunderClan would be grieving.

Tawnypelt nudged Tigerheart to one side, flicking her tail toward the patrol. "Take your catch into camp," she told them. "The fresh-kill pile needs filling." As they obeyed and disappeared through the bramble tunnel, Tawnypelt looked into Tigerheart's eyes. "Do you know anything about Dovewing's disappearance?"

"No." Tigerheart's pelt burned as he struggled to return his mother's gaze innocently. "Why should I?"

"I saw the way you were with her when we were living with ThunderClan. You ate with her and talked with her like she was the only cat in camp. And it wasn't just me who noticed. Ivypool asked specifically if *you* knew anything about Dovewing's disappearance. She's clearly suspicious. She's on her way to SkyClan right now to ask them if they've seen Dovewing.

But I know she doesn't believe they'll have any answers." Her whiskers twitched. "Was there anything going on between you and Dovewing?"

Tigerheart hesitated, then avoided the question. "I don't know where Dovewing is."

Tawnypelt's eyes narrowed. Tigerheart could sense doubt glittering behind them. But she didn't ask again. "Shadow-Clan needs you, Tigerheart. Your father needs you."

Anger surged beneath Tigerheart's pelt. "You think I don't know that?" *If I didn't, I'd be with Dovewing right now! I'd have followed her wherever she went.*

Tawnypelt held his gaze for a moment, then turned away. "A warrior is loyal to his Clan above all things."

As she headed back to camp, Tigerheart called after her. "You don't need to tell me about the warrior code!" She had no idea what he was giving up to stay loyal to his Clan. Not just Dovewing, but his kits. He might never know them.

As she disappeared through the bramble tunnel, urgency tugged at his paws. He headed for the ThunderClan border, rain splashing his pelt. He had to speak with Ivypool before she sparked suspicion in any other cats. He didn't want all the Clans silently believing that he was responsible for Dovewing's disappearance. It had been Dovewing's decision. Ivypool had to know that. *Should I tell her where Dovewing was heading?* His belly twisted. *I can't betray her! What if ThunderClan follows her and brings her home?* He slowed. *Would that be so bad? She's not safe alone.* His thoughts were spinning as he crossed the border. Tawnypelt had said Ivypool had gone to SkyClan. He could intercept her on her way home, before she reached her camp. Climbing a leaf-strewn rise, he ducked through bracken and shadowed a ThunderClan trail. He tasted Ivypool's scent before he heard her call.

"Tigerheart." There was anger in her yowl. He stopped as she marched toward him. She was alone, her pelt bristling as she glared at him. "You're on our land. And I know why. You've come to lie to me again. You're here to persuade me that you have nothing to do with Dovewing's disappearance. But you know where she is, don't you?"

"No."

"You *knew* she was going to leave!" Ivypool accused.

"I did," Tigerheart admitted. "I tried to stop her, but she was determined."

"Where has she gone?"

A huge Twolegplace with nests that reach into the sky . . .

He could still hear Dovewing's words clearly. He pictured the desperation in her green eyes as she told him. He couldn't betray her. She was convinced that their kits' lives depended on finding a gorse-spined den. He looked at Ivypool. "I tracked her as far as the Thunderpath beside the marsh."

"But no farther?" Ivypool's eyes flashed with disgust. "Did the monsters scare you away?"

"My Clan needs me," Tigerheart meowed simply. "I couldn't abandon them."

"But you could abandon Dovewing?" Ivypool flexed her claws.

She abandoned me! Frustration flared in Tigerheart's belly. "I thought you didn't *want* us to be together," he snapped.

Ivypool spat at him. "Do you think I'd prefer she was out there *alone?*"

Guilt swamped Tigerheart. Ivypool was right. He had chosen to stay with his Clan. He'd left Dovewing to face the land beyond the forest alone.

Ivypool thrust her face closer. "I always knew you were trouble. You never cared about Dovewing. If you had, you'd never have let her leave." With a snarl, she lashed her claws across his muzzle.

Tigerheart didn't flinch. He deserved it. He felt the sting of torn flesh and the wetness of blood welling on his nose. Without moving, he held Ivypool's gaze. "I love her," he confessed. "I should have stopped her, but I couldn't." He'd let Scorchfur and Juniperclaw keep him from meeting her. If he had let his Clanmates go to SkyClan, he could have met Dovewing before she left. He might even have been able to persuade her to stay. Instead he'd given up everything he loved for his Clan. His eyes grew hot with grief.

Ivypool stared at him with hatred. "You're a coward. And a fox-heart. Dovewing deserved a better mate than you." Tail lashing, she turned away and left him alone beneath the dripping pines.

She's right. His throat thickened with grief, almost choking him. *Dovewing, I'm so sorry.*

CHAPTER 7

❧

"The rain has driven the prey too far underground." Grassheart lifted a clump of soggy leaves and peered underneath. "There's a mouse hole here." She reached in but dragged up nothing but mud.

Tigerheart's belly rumbled. The rain still hadn't ceased. The scratches Ivypool had given him still stung. They hurt worse in his sleep, when he dreamed of Dovewing wandering alone. Each morning he woke to a fresh ache in his heart. The fresh-kill pile had dwindled to nothing as the forest creatures hid from the endless torrent. As he stood with the patrol now, he grunted at Grassheart. "Prey must search for food eventually. It'll starve quicker than us." He tasted the air but smelled nothing but wet wood.

Juniperclaw paced behind him. Strikestone and Snakepaw huddled beneath the shelter of a bramble, their pelts slicked against their skinny frames.

"There might be frogs in the ditches," Juniperclaw suggested. "We could catch those."

"There's probably *fish* there by now," Grassheart snorted. "They've been flooded for days."

"Tawnypelt led a hunting patrol to the ditches this morning

while you were marking the borders," Tigerheart told Juniper-claw. "They came back with a drowned vole and four slugs."

Snakepaw shuddered, her nose wrinkling. "Perhaps we could look around the beech patch near the SkyClan border," she suggested. "The beechnuts might attract something tastier than slugs."

Tigerheart glanced at the honey-brown tabby. It was a good idea. He flicked his tail. "Nice plan, Snakepaw."

She glanced shyly at her paws. Grassheart shook the rain from her pelt and headed toward the patch of forest where, moons ago, beeches had found a gap among the pines and had grown vigorously, as though celebrating their small victory over the evergreens.

Their leaves were browning in the leaf-fall chill. Some hung limply on bare branches. Most lay on the ground in sodden swathes around the roots. The small opening to the sky let more rain in and Tigerheart narrowed his eyes against it as he reached the beech patch. Beyond it, the ground sloped upward toward the SkyClan border nearby. Spiky beechnuts scattered the ground, their skin peeled open, the nuts gone.

Grassheart kicked miserably at an empty shell. "It looks like the prey has already been and gone."

"They didn't get everything." Snakepaw tapped an unopened beechnut with her paw, her eyes bright.

Tigerheart flicked his tail toward his Clanmates. "Let's surround the beech patch and wait. It might take a while, but something is bound to come looking for food eventually."

He threaded through the battered bracken stalks sprouting beside a beech and crouched just outside the cluster of trees. The rest of the patrol did the same, encircling the beeches. As Tigerheart flattened himself against the ground, hoping his pelt would blend against the moldering leaves, his Clanmates hunkered down until he could hardly see them.

Now we wait. He braced himself against the cold that began to seep through his pelt. As his belly rumbled with hunger, he thought of Dovewing. He had tried to keep himself busy since she'd left, but there were always moments of stillness when his thoughts would slide toward her. Where was she? Was it raining there too? Was she wet and hungry? Their unborn kits would need food, and so would she. Would he ever see her again? Would he ever meet his kits? Grief swelled in his chest. He tried to push it away. But the scent of her still lingered in his fur despite the rain. Perhaps he was imagining it. He no longer knew.

Paw steps thudded the ground nearby. He stiffened, his eyes widening. *Prey?* His heart leaped as a rabbit raced across SkyClan's border toward the beech patch. He saw Juniper-claw's eyes widen with excitement beyond the bracken. *Not yet.* He flicked his tail to order the warrior to wait. He wanted to make sure the rabbit was surrounded. It wasn't going to escape.

Suddenly a SkyClan warrior crashed across the border and streaked after the rabbit. *Plumwillow!* The she-cat's gaze was fixed on her quarry. Her fur was fluffed with excitement. She'd clearly been chasing it for a while. As the rabbit reached the edge of the beech patch, Plumwillow leaped. Fast as a bird, she swooped onto the terrified prey and, clamping her jaws around its neck, snapped its spine with a killing bite.

Her eyes shone as she straightened and rested her paw on the rabbit's fat flank.

"What are you doing?" Juniperclaw's angry yowl made her stiffen. She turned, eyes wide, toward the ShadowClan warrior as he strode from his hiding place among the bracken.

Grassheart marched between the beeches, fur bristling with indignation. "That's *our* rabbit!"

Plumwillow blinked at them in surprise. "But I caught it."

"On *our* territory!" Juniperclaw glared at her.

"I started chasing it on SkyClan land," Plumwillow argued. "That makes it SkyClan prey."

As Snakepaw followed Strikestone to join their Clanmates, Tigerheart padded from the bracken. Rain pounded the forest floor around the cats as they eyed one another angrily. "Perhaps SkyClan doesn't understand our ways yet," he meowed sympathetically. He dipped his head to Plumwillow. "Prey belongs to the Clan where it's caught."

Plumwillow tipped her head. "Really?" She sounded unconvinced. "What about the rabbit Sandynose and Rabbitleap caught for you? That was caught on SkyClan land, wasn't it? And yet you took it because it ran from ShadowClan territory." She blinked rain from her eyes.

Juniperclaw snorted. "If Sandynose and Rabbitleap want to give away prey, that's up to them. We have a hungry Clan to feed."

"So do I." Plumwillow pulled the rabbit closer. "Is Shadow-Clan's hunger more important than SkyClan's hunger?"

"No Clan's hunger is more important." Tigerheart saw Strikestone flexing his claws. Juniperclaw's hackles were twitching. His Clanmates were ready to fight for this prey. "That's why we have the warrior code. To help settle disputes like this."

Plumwillow eyed the ShadowClan cats warily, then lifted her chin. "If you want *my* prey, you'll have to take it from me. I chased it and I caught it. It belongs to SkyClan."

Juniperclaw's whiskers twitched menacingly. "Is this how SkyClan shows respect for us? When we gave you some of our territory, we were doing you a favor. Now you steal our prey."

"I'm not stealing." Plumwillow's eyes flared with anger. "And when we moved into our new home, we did *you* a favor. You admitted that you weren't strong enough to patrol a large territory. With us patrolling, you know your border is safe from *rogues*." She emphasized the last word with satisfaction.

Grassheart stared in disbelief. "Does SkyClan think it's *protecting* us?"

Plumwillow flicked her tail. "There are barely enough of you to make a Clan. *Of course* we're protecting you. So is ThunderClan. We are keeping your borders safe while you recover."

Tigerheart quickly padded between his Clanmates and Plumwillow. The SkyClan warrior wasn't making this easy. But she did have a point: Having friendly allies on their borders was useful. Would ShadowClan be wise to antagonize

SkyClan by stealing Plumwillow's catch? Was she really prepared to fight for it? The ShadowClan cats might be weak, but four warriors and an apprentice could easily hurt a lone warrior. He checked the slope to see if Plumwillow was part of a patrol, but it was deserted. *She's brave.* He admired her courage. It reminded him, with a twinge, of Dovewing.

"Tigerheart?" Juniperclaw was glaring at him. "Let's take this rabbit and go."

"No." Tigerheart faced his Clanmate. Plumwillow *was* right. She had chased this prey down and killed it. "ShadowClan owes SkyClan for the rabbit Sandynose and Rabbitleap caught for us."

"What about the warrior code?" Grassheart looked outraged.

"Prey belongs to the Clan where it's caught," Snakepaw reminded him.

"I know what it says." Tigerheart shifted his paws. First his mother, now an apprentice. Did everyone think they knew the warrior code better than he did? Irritation pricked beneath his pelt. He could be with Dovewing now, not settling stupid squabbles over prey. He lashed his tail. "The rabbit came from SkyClan land, and Plumwillow was barely over the border when she caught it ."

Juniperclaw stared at Tigerheart, wide-eyed. "Are you serious?" He lowered his voice to a whisper. "You know how much we need this prey."

"But we are warriors," Tigerheart hissed back. He raised his muzzle. "The warrior code says that warriors are honorable and *fair*. Taking Plumwillow's prey now wouldn't be fair. But in the future, let's all remember that prey belongs to the Clan who owns the land on which it's caught." He eyed Plumwillow sternly. "Right?" She nodded curtly.

Snakepaw glanced at Strikestone, doubt shimmering in her eyes.

Strikestone shrugged at her. "He's the deputy."

"That's right," Tigerheart growled. "You will do as I say. Which is to let Plumwillow take her prey and go back to her territory." He urged Plumwillow to hurry with a warning look.

The SkyClan cat picked up the rabbit, nodded quickly at him, and headed for the border.

Juniperclaw lashed his tail as she disappeared over the rise. "Are you crazy?"

Tigerheart ignored him. "Let's get back to hunting." He returned to his position among the bracken and crouched down to watch the beech patch once more.

Juniperclaw exchanged an angry look with Grassheart while Strikestone nudged Snakepaw toward the undergrowth. Gradually they returned to their positions and dropped into hunting crouches.

Tigerheart's pelt prickled uneasily. Had he made the right decision? *Of course I did.* Rules were rules, but warriors needed to have common sense too. Surely, at the moment, a good relationship with SkyClan was more important than a single rabbit? *But ShadowClan is hungry.* He felt rainwater reaching through his pelt. He couldn't push away a thought nagging at the back of his mind. He shivered as he pictured Dovewing far away, her green eyes hollow with hunger as a bigger, stronger cat stole the prey she'd just caught. Had his worry about Dovewing made him kinder to Plumwillow than he should have been?

"Is that it?" Rowanstar stared at the vole and the bedraggled squirrel Tigerheart's patrol dropped onto the meager fresh-kill pile.

"We were lucky to find that," Tigerheart told him. "We'd have nothing if Snakepaw hadn't thought of stalking the beech patch." He glanced appreciatively at the honey-brown apprentice. Her gaze warmed with pride.

"Nothing?" Juniperclaw pushed past him and glared at Rowanstar. "Why don't you tell our leader about the rabbit you gave away?"

Rowanstar's gaze flashed toward Tigerheart. "What happened?"

Tigerheart saw anger in his father's gaze. "It was the right thing to do," he meowed. "Plumwillow had chased it and caught it."

"On our territory," Grassheart put in.

"She had only just crossed the border," Tigerheart reminded her, irritably. He'd abandoned Dovewing for his Clanmates, and now they betrayed him. He shot her a reproachful look.

Rowanstar growled. "If it had crossed the border, it was our prey. That's what the warrior code says."

"But what about the rabbit Sandynose gave us a quarter moon ago?" Tigerheart argued. Wasn't *anyone* going to support him? "If you believed so strongly in upholding that rule, you'd have insisted on returning it."

"If SkyClan wants to behave like soft-bellies, then let them. We don't have to starve just so we can be like them. We're ShadowClan." Rowanstar lifted his muzzle. "And that means something."

Tigerheart's pelt crawled with resentment. *Now* Rowanstar was behaving like a leader—over a *piece of prey*!

"I did the right thing," Tigerheart felt certain now. His worry over Dovewing hadn't influenced him. His instinct had been true: Warriors should be fair, and keeping peace with their neighbors was more important than one catch. "It was clearly Plumwillow's rabbit. And if there's one rabbit in the forest, there must be more. Let's catch our own prey, not steal from other Clans."

Rowanstar narrowed his eyes. "It was *our* rabbit," he growled softly. "We have to make SkyClan pay for stealing it."

"I gave it to them!" Frustration rippled beneath Tigerheart's pelt.

But his father wasn't listening. The ShadowClan leader nodded to Juniperclaw. "Come with me." Glancing around the clearing, he called to the cats watching around the camp. "Snowbird, Whorlpaw, Scorchfur, Flowerpaw, Grassheart, Stonewing! Follow me."

He marched out of camp. His Clanmates followed, exchanging approving glances, their pelts rippling with excitement. Tigerheart dug his claws into the ground. He'd stayed to save his Clan, and they weren't even listening to him. Was

Rowanstar really going to start a war over a rabbit?

He felt fur brush his flank. Tawnypelt's mew sounded in his ear. "It looks like old times," she murmured wistfully as the warriors disappeared from camp.

Tigerheart didn't look at her. "He's wrong."

"He's fighting for his Clan." There was relief in her mew. She was clearly pleased to see Rowanstar being so strong. "Why don't you go with him? He wants to teach you how to lead. It'll be your turn one day."

Dread dropped like a stone in Tigerheart's belly. *My turn.* He was going to be tied to ShadowClan forever. What about Dovewing?

Tawnypelt nudged him forward. "Go on."

Reluctantly, Tigerheart followed his father and Clanmates out of camp. Perhaps it wasn't too late to stop the war Rowanstar seemed so intent on starting. As he hurried through the woods, tracking the path of scuffed pine needles, he couldn't help thinking Plumwillow had been right. *We are keeping your borders safe while you recover.* ShadowClan was weak. It needed *allies* on its borders while it recovered, not enemies.

He remembered his dream and saw the strong sunshine glinting on his pelt as the shadows deepened around him. He saw the long, dark shadow he cast. *I must be the sun from Puddleshine's vision. Rowanstar is only leading them into trouble.*

He caught up with the ShadowClan patrol as they neared the SkyClan camp. Surely SkyClan would hear them coming? They weren't trying to hide their paw steps, and he could hear their voices before he saw them.

"We'll show them!" Juniperclaw muttered angrily.

"No one steals our prey," growled Snowbird.

"Tigerheart." Rowanstar turned to look at him as he slid past Stonewing and Scorchfur. "You've come to see how a Clan fights for its honor." Pride burned so fiercely in his father's eyes that Tigerheart felt a twinge of pity. *You are wrong.* But Juniperclaw and Snowbird were plucking excitedly at the ground while Grassheart and Scorchfur's pelts rippled. They were clearly relishing the prospect of a battle.

The wide stretch of bracken that hid the entrance to Sky-Clan's camp shivered. Leafstar pushed her way through. Plumwillow, Sandynose, and Sparrowpelt followed at her heels. The warriors stopped and stared quizzically at the ShadowClan patrol.

"Is something wrong?" Leafstar asked.

"You stole a rabbit of ours." Rowanstar cut straight to the point.

Juniperclaw snorted, and Stonewing raised his hackles aggressively.

Leafstar looked puzzled.

"I chased a rabbit over the scent line and killed it on ShadowClan land," Plumwillow explained.

Leafstar's gaze remained fixed on Rowanstar as Plumwillow went on.

"But Tigerheart said I could keep it, so I brought it back to camp."

"Tigerheart was wrong." Rowanstar glared at Leafstar. "SkyClan should know better than to take prey killed on another Clan's land. Or perhaps you forgot the warrior code while you were in the gorge."

Leafstar's fur twitched irritably along her spine, but her eyes remained calm. "We know the warrior code. And so, I assume, does Tigerheart. He let Plumwillow take the rabbit. I guess he had his reasons."

Tigerheart shifted uneasily. He still believed he'd made the right decision. SkyClan was worth keeping as an ally. But his Clanmates clearly disagreed. Scorchfur shot him a look of reproach. Tigerheart ignored it. This was Rowanstar's moment. Perhaps this challenge to SkyClan would regain him the respect and loyalty of his Clan.

It might also make enemies when ShadowClan needed enemies least.

"Tigerheart was wrong," Rowanstar growled again.

Leafstar whisked her tail lightly. "Even if he was, we can't give back what we've already eaten."

"Already?" Juniperclaw glared distrustfully at Leafstar.

"Do you think I'm lying?" Leafstar returned the warrior's gaze unwaveringly.

"I think SkyClan should be taught some respect," the black tom hissed. He glanced at Rowanstar, as though asking permission to attack.

Rowanstar glanced around his warriors, then flicked his tail. "Battle stances!" he ordered.

No! Tigerheart's pelt bushed with alarm. As Juniperclaw, Scorchfur, Grassheart, and the others crouched, ready to leap, he shot between the two groups of warriors. "We can't fight over a rabbit!" he yowled. He glared at his Clanmates, facing them with bared teeth.

They blinked at him, shock freezing them where they stood.

"We need SkyClan's friendship more than we needed that rabbit!" Tigerheart stared imploringly at his father, willing him to understand that good neighbors meant strong borders.

Rowanstar's fur pricked. His brow furrowed as he returned Tigerheart's gaze. Before he could speak, Leafstar cut in.

"If it's a rabbit you want, we will give ShadowClan the next rabbit we catch."

Relief washed Tigerheart's pelt. At least one leader was ready to be sensible. He looked hopefully at Rowanstar. "That sounds fair," he meowed.

Rowanstar was still staring at him. Tigerheart saw anger in his father's eyes. His Clanmates began to shift nervously, as though uncertain what to do. They glanced at Rowanstar, but the ShadowClan leader's attention was fixed on Tigerheart.

"I guess having their next rabbit sounds reasonable," Snowbird mewed grudgingly.

"I suppose it shows respect," Stonewing conceded.

Tigerheart saw his Clanmates' fur flatten as they eased out of their battle stances. He tore his gaze from Rowanstar and nodded at Leafstar. "That sounds like a fair settlement." He hoped she could read the gratitude in his gaze.

"We'll leave one at the border as soon as we catch it." She paused, her gaze flicking meaningfully around the

ShadowClan cats. "As a gesture of goodwill." With a flick of her tail, Leafstar turned toward SkyClan's camp and led her warriors through the bracken.

As they disappeared, Tigerheart looked nervously at his Clanmates.

"I suppose we do get a rabbit." Strikestone began to head toward the border. "And no blood shed."

"I still wish we could have left them with a scratch or two," Juniperclaw grunted as he followed. Snowbird and Grassheart glanced accusingly at Rowanstar, and then headed away. Flowerpaw and Snakepaw hurried after them.

Tigerheart gazed at his father, his heart pounding in his ears. Rowanstar still hadn't moved. "I solved the problem," he offered, hoping his father would see that Leafstar had conceded defeat in offering to replace the rabbit, even though it hadn't been taken without permission. That was surely a victory?

"How dare you undermine me?" Rowanstar's mew was ice-cold.

Tigerheart's paws felt suddenly heavy. Of course Rowanstar would misunderstand his intentions. He'd been trying to keep the peace because ShadowClan's security was more important than its leader's pride. "It would have been wrong to make enemies of SkyClan now." Was he wasting his breath? "We're not strong enough to protect our own borders. We need them to remain allies."

Rowanstar shot him a look of disgust, then barged past him.

Tigerheart followed, feeling sick. He'd done what was right for his Clan, but he knew he'd crossed a line his father would not easily forgive. It hurt to disappoint him. Worse, it worried him to know that Rowanstar could be so shortsighted. How could Tigerheart ever hope to protect ShadowClan if his father wasn't smart enough to see beyond a piece of prey? Hopelessness flooded him. He could keep the love of his father or he could save his Clan. What choice was that? Was this what he'd abandoned Dovewing and his kits for?

CHAPTER 8

Tigerheart hunted alone until nightfall. The three mice and two
shrews he added to the fresh-kill pile meant that all his Clanmates could eat. They'd find the flesh sweet and soft, but they
wouldn't taste the bitter resentment that had driven him to
hunt so determinedly.

He crouched now beneath a jutting knot of brambles
beside the warrior den. The night was cold, and his sodden
fur did little to keep out the chill. The rain pounded the clearing. Snowbird and Scorchfur were patrolling the borders.
The rest of his Clanmates had long since withdrawn to their
dens. Tigerheart didn't want to go to his nest yet. He didn't
want to listen to Stonewing and Grassheart snoring. He knew
he wouldn't sleep. Worry about Dovewing would crowd his
thoughts the moment he closed his eyes. It pricked at his belly
now. Had she found somewhere safe and dry to shelter for the
night? Perhaps she was keeping ahead of this relentless rain.

He saw two shapes move outside Rowanstar's den.

"Go and talk to him." Tawnypelt mew was muffled by the
downpour. Tigerheart saw her nudge Rowanstar toward him.

As his father approached, he straightened and sat up,

curling his tail tightly around his paws. Rain streamed from his whiskers.

"You shouldn't have interfered." Rowanstar stopped in front of him.

Tigerheart could see anger still burning in his father's gaze and, behind it, hurt. "I'm sorry." He dipped his head. He might have been right about the rabbit, but he knew how much he'd humiliated his father by stepping between his Clanmates and SkyClan. "I just didn't want to see anyone get hurt." He wondered if he should remind him that it would be a good idea to stay friendly with SkyClan. He decided to appeal to Rowanstar's kindness instead. "After all we suffered with Darktail, I didn't want to see more cats wounded."

Rowanstar seemed to flinch; the memory clearly pained him. "I understand how you feel, Tigerheart. You care about your Clanmates. You are a good warrior, but leading a Clan that has been torn apart by rogues is hard enough. Leading a Clan when your son and deputy publicly challenges your decisions is impossible." He gazed at Tigerheart, his eyes glittering solemnly in the darkness.

"I didn't mean to undermine you," Tigerheart meowed quickly. "I just wanted to do what was right."

Rowanstar held his gaze. "Your plan worked. SkyClan promised to return what they stole and everyone was left unscathed." He stared at the muddy earth for a moment before lifting his gaze to meet Tigerheart's once more. "I am proud of you. I know that one day you will be a great leader. But it is hard to be eclipsed."

Sympathy welled in Tigerheart's chest. Rowanstar wanted to do the best for his Clan, but he didn't always seem to know how. Had it always been this way? Had he been out of his depth since StarClan named him leader? *Perhaps I was too young to realize until now.* Tigerheart gazed softly at his father. "How did you know you wanted to be leader?"

Rowanstar blinked back at him. "I'm not sure I did. But when Blackstar made me deputy, I realized the difference between being a leader and a warrior." Tigerheart leaned forward, pricking his ears as Rowanstar went on. "A leader's loyalty and heart lie with his Clan. A warrior's loyalty and heart lie with his leader." His gaze seemed to reach deep into Tigerheart, tugging guilt from his belly. *He's telling me to trust him. But how can I when I know better? When the sun is strong, the shadows are strong.*

"Do you want to lead this Clan?"

Rowanstar's blunt question took him by surprise. Had his eyes betrayed his thoughts?

"Wh-when my time comes," Tigerheart stammered. "But there's no need to think of that now. You have moons left."

"I mean now." Rowanstar's gaze remained steady. "Leaders have stepped down before and handed leadership to their deputy if it's what is best for the Clan. I will support you if you wish to take my place. I can see that you are strong and wise, despite your youth. If you are ready to lead, I won't stand in your way."

Tigerheart could hardly believe his ears. "Now?" Suddenly the rain seemed to harden, filling his eyes and his nose, pressing in on every side until Tigerheart felt he was drowning. *Leader?* The responsibility snatched his breath. Every cat in the Clan would look to him for guidance, and rely on him to protect them. *And I'd never be able to join Dovewing.* His heart seemed to split with pain. His paws ached to run from the camp and keep running until he could escape from the endless rain and responsibility and think only of her and his kits.

He realized Rowanstar was staring at him questioningly. "I—I . . ." He could do no more than stutter.

"You aren't ready," Rowanstar answered for him gently. He dipped his head sympathetically. "You are still young and inexperienced. It takes courage to lead."

"I'm not scared," Tigerheart meowed quickly. "But there are other things I have to think about—"

Rowanstar hardly seemed to hear him. He seemed caught up in his own thoughts. "But if you don't wish to lead, then you must learn to follow." He lifted his chin, as though unaware of the lashing rain. "When I make a decision, you must obey. No arguing. No contradicting. You must follow me without question."

Tigerheart nodded. What else could he do but agree? If he refused to lead, then he couldn't undermine his leader. "I can do that," he promised.

"I hope so," Rowanstar meowed gravely. With a flick of his tail, he turned away and stalked back to Tawnypelt, who was waiting outside his den. Together they disappeared into its shelter.

Tigerheart crossed the clearing. He wanted to look up at

the open sky, where the branches of the encircling trees didn't touch. He stared at the gloomy clouds, which hid the night sky, and breathed deeply through the rain. He'd had a chance to lead ShadowClan. Should he have taken it?

As doubt swirled around him, paw steps sounded at the camp entrance.

Scorchfur and Snowbird padded into camp. Scorchfur was carrying a rabbit between his jaws. He dropped it at Tigerheart's paws. "SkyClan left this at the border."

Snowbird looked at the rain-soaked rabbit. "I guess the argument is settled."

"You were right to stop the battle." Scorchfur dipped his head to Tigerheart. "You showed SkyClan that ShadowClan deserves respect without blood being shed."

Snowbird glanced around the deserted clearing. "Rowanstar would have let us fight," she breathed in a hushed mew. "Puddleshine would be treating our injuries right now. But we have a rabbit instead of wounds because of you."

Scorchfur nodded. "If you'd been leader in the first place, ShadowClan wouldn't be in the state it is now."

Tigerheart stiffened. "That's not true. Rowanstar hasn't caused our suffering. That was Darktail's fault."

"If we'd had a strong leader, Darktail would never have been able to take over," Snowbird argued.

"Rowanstar doesn't know how to lead," Scorchfur agreed. "From now on, we will only take our orders from you."

Tigerheart's belly tightened. *No!* He'd just promised his father he wouldn't undermine him. "You can't—" But

Snowbird was already heading to her den. Scorchfur had picked up the rabbit and was carrying it to the fresh-kill pile.

I'm not leader, but I must lead. Tigerheart's thoughts spun. *Without letting Rowanstar see what I'm doing.* How was that possible? He felt trapped, tangled by the need to help his Clanmates while honoring his father. Would he ever be able to escape Shadow-Clan's plight? *What about Dovewing? What about my Clan?* His heart ached while questions twisted his thoughts into knots. *What about me? Am I destined to be alone, separated forever from Dovewing and my kits?*

CHAPTER 9

❧

Tigerheart shifted in his nest. Snowbird and Scorchfur's words earlier that night still rang in his ears. *From now on, we will only take our orders from you.* The den was damp. The moss at the bottom of his nest was soaked with rain. It chilled his pelt. Stonewing and Grassheart breathed softly beside him, lost in sleep. Strikestone turned in his nest with a grunt and began to snore. Tigerheart pushed himself deeper into his nest and tried to sleep.

What should he do? He couldn't please everyone. The cats he cared about all wanted something different from him. Dovewing wanted a mate; his unborn kits needed a father; Rowanstar needed his obedience; his Clanmates wanted his leadership. He couldn't help one cat without hurting another.

StarClan, guide me! He sat up in his nest, staring at the roof of the warriors' den. The stars were so far away, above the brambles, above the rain, beyond the thick clouds. Could his ancestors even see what was happening?

What does my instinct tell me? Protect my kits. Protect my Clanmates. Protect my father. How could he do all three? *My dream.* He pictured the sun shining on his pelt, his shadow stretching darkly

behind him. Was there guidance in the vision that he'd failed
to understand?

Puddleshine will know.

Tigerheart stepped softly from his nest and slid from the
den. He hurried through the pouring rain to Puddleshine's
den. Gentle snoring sounded inside as Tigerheart ducked
through the narrow entrance. In the darkness he could
just make out Puddleshine's shape in his nest. Tigerheart
approached quietly and stood beside him. "Puddleshine," he
breathed, wanting to wake the cat gently.

Puddleshine's eyes opened sharply. The medicine cat
leaped up and scrambled to the back of his nest. Hissing, he
narrowed his eyes defensively.

Tigerheart stiffened with alarm. Why was Puddleshine so
scared? "It's me. It's okay. Everything's fine," he soothed.

Puddleshine blinked at him, his arched spine dropping as
he relaxed. Pelt ruffled, the brown tom hopped from his nest,
his white splotches glowing faintly in the gloom. "Sorry," he
mumbled thickly. "I was dreaming. A cat was looming over me
in the dream, and I woke up and you were . . ." His mew trailed
away as though thoughts distracted him. His gaze dropped
for a moment; then he stiffened. "It was you!" He blinked at
Tigerheart. "*You* were the cat I was dreaming about."

Alarm jabbed Tigerheart's chest. Had StarClan sent a sign
after all?

"You were standing in front of me. I felt cold, even
though the sun was shining. There was blue sky, but I felt
chilly. . . ." He shivered. "Like the coldness of a cave that has

never felt the warmth of the sun."

"The sun?" Tigerheart echoed, his moth dry. *Another dream about the sun.* "What was I doing?"

"You stood over me, dark and huge, and I realized that the sun was streaming all around you. But you were blocking it." Puddleshine's mew slowed thoughtfully. "You were blocking the sunshine."

Tigerheart stared at him, his thoughts flitting to his own dream. His pelt had shimmered in the sunshine. *But the shadow I cast was darker than anything else in the camp.* Suddenly he knew what the dream meant. He wasn't the sun after all! He was getting in the way of the sun! Hadn't his father faded in the dream? "I shouldn't be here," he mewed. Regret choked him as the idea cut through his muddled thoughts as clearly as the warning screech of a magpie. He'd let Dovewing leave without him for nothing. He'd wasted so much time. "If the sun is to be strong and the shadows are to be strong, I must go."

"No!" Puddleshine leaned toward him. "You were casting a shadow, that's all. Isn't that what we need? Yours was the strongest shadow of all."

Tigerheart hardly heard him. His own thoughts were spinning, faster and faster. No wonder he'd been confused. So many mixed messages. How could he support his father and lead his Clanmates at the same time? Of course it was impossible. He shouldn't even be here. He should be at Dovewing's side. The longer he stayed, the harder it would be for his father to lead ShadowClan back to greatness.

"Tigerheart!" Puddleshine's eyes gleamed in the darkness. "ShadowClan needs you."

Tigerheart blinked at him. "Don't worry, Puddleshine. I know exactly what to do." He dipped his head to the medicine cat. "Thank you for helping me."

"Where are you going?" Puddleshine called as Tigerheart turned to leave the den.

"I need to get some sleep," Tigerheart told him. It was true. He hadn't slept well in days. But he wasn't going to sleep now. He had something far more important to do. "Go back to your nest," he told Puddleshine, and hurried out into the rain.

He scanned the clearing. There was no sign of movement. He could only smell the warm scent of sleeping cats curled in damp nests. He checked Puddleshine's den. The medicine cat hadn't followed him out. He pricked his ears and heard the rustle of Puddleshine's nest as the tom climbed back into it.

Dipping his head in farewell to his sleeping Clan, he crept quietly to the camp entrance. He slunk through the tunnel and padded softly into the forest. Only when he was clear of the camp and felt sure the pounding of the rain would disguise the sound of his paw steps did he break into a run. *I'm coming, Dovewing.* For the first time in days, his heart felt light. It chimed in harmony with his thoughts. He raced for the Thunderpath, like a bird flying for warmer lands, not knowing what his journey held, but certain that he must make it—that making it was the most natural thing he could do. Somewhere, far beyond the Thunderpath, Dovewing was managing alone. He was going to find her and, in another moon, welcome his kits to their new home in the strange gorse-spined den.

CHAPTER 10

❧

Tigerheart slept for a while before dawn. He had crossed the silent Thunderpath easily and let the landscape guide him because he guessed that was what Dovewing would have done. The marshland had led to fields. Hedgerows had led to valleys, which skirted hills and drew him on over farmland where ridges and hollows seemed to create natural paths. All the while he had prayed to StarClan that he was heading the right way, imagining what Dovewing might see and trying to follow her paw steps, trying not to think of the hurt that must have clouded her thoughts as she'd traveled. He had left her to make this journey alone. *I'm sorry, Dovewing. I'm coming now.*

The days of rain had washed all scents clean, and there was nothing to guide him but hope. As he'd sensed dawn easing the darkness, he'd found shelter in a rocky outcrop and slept. Daylight had woken him, and he'd hunted and caught a mouse. It had warmed him and refreshed his hope that Dovewing lay ahead.

He pushed on, his heart lifting as he saw clear sky opening beyond the gray clouds ahead. As he padded clear of the rain shadow that had drenched the forest for so long, sunshine warmed his pelt. Before long, he felt drier than he had for days. He fluffed out his fur happily. ShadowClan was far behind him, and with every paw step he felt lighter. The worry that had felt like a weight in his chest for so long slowly lifted. He would find Dovewing, even if he had to walk forever.

As the sun began to slide toward the horizon, throwing lazy shadows across his path, he saw a Twolegplace sprawling across the valley ahead. It cluttered the hollow between the enclosing hills with low stone nests, and he could make out a maze of Thunderpaths weaving through it. Instinct told him to go around, but where there were Twoleg nests, there were kittypets. And kittypets might know of the gorse-spined den Dovewing had seen in her dream. Fluffing his fur against the deepening chill of the afternoon, he turned his paws toward the Twolegplace.

He crossed a meadow edged by Twoleg nests. Twoleg smells reached his nose as soon as he neared the small patches of fenced land that lay behind them. Monster stench rolled over him. Strange food scents confused him. How could any cat hunt when prey-scent was hidden by such unnatural odors?

Perhaps that was why kittypets ate the food their Twolegs gave them.

As he wondered about kittypets, a thought lit him with hope. Dovewing might have come this way in search of information about the gorse-spined den, just as he had. A kittypet might have spoken to her. He'd know for sure that he was traveling in the right direction. He reached a wooden fence and jumped. Hooking in his claws, he hauled himself up, sending splinters of sharp-smelling wood showering down behind him. At the top, he warily surveyed the patches of green behind each Twoleg nest. Birds twittered in the trees, which sprouted here and there among the patches. His fur smoothed along his spine with relief. There were no Twolegs, and no scent of dog. No kittypets either. He frowned. He'd have to push deeper into the Twolegplace to find a cat to ask about Dovewing. He spotted an opening between the two closest nests, jumped down, and crossed the grass. Ears pricked, he pushed past a bush and slipped into the shadowy gap.

He crept through it, relieved to see light at the end of a stone-lined path. He hurried along it, his pelt prickling. Monsters were rumbling in the distance. The whooping of Twoleg kits pierced his ear fur. He slowed as he reached the end of the gap and peered out uneasily. A Thunderpath ran between two rows of nests. Stretches of grass, dotted by bushes and young trees, lay beside it. Had Dovewing been here? Longing seared his heart. He should have been with her. He tasted the air, wrinkling his nose. There was no familiar smell to guide him, but he couldn't stay where he was. He darted from the shadows and hurried that way, ducking beneath a low-spreading willow as a monster growled along the Thunderpath a few tail-lengths ahead. He crouched, waiting as it passed.

His heart fluttered like a trapped bird. He just needed to find one friendly kittypet.

Suddenly an excited *mrrow* sounded behind him. He spun. His pelt bushed as a soft bundle of fur flew at his face. It toppled clumsily over him and knocked him off his paws. As he rolled clear, he smelled kittypet. A tom, but a young one, his scent faint. Tigerheart darted from beneath the willow, and as the kittypet chased after him, he saw that it was a splotchy ginger tabby, thick-furred and hardly bigger than Whorlpaw. Its yellow eyes flashed excitedly. With a squeak, it reared for another lunge. Tigerheart batted it away. Was this how all kittypets fought?

The ginger tabby seemed unconcerned by the clumsiness of his attacks. Paws fluttered around his ears like butterflies as Tigerheart ducked another flurry. Then the kittypet bounced around him, ears twitching, fur bushed. "Come on!" he mewed eagerly. "Fight back!"

Tigerheart swallowed a purr. Did the kittypet seriously think this was a real fight? Tigerheart kept his claws sheathed as the tabby flung itself at him once more. He ducked the flailing paws and jabbed his nose beneath the kittypet's belly. Flicking his head up, he flipped the tom onto its back.

"Wow! Nice!" The kittypet scrambled to its paws and turned on Tigerheart. It ducked beneath Tigerheart's belly as though trying to copy his move, but when it tried to push up, Tigerheart hopped neatly out of the way. The kittypet spun. "Where'd you go?"

"I'm over here." Tigerheart sat down and watched the befuddled tabby drop into an ungainly attack crouch. He lifted a paw as the tabby began to wiggle its hindquarters. "Stop."

The tabby blinked at him. "Why? Am I winning?"

Tigerheart eyed him. "I'm not looking for a fight," he meowed.

The tabby paused. "But I was winning, right?"

Something seemed to catch the tabby's eye, because his gaze flashed to the Twoleg den behind Tigerheart. His pelt fluffed excitedly. "Got to go!" he mewed. "Let's fight again soon."

Before Tigerheart could speak, the kittypet hared past him, leaped a stretch of small shrubs, and disappeared into the shadows between two nests.

Tigerheart stared after him. What was that all about? If the kittypet was defending its border, then it wasn't very good at it. Perhaps it was just hoping to scare him off. Did the tabby think that a few soft jabs were enough to scare a warrior away? Kittypets must have bees in their brain. He shook out his pelt and crossed the grass. Following the Thunderpath, he skirted the row of Twoleg nests. The sun was slipping toward the hillside.

"Hi." A gentle mew made him stop. He looked toward the Twoleg nest where the voice had sounded. A pale cream she-cat was crouched on a wide wooden ledge jutting from the front. She glanced down at him, her fluffy tail twitching at the tip. "You're not from around here. Are you lost?"

Tigerheart eyed the kittypet and saw softness in her gaze. "I'm looking for someone." He padded toward the ledge and blinked at her hopefully. "A gray cat called Dovewing. Have you seen her? She might have passed this way a few days ago. She was looking for a den with spikes on the roof like gorse spines."

The kittypet looked puzzled. "Spikes?"

"It's in a Twolegplace where the nests reach into the sky," Tigerheart explained.

The kittypet glanced at the low Twoleg nests surrounding hers. "It won't be here, then," she mewed apologetically.

"Perhaps you saw Dovewing?" Tigerheart's belly ached with hope as he searched the kittypet's face for recognition.

"Fight!" An excited yowl sounded behind him, and he turned to see the ginger tabby rushing toward him once more.

Frustration spiked Tigerheart's pelt. *Not you again!* He reared to meet the tom's attack, flipped the kittypet's hind paws from beneath him with a swipe of one paw, and knocked him to the ground with another. He pinned him there, his claws sheathed, his paws buried deep in the tabby's fluffy pelt. The kittypet was so soft it was like pressing into moss.

"Hey!" the kittypet wailed indignantly, trying to wriggle free of Tigerheart's grip.

"I don't have time to fight," Tigerheart meowed firmly. "I'm looking for someone. If I let you up, will you back off?"

The kittypet squirmed. "But why? I'm having fun!"

"Just back off," Tigerheart growled.

The kittypet stopped squirming. "Okay."

Tigerheart let him go.

The kittypet leaped to his paws and backed away, his eyes bright. "That was an awesome move," he mewed. "Can you show me how you did it?"

"I said I don't have time." Tigerheart's pelt prickled with irritation. Every moment that passed, Dovewing was getting further away.

"Do you need to get back to your Twolegs?" the kittypet tom asked.

"I don't have Twolegs," Tigerheart told him. "I'm a warrior."

"A warrior!" The kittypet's eyes widened in wonder. "That's why you fight so good. I've heard about warriors. Have you been one for long?"

"Since I was born." Tigerheart supposed that was a bit inaccurate—he'd been a kit and an apprentice first—but that didn't seem worth explaining to this kittypet, whose eyes widened with interest.

"Do you live in the wild?"

"Yes."

"Why?"

Tigerheart paused. What a mouse-brained question. "Why do you live with Twolegs?"

But the kittypet seemed more interested in Tigerheart's life than his own. "Don't you get cold and hungry?"

"Sometimes."

"Do you really fight foxes and badgers?"

"When we have to." Tigerheart's pelt rippled along his spine. This was taking too long.

"Fuzzball," the she-cat cut in gently, clearly sensing Tigerheart's impatience. "Give him a break."

"*Fuzzball?*" Tigerheart's whiskers twitched in surprise. "Is that your name?"

Fuzzball blinked at him. "Of course."

Didn't this kittypet mind having such a dumb name? Tigerheart stared at him. "I've never heard of a cat called Fuzzball before."

"What's your name?" Fuzzball asked.

"Tigerheart."

The ginger tabby's eyes widened, impressed. "That's a great name!" He blinked at the she-cat. "Tigerheart." Saying the name seemed to please him, and he purred. "I want to be called Tigerheart."

The she-cat blinked at him fondly. "I think Fuzzball suits you better."

"Not as much as Tigerheart would!"

As Fuzzball puffed out his chest, the she-cat dipped her head to Tigerheart. "My name is Rose. I'm sorry we can't help you find your friend, but you said that she was looking for a place with nests that reach the sky." She turned to Fuzzball. "Do you know where that is?"

Fuzzball looked pleased to be asked. "No." He blinked at Tigerheart. "But Ajax might. He told me that he and his Two-legs once lived in a den so high he could look down at the birds."

Tigerheart pressed back a shudder. Why would anything without wings want to live in the sky?

"Come on." Fuzzball headed around the side of the Twoleg nest. "I'll take you to Ajax."

Tigerheart nodded quickly to Rose. "Thanks for your help."

She tipped her head. "Good luck!" she called as he followed Fuzzball. "I hope you find your friend."

Fuzzball wasn't a good fighter, but he did know how to travel through Twoleg territory. Tigerheart hurried to keep up as the ginger kittypet led him through a maze of paths and tracks that wove between Twoleg nests, over grassy clearings, and around fences. The tom showed no fear as he dodged beneath monsters sleeping in front of nests and slid between them as they dozed beside Thunderpaths.

"Here," he meowed, stopping at last on the grassy square behind a yellow Twoleg nest. While Tigerheart caught his breath, overwhelmed by the countless new scents that filled his nose and distracted by noises he didn't recognize, Fuzzball lifted his muzzle and yowled. "Ajax!" He looked expectantly at the nest.

A moment later, a clear flap clattered open near the bottom and a burly black-and-white tom squeezed out. He lifted his tail as he saw Fuzzball. "Hey, Fuzz! Are you looking for a fight?" His eyes sparked warmly.

"Not today," Fuzzball purred back. "Although this cat could teach you a thing or two about fighting. He totally beat me."

"*Rose* could beat you in a fight," Ajax teased.

Fuzzball flicked his tail. "One day I'm going to be the best fighter in the neighborhood."

Ajax wove around him, brushing pelts with the fluffy tom. "Perhaps," he conceded. "But you need to spend less time at your food dish and more time patrolling your territory."

Tigerheart's ears pricked in surprise. "Do kittypets patrol territory too?"

Ajax swung his wide head toward Tigerheart and narrowed his eyes. "Of course. If we have territory to patrol."

"But you're not warriors," Tigerheart pointed out.

"What's a warrior?" Ajax poked his muzzle forward and sniffed Tigerheart.

"Haven't you heard of warriors?" Fuzzball whisked his tail. He seemed happy to know more than his friend. "They're strays that live in the wild."

Ajax blinked sympathetically at Tigerheart. "Couldn't you find a Twoleg to take you in?"

Tigerheart's pelt bristled. "I wouldn't *want* a Twoleg to take me in."

Fuzzball lifted his muzzle. "He likes being a stray."

"A *warrior*," Tigerheart corrected.

"Well, whatever you are . . ." Ajax circled him slowly. "You look lost."

Tigerheart warily eyed the Twoleg den behind Ajax. What if a Twoleg came out? "I'm traveling somewhere to find a friend," he explained.

"His friend was heading for a place with nests that reach to the sky, like the one you used to live in," Fuzzball told Ajax.

"She had a dream that told her there was a den there with a spiky roof," Tigerheart added.

"*She?*" Ajax exchanged meaningful looks with Fuzzball. "Is this a romantic quest?" He didn't wait for an answer. "If you're looking for romance, there are plenty of she-cats here."

"This one's special." Tigerheart's pelt prickled hotly. Didn't kittypets fall in love?

"Whatever." Ajax shrugged. "If your friend was heading for a place with sky-high nests, she was probably looking for the Twolegplace I come from." The black-and-white tom glanced at his Twoleg nest disdainfully. "It's *way* bigger than this place. I used to live in a *huge* den filled with Twoleg nests. From the window, the Thunderpaths below looked tiny. Everything looked tiny. Twolegs looked like prey from up there. Even the monsters looked like prey."

Tigerheart swallowed. Dovewing was in a place where the dens reached so high that the monsters looked *tiny*. He had to get to her. "Is there a den there with big spikes like gorse thorns on the roof?"

Ajax narrowed his eyes. "Like gorse thorns?" He seemed to be thinking. "That sounds like a Twoleg gathering place."

Tigerheart blinked at him confused.

"I could see a gathering place from my old home," Ajax told him. "Every quarter moon, Twolegs would go there and yowl together."

"Why?" Fuzzball asked.

"It's something Twolegs do." Ajax sniffed.

Tigerheart's heart sparked with hope. Dovewing had been right. There *was* a gorse-spiked den. He was heading the right way. "How do I get to that Twolegplace?" he asked Ajax.

Ajax looked over his shoulder at his Twoleg nest, then swished his tail. "Follow me. I'll show you."

As he headed across the patch of grass behind the nest, Fuzzball glanced nervously at Tigerheart. "Are you sure you want to go there?"

Tigerheart nodded. "I have to."

Ajax called to them from across the grass. "Are you two coming?"

Tigerheart hurried toward him. He let the two kittypets take the lead. They were clearly more skillful at dodging Twolegs and monsters. They kept to shadowy gaps between nests, and when they needed to cross a Thunderpath, they knew exactly when to dart between the monsters. When they saw Twolegs on the pathways, they slipped around them, ducking nimbly if a Twoleg bent to touch them.

"If you can learn to dodge Twolegs and monsters like that," Tigerheart puffed as they reached a clear stretch of grass on the outskirts of the Twolegplace, "you can learn to fight."

Fuzzball blinked at him hopefully. "Do you really think so?"

"Sure." Tigerheart looked back in relief at the dens and paths that cluttered the landscape behind him. "You just need to work out a few battle moves and practice them until you can do them without thinking."

Fuzzball purred.

Ajax was padding on, crossing the scruffy grass. Tigerheart followed him. He could see two shiny tracks cutting across the scrubland ahead. A few tree-lengths away, a small nest sat on a wide stone ledge that edged the track squarely. Ajax stopped and nodded toward it. "That's where Twolegs wait for the Thundersnake to arrive."

"Thundersnake?" Tigerheart pelt prickled with unease. "What's that?"

Ajax stared at him. "You don't know? Are you kidding?"

Tigerheart fluffed out his fur self-consciously. "We don't have Thundersnakes in the forest."

Fuzzball padded between him and Ajax. "A Thundersnake is a huge monster that travels along the Silverpath." He nodded toward the shiny tracks that lay a few tail-lengths in front of them.

"The Silverpath leads to the big Twolegplace." Ajax added.

"That's why the Twolegs are waiting. When the Thunder-snake arrives, they'll climb into its belly and let it carry them there."

Climb into its belly? Shuddering with horror, Tigerheart followed his gaze and saw Twolegs milling on the ledge now. Some were gazing eagerly along the track. Others hung back or paced. Tigerheart could sense impatience in the Twolegs' restless movements. "How long till the Thundersnake comes?"

"Soon." Ajax turned his head and looked expectantly along the shiny tracks.

Tigerheart watched the Twolegs on the ledge. One of them put down the heavy bundle it was carrying and crouched beside it. The Twoleg used its forepaws to open up the bundle, revealing colorful pelts crammed inside. "What's that?" Tigerheart nudged Ajax.

Ajax turned to look. "It's a shell," he grunted. "Twolegs use them to carry their spare pelts around." He stiffened and looked back along the track. "The Thundersnake's coming."

Tigerheart followed his gaze. His ears twitched as the tracks began to hum. He felt the air tremble around them as their vibration grew stronger. Suddenly a monster appeared where the tracks dipped behind a ridge. It rumbled toward them like a storm.

Tigerheart's paws froze in fear. The Thundersnake was huge—far bigger than any monster he'd seen before. The earth shook as it pounded closer. Its paws carved a path along the tracks, which seemed to scream beneath its weight. He glanced at Ajax and Fuzzball. Why weren't they running away? He held his ground beside them, fighting the urge to flee as the Thundersnake screamed closer. It roared past them like forest fire. Hot air blasted from its flanks, which flashed by, flank after flank, until Tigerheart wondered if the Thundersnake would ever end. He narrowed his eyes against its choking stench and dug his claws into the earth. Its wind tore at his pelt, and he flattened his ears against its deafening howl. Stiff with terror, he held his breath as the world seemed to explode around him. Was this really where Dovewing's dream was supposed to lead?

CHAPTER 11

Tigerheart pressed himself against the earth, trying not to tremble as the Thundersnake's long tail slowed a short distance in front of him. Finally its flanks drew level with the stone ledge, and the creature rumbled to a halt. The waiting Twolegs didn't flinch as it growled to itself beside the ledge. How could they be so calm? Twolegs were even stranger than he thought. When gaps opened in the side, the Twolegs on the ledge shifted away as other Twolegs streamed out, then began to push past them and climb into the belly of the snake. Tigerheart's pelt bristled with fear. Why were they so trusting? Did they really believe the Thundersnake would let them out of its belly when they reached the Twolegplace? What if it was hungry?

"Quick!" Ajax hissed in Tigerheart's ear. "If you run, you can get inside."

Tigerheart stared at him in horror.

"Go on!" Ajax nudged him toward the ledge. "You have to get in before it closes back up. Then the Thundersnake will take you to the Twolegplace."

"I'm not getting into the belly of a Thundersnake!" Tigerheart blinked at him.

"Twolegs do it all the time," Ajax argued.

"But Twolegs are crazy," Tigerheart pointed out.

"He's right," Fuzzball agreed.

"*I've* been inside a Thundersnake," Ajax reminded them.

"And it let you out?"

"Of course."

"What was it like inside?" Tigerheart couldn't imagine it had been safe.

Ajax looked thoughtful for a moment. "It was loud and smelly and full of Twolegs. And my Twoleg carried me in a cage." He shifted his paws. "Okay. It wasn't the best day of my life, but I survived, and how else are you going to get to the Twolegplace?"

"I'll walk."

"It'll take forever." Ajax stared at him. The Thundersnake suddenly hooted and began to shudder. "Hurry!" He flicked his tail. "It's about to leave."

"Good." Tigerheart glanced toward the Thundersnake, relieved as the gaps closed. He let his fur smooth as the great creature began to pull away from the ledge.

"You can't walk all the way to where you're going," Ajax argued. "It's too far."

"I can walk anywhere," he told Ajax. "My Clan once walked over a mountain range to find a new home."

Ajax shrugged. "I don't know who your Clan is, but they sound as crazy as Twolegs."

"They sound awesome." Fuzzball was staring at him, wide-eyed. "Are they your family?"

"Some of them." A pang of loss jabbed Tigerheart's belly as he thought of Rowanstar and Tawnypelt. He might never see them again. He changed the subject. "I'll follow the Silverpath. It will take longer, but I trust my own paws more than I trust a Thundersnake."

Ajax shrugged. "If that's what you want." The black-and-white tom looked at the sky. The sun was sliding toward the hilltop behind them. "When will you leave?"

"You can stay with my Twolegs tonight," Fuzzball offered. "They feed strays." His tail twitched. "I'm always having to share my food."

"*Warriors* can feed themselves." Tigerheart meowed pointedly. He scanned the scrubland. The low-growing shrubs were bathed in golden light. Prey would be moving between them. He blinked at the two kittypets. He was grateful for their help, even if they did keep calling him a stray. "Thanks for the offer, Fuzzball, but I want to leave soon. I'll eat here first, though."

"How?" Fuzzball blinked at him. "There aren't any food dishes here."

"Who needs food dishes?" Tigerheart whisked his tail. "Let's hunt."

"Catch our own food?" Ajax looked unconvinced.

Fuzzball paced excitedly. "Hunt? I'd love to. I've chased the birds in my garden and tracked a mouse once, but I've never caught anything."

"You will today." Tigerheart dipped his head to the young tom.

"I guess it sounds interesting." Ajax wandered over the Silverpath, his fur gleaming in the afternoon sun, and headed onto the scrub. "I'd like to stretch my legs before I go home."

Tigerheart leaped over the Silverpath, careful not to touch it. It gleamed suspiciously, and stank of Thundersnake scent. Fuzzball followed him. On the other side, Tigerheart tasted the air. As the Thundersnake stench settled, he smelled the aroma of leaves and, breathing deeper, could just taste the musky scent of prey. He licked his lips. "Let's go this way." Keeping low, he pushed between two spiky bushes and followed a scuffed trail through the scrub. His nose twitched excitedly as the scent of prey grew stronger. He saw peck marks around the stems of the bushes and could smell that they were fresh. It must be a bird, a large one by the look of it.

Fuzzball and Ajax set the bushes rustling behind him as they followed.

"Are we tracking something?" Fuzzball asked loudly.

"Hush!" Tigerheart glared at the kittypet over his shoulder. If he carried on yowling like that, he'd scare their prey away.

Fuzzball looked apologetic and followed quietly for a few moments before yowling again. "I can smell something nice. Is that what we're hunting?"

Ahead, a fat grouse fluttered noisily into the air, its beating wings sending dust swirling over the scrub.

Tigerheart flattened his ears in frustration. He turned on Fuzzball. "We're not here to talk. We just hunt, okay?" he whispered through gritted teeth. He nodded to a side trail leading away between the bushes to one side. "I need you to go down there until you can't see me anymore and then sit as quietly as you can and listen for badgers."

"Badgers?" Fuzzball frowned at him, puzzled. "There aren't any badgers here."

"Then listen for foxes, or dogs." *Anything! Just keep out of my way.* As he nodded Fuzzball away, he saw that Ajax had disappeared. He rolled his eyes as he thought, *This is like leading a patrol of kits.* Then he purred, remembering that he should try to get used to this. He would be seeing his own kits very soon, and—one day—he'd be teaching *them* how to hunt. "Where did Ajax go?"

"I don't know," Fuzzball answered cheerfully. "I guess he got distracted. There are lots of good smells here." He looked along the trail where Tigerheart had nodded. "So I go that way, right?"

As he spoke, Tigerheart heard the thump of a rabbit's paws. He stiffened, scanning the bushes for movement.

Fuzzball raised his front paws off the ground and peered over the top of the bushes like a squirrel. "I see a rabbit! It's over there!" With a yowl he plunged into the undergrowth.

Pushing back frustration, Tigerheart strained to hear past Fuzzball as he crashed through bushes like a dog.

Ajax ambled along the trail toward him. "Caught anything yet?"

Tigerheart dug his claws into the earth. Why had he invited these two kittypets along? With all the noise they were making, he'd never catch any prey. He swallowed back irritation. Hunger was making him irritable.

Fuzzball's yowl split the air. "It's heading toward you!"

Tigerheart turned in surprise as brown fur flashed past him and disappeared between the bushes. He pelted after it, his fur prickling with excitement. The rabbit was plump but fast. It swerved beneath a sage bush. Tigerheart dived after it, his belly brushing the earth as he skidded under the low branches. The rabbit shot out the other side and veered toward the hillside, which sloped upward beside them. Tigerheart raced after it, fighting to keep his balance as he made a tight turn and cut across the rabbit's path. It pulled up, its eyes wide with horror as it saw him. He slammed his paws onto its shoulders and made a fast killing bite.

Paws pounded toward him. "You got it!" Fuzzball's excited face popped out from the bushes. He stared in delight at Tigerheart's catch. "*I* flushed it out!" he announced proudly.

Tigerheart looked at him, swiping the blood from his mouth with his tongue. "Yes, you did." Fuzzball was a mouse-brain. But he was good-hearted. And at least they'd caught prey. He picked up the rabbit and carried it toward an open stretch of earth on the hillside. Laying it down, he settled beside it, relishing the warmth of the evening sun as it began to melt behind the far hill.

As Fuzzball trotted after him and sat down, Ajax nosed his way from the bushes and sniffed the rabbit, his nose wrinkling. "What do we do now?"

"We eat it." Tigerheart leaned forward and tore a lump of flesh from the rabbit's flank. It was warm and juicy in his mouth. "Try some." He pushed it closer to Fuzzball.

Fuzzball sniffed it gingerly, then grabbed a small mouthful. He chewed for a while and then mewed, with his mouth full, "It's all fur." He sounded disappointed.

"Here." Tigerheart grabbed the rabbit in his paws and tore away a hind leg with his teeth. He laid the bloody stump in front of Fuzzball. "There's plenty of meat there."

Fuzzball stared at it, swallowed, then leaned close and took a second mouthful. He chewed unenthusiastically. "Is this what you eat all the time?" he asked warily, as though afraid of the answer.

"Sometimes we eat mice or voles or birds," Tigerheart told him.

"Does it all taste like this?" He licked his lips clean and shuddered.

"Not really." How could any cat think a rabbit could taste like a mouse or a bird?

Ajax sat down, keeping his distance from the rabbit. "I think I'll wait till I get home. It doesn't smell like *real* food. And it looks a bit bloody."

"Of course it's bloody. It's prey." Tigerheart blinked at him. Kittypets didn't seem to enjoy anything about being a cat. He felt sorry for them. But they seemed happy, and he was happy too, here in the sunshine. The rabbit was tasty and it was all his. For once there were no Clanmates to share it with, and these kittypets didn't seem to want any. If the journey was as long as Ajax had suggested, he'd need all his strength. He began to purr as he chewed. He'd found a trail that would lead him to Dovewing. He felt freer than he had in moons. His paws itched to begin the next part of his journey.

Quickly, he finished his meal, gulping down most of the rabbit. The kittypets had given up eating and watched him in awed silence, as though they were watching a squirrel chew its own leg.

He sat up and licked his lips, his belly full. "Thanks for your help." He dipped his head to Ajax and Fuzzball.

Ajax looked along the Silverpath, which followed the valley and curved behind a hill. "You're really going to walk?"

"Yes." Tigerheart fluffed out his fur. For the first time he wondered if Dovewing had walked. Perhaps she'd found enough courage to climb into the Thundersnake's belly. *She's braver than me.* Would she forgive him for not making the journey with her? What if he found her and she sent him away? *She can't. They're my kits too.* He wanted to help her raise them. "I have to get going." Standing here worrying wasn't going to change anything. He headed toward the Silverpath.

"Good-bye!" Fuzzball called after him. "When you come back, will you take me to meet your Clan?"

Tigerheart glanced back at the orange tom, affection swelling in his chest. *Dumb kittypet.* He imagined the look on the faces of his Clanmates if he walked into camp with Fuzzball at his side. What if he tried to show them his hunting skills? Tigerheart's whiskers twitched with amusement until a thought struck him like cold water. Would he ever walk into the ShadowClan camp again? Had he seen his Clanmates for the last time?

He quickened his step, forcing his thoughts forward as he

reached the Silverpath. He hopped between the tracks and followed them, picking his way over the wooden slats and between the scattered stone chips. Dovewing lay at the other end. He lifted his chin as the sun dipped behind the hill and cold shadow closed over him.

By the time he'd followed the curve of the Silverpath around the foot of the hill, his paws were sore, grazed by the sharp stones. He jumped over a track and padded onto the grass at its edge. The grass was damp with dew and soothed his pads. The evening was deepening quickly into night. Stars specked the sky, and the moon showed, pale and distant. Tigerheart strained to see where the Silverpath led. It seemed to reach toward the hill rising ahead of him, but he couldn't see its silver glint on the slope beyond it. Was a Thundersnake strong enough to haul itself up such a steep rise?

As he neared, he realized that the path seemed to end as it reached the shadowy base of the hill. Anxiety churned in his belly. Was this a dead end? Had he followed the wrong Silverpath? As he neared, peering into the darkness, he realized with a jolt that the Silverpath disappeared *into* the hillside. He narrowed his eyes, making out an opening. Was this a Thundersnake den? Had it taken the Twolegs into its underground lair? He stiffened against the fear sparking beneath his pelt and forced himself to keep walking. *Don't be such a kit,* he told himself sternly. Why would Twolegs get into its belly? They must know where it was going. Ajax had been inside, and it had carried him from his old Twolegplace to here. *It must be a tunnel.* Tigerheart relaxed a little. *Of course it's a tunnel. I just have to walk through it.*

Heart pounding, he approached the yawning hole. The utter blackness inside alarmed him. *Did Dovewing come this way?* He stepped into the darkness and shivered as it swallowed him. Pressing against the smooth stone wall of the tunnel, he used it to guide him. His gaze, usually so sharp in darkness, could make out nothing except more darkness. He put one paw gingerly in front of the other, acutely aware of his whisker tips as he felt for obstacles ahead. An icy breeze swept his pelt as wind streamed through the tunnel. He fluffed his fur against the chill, his heart pounding as he strained hopefully to see moonlight.

As he walked, he glanced backward and saw that the opening behind him had disappeared into shadow. He was completely enclosed by darkness. A sound stirred his ear fur. He stiffened as he heard a low rumble. His whiskers quivered as the Silverpath beside him began to tremble. A light showed ahead. The end of the tunnel? Even as hope pricked in his belly, he knew he was wrong. The sour stench of a Thundersnake tainted the breeze. Its roar slowly grew as the light shone brighter. A Thundersnake was heading toward him.

Tigerheart froze in terror. Was there room enough to hide? Jerking into action, he squeezed himself against the side of the tunnel and pressed down onto his belly so that he was flat against the earth. The breeze hardened, battering his face like freezing water. Even when he narrowed his eyes to slits, the glare of the Thundersnake's single eye stung his gaze. Its roar grew until Tigerheart thought his ears would burst. He flattened them and pressed himself harder against the wall and the earth. Tucking his nose under his paws, he braced himself for the Thundersnake to strike. It tore past like a hurricane. The earth shook. The air screamed. The Thundersnake's roar seemed to howl into every part of him until he felt that its fury would tear him apart.

Then it was gone. The noise died; the wind dropped. For a moment, Tigerheart wondered if he'd been deafened. Then he heard water drip onto stone nearby. Limp with fear, he lay still until he stopped trembling. His heart slowed, and he steadied his breath. As he pushed himself shakily to his paws, exhilaration swept through him. *I survived.* He'd never felt so close to death before. *Is this what losing a life feels like to a Clan leader?*

He lifted his muzzle and padded on through the darkness, quickening his pace a little. He wanted to get to the end of this tunnel fast. Stubbing his claws on a stone in the dark would be far less awful than facing another Thundersnake.

As he hurried on, praying for moonlight, a new scent touched his nose. He stopped, his heart quickening. He leaned down, quickly sniffing the ground. Fluff tickled his nose, its scent so familiar that his heart nearly burst with joy. Dovewing's fur! No blood, no fear-scent, just a few strands of her pelt, as though she had stopped to scratch an itch and had left a shower of fur behind. She had come this way! Tigerheart's chest seemed to burst with joy. He was on the right trail. Dovewing had to be waiting for him at the end.

CHAPTER 12

❧

Tigerheart woke, his heart pounding. He'd dreamed of ShadowClan. He'd been among them, but watching unseen, like a spirit from StarClan. They weren't aware that he was there. He wasn't even sure these dream cats would have known him, for they seemed to inhabit a reality he barely recognized.

The pines around the camp had seemed so thick they hid the sky. Darktail had stalked the clearing, and, hollow-eyed, his Clanmates had followed his orders to defend the border from a predatory SkyClan. Tigerheart had tracked them to the scent line and watched in horror as they battled desperately while SkyClan drove them back. Ivypool fought alongside SkyClan, her eyes shining with spiteful triumph as ShadowClan cats fell one by one. Scorchfur lay shrieking in agony, blood oozing from his flanks. Whorlpaw wailed over Snakepaw's battered body. Flowerpaw backed away as Hawkwing snarled at her, lips drawn back. Snowbird dropped to her belly as Leafstar's claws left red trails across the white warrior's face. And all the while Darktail had slipped among the shadows, urging them to fight, driving ShadowClan to more suffering—never entering the battle, but always goading them to sacrifice more.

Tigerheart's fur rippled as he pushed himself to his paws and blinked in the watery dawn light. The nest where he'd slept was hardly more than a pile of leaves, gathered in a drift against a fallen tree. He'd been traveling for days, following the Silverpath by day, hunting and sleeping by night. His paws ached from walking, and he felt colder each day. He'd grown almost numb to the roar and the wind of passing Thundersnakes and more than once had eaten prey one of them had killed. Or at least he guessed the Thundersnake had killed it, because he'd found it lying beside the track, sour with death. For the first time in his life he had tasted deer flesh. It was stale, not far from rotting, but he'd eaten it gratefully. He was ashamed to eat crow-food, but eating what the Thundersnake left gave him more time to travel.

Twoleg nests had grown more numerous in the past day. He'd slept farther from the track last night, away from the dens clustering around the Silverpath. He guessed he would reach another stopping place soon, where Twolegs could bustle in and out of the Thundersnake. He glanced around the small copse where he'd spent the night and tasted the air. He'd hunted and eaten before he slept, but he was hungry again. There were no fresh prey-scents left here. He would have to hunt as he walked.

As he padded from the shadow of the trees into a thin drizzle, last night's dream haunted him. Guilt wormed in his belly. Had he left ShadowClan unprotected? *StarClan, take care of them.* He fluffed out his pelt against the rain and focused on

Dovewing. She needed him. His decision to leave had been right. Hadn't Puddleshine seen his shadow block the sun?

He pushed his way through the wet grass and slid between two dens, emerging onto the Silverpath beyond. A puddle gleamed where water pooled between the tracks. Thirsty, Tigerheart stopped beside it and drank. He shuddered at the foul taste and padded on, feeling queasy and longing for the fresh rainwater pools of the forest.

The rain was hardening, and the damp reached through his fur as he followed the Silverpath down a gentle slope, where the cluster of Twoleg nests thickened. He could smell Thunderpaths and hear the rumbling of monsters beyond them. The track reached deeper into the earth, the land rising on either side in steep banks until Tigerheart's paws began to prick nervously. Twoleg fences walled the top of the banks. He was hemmed in now, like prey in a gorge. Ahead, a Thunderpath spanned the track, arching above it. Tigerheart glanced nervously over his shoulder. *Don't let a Thundersnake come now.* He quickened his pace, hoping that the Silverpath would lead into countryside once more.

Ahead, a flat stone ledge sat squarely beside the track. Another stopping place for a Thundersnake. It was slick with rain. Tigerheart scanned the ledge nervously, relieved when he saw no Twolegs waiting there. As he hurried past it, a mouse darted across the track. He pricked his ears. His belly was still hollow, so he dropped into a hunting crouch and watched the mouse scamper over the track and scrabble up the steep slope onto the stone ledge. Eyeing it hungrily, Tigerheart wondered whether to follow. The ledge was deserted. It would be easy enough to jump up, catch the mouse, and carry it to eat in a quiet spot beyond the Thundersnake's resting place. He was hungry enough to risk it.

The mouse scurried across the wide stretch of stone. Tigerheart leaped onto the ledge. He tracked it, his pads slapping softly against the wet stone. The mouse hurried for shelter where the ledge met a wall, and ran along the edge. Heart quickening, Tigerheart broke into a run, racing after the mouse. He leaped and caught it between his front paws. He hooked it up and snapped its spine in his jaws. The sweet odor of fresh prey flooded his mouth.

Suddenly, something clacked on the stone behind him. He turned to see a Twoleg walk onto the ledge. Another followed, then a third. Panic shrilled through his body as one turned and stared at him, its eyes widening in surprise.

Without thinking, Tigerheart raced for a pile of Twoleg shells. They were heaped on wooden slats, piled as high as the bramble walls of the ShadowClan camp. Gaps opened between them, large enough to squeeze between but small enough to hide in. He nosed his way inside the pile, the mouse still in his jaws. Wriggling deep, he caught his breath. The sound of Twoleg paw steps grew. Peering out between two shells, Tigerheart could see the ledge growing busy with more Twolegs. A Thundersnake must be coming. Once the creature had passed, the Twolegs would leave, and the ledge would be empty once more. All he had to do was wait.

He drew back as one of the Twolegs walked toward the pile

of clutter. A heavy shell dangled from its paw. With a grunt, the Twoleg heaved it on top of the pile and walked away. The shells around Tigerheart shifted slightly, then settled again. Tigerheart drew back into the shadows and began to eat his mouse. No one could see him here, so he might as well satisfy the hunger growling in his belly.

As he swallowed the last morsel, he heard a Thundersnake rumbling to a stop at the ledge. *Good.* The Twolegs would be gone soon, and he could start traveling again. He settled in deeper among the shells.

Then, with a lurch, the pile of shells began to trundle toward the Thundersnake. *I'm moving.* Shock spiked through Tigerheart's pelt as he felt the pile roll across the ledge, the shells rocking around him.

He tried to get out, but a shell was squashing his tail. As the pile of shells rolled into the gloom of the Thundersnake's belly, he tugged it free and scrambled from the pile. His pelt bushed as he saw the gap in the Thundersnake's side sliding shut. The bright air outside narrowed to a slit and, by the time he'd reached it, disappeared.

He pawed at the curious wall, as if his small claws could cut a hole through which he could pass. But it was useless.

I'm trapped inside the Thundersnake!

As darkness closed around him, Tigerheart tasted the air. It was rank and musty, the scent of Twolegs faint and stale. He peered out from the pile of shapes. Other piles and larger shells were strapped to the walls and fastened to the floor.

Tigerheart felt a prickle of relief. This must be the part of the Thundersnake where Twolegs stored their clutter. He tried to steady his breathing. At least he wasn't trapped with Twolegs.

As the Thundersnake rumbled beneath his paws, he crept out and picked his way around the clutter, searching for a way out. Light seeped in through a gap high up in the wall. Quickly he scrambled up a cold, hard branch and crept cautiously along it until he could peer out of the Thundersnake.

He saw Twoleg nests flashing past, taller than any he had seen before. From here he couldn't see their tops, but as the Thundersnake raced on, they began to grow wider, their stone walls darker. Suddenly the Thundersnake plunged into darkness. Light flickered inside its belly, but beyond the clear walls, blackness pressed against its flanks as the Thundersnake rumbled deeper into darkness. *It's just a tunnel,* Tigerheart told himself as his claws scraped against the hard surface. The Thundersnake began to slow. Tigerheart looked for daylight beyond the clear walls, where the darkness was easing. But there was no sign of sky, or of daylight. A harsh yellow glow lit a stone cave outside as the Thundersnake slid to a halt. *It's brought me to its lair. I feel like a piece of prey!*

Tigerheart pressed harder against the floor, terror swamping him as the gaps in the flanks opened and the Twolegs began to stream out.

He froze. *What do I do?* Surely it was crazy to step into a Thundersnake's den? Through the gap he saw another Thundersnake. It sat a tree-length away, at the other side of the ledge, humming while Twolegs crowded past it. This was a Thundersnake camp!

Dread crawled through his fur. Tigerheart stared at the Thundersnake camp, willing himself to move. If he didn't, he might never find Dovewing. *I have to be brave,* he told himself.

Then he pelted through the gap in the Thundersnake's flank, out into its heaving nest.

CHAPTER 13

Tigerheart fled along the ledge between two Thundersnakes. The stone was slippery beneath his paws; his claws slithered over it, unable to get a grip as he dodged back and forth, swerving around Twolegs. They yelped as he shot past them. He wanted to get away from the snakes, away from the Twolegs, but the great cavern seemed to stretch away in every direction. He saw tunnels opening at its edges, but the dazzling light almost blinded him, and he couldn't see where they led. Twoleg voices echoed from the walls and the high, domed roof. Clanking and rumbling made the air tremble. Countless scents overwhelmed his senses.

Heart bursting with terror, he cleared the snakes and glanced back, shocked to see yet more Thundersnakes flanking them. Twolegs hurried to and from them, disappearing into one, pouring out from another.

Instinctively, Tigerheart headed for a wall. Like prey, he craved shelter. He ran for the nearest one and crouched in its shadow, scuttling backward until he'd edged himself into a corner where two walls met. The Twolegs ignored him. Though they'd yelped as he'd passed them, none seemed interested in following him. He huddled in the shade of the walls and stared.

The cavern was huge. Brightly lit dens in the walls thronged with Twolegs. Arches and tunnels showed between them. Steadying his breath, Tigerheart let his panic ease and tried to think. If he could get used to the acrid stench of Thundersnakes and Twolegs, he might be able to detect fresh air. He slowed his breathing and narrowed his eyes. Opening his mouth, he let the jumble of scents bathe his tongue. At first it was overwhelming and he felt sick, but gradually he grew accustomed to the strange smells, just as his ears adjusted to the unending cacophony.

A few scents smelled tasty, others were sour, and some were bitter or rancid, but none tasted of fresh air. He would have to creep out of his hiding place and explore one tunnel at a time. Surely one must lead up into daylight?

Keeping low, he slipped along the wall to the front of a brightly lit den. A Twoleg padded out and headed across the cavern. Tigerheart hurried across the entrance and ducked around the far wall. A tunnel, lit by harsh light, opened ahead of him. He opened his jaws, hoping to taste fresh air that would guide him out, but only harsh scents landed on his tongue. *It leads away from the cavern, though.* Perhaps it would join another tunnel that would take him out of this warren.

The slick stone floor was cold beneath his paws, and he hurried, relieved that no Twolegs were using the tunnel. It opened quickly into another cavern, smaller and without Thundersnakes, but edged by more brightly lit dens. He scurried past each one, ignoring the surprised barks of Two-legs as he dodged around them. Mouth open, he tasted the air for the way out. He scanned the high walls, hoping to see a clear stretch that would show him the sky. But the walls were covered in strange images and shapes that gave no clue as to how he might get outside.

Suddenly a scent touched his tongue that made him freeze. *Cat.*

Another cat was here! He smelled tom scent with a rush of surprise that made him scan the cavern more closely. The scent was both fresh and old, as though a cat visited this place regularly. Did a cat *live* here?

Accustomed now to the idea that the Twolegs here wouldn't chase him, and that he only had to avoid their clumsy paws, he paused beside the opening of a brightly lit den and took a moment to analyze the tom's scent. It was stale here, but fresher beyond the den entrance. He headed toward the fresher scent, pleased to find it so strong that he knew the tom must have passed this way very recently.

Tracking the smell, he wove through the stone columns that stood like trees around the cavern. The trail led him toward a small opening in the lower part of a wall. A hard mesh lay in front of it, as though it had fallen away from the opening. Tigerheart ducked inside, relieved to find it dark here, and the scent of the tom much stronger.

A hiss from the shadows made him freeze.

"I'm Tigerheart," he mewed quickly. "I'm not here to fight. I just need some help." He unsheathed his claws warily. This tom might not want to welcome a new cat onto his territory. As his eyes adjusted to the gloom, he saw a skinny black-and-white cat glaring at him through slitted eyes.

Back arched, the tom showed its teeth. "Get out or I'll shred your muzzle."

Tigerheart backed away. "Please," he begged. "I just need to find my way out of this place." He tried not to wrinkle his nose. The tom smelled like Twoleg leavings.

His gaze flitted over Tigerheart. Slowly his arched back relaxed. "You're not here to steal food?"

"I don't need to steal food," Tigerheart told him. "I can hunt."

"You don't want to fight?" The tom sounded suspicious.

"No." He waited while the tom breathed deeply, clearly testing his scent.

"You don't smell like a rot pile cat," he conceded.

"What's a rot pile cat?" Tigerheart wondered if there were different Clans here too.

"There's a gang of cats that hangs around the rot pile behind the station," the tom explained. "They're always trying to drive me away. I don't know why. The Twolegs here leave enough trash for every cat."

Rot pile? Station? Trash? This cat used odd words. He stared at the tom, suddenly aware how far from home he was. He didn't even understand the language. His pelt prickled nervously. He puffed out his chest. "Why don't you fight them?"

"There are three of them." The tom looked at him like he was a mouse-brain. "There's only one of me."

"Don't you have Clanmates here?"

"Clanmates?" The tom stared at him, puzzled.

Tigerheart groped for a word this cat could understand. "Kin."

"I'm the only cat in the station."

"Is that what this place is called?" Tigerheart pricked his ears. "I thought it was a Thundersnake nest."

The tom blinked at him. "You're not from the city at all, are you? Only outsiders call trains *Thundersnakes*."

City? Tigerheart blinked back. "I'm from the forest. I'm looking for my friend."

"Is your friend from the forest too?"

"Yes."

The tom tipped his head. "I didn't know there were strays in the forest."

"We're not strays," Tigerheart corrected him. "We're warriors."

For the first time the tom looked interested. His gaze sharpened, glittering in the dingy light seeping into the den. "A warrior? Does that mean you fight?"

Tigerheart didn't like the inquisitive edge in the tom's mew. "I can fight if I have to," he mewed cagily. *What does he want?*

The tom dipped his head. "I'm Dash, by the way. I live here."

"I guessed." Tigerheart wasn't ready to warm to this prickly cat. He seemed to be planning something.

"So?" Dash leaned closer. "Do you know where your friend was heading?"

Tigerheart avoided answering Dash's question directly. "Is there a big Twoleg den here with a roof that has gorse spines sticking up to the sky?"

Dash frowned. "Gorse spines?"

"Like this." Tigerheart held up a paw and fanned out his claws.

Dash tipped his head. "There's a big den with a couple small thorns, and one big thorn. It's a Twoleg gathering place."

A Twoleg gathering place! That's what Ajax had called it! Could it be the gorse-spined den Dovewing had dreamed about? He had to check. "Is it near here?"

"It's not far."

"Can you show me?"

Dash looked down at his paws. "I can help you—if you help me."

"You need help?" Tigerheart's eyes narrowed. Dash sounded cagey. Was he going to ask Tigerheart to do something bad?

"I told you," Dash meowed. "The rot pile cats have been trying to drive me away. If they thought I had a tough friend, they might leave me alone."

"You want me to help fight them." Why hadn't he just asked straight out?

Dash looked away. "I'm not so good at fighting."

"Of course you are. You're a cat."

"So are they," Dash pointed out.

Tigerheart felt a glimmer of pity for the tom. No cat liked to be bullied. "Do they belong to a Clan?" He wanted to know what fighting skills they had.

"Clan?" Dash looked confused. "We don't have Clans in the city. They're just strays."

Strays. Hopefully they wouldn't know any warrior moves. Tigerheart jerked his nose toward the entrance to Dash's den. "Can you show me where they are?"

"They'll be around the rot piles." Dash padded past him and slipped out into the cavern.

Tigerheart followed, relieved to have a guide this time. He trailed Dash as the station cat skirted a long wall, then turned to climb a tunnel that sloped upward. Twolegs streamed past them, unheeding, as the tunnel divided and then turned sharply. Tigerheart was met by fresher scents, and his fur prickled with excitement, even though they were slightly tainted by monster stench. Dovewing might be out there—she might be nearby. And if he could deal with these rot pile cats, Dash would take him to look for her.

He quickened his pace as Dash turned in to a narrower tunnel where there were no Twolegs.

Dash hurried along it. A wall blocked the end, but Dash nodded toward a piece of mesh, like the one lying outside his den. "The way out is through this vent." The mesh hung loosely over a small opening; Dash nosed it open easily and slid through. Tigerheart followed the station cat into a small dark tunnel. A cold breeze funneled over him as he glimpsed light at the end. It wasn't the harsh yellow of the station, but cool, bright daylight.

Relief swamped Tigerheart, and the panic that had been

sparking at the edges of his thoughts since he found himself in the belly of the Thundersnake began to ease. He breathed deeply as he squeezed past another vent into the open air.

Once outside, Tigerheart immediately smelled crow-food. The sour stink bathed his muzzle. Dash was gazing toward a stretch of ground where four huge red shapes—like square monsters—stood, overflowing with stinking Twoleg waste.

"Those are the 'rot piles'?" Tigerheart guessed. He drew back into the shadow of the station wall.

"Yes." Dash crouched beside him. From their hiding place, Tigerheart could see two mangy toms sniffing around the base of one of the rot piles while a big brown tabby she-cat dug through the litter at the top.

"That's them," Dash whispered.

"Which one is the meanest?" Tigerheart asked.

"Floyd." Dash nodded toward the smaller of the toms. He was brown and white, his muzzle filthy and his ear tips torn from fighting.

"Okay." Tigerheart assessed the three cats quickly. "You're going to have to help—"

"But I can't fight," Dash protested in a whisper.

"You only need one move." He turned on Dash and slowly but firmly swept one paw under the station cat's front paws, tugging them from beneath him, then swept another softly over his ears.

Dash stumbled, but Tigerheart caught him before his flank hit the ground.

"You try it on me," Tigerheart ordered.

Dash blinked at him, recovering from his surprise, then frowned thoughtfully. After a moment of concentration, he jabbed clumsily at Tigerheart's front paws, managing to hook them with speed rather than accuracy, and then swung an awkward blow that caught one of Tigerheart's ears.

"Not bad." Tigerheart stumbled and regained his balance. "I'll drive the she-cat from the top of the rot pile. As soon as she lands, you do your move on Floyd."

"On Floyd?" Dash looked alarmed. "But what if he fights back?"

"Don't worry. You just need to start the fight. I'll finish it," Tigerheart promised. "But it has to look like you attacked them, or they'll keep hassling you."

Dash nodded.

"Remember," Tigerheart encouraged, "you're fighting for your territory, okay?"

Dash's eyes flashed anxiously. Tigerheart didn't give him a chance to argue. "Follow me." He marched across the stone and leaped onto the rot pile where the tabby was rummaging. His paws sank right into the garbage. He swallowed against the nausea that swept over him as he felt wetness seep into his fur.

The tabby looked at him in surprise. Her warm scent touched his nose. "Hi." She flicked her tail at him flirtatiously. "You're new around here."

A hiss sounded from below. "Mae! Who are you talking to?"

Mae picked her way across the stinking rubbish and peered over the edge. "Just a stranger." She glanced back at Tigerheart and winked. "It's nice to see a tom who looks like he can feed himself."

Tigerheart glanced at Dash, who was padding across the stone toward the two toms. "I've moved into the station with Dash," he meowed quickly. "And we don't think there's enough food around here to share with you three." He flattened his ears and gave her a warning hiss.

Her gaze hardened instantly. "Do you really think you and that fleabag can drive us away?" She curled her lip. "We're the ones who own these bins. The sooner you learn that, the better." With a hiss, she flung herself at him. He leaped clear, the garbage shifting beneath his paws. This wasn't an easy place to fight. As he turned to meet another attack, his paws sunk deeper. Below, he heard an angry yowl.

"You think you can fight now, station cat?"

Struggling to get a paw hold, Tigerheart reared to meet Mae's attack. He wrapped his paws around her and, holding on hard, threw himself onto his side and rolled over the trash toward the edge of the rot pile. Then he dropped over the edge, dragging her with him. As his paws met the stone, he let his hind legs fold beneath him, absorbing the impact of the landing while he still held Mae.

She struggled and hissed in his grip. Behind him he heard an angry yowl. He glanced backward and saw Floyd collapse onto the stone as Dash swung a blow at his cheek. *Well done!* He flung Mae away and leaped between Dash and Floyd while the ragged tom found his paws.

"Hi," Tigerheart snarled. "I'm Dash's new friend." He

sliced his claws across the mangy tom's face.

He heard the tabby hiss behind him and kicked out his hind legs. His paws slammed into her chest. She grunted and staggered away.

The other tom stared, unmoving, from beside the rot pile. Floyd backed away, hissing. Tigerheart padded to Dash's side as Mae glared angrily at Floyd, her pelt ruffled.

"Is that it?" she growled at the brown-and-white tom. "Aren't you going to fight him?"

"*You* fight him," Floyd spat back. "His claws are sharp." He dabbed at his bloody muzzle with a paw.

"He threw me off the rot pile!" Mae snapped indignantly. She looked at the other tom. "What about you, Scrap? Aren't you going to defend me?"

Scrap looked nervously from Tigerheart to Dash. "Why don't we just go and find somewhere else to eat?" he mewed. "There are some more rot piles just down the street."

Tigerheart showed his teeth. "Good idea." These cats were mouse-hearts. "Go scavenge somewhere else. This is Dash's territory."

The rot pile cats glanced at one another uncertainly. Then Floyd shrugged. "I guess we could find other rot piles. There's no decent food here anyway." He turned and headed down the stone path that led toward a gap where monsters rumbled past. Scrap followed him, glancing reproachfully at Dash. Mae shot Tigerheart a look. "You didn't have to get *mean*."

"You've been bullying Dash." Tigerheart glared at her.

"It's his own fault for being so pathetic." She hissed at

Dash and headed after the others.

"At least he's willing to fight for what's his!" Tigerheart yowled after her.

"Yeah!" Dash fluffed out his fur. "So don't come back here."

Tigerheart glanced at him. "Are you going to be okay once I'm gone?"

"Sure." Dash blinked at him happily. "Now that I've seen how easily they give up."

"If they ever learn how to work together, they might be dangerous," Tigerheart warned.

"They won't." Dash watched them as they disappeared around the corner. "Cats tend to look out for themselves around here."

"They look out for one another where I come from," Tigerheart told him, trying to ignore the prickles of sadness in his chest as he thought about how much fun it was, hunting with his Clanmates.

"Why?"

Tigerheart stared at him. Couldn't he guess? "Cats are stronger when they work together."

"But isn't it easier when you only have to take care of yourself?" Dash seemed perplexed.

The tom's words sparked guilt in Tigerheart's belly. Wasn't that the thought he'd had when he left ShadowClan? *No! I'm going to find Dovewing. She needs me.* He blinked at Dash. "You didn't seem to be doing so well at taking care of yourself."

"I made you help me." Dash swished his tail. "That was pretty smart."

"You didn't *make* me do anything," Tigerheart told him. "I wanted to help you."

"Really?" Dash looked surprised.

"Really." Tigerheart glanced along the stone path that the rot pile cats had taken toward the Thunderpath. "Is the Twoleg gathering place that way?"

Dash followed his gaze. "Yes." He glanced hungrily at the rot pile. "Do you want some food first?"

Tigerheart still had the scent of rancid trash on his paws. "No, thanks. I'll hunt later." He craned his neck, looking up at the dens towering around him. It was like being in a forest, with slivers of sky cutting between the soaring rooftops. The sun was sliding slowly behind them.

Dash was still looking at the rot piles. "Come on, let's rummage for food. You'll like it. Some of it's really good."

"No, thanks." Tigerheart wished Dash would stop offering. He wanted to find out if the gathering place was the thorn den Dovewing had been looking for. "I don't eat crow-food unless I have no choice."

"*Crow-food?*" Dash frowned.

"Scraps," Tigerheart explained.

"Crow-food." Dash repeated thoughtfully. He was quiet for a moment, as though thinking; then he shrugged. "I guess if it's good enough for a crow, it's good enough for me."

Tigerheart's pelt pricked uneasily. Why did Dovewing believe it was better to raise their kits in a place where cats thought of themselves as no better than crows? "Come on." He headed along the stone path, flattening his ears against the rumbling of the monsters at the end.

Dash fell in beside him as they reached a monster sleeping beside a wall. It had lost one of its paws, and its pelt was dull. Tigerheart wondered if it was dead. Dash padded past it, unconcerned, and Tigerheart followed. At the end of the path, wind whisked around the corner. It stung his eyes so that the monsters and Twolegs, streaming past, blurred in front of him. Tigerheart hesitated, fear sparking beneath his pelt as Dash padded onto the stone walkway that edged the Thunderpath.

"Come on." The station cat beckoned Tigerheart with his tail.

Tigerheart forced himself out into the flood of movement. A stinking breeze washed his pelt. The glittering walls and towering dens made him dizzy. Roofs cut a jagged line through the sky. He dodged a Twoleg and pressed against a wall. "Why do the Twolegs here need such big dens?" he asked, trying to distract himself from the panic welling in his chest.

"There are a lot of Twolegs in the city." Dash ducked beside him as Twolegs streamed past them. "I guess they've all got to sleep somewhere."

Tigerheart blinked at the station cat. How did he stay so calm? Beyond the Twolegs, monsters were crawling along the road in an endless stream, honking at one another like geese. He was glad Ajax and Fuzzball had shown him how to slip around Twolegs and monsters in their small Twolegplace. That had seemed busy. This was overwhelming. He stared at Dash with wide eyes. "How do you get around here? It's so crowded!"

Dash shrugged. "Everything keeps moving, but not very fast, and the Twolegs and monsters aren't interested in cats. Just keep your head down and don't get in anything's way and you'll be fine. Follow me." He skirted the wall, following the stone walkway until a Thunderpath crossed it.

"Where now?" Tigerheart stared at the gap between the dens where two Thunderpaths crossed. Lights flashed on sticks, red and green, above their heads.

"Wait until that light shows green." Dash nodded to a light shaped like a Twoleg. "Then we cross the Thunderpath with the Twolegs. Just don't trip them. That makes them mad."

Tigerheart stared at the green light as it suddenly brightened. The monsters stopped as though an invisible wall had dropped in front of them, and the Twolegs streamed over the Thunderpath.

"Now!" Dash nudged Tigerheart forward with his shoulder.

Tigerheart hurried beside him. His heart pounded with terror. He focused on the Thunderpath, smooth beneath his paws, and forced himself not to break into a run. Twolegs flowed around them, and he didn't want to risk tripping them. Relief washed over him as he reached the walkway on the other side. Dash guided him forward along another stone walkway that lined an even wider Thunderpath.

Tigerheart kept his eyes fixed ahead. The noise and bustle around him made his head swim. How had Dovewing found her way through these noisy crowded trails? "Is the gathering place far?"

"Just a little farther." Dash picked up his pace as the crowd of Twolegs began to thin. He turned a corner onto a quieter walkway, narrower and with fewer Twolegs and monsters teeming between the dens.

They crossed more Thunderpaths, each a little quieter than the last, until finally Tigerheart saw a break in the dens and a stretch of green ahead. His heart soared at the sight of grass and trees. In the center sat a den, squat compared to the towering dens that surrounded it. Its stone walls were punctuated by stretches of colored stone that reflected the late afternoon light like shattered rainbows. A sloping roof stretched along the den like a bony spine. On either side, small spikes poked into the sky, and in the middle, one huge spike looked as though it were trying to spear the clouds. "The gorse thorns!" Tigerheart stopped and stared. Was this the den Dovewing had dreamed of? Surely it must be. He'd followed the Silver-path and here it was.

Dash stopped. "You can find your own way from here." He dipped his head to Tigerheart. "Thanks for chasing Floyd and the others away. I'll be able to sleep easier for a while."

Tigerheart dragged his gaze from the thorn den. "If they come back, don't forget the fighting move I taught you."

"I won't." Dash blinked at him happily. "Good luck. I hope you find your friend."

"So do I."

As Dash turned back along the pathway, Tigerheart stared at the gathering place. It seemed empty. The stretch of grass surrounding it was deserted. Thin slabs of stone stood upright in neat rows. Tigerheart hurried forward and, relieved to feel grass underpaw once again, wove between them. He tasted the air, hoping to catch Dovewing's scent. His heart tightened as he scanned the great, glittering den. *I'm here. . . . I just hope that Dovewing is here too.*

CHAPTER 14

The thin stone slabs cast long shadows as the sun slid behind the huge dens. Tigerheart shook out his fur. The rumbling of monsters was quieter here. This patch of green seemed sheltered from the noise and movement of the heaving city by the trees growing among the slabs. Their branches crisscrossed the sky, rattling softly in a breeze that carried reminders of forest scents among the Twoleg stench. Tigerheart remembered with a pang the secluded glade where he and Dovewing had met in secret. Would she forgive him for not meeting her there before she left? He tasted the air anxiously, hoping to catch a scent that would lead him to her.

"Who are you?" A growl sounded on the evening air.

Tigerheart unsheathed his claws defensively and scanned the stones.

Green eyes glared through the fading light. A tortoiseshell she-cat faced him, her black muzzle thrust forward. Two toms flanked her, one small but well-muscled with a brown-and-black splotched pelt, the other smoky gray and long-furred.

The three cats padded slowly toward him, flattening their ears aggressively as they neared.

"I'm looking for someone," Tigerheart told them quickly. His heart lurched as he wondered if Dovewing had met these cats. They didn't seem welcoming. What if they'd chased her off? Or hurt her?

The toms halted as the tortoiseshell flicked her tail. She padded closer to Tigerheart, showing her teeth. "Who are you?" she repeated slowly.

"My name's Tigerheart." He glanced at the gathering place behind the tortoiseshell. The sun had dropped behind the skyline and swept it into shadow. Without its glittering walls and glinting roof, it looked gloomy and forbidding. "My friend traveled a long way to find this place. And I've traveled a long way to find her."

Curiosity glittered in the tortoiseshell's gaze. "You're looking for a she-cat?"

"She's my mate." Tigerheart felt his throat tighten. Saying the words opened grief in his chest that he'd ignored for so long. He'd forgotten how much he missed Dovewing. "She's carrying my kits."

The tortoiseshell tipped her head. Her ears pricked. Her gaze lost its menace. "What's her name?"

"Dovewing." Tigerheart's mew was thick with emotion. He felt suddenly weary.

She glanced over her shoulder at the brown-and-black tom. "Ant. Go and see if there's a cat with that name here."

As he hurried away, she snapped her gaze back to Tigerheart.

Tigerheart blinked at the tortoiseshell hopefully as Ant

disappeared into the shadows around the gathering place.

"My name's Fierce," she told him. She nodded toward the gray tom. "That's Cobweb."

"Do you live here?"

Fierce eyed him distrustfully. "How long have you been traveling?"

"Days."

"You must be tired."

Tigerheart lifted his chin, ignoring the weariness dragging at his bones. "Not too tired to keep traveling if I have to. I need to find Dovewing." Perhaps if he kept pressing, she'd tell him if Dovewing had been here.

Fierce didn't reply, but stared at him in silence.

Tigerheart stared back, desperately trying to read her green gaze. Was she hiding something? He saw nothing but the reflection of harsh Twoleg lights, which were beginning to glimmer behind him.

Cobweb shifted restlessly as the twilight deepened. At last, Tigerheart saw movement in the shadows. Ant was hurrying between the stone slabs. He stopped beside Fierce and whispered in her ear.

Tigerheart held his breath. Was Dovewing here?

"She says she'll see you," Fierce meowed curtly. "Follow me."

Joy burst in Tigerheart's chest. "She's here?" He could hardly believe it.

Fierce turned away and padded toward the gathering place. Tigerheart's paws trembled with excitement as he followed. He'd found her! Dovewing was here! Ant and Cobweb fell

in behind him as he wove between the slabs. Fierce led him
to an opening in the ground where stone steps led down to a
stretch of clear wall. The stones beside the clear wall had been
dislodged so that a gap opened beside it. Fierce slid through it
and Tigerheart followed. He emerged onto a ledge that looked
down into a large square cave. He scanned it nervously. "Do
Twolegs come here?"

"Not anymore." Fierce paused on the ledge.

Smooth walls lined the cavern. Twolegs must have carved it
out. It was lit by stretches of transparent stone set high in the
walls, which let evening light filter through. Twoleg clutter sat
in piles against the walls here and there. He couldn't believe
that Dovewing, a warrior, would ever have chosen to make a
home here. *How convinced was she that her dreams were a bad omen for
our kits?* he wondered.

He saw a cat move among the shadows. Another crossed
the wide, shiny floor.

"Where's Dovewing?" He pushed past Fierce.

"Wait." She nudged him out of the way and hopped down
onto a wooden ledge below and then onto the floor.

He stared at her as Cobweb and Ant brushed past him and
followed her down.

I can't wait any longer! "Dovewing!" His mew echoed through
the shadowy space.

"Hush!" Fierce shot him a warning look. "There are sick
cats here. They don't need you making a racket." She beckoned him with a sharp flick of her tail, and he jumped down
onto the wooden ledge she'd used. It wobbled beneath his

paws, and he dropped quickly to the floor, which felt cool and smooth, tainted by a sharp Twoleg tang. As he followed Fierce, the floor felt tacky, and it peeled stickily away from his pads with each step.

Cobweb and Ant flanked him, moving noiselessly over the floor.

Tigerheart smelled sickness as they passed a nest made of furless pelts. A one-eyed tabby leaned into it and lapped the dull fur of a stinking she-cat who lay there limply. Another cat carried a wad of something soft toward a hollow stick that jutted from the wall and dripped water onto the floor. She placed the wad beneath the drip and stood back while it soaked up the moisture. Fierce followed his gaze. "She's collecting water for cats too sick to walk to the drip-pipe."

"Is that where you drink?" Tigerheart stared at the stinking patch of damp spreading around it.

"Cats who aren't sick drink outside. The drip-pipe provides water for the rest," Fierce explained matter-of-factly.

Another nest caught Tigerheart's gaze, where a cat lapped the paw of another. It was hard to see in the shadows, but he smelled blood and herbs. "Is that a medicine cat?"

"A what?" Fierce looked at him.

"A cat who takes care of sick cats."

Cobweb followed his gaze. "That's Bracken. He's treating Rascal's rat bite."

"We all take care of sick cats here," Ant explained.

Tigerheart noticed that old wounds scarred Ant's cheek. Cobweb had half an ear missing, and Fierce leaned as she

stood—one of her legs was shorter than the others. Were all
the cats here wounded or sick? His belly tightened. Was that
why Dovewing was with them? Was she sick? "Where is she?"
he repeated anxiously.

"You mean Dovewing?" Fierce began walking again.

"Yes!" Anxiety pricked beneath Tigerheart's fur as they
passed a nest where two cats slept, curled together, their
breathing rough.

"She's here." Fierce ducked beneath a wooden ledge that sat
on wooden legs. A pile of furless pelts made a nest against the
wall at the back.

Tigerheart tasted a familiar scent, faint among the jumble
of odors. His heart leaped into his throat. "Dovewing?"

He saw her gray fur move among the strange pelts, and as
his eyes adjusted to the shadow, he made out her face. She was
staring at him, her eyes wide.

"Dovewing!" His heart overflowing with joy, he darted to
her and pressed his cheek against hers.

She pulled away with a hiss. "You didn't meet me!"

Flinching as though she'd raked claws across his muzzle,
he backed away. Pain sliced his heart. "I'm sorry. I tried. I
was on my way, but Scorchfur and Juniperclaw were going to
leave and I had to stop them and then a badger attacked us. By
the time I reached the glade, you were gone! I tried to follow,
but there were too many monsters and my head hurt." The
words poured from him, garbled and confused. He hadn't
really thought about what he was going to say, and now the
words seemed to tumble around each other, like play-fighting

kits. *Please understand!* "I hit my head when we fought the badger, and I couldn't cross the Thunderpath. And then I had a dream that told me I couldn't leave ShadowClan. I wanted to. But ShadowClan might have disappeared if I'd come."

Dovewing looked past him. Fierce, Cobweb, and Ant had withdrawn and were watching from beyond the ledge, their gazes protective but not prying. She nodded at them and they moved away. Then she turned to Tigerheart. "If your Clan needed you so much, what are you doing here?"

"I was wrong. I thought I was the sun, but I was the shadow. . . ." He trailed away, realizing he must sound crazy.

Dovewing seemed unfazed. Her cold gaze didn't waver. "So your Clan won't disappear without you now?"

"No." Tigerheart gazed at her, desperately hoping to find enough warmth in her gaze to cling to. "I hope not. I don't know. I just had to find you. ShadowClan must look after itself."

"So you only chose me when you thought your Clan didn't need you anymore?"

Dovewing's question silenced him. He'd chosen her because of Puddleshine's dream. But what if he *had* been the sun? Would he have stayed forever and become Clan leader? "I chose you as soon as I knew that you needed me more than my Clan did."

That was the truth.

But what if ShadowClan had needed me more?

He pushed the question away. Dovewing must believe that he would choose her over anything—even his Clan.

"I love you." He stared at her desperately. "I want to take care of our kits. I couldn't stay away."

For the first time, grief shimmered in her eyes. "You *tried* to follow me?"

Tigerheart nodded. "I followed you, but the badger and the dream and—"

"You're here now." Dovewing heaved herself to her paws.

For the first time, Tigerheart saw how swollen her flanks had grown. He hurried to her and rubbed his muzzle lovingly along her jaw. "I've missed you so much. How did you make the journey alone? Did you follow the Silverpath?"

Dovewing sat down heavily. He could hear her panting, and suddenly he realized he could smell blood. He sniffed her. His whiskers brushed a wound on her shoulder, and the tang of blood and herbs filled his nose. "You're hurt!" He blinked at her, his heart quickening. "Did it happen on the way? Did something attack you?"

"I'm okay," Dovewing reassured him gently. "It's just a fox bite, and Spire has treated it. It's healing fast."

"A *fox* bite?" In a flash, Tigerheart relived every nightmare that had haunted him since she'd left. She'd been so vulnerable on her own. How had he ever left her to make the journey without him?

"It happened while I was out with the guardian cats," she told him gently, easing down into her nest.

"The guardian cats?" Tigerheart blinked at her dumbly.

"These cats here." Her gaze swept around the cave. "They take care of one another. And of strangers who need help or healing." Her eyes rounded as she stared at him. "You see? My dream was right. I was meant to come here. Our kits will be safe."

For how long? Tigerheart's thoughts spiraled. Sure, the guardian cats seemed kind and helpful, like a whole Clan of medicine cats. But what about Dash, a cat who didn't even understand that cats were stronger together? Or Floyd, Scrap, and Mae? They only thought of themselves. Was this really a good place to raise kits? How could they ever learn to become warriors if they were surrounded by strays and loners?

Dovewing was still looking at him, her eyes huge and dark, glittering in the shadows. She needed him to be strong. She needed him to be a warrior. She needed him to stand beside her.

"Our kits will be safe here," he agreed. He stepped into the nest and curled around her, his belly softening as he felt the warmth of her pelt against his. He wrapped his tail tightly around her and tucked his muzzle behind her ear. "Your dream was right. It has brought us here." The nest was comfortable, the furless pelts soft against his spine. He relaxed into them and closed his eyes. "Are you hungry?" he murmured sleepily as she snuggled into him, purring. "I'll hunt for you soon. I want our kits to grow healthy and strong."

"I can hunt," she whispered. "There are plenty of mice around the gathering place."

"But I want to get used to taking care of my kin." Tigerheart's words were slurred by sleep.

"You always have," Dovewing murmured. "And you always will."

Her scent filled his nose as he nuzzled deep into her fur. Happiness moved through him like a greenleaf breeze and seemed to lift him gently up. As he breathed softly and deeply, drawing in her warmth, he floated into sleep.

"Wake up, sleepypaws."

Dovewing's gentle mew nudged Tigerheart from his slumber. *Dovewing!* He'd found her. Fresh joy flooded him. He smelled the scent of mouse and opened his eyes. Surprise spiked through his fur as daylight flooded his gaze. It was morning! He'd slept all night. He lifted his head sharply. "I was going to hunt." Confused, he gazed around the den. Slowly, memories of his arrival—the Thundersnake, Dash, the rot piles, the guardian cats—flooded back.

"I brought you this." She nudged a mouse toward him. "You must be hungry."

He was. His belly was as hollow as a deserted rabbit hole. He licked his lips. "But I was going to hunt for you."

"Are you frightened you'll forget how to catch a mouse?" Dovewing's green eyes sparkled teasingly. She looked happy. "Don't worry, Tigerheart. You'll have plenty of chances to refresh your memory. There are a lot of mouths to feed here."

Tigerheart followed her gaze around the cave. In the bright morning light, it seemed friendlier. But the smooth walls and shiny floor and Twoleg clutter still felt strange. He leaned closer to Dovewing. "We're living in a Twoleg den. Don't you find it odd?"

She shrugged. "Not anymore. Twolegs don't use it," she

told him. "They meet upstairs every few days, but they don't live there, and they never come down here."

Tigerheart glanced at the flat, square ceiling. "But they built this den. Why don't they use it?"

Dovewing hooked the mouse up with her claw and dropped it into the nest. "Stop worrying and eat."

The mouse tasted musty. There was no forest sweetness in its flesh, but he was grateful for it. As he began to eat, Dovewing glanced over her shoulder. A skinny black tom was padding toward them. Dovewing climbed into the nest beside Tigerheart and pressed against him. Was she frightened of this tom? He didn't look dangerous, and a small white-and-ginger kit was following him.

"Is this the cat you were talking about?" The kit wove excitedly around the black tom as he stopped beside the nest.

Tigerheart chewed his mouse, curiosity pricking in his fur. The black tom blinked at him slowly. There was a remote look in his eyes that made Tigerheart wonder what he was thinking.

"Yes. He must be the second one." The tom's gaze flicked over Tigerheart. "I was expecting two cats. Now they're both finally here."

Tigerheart frowned. What was he talking about? Had he known they would be coming? How?

Dovewing shifted beside him. "This is Spire." She dipped her head. "He's a healer here."

The kit puffed out his chest. "He's the *best* healer here. He knows things no other cat knows. And he dreams things. I'm

Blaze, by the way. I help Spire. And he looks after me."

Spire did not acknowledge the kit's words. Instead he just turned and began to pad away, as abruptly as he had come.

Tigerheart blinked at the healer, swallowing his mouthful. He'd seemed interested in their arrival. Didn't he want to stay and talk? "Nice to meet you," he called.

But the tom didn't seem to be listening. His head was tipped back, and he was staring into midair, mumbling to himself. Then he dropped his gaze and shook his head, as if answering a question only he could hear, asked by some cat only he could see.

Blaze hurried after him. "Are you hungry, Spire? Shall we go and look for food?"

Fierce padded past the kit. She flicked her tail fondly along his spine. "Go and ask Mittens to help you hunt," she told him.

"Okay." Blaze caught up to Spire and nudged him toward a tabby tom basking in a strip of sunshine.

Fierce headed toward Dovewing's nest. Tigerheart swallowed the last morsel of mouse as she reached them. Cobweb and a tabby she-cat were with her.

"I see you've met Spire," Fierce meowed.

"He said he was expecting us," Tigerheart told her.

"Spire says a lot of things." Fierce flicked her tail. "Most of it is nonsense. He gets confused. But we look after him. And he's a good healer."

"Blaze mentioned that." Tigerheart looked across the cavern at the kit. He was nosing the tabby to his paws.

Fierce purred. "Blaze is good for him. Keeps Spire's paws

on the ground even though his thoughts are in the clouds. I have no idea why a kit wants to spend so much time with such a strange cat, but they take care of each other."

Tigerheart looked at Dovewing. "You said Spire treated your fox bite," he said. "Do you think he is a medicine cat?"

Dovewing shrugged. "I really don't know. He says he has dreams . . . but I don't think they come from StarClan. Sometimes it seems like he just sees things that aren't there." Her fur ruffled. "I just wish he didn't keep looking at me like he knows something about me." She looked up at Fierce. "And he was acting weird with Tigerheart just now, too."

Fierce's eyes rounded with interest. "Really?"

Beside her, the tabby she-cat's ears twitched. "Sometimes Spire gets his weird dreams mixed up with reality. He probably thinks you can fly." She purred at Tigerheart.

"This is Cinnamon." Fierce introduced the brown tabby, who shifted her white paws shyly and dipped her head in greeting.

"Hi, Cinnamon."

As Tigerheart nodded in return, Fierce blinked at Dovewing. "I'm glad your mate has come at last." She turned to Tigerheart. "Dovewing's told us about you."

Tigerheart wondered guiltily what Dovewing had said. "I should have made the journey with her." His pelt prickled self-consciously. Did they think he'd let her down?

"You're here now," Fierce meowed. "And I'm hoping you can help us. Dovewing says you're a warrior too."

Cobweb leaned forward. "She says *all* cats are warriors

where you come from. She says you live in Clans. It sounds like a strange way of life."

"No stranger than this." Tigerheart glanced around the cavern. These cats were different from Dash and the rot pile cats. They understood what it meant to take care of one another. "How did you come to live like this?"

Fierce shrugged. "Who knows? Sick cats come and go. Some of us with wounds that will never fully heal stay on." She glanced at her short leg. "It's safer to have friends. And we each do what we are best at. Some heal; some hunt; some guard."

Cinnamon's gaze flicked over Tigerheart. "He looks fit. He might be useful."

"Of course he'll be useful," Dovewing lifted her muzzle proudly. "I just wish I could help too."

Fierce looked at her sternly. "You need to worry about keeping those kits safe. Look what happened last time you tried to help." She glanced at Dovewing's shoulder wound.

Dovewing's eyes flashed with frustration. "I didn't think my belly would get in the way of my fighting moves."

Alarm flickered in Tigerheart's belly. "You've been fighting?"

"We're having trouble with a fox," Fierce told him.

"It's stopping us from gathering herbs," Cobweb explained.

Cinnamon flicked her tail-tip. "Dovewing said that a few warrior moves would get rid of it, but hers aren't too good at the moment."

"She tried to teach us some," Cobweb chipped in.

"Dovewing is too close to kitting to train us properly,"

Fierce meowed. She glanced over her shoulder at the cats moving around the cavern. "We've learned a few moves, but she says we'll need to fight together if we want to drive off a fox."

"It looks like you already work well together." Tigerheart gazed around the Twoleg cave. Ant was waiting beside the drip-pipe with a wad of furless pelt to soak up water. A tortoiseshell she-cat was stripping tiny leaves from a twig and laying them on the side of Rascal's nest. A brown-and-white tom was jumping down from the cave entrance beside the clear wall. A rat dangled from his jaws. He carried it to the nest where the sickly she-cat lay. "Where did you learn your medicine skills?"

"A stray named Pumpkin stayed with us. He'd lived with forest cats and learned that herbs could be useful," Fierce explained.

Forest cats? Had Pumpkin stayed with a Clan? Tigerheart had never heard talk of such a cat. He wondered if Pumpkin might have stayed with SkyClan while they were still at the gorge.

Fierce went on. "He knew a few herbs and taught us what they looked and smelled like. Since then he's moved on, and we've experimented with new herbs and found what works and what doesn't. We realized that common sense is as important as herbs when it comes to treating the sick and injured. We've collected a lot of knowledge about healing. But fighting needs different skills. We were hoping you could teach us."

That must have been why Spire was relieved he had come.

He'd been hoping some cat would help them drive the fox away from the herbs.

"Well?" Fierce was staring at him.

Tigerheart dipped his head. He admired her directness. Her request was simple, and she offered nothing in return. How different she was from Dash. He was relieved that not all city cats were the same. "So the fox is keeping you from the herbs?"

"Nothing much grows here," Cobweb chimed. "But we found a space where we can get nearly all the herbs we need. We've gathered leaves there for moons."

Tigerheart nodded. "But now the fox has taken over the land." He glanced at Dovewing's wound. "Was it the same fox who did that?"

"Yes. We need to drive it away and gather herbs before the cold weather kills the plants." Fierce looked at him unwaveringly. "Will you help us?"

"Of course." If this place was going to be their home for now, Tigerheart would defend it as fiercely as he'd defend ShadowClan territory. "Show me this land. I want to know what we're dealing with."

He felt Dovewing stiffen beside him. "You'll be careful, won't you?"

"This patrol will just be to check out the fox's territory," Tigerheart told her. "Let's find out whether it's dug a den or is just passing through." He looked at Fierce. "It may just be a youngster looking for somewhere to settle, or it could be a mother looking for somewhere to raise cubs. Whichever it is,

WARRIORS SUPER EDITION: TIGERHEART'S SHADOW 149

it's better to know. It could be serious trouble."

Fierce dipped her head. "Thank you." She turned toward the cavern entrance, flicking her tail decisively. "I'll lead you there. Cobweb, Cinnamon, Ant." She raised her voice as she called across the space to where the scarred brown-and-black tom was swallowing the last mouthfuls of a mouse. Ant looked up eagerly.

"We're going to show Tigerheart the herb patch," Fierce told him.

"Are we going to fight that fox?" Ant hurried to join them.

"Let's check it out first," Tigerheart told him. "Fighting foxes is one thing; driving them away for good is another."

Fierce crossed the cavern and leaped onto the wooden ledge. As Tigerheart followed with the others, she scrambled through the gap beside the clear wall and disappeared outside. Tigerheart paused on the wooden ledge while Cobweb, Cinnamon and Ant filed past him. He glanced back at Dovewing. She was settling into her nest, yawning. Affection flooded him as he watched her curl into the old pelts. Her belly was swollen with his kits. Before long, they'd be a family. A purr rumbled in his throat. *Thank you, StarClan, for guiding me here.*

CHAPTER 15

Tigerheart followed Fierce, Ant, Cinnamon, and Cobweb, hardly daring to glance sideways for fear of losing them as they dodged between towering dens and teeming Thunderpaths. The howl of the city was even louder this morning. Twolegs swarmed everywhere. Clear walls reflected bright sunlight. Monsters barked and shrieked.

Hurrying after Cobweb, Tigerheart kept his ears pressed flat as they ducked beneath a sleeping monster and waited for a moment, then darted through a flood of monsters that had ground suddenly to a halt. How did they know when it was safe to cross? How did they remember the route? Scents overwhelmed him. The noise and movement disoriented him. He prayed he wouldn't lose sight of the guardian cats. If he did, how would he ever find his way back to the gathering place and to Dovewing?

The thought alarmed him, and he focused even more determinedly on Cobweb's tail as it disappeared around a corner onto a quieter stretch of stone.

Fierce slowed and glanced at the blue sky, which showed in a strip between the Twoleg dens on either side. Tigerheart felt like he was looking up from the bottom of a huge canyon. "Are we nearly there?" he asked. It seemed a long and dangerous route to the herb patch.

"The dens disappear at the end of this alley," Fierce told him. "No more Twolegs, just monsters and Thunderpaths."

Just monsters and Thunderpaths! She sounded so casual. "Won't that be dangerous?"

"It's okay," Ant reassured him. "We know a safe route."

Tigerheart glanced at the tom skeptically. Was *any* route safe in this place?

At the end of the alley, the land opened out. The Twoleg dens ended, and ahead of them stretched a maze of Thunderpaths. Monsters zipped along them, the air foul with their fumes. Tigerheart blinked in surprise as he saw a Thunderpath arching over the others. Its vast legs plunged wide stone paws into the earth below.

Cinnamon pointed her muzzle toward a green slope beneath the soaring Thunderpath. "That's where the herbs grow."

Tigerheart stared across the Thunderpaths twining between him and the herb patch. "How in StarClan do we reach it?"

"This way." Fierce hurried along the side of a wide Thunderpath. Monsters whipped past them, tugging at his fur. Their roar made his ears tremble, but Tigerheart saw with a rush of relief that Fierce was heading toward a ditch beside the Thunderpath. There was a gap beneath it. *A tunnel!*

Excitedly, he followed Fierce, Cobweb, Ant, and Cinnamon

into the dark hole. It was no bigger than a badger run. Its smooth, rounded walls echoed as they splashed through the shallow water running along the bottom of the tunnel. Tigerheart wrinkled his nose as he felt slimy stone beneath his paws and smelled the stench of ditch water. But at least it would get them safely to the other side of the Thunderpath.

Fierce led them from one tunnel to another until, at last, they emerged on the green slope beneath the flying Thunderpath.

Tigerheart looked up nervously at the wide stone path that arced over their heads. Its wide leg was planted firmly at the top of the slope. Low bushes and grass sprouted against it. The slope was dotted with scrubby plants, their leaves dusty from the stench of the Thunderpath. "Are these the herbs you use? Don't they taste bad?"

"We wash them before we use them to get the monster stink off," Fierce told him.

Cobweb was already hurrying toward the stone leg, sniffing eagerly at one of the plants. "The willow herb is doing well."

Ant wove around a dark green bush topped with white-and-yellow flowers. "The feverfew is ready for gathering."

"At least foxes don't eat herbs." Fierce was glancing around the slope warily.

Tigerheart followed her gaze. He tasted the air, reaching for the scent of fox among the monster stench. He caught a whiff and stiffened. The smell was fresh. "We should stick close to one another," he warned Fierce.

Fierce signaled to the patrol with her tail. "Let's check the herbs once we've solved the fox problem."

"But it's night-chill already," Cobweb meowed anxiously. "If we wait until ice-chill, the frost will have killed the freshest leaves."

Tigerheart guessed that night-chill must be leaf-fall, and ice-chill was leaf-bare.

Fierce glanced along the slope. "We're still half a moon away from frost."

"If we're lucky," Cobweb argued. "If we don't gather herbs soon, we'll have to wait until warmingtime."

Does he mean newleaf? Despite their strange words, these cats faced the same problems as medicine cats in the forest. Hadn't Puddleshine been pressing Rowanstar to send out herb-gathering parties in the quarter moon before Tigerheart left?

"Let's check the whole slope," he suggested. "I want to find out if this fox has made a den. And I need to find more of its scent. I'm not sure if it's a dog fox or a vixen." A vixen would be harder to drive out, especially if she'd already dug a den.

Fierce dipped her head and began to lead the patrol through the bushes. Tigerheart pricked his ears. The fox had been here recently, but he knew that foxes tended to sleep during the day. Perhaps they'd catch it napping. He picked up a fox scent and whispered to Fierce. "This way." Heading into a stretch of long grass, he followed the scent trail that drifted from the green stems. The Thunderpath soaring overhead cut a wide shadow over the slope. Tigerheart shivered in the chilly wind that funneled beneath it. Cobweb and Ant pressed close behind. Cinnamon and Fierce followed. As Tigerheart led the patrol uphill, a huge monster roared on the Thunderpath at the bottom of the slope. He flattened his ears against the roar and narrowed his eyes, scanning for movement ahead.

A growl sounded beside them. Tigerheart's chest tightened. *The fox!* He turned, unsheathing his claws as red fur exploded from the grass. It sent Cobweb and Ant tumbling. Tigerheart smelled dog fox. Thinking fast, he leaped as it snapped at Cobweb, who was struggling to find his paws. Hooking his claws into the fox's fur, Tigerheart tugged it back in time for Cobweb to escape.

Ant was already back on his paws. With a hiss, the tom swung a paw at the fox's nose. The fox lunged at him, its eyes sparkling with rage. Ant ducked just in time and, dodging beneath the fox's chin, spun and aimed another blow at its muzzle. Fierce leaped onto the fox's back and sank her teeth into its shoulder. Cinnamon snapped at its hind paw and sank in her teeth. The fox yelped and shook Fierce off, turning to snarl at Cinnamon.

Tigerheart hesitated, watching the guardian cats fight. They were brave and fast, but their attacks were hasty and uncoordinated. Each cat fought as if facing the fox alone. Each attack distracted the fox from the one before, but none was fierce enough to frighten it. *They're just making it angry.* Tigerheart could see frustration flashing in the fox's eyes as it responded to each assault, turning to meet one and then another. With a sudden bark of rage, it darted at Cobweb, sank its teeth into the tom's spine, and shook him. Cobweb shrieked with pain and fear.

Tigerheart flung himself beneath the fox's belly. "Bite its tail!" he ordered Fierce. "Get on its back!" he yowled at Ant. "Claw its throat!" he told Cinnamon. As the three guardian cats leaped to obey, Tigerheart twisted under the fox's belly and began churning his hind paws at the soft flesh above him.

As the cats swarmed around him, the fox yowled in pain. Cobweb dropped to the ground. His flank thumped the earth, and for a moment, he was still. Tigerheart glanced at him. Was he dead? Then the smoky gray tom twitched and groaned on the grass. The fox turned on the others. Tigerheart darted from beneath its belly and leaped to stand beside them. The fox stared at them as Cobweb scrambled to his paws. Tigerheart felt a surge of triumph as doubt flashed in the fox's eyes. *It's scared.*

Suddenly the fox's gaze flicked past them. Its expression changed in an instant. Joy, so malicious that it made Tigerheart's blood freeze, sparked in its eyes. A growl sounded behind them. *Two* foxes. He spun and saw a vixen padding toward them, her teeth bared.

"Cobweb! Get up!" Tigerheart stared desperately at the injured tom. "We've got to get out of here." These cats didn't have the skill to fight two foxes at once.

Fierce flung herself toward the dog fox, hissing and snarling, swiping her paws so wildly that it drove the fox backward. Ant darted toward Cobweb and nudged the smoky tom to his paws. Tigerheart turned to face the advancing vixen. Cinnamon pressed against his side. Together they reared as the fox leaped at them. Flailing wildly, they pushed it back. "Run!"

He yowled at Fierce and Ant as they helped Cobweb down the slope. His gaze flicked to Cinnamon. "You too!"

She searched his gaze. "What about you?"

"I'll follow," he promised.

As she raced after her friends, Tigerheart faced the foxes alone. They slid together and snarled at him menacingly. Fear closed his throat. He wanted to give the guardian cats a chance to get Cobweb clear. But he couldn't fight two foxes either. He backed away as they advanced. Blood roared in his ears. Showing his teeth, he bushed out his fur. As he glanced down the slope and saw Fierce guiding Cobweb and the others into the tunnel, the foxes rushed him. Their eyes glittered with glee. Swiping out one paw, then another, Tigerheart caught the muzzle of each. But they were on him. The force of their hard, strong bodies knocked him backward. He landed clumsily and turned. He had to flee. Hot breath bathed his tail as he hared down the slope. The tunnel was only a tree-length away. *Run!* The others had already disappeared into the shadows. He leaped for the entrance, panic scorching through his heart. Sharp teeth caught his tail. Agony seared like fire as he felt his fur rip. Ducking into the tunnel, he ran. Water sprayed out behind him as he pelted through the darkness. His tail shrilled with pain, and he glanced over his shoulder. Two pairs of eyes peered down the tunnel. The foxes had stopped at the entrance and were watching him flee.

Ahead, he could make out the shapes of the guardian cats against the flood of light at the far end of the tunnel. He splashed his way through and emerged a few moments after them onto the dirty strip of grass between two Thunder-paths. Deaf to the monsters streaking past either side, he stared wide-eyed at the guardian cats. "They're mates," he puffed. "The foxes are mates." He saw by the darkness in Fierce's eyes that she understood. If a pair of foxes had taken over their herb land, before long there would be cubs—and so many foxes that they would never be able to gather herbs there again.

CHAPTER 16

❧

"We're healers, not fighters." Pipsqueak, *a* brown-and-white tom, squared up to Tigerheart in the middle of the cavern beneath the gathering place.

"But Fierce says the cats who stay on here each have their own role," Tigerheart reminded him. "She said some heal, some hunt, and some guard."

Dotty, a pale white-and-ginger she-cat, padded to Pipsqueak's side. "Keeping watch and warning if danger is near is different from mounting an attack on a pair of foxes."

In the two days since the fight with the foxes, Tigerheart's tail had healed, thanks to the poultice Spire had smeared over the torn fur. At first Tigerheart had been concerned that Spire was inexperienced, because he kept mumbling, "Is this right?" as he prepared the salve. But after a while, he began to wonder— could Spire be seeking guidance from some unseen mentor?

The guardian cats' herb store was running low, and a chill in the air warned that frost might come sooner rather than later. Frost would kill the leaves the healers needed to see them through leaf-bare. Besides, they needed to drive the foxes away before the pair settled into a den. They couldn't afford to wait until any cubs were born; Tigerheart knew that as soon as the vixen was expecting, the foxes would be fighting for their young. It would be impossible to win a battle for the land, and the guardian cats' precious herb source could be lost within a moon.

Tigerheart had assembled the guardian cats in a circle while Dovewing rested in their nest. He wanted to teach them how to fight.

Tigerheart glanced around the circle. Fierce hung back, curiosity flashing in her bright green gaze. Blaze was watching excitedly beside Spire. The strange healer's gaze was drifting as usual, following the dust motes that hung in the shafts of sunshine cutting the air. Ant and Cinnamon shifted their paws impatiently. Tigerheart knew that they, at least, wanted to learn battle moves. Cobweb was still recovering from the bitemarks the fox had left on his back. But Boots, the one-eyed tabby who had tended to him, said the wound was superficial: Cobweb's spine was unharmed. The long-furred gray tom watched from his nest now, his eyes still dull with pain while Boots sat beside him. Rascal and Mittens, the tabbies known best for their hunting skills, eyed Tigerheart with interest, exchanging glances as Pipsqueak and Dotty stared at him challengingly.

Peanut, a healer cat, caught Tigerheart's eye. "We need to restock the herb store soon," she mewed, flicking her gaze from Tigerheart to Dotty. "And if that means fighting, we should fight. Cats' lives may depend on it."

Dotty stared back at her. "*You* won't be doing the fighting," she pointed out. "You're a healer here. You barely hunt."

Fierce padded forward at last. Tigerheart's belly sparked with hope.

"If you don't want to fight, then don't fight," she mewed casually.

Tigerheart stared at her. "You should encourage them!"

Her eyes widened. "Why me?"

"You're the leader." She acted like one, and all the cats dipped their heads in respect when they greeted her.

"You seem to have misunderstood." Fierce flicked her tail. "We are equals here. This isn't a *Clan*." She spoke the word as though the strangeness of warriors was beyond her understanding.

Irritation pricked in Tigerheart's pelt. "If you want to protect your territory, you're going to have to start thinking like a Clan."

"We don't *have* territory," Dotty mewed querulously. "We simply shelter here and take care of one another."

"What's the land you gather herbs on if not *territory*?" Tigerheart challenged.

"It's just land," Pipsqueak meowed.

Tigerheart's ears twitched. "So you don't mind foxes taking it?"

"Of course we mind," Pipsqueak snapped. "We need the herbs."

"Then you're going to have to fight for them!" Tigerheart raised his voice, looking pleadingly at Fierce. Hadn't she asked him directly for this help? Why wasn't she supporting him now?

Fierce padded around Pipsqueak and Dotty. "This warrior does have a point," she mewed casually. "We all joined this community because we needed help or shelter. Without herbs, some of us wouldn't be here now, and we owe it to future visitors to give them the same care we received."

Pipsqueak tipped his head thoughtfully. "Are you telling us to fight?"

Tigerheart's belly fluttered with hope.

Fierce glanced into a shaft of sunlight. "If we learn fighting skills, we can drive the foxes away and gather all the herbs we want. But it's your choice. Learn to fight or don't. It's up to you."

Dotty narrowed her eyes. "Are *you* going to let this warrior teach you how to fight, Fierce?"

"Of course." Fierce stopped in front of Tigerheart. "I think he has a lot of useful knowledge. It seems foolish not to learn from him."

He blinked at her gratefully. She was going to convince them!

Ant padded forward. "I want to learn how to fight too."

"And me." Cinnamon joined him.

Rascal and Mittens looked at each other.

"There are foxes everywhere in this city," Rascal meowed.

"And dogs." Mittens whisked his tail. "We'd be pigeon-brained not to learn some fighting skills from a *warrior*."

Tigerheart blinked at Pipsqueak and Dotty. Were they going to agree too?

"I guess there's no harm in learning," Pipsqueak conceded.

"So long as this outsider doesn't start thinking of himself

as our leader," Dotty mewed.

"We're equals here," Pipsqueak reminded Tigerheart.

"I only want to help." As Tigerheart dipped his head modestly, his thoughts flitted back to ShadowClan. Scorchfur and Snowbird had practically begged him to lead them. Here the cats didn't want anyone to lead them, especially not him. His frustration with the guardian cats melted away. It felt good not to be weighed down by responsibility. These cats only wanted to learn a few battle moves that would help them save their herb patch. Their simplicity warmed him, and he purred. "Let's start." He padded to the center of the cavern and dropped into the first battle crouch Oakfur had ever taught him. He looked around at the watching cats. "This is the easiest position to launch most battle moves from."

Before long, the guardian cats were practicing moves on one another while Tigerheart wove among them, adjusting crouches and advising which paw was the best to lead with or to push back on. As he moved from one cat to another, he remembered training Sleekpaw. He had spent long days in the forest with his apprentice, going over moves that could defeat ThunderClan, or confuse a RiverClan cat, or unbalance a lithe WindClan warrior. That was before the apprentices had turned on their own Clan, before the rogues had come and trouble had torn ShadowClan apart. The memory pierced his heart like a thorn, and he jerked his thoughts back to the present. These cats were learning how to defeat foxes, not warriors. There were no rogues here, or Clans to betray.

Tigerheart looked toward the nest where Dovewing was

sleeping, her chin hooked over the side. She looked so peaceful and content, her eyes closed, her ears twitching as she dreamed. She and their kits were all he needed to worry about now.

Fierce's mew surprised him. "I think we've learned enough basic moves. We need to come up with a plan."

Dovewing opened her eyes and gazed sleepily at the cats. Tigerheart blinked at her reassuringly and turned to Fierce. "A plan to deal with the foxes?"

Fierce nodded.

"We need to remember that we are not fighting alone, but together." Tigerheart remembered the skirmish on the slope. The cats had fought bravely but had been uncoordinated. He looked seriously around the guardian cats, who had turned to face him. "Be aware of the cats around you. Fit your moves with theirs. Let your attacks fill gaps they have left. See openings you can use, and always distract your enemy if you see your Clanmate in trouble." He corrected himself as he saw confusion flutter in their gazes. "If you see your *friend* in trouble." He hesitated. Did these cats see one another as friends, or merely as cats they lived beside?

Gray fur moved at the edge of his vision. Dovewing was padding toward them. "I've been thinking about how to start the attack on the foxes." She stopped beside Tigerheart and sat down heavily, clearly still sleepy. "If the patrol can take up positions around the slope, one cat can wait in the middle as bait."

"Bait?" Tigerheart looked at her, unease rippling through his fur.

"To make the foxes think there's no threat, so we can catch them off guard." she explained. "A cat who looks harmless." She shifted her swollen belly as though it was uncomfortable. "Like me."

"No!" Fierce cried out before Tigerheart could open his mouth.

"How could you put your kits in danger?" Dotty looked at her in shock.

"You're too fat to run away," Ant pointed out.

Tigerheart stared at Dovewing sternly. "You're not going anywhere near the herb patch."

"But I want to help," Dovewing objected. "And I'll worry about you if I'm not there."

"I could be the bait." Spire padded forward. For once, his gaze was fixed on the other cats. He looked from Fierce to Tigerheart, his yellow eyes glittering. "I'm skinny and small, and I look harmless and half-crazy most of the time."

"You don't look half—"

Spire cut Fierce off. "I know my thoughts wander and I often seem lost. But I'm no fool. These foxes need to go. That herb patch is important. I'm fast on my paws, and I trust you to protect me." His gaze swept around the guardian cats.

They nodded solemnly.

"Are you sure?" Fierce asked. "You'll need to keep your mind on what you're doing."

"I'm sure," Spire promised her. "And I will."

Tigerheart searched the strange tom's gaze anxiously. "You'll . . . *concentrate*?" He still wasn't sure what to make of

Spire's conversations with invisible cats. Surely he couldn't be talking to StarClan. But Tigerheart couldn't help worrying what might happen if one of them suddenly wanted to talk to him while he was out playing fox bait.

Spire flicked his tail. "Yes." He winked at Tigerheart. "I know you think I'm a featherbrain, but there's more to me than meets the eye. You'll grow to like me eventually. We might even become friends one day."

Tigerheart blinked at him. Would they be here long enough to become good friends with any of these cats? Once Dovewing had kitted and the kits were weaned and ready to travel, he'd thought that perhaps he'd be able to persuade Dovewing to return to the Clans. And yet, why should they? He liked the simplicity of this group: There were no leaders, no grudges, and no responsibility except to take care of the weak. Did he really want to rush back to a Clan on the brink of collapse and be caught up once more in a storm of distrust, betrayal, and recrimination?

Blaze bounced forward and began brushing around Spire. "You're so brave! I want to come with you. I could be bait with you. A fox wouldn't suspect a kit."

Spire touched his muzzle to the top of the kit's head. "You have to stay here with Dovewing. You can keep her busy so she doesn't worry about Tigerheart."

Tigerheart's whiskers twitched with amusement as the healer flashed him a knowing look. Spire knew exactly how to distract Blaze—perhaps he wasn't so crazy after all.

Blaze puffed out his chest. "I can do that." He hurried

toward Dovewing. "I'm the *best* at keeping cats busy. Spire tells me I keep him busy all the time. With me around, you won't even *think* about Tigerheart."

"She won't need to." Fierce lifted her chin. "With a little more training, we will be able to fight those foxes off easily."

Rascal narrowed his eyes thoughtfully. "How do we make sure they stay away?"

Mittens nodded. "We don't want to have to fight them every time we gather herbs."

The guardian cats looked toward Tigerheart expectantly. He blinked at them. He couldn't believe he hadn't told them already. "That's simple. We'll block up their den. My mentor taught me that if you block a fox's den, it never comes back. Foxes are far too lazy to dig the same den twice."

Fierce padded around the circle of cats, her tail whisking. "Let's get back to training then. The sooner we drive those foxes away, the better."

The next day, as the sun lifted over the soaring Thunderpath and cast the herb patch into shadow, Tigerheart crouched between the bushes near the top. From here he could see the scrub and grass twitching below. The guardian cats were hiding there. In the center, where the foliage opened onto a clear stretch of grass, Spire padded around distractedly. He gazed into the air and batted invisible prey. Tigerheart hoped he was pretending.

When he saw the gleam in Spire's eyes, he realized that the skinny tom knew exactly what he was doing. With a flick of his tail, Spire lifted his head and let out a mournful yowl.

Tigerheart's pelt prickled. That would get the foxes' attention, surely?

A growl sounded from the top corner of the patch, where the stone leg of the soaring Thunderpath reached into the earth. Tigerheart jerked his muzzle toward the sound and saw a red pelt streak through the scrub. It darted toward Spire, lips drawn back in a threatening sneer. Spire blinked at it, then shot away beneath a low-spreading juniper. As the fox raced after him, Fierce exploded from her hiding place. With a hiss, she swiped her claws along the fox's flank.

It turned, snarling at her, its gaze turning quickly from surprise to fury. Slinking low to the ground, it advanced on her. Tigerheart forced his paws to stay still. He wanted to rush in to help, but he had to trust that the guardian cats would stick to their plan. Relief sparked in his belly as Cinnamon and Ant leaped from their hiding place and flanked the fox. Pipsqueak leaped out behind it. The fox was surrounded. It spun, its long body curving as it took in the sight of four cats. Alarm sparked in its gaze. It showed its sharp teeth and dropped its head. Tigerheart's breath caught in his throat. A cornered fox was more dangerous than a full set of badgers. Wildness shone in its eye, and it lunged for Fierce, its jaws snapping at her paws as she leaped clear. Cinnamon and Ant leaped at its flanks, tearing at its pelt with outstretched claws. Pipsqueak caught hold of its tail and bit in hard.

Yelping with pain, the fox thrashed desperately as the guardian cats clung on. Fierce hissed at it and raked her claws across its muzzle.

Tigerheart still held his breath. The vixen must be close.

Foxes rarely left each other's side once they'd mated. He saw red fur near the Thunderpath leg. That must be where the den was. "She's coming!" With a yowl, he charged forward, blocking the vixen's path to its mate. As it crashed from the undergrowth, he faced it. Anger bristled through its pelt as it saw him. Instantly it tried to snatch at his ear, its jaws snapping shut a whisker away as he ducked clear. With relief, he saw Rascal and Mittens dart from their hiding places. Dotty leaped from hers, aiming for the second fox's tail as they'd planned. As she sank her teeth into the thick brush, Rascal and Mittens copied Cinnamon and Ant's tactic and leaped for the vixen's flanks. Tigerheart faced its muzzle, triumph surging in his chest. It staggered under the weight of the others. He swiped his claws across its nose. Confusion and panic lit its eyes. Its mate had been dragged to the ground. Fierce, Ant, Cinnamon, and Pipsqueak clawed at it with such speed and ferocity, it could only flail its paws and snap. With a yelp, the vixen called to its mate. The dog fox scrabbled free of its attackers. Shrieking in terror, both fled through the scrub, their shredded tails bobbing behind them as they disappeared from the herb patch.

Fierce met Tigerheart's gaze, her fur bushed with excitement. "We did it!"

Cinnamon, Ant, and Pipsqueak wove around each other happily while Rascal, Mittens, and Dotty congratulated one another.

"You moved so fast!" Dotty told Mittens.

"You got such a good grip on its tail, it didn't know what to do!" Rascal praised her.

Tigerheart shook out his fur, a purr rippling through him as he let his eyes rove over all the guardian cats. None of them had been hurt, and the foxes had fled. They had won!

He glanced toward the wide stone leg where the foxes had been nesting. "Let's block up their den in case they find the courage to come back."

His paws ached by the time he slumped down beside Dovewing in the cavern. Late-afternoon sunshine filled the Twoleg space with rosy light. He'd spent the afternoon with the others, hauling rocks and earth to the foxes' den and filling it so thoroughly that no fox would ever have the patience to unearth it.

Rascal and Mittens had left the patrol early to hunt, and they slid through the entrance now, mice dangling from their jaws. They jumped from the ledge and crossed the space, where the guardian cats had gathered to celebrate their victory. Dropping their catch in the middle, they nodded to Fierce, who was washing mud from her paws.

"We met Boots and Bracken while we were hunting," Mittens told her. "They're bringing more prey. There will be food for every cat."

Fierce nodded to the tabby tom, her eyes shining. "Thank you."

Mittens picked up two mice by their tails and carried them toward Tigerheart and Dovewing. He dropped them at their paws. "Thanks for your help today."

"Thanks for yours." Tigerheart pointed his muzzle toward

a huge pile of herbs at the side of the cavern. "Spire and Peanut gathered a lot of leaves."

Spire was lying next to Blaze nearby, his gaze clear and happy. "Once I've sorted and dried them, we'll have enough herbs for a moon."

Blaze snuggled closer to the skinny tom. "Will you teach me which herb is which?"

"Of course." Spire lapped the kit's head.

Pipsqueak and Dotty stretched happily in the sunshine pooling on the floor.

"I didn't think we could actually do it," Pipsqueak admitted.

Tigerheart blinked at him. "When cats work together, they can do anything."

As he spoke, Boots and Bracken jumped down from the entrance. They were carrying prey as they'd promised and dropped it beside the rest.

Tigerheart rubbed his cheek against Dovewing's as he watched the guardian cats settle beside one another to eat. "I'm glad we came here," he murmured.

"Really?" She blinked at him, her eyes round.

"We've helped these cats. And everyone seems happy." After the unease and mistrust that had permeated Shadow-Clan for so long, the simple worries and joys of the guardian cats seemed a relief.

Dovewing's gaze softened. "So . . . are you starting to feel like you belong here?"

Tigerheart felt his spine stiffen. That wasn't what he'd

meant. "I guess," he told her. "For now."

Dovewing said nothing. She just leaned against him, and Tigerheart felt the contented purr as her ribs swelled to nudge his. "I'm so happy you like it here. . . ," she murmured.

Tigerheart's belly churned. Fighting beside the guardian cats had felt good, but he'd still assumed that, eventually, they'd return to the lake . . . even though, lately, his Clanmates seemed more interested in fighting one another than their enemies. After all, he and Dovewing were warriors. Surely they would raise their kits to be, too?

Life here might be simpler, he thought, *but, without kin—without a Clan—will our kits be anything but strays?*

CHAPTER 17

❧

Tigerheart opened his eyes. Dawn light filtered through the high stretches of clear wall. Dovewing was sleeping beside him. He let himself wake slowly. In the days since he'd helped chase the foxes away, he'd grown accustomed to the slow pace of life among the guardian cats. There were no dawn patrols, no borders to mark, no dens or camp walls to repair. He could hunt when he liked, bringing food back for the others as well as for Dovewing and himself. He'd accompanied a patrol to the herb patch to gather leaves and checked the blocked fox den. There was no sign the foxes had returned; their scent was all but gone, replaced by Thunderpath smells.

Now he gazed lazily around the cluttered cavern. The guardian cats were still sleeping, except Boots, who was murmuring softly to Marigold, the old black cat who had hardly left her nest since Tigerheart had arrived. Marigold listened, her gaze distant and dull. Boots stopped talking and began gently lapping her head, working his way along her spine with gentle strokes.

Tigerheart guessed that the old cat was dying. He was glad she had the care and protection of the guardian cats. For a moment he wondered how often strays must die alone, in a chilly makeshift den, with no help for their pain. The thought stung him, and he pushed it away. He wasn't a stray; he never would be. And he'd make sure his kits never became strays either.

He stood up and stepped from the nest, turning back to tuck a few pelts around Dovewing so she didn't feel the chill of his absence. He padded into a stream of early-morning light and began to wash. The sound of his tongue rasping over his fur was loud in the silent cavern. Boots lifted his head and blinked at him, then returned to washing Marigold.

Fur swished nearby, and Tigerheart turned to see Spire creeping from his nest. The skinny black tom glanced back at Blaze, still sleeping among the furless pelts, then tiptoed across the cavern floor and leaped onto the ledge that led to the entrance.

Quiet as a mouse, the tom slid out the gap into the pale morning.

Why had he left Blaze? Spire normally took the kit everywhere with him. What was he up to? Curious, Tigerheart hopped onto the wooden ledge, waited until Spire had slipped out of sight, and then leaped up and squeezed through the gap in the wall. Stone dust trickled into his fur, and he shook it free as he padded out of the shadow of the gathering place. The leaf-fall sunshine was bright, the air cold, and a blue sky arced above. The lines of stone slabs, sitting upright in the dewy grass, striped the clearing with shadow. Tigerheart saw a shape move between them. Spire was weaving his way toward a tall chestnut tree at the edge of the clearing. A Thunderpath lay beside it, monsters rumbling sedately past. Tigerheart had grown so used to them, he hardly noticed. His gaze was following Spire.

Tigerheart lingered behind a stone slab and watched as Spire reached the chestnut tree. The tom sat down and stared across the stretch of grass, which was divided by a smooth stone path that led to what Tigerheart guessed was the Two-leg entrance to the gathering place. Was Spire waiting for something? Tigerheart padded closer, his pelt tingling with curiosity. Keeping quiet, he stopped behind the stone slab nearest the chestnut tree and, hidden from view, watched to see what Spire would do next.

"Is this what warriors do?" Spire asked pointedly.

Tigerheart stiffened, confused for a moment—he hadn't expected to hear the word *warrior* from one of the guardian cats, though it didn't sound quite so strange out of Spire's mouth. But he had been sure that he hadn't been seen or heard as he approached.

"I came outside to get a chance to think," Spire went on.

Tigerheart padded sheepishly from his hiding place and dipped his head to the skinny black tom. "I wondered why you'd left Blaze," he mumbled. "You usually take him everywhere."

"He usually *follows* me everywhere," Spire answered tartly. "But even a crazy cat likes me needs solitude once in a while."

"I'm sorry." Tigerheart backed away. "I'll leave you alone."

As he spoke, a monster drew up at the end of the smooth

stone path, and a brightly pelted Twoleg got out and began to walk toward the gathering place. Tigerheart froze and waited as the Twoleg disappeared inside.

"The entrance is open," Tigerheart mewed in surprise. The wooden slabs that usually barred the entrance to the gathering place stood open. "Will they find the cavern?"

"They won't even look for it," Spire told him matter-of-factly. "It's their yowling time. They do it every quarter moon, and in the evenings sometimes too."

Another monster pulled up and stopped at the edge of the Thunderpath. Several Twolegs climbed out and headed toward the gathering-place entrance.

Tigerheart hesitated. He knew Spire wanted to be alone, but he wanted to know what yowling time was. He'd leave soon, but for now he'd watch. Another group of Twolegs were heading up the smooth stone path toward the wooden entrance. Soon more were flocking toward the thorn den, and Tigerheart glanced guiltily at Spire, whose gaze hadn't shifted from the Twolegs. "I should go." Reluctantly, he turned toward the cavern.

"Stay and listen if you want." Spire shifted his paws.

"But you wanted to be alone," Tigerheart reminded him.

"Being pestered by a kit is not the same as sitting with a warrior." Spire didn't look at him. He was absently watching more Twolegs arrive. He must have watched it many times before.

Tigerheart padded to the tom's side and sat beside him.

"I like having Blaze around," Spire meowed suddenly, as

though he felt he had to explain. "But kits ask lots of questions, and this morning I need to think."

Tigerheart remembered with a pang how Grassheart's kits had asked questions relentlessly, and had wanted to play when Grassheart longed to doze quietly in the sunshine. The apprentices had kept them busy, teaching them games and hunting moves, and the elders had joined in, giving Grassheart a chance to rest. Would his kits ask questions? How would he and Dovewing cope without Clanmates to help them?

"I had a dream." Spire interrupted his thoughts. "I saw a tree fall. . . ." The tom's eyes had glazed; his mew had drifted into thoughtfulness. "It cut through a shadow as black as night."

A *shadow?* Tigerheart stiffened. Spire might not be a medicine cat, and they were far beyond the reach of StarClan—but there was something about the way that he described his dream that made Tigerheart feel it might be significant.

"Where it cut through," Spire continued, "I could see beyond."

Tigerheart's pelt prickled with foreboding. "What could you see?"

Spire looked at him, his gaze clearing suddenly as though waking from a trance. "Light."

Tigerheart's thoughts spun in a way they hadn't since he'd left ShadowClan. He'd thought he was free of omens and worry. But now, this cat, who had never even heard of StarClan, was talking of dreams like a real medicine cat. His dream sounded like one Puddleshine might have had. And it was about shadows. *Always shadows!* Tigerheart shivered. "The tree." He stared at Spire. "The one that sliced through the shadow . . . What sort was it?" *Could it represent Rowanstar?*

Spire shrugged. "It was a tree. A tall one. An old one."

"Was it a rowan tree?"

"I don't know," Spire told him. "A tree is a tree."

"But it's important!" Was his father going to destroy ShadowClan like the tree in Spire's dream? Or would he cut through the shadows that threatened to swallow the Clan and find a way to light beyond? "How did you feel when you saw the tree cut the shadow? Were you scared?" Tigerheart leaned closer. "Or did you feel hope?"

"I didn't feel anything, apart from curiosity." Spire looked at him blankly. "Why? Docs the dream mean something to you?"

Tigerheart looked away. "I don't know." He stared at the ground. Spire wasn't a Clan cat. How could his dream have anything to do with ShadowClan? "You dream a lot, right?"

"Yes." Spire curled his tail over his paws and looked back toward the Twolegs streaming into the gathering place. "Sometimes when I'm awake."

Tigerheart forced his fur to smooth. *Maybe they aren't real visions,* he told himself. *Maybe Spire just has . . . a good imagination.*

The gathering place began to hum with Twoleg murmuring. Then the noise swelled suddenly, and the murmurings joined into one voice that yowled in a way Tigerheart had never heard before. Their yowling lifted and fell, hardened and softened, like the song of a bird in greenleaf. Tigerheart stared at the great den. The huge thorn jutting from its roof sparkled against the cloudless sky as the Twolegs wailed inside.

Spire blinked at him. "Let's go back into the cavern," he meowed. "The yowling sounds more interesting from down there."

Tigerheart's ears twitched. He hurried after Spire as the tom headed toward the gap in the wall. Dovewing would wonder where he'd gone.

I'm coming. He broke into a run. Dovewing needed him. That's why he'd come here. *Forget about ShadowClan.* Why had he let Spire's dream spook him? *But what if StarClan is trying to reach me?* He pushed away the nagging doubt. ShadowClan had Rowanstar. *I'm needed here now, not there.*

He nosed through the gap ahead of Spire and jumped down to the wooden ledge. Dovewing was awake, sitting in a pool of sunshine, watching Blaze and Ant play fight.

"Am I doing it right?" Blaze looked eagerly at Dovewing as he wrapped himself around Ant's forepaw and began churning his leg with his hind paws.

"You're doing great!" Dovewing purred.

Spire landed on the ledge beside Tigerheart, and Blaze's gaze flashed toward them.

"You're back!" He released Ant's leg and rushed to meet Spire as the black tom jumped down from the ledge. "Did you go to watch the Twolegs yowling?"

Spire had been right. The cavern throbbed with the noise above. Tigerheart caught Dovewing's eye and blinked at her affectionately. He followed Spire down from the ledge and crossed the floor to meet her. "The noise is really something."

Ant, sitting where Blaze had left him, lifted his head. "The first time I heard it, I thought dogs were howling upstairs."

"It does sound like that," Dovewing mewed. "Isn't it strange?"

Tigerheart's fur brushed hers as he sat down beside her. "Twolegs are weird."

"Where did you go?" she asked him softly.

Before he could answer, Ant stretched. "Thanks for the fighting tips. I'm going to hunt." He nodded to Tigerheart. "Do you want to come?"

"Maybe later," Tigerheart told him. He wanted to speak with Dovewing first. Spire's dream had shaken him.

Ant flicked his tail. "Okay."

As the brown-and-black tom headed toward the cavern entrance, Tigerheart leaned closer to Dovewing. "I followed Spire," he told her. "He told me he'd had a dream."

Dovewing shifted her paws as though easing her swollen belly into a more comfortable position. "Fierce says he dreams all the time."

"I know," Tigerheart mewed, frowning. "He said that sometimes he even dreams when he's awake." Worry was tugging in his belly. "The way he talked about it, it seemed a lot like a dream Puddleshine might have."

"How?" Dovewing blinked at him, concern glittering in her green eyes.

"He dreamed about a shadow and a falling tree. The tree cut through the shadow, and he could see light beyond."

Dovewing flicked her tail impatiently. "I suppose you think that has something to do with ShadowClan."

"Perhaps it does."

"Why? Spire's not a medicine cat. And these cats all live so far away from the Clans, they had no idea we even existed. Why would StarClan speak to him?"

"Perhaps because they want to reach me here."

Dovewing rolled her eyes. "Because you're *so* important to ShadowClan."

Anger sparked in Tigerheart's pelt. "I *am* important to ShadowClan. I'm their deputy, remember?"

"You *were* their deputy," she reminded him. "But you gave all that up to be here with me."

Not forever. He searched Dovewing's gaze. Did she really think they would never go home?

She blinked back at him, doubt furrowing her brow. "You did give it up, didn't you?"

Guilt jabbed Tigerheart's belly. "I wanted to find you. . . ."

Her green eyes blazed angrily. "So you could bring me back?"

"No!" he yelped. "Well, yes . . . I don't know, exactly! I just knew that I wanted to be with you." His head drooped as he kneaded the ground in confusion.

"You can be with me *here.*"

Tigerheart felt like a huge paw was pushing down on his head. He couldn't bear to look up at her, because he feared what he would see in her eyes. Disappointment? *Betrayal?*

"Tigerheart?" She was searching his gaze now, fear sparking in her eyes. "You gave up ShadowClan to be here with me, right?"

Grief swept through him like a storm tearing through forest. "I . . . I guess I didn't know it might be forever," he meowed helplessly.

"And now because some cat has a dream," she hissed, "you want to go back? I seem to remember it was not so long ago that you weren't taking dreams quite so seriously."

Tigerheart felt a pang of guilt, but stood up straight and looked at her. "Do you *really* believe we can stay away from our Clans forever? Can you really raise our kits *here*? They'll never know what it's like to have Clanmates, or to have a mentor, or to be willing to fight for their territory." He stared at her. "You want to raise our kits as *strays?*"

Pain flashed suddenly across Dovewing's face.

Tigerheart's breath caught in his throat. "I'm sorry," he yowled, pressing himself against her. "I didn't mean to be so harsh. . . ."

Dovewing gasped and staggered. "It's not that, you mousebrain!"

Panic flashed in her eyes. She shot him a desperate look as she dropped into a crouch. Heart pounding in his ears, he scanned the den for a healer.

Fierce was already crossing the floor toward them. She flicked her tail toward Spire. "Dovewing needs help."

Spire hurried to join her.

"What's wrong with her?" Tigerheart wailed as they reached him.

Dovewing panted beside him. "The kits are coming."

Terrified, Tigerheart turned to Spire. "Is it time?"

Spire blinked at him calmly. "I think that your kits have decided it is."

CHAPTER 18

🍀

Fierce guided Tigerheart away as Spire helped Dovewing to her nest.

"She needs me." Tigerheart looked at her, contorted with pain as she slumped among the furless pelts.

"The healers will take care of her." Fierce nodded to Peanut, who was already hurrying toward the sound of Dovewing's wailing. "Peanut's had kits of her own, and she's helped cats in their kitting before." She blinked gently at Tigerheart. "We get a lot of queens through here. Spire and Peanut know what they're doing."

"I want to be with her." Tigerheart's chest was so tight he could hardly find his breath.

"First you need to calm down." Fierce fixed her gaze on his, her eyes shimmering. "I know it's your first litter, but it will be okay."

"It's my fault she started kitting." Guilt surged beneath his pelt. "I upset her."

"If a queen started kitting every time some cat upset them, there'd be a lot of unexpected deliveries," Fierce soothed.

"I shouldn't have said anything." Tigerheart's thoughts whirled. Why in StarClan had he mentioned Puddleshine's dream? Dovewing already had so much to worry about right now.

"Tigerheart!" Dovewing's cry cut into his thoughts.

He jerked his muzzle toward her. She was glaring at him, pain glittering in her fierce gaze. "Stop sitting there like a rabbit and do something useful!" She gasped as Peanut leaned into the nest and stroked her belly with a paw.

Tigerheart stared in panic. "What can I do?"

"Fetch me a stick to bite on," Dovewing panted. "I don't want these cats to hear me squealing like a kit!"

Tigerheart nodded and hurried to the gap in the wall. He scrambled outside, then raced to the tall chestnut tree he'd sat under with Spire. The Twolegs were still yowling inside. A monster rumbled past. White clouds dotted the sky. Tigerheart scanned the grass, spotting a sturdy stick lying beneath the tree. He bent down and bit it, relieved to feel it firm between his jaws. No bark splintered from the smooth stem. It would be perfect for Dovewing. Quickly he carried it back to the cavern, struggling to maneuver it into the gap. He pushed it through, end first, and it fell onto the ledge and bounced on the floor.

Fierce and Rascal turned to watch it tumble to a halt. Blaze hurried across the cavern and stood beside it. "What's this for?" he asked as Tigerheart landed next to it.

"It's for Dovewing." Tigerheart snatched it up and carried it toward Dovewing's nest.

"What does she need a stick for?" Blaze followed him.

"To bite on." Tigerheart struggled to speak through the

stick. He dropped it beside the nest. "It will help with the pain."

Blaze stopped beside him and stared at Dovewing. Peanut had climbed into the nest and was soothing her with gentle laps behind her ears. Spire leaned in and ran his paws over her belly. Dovewing convulsed, a spasm jerking her body. "Why do cats have kits?" Blaze asked.

Spire turned from Dovewing and met the tom-kit's gaze. "Blaze," he meowed softly. "Dovewing will need water. Find a rag and soak it under the drip-pipe. Then bring it here. But wait until it's dripping wet before you bring it back."

Blaze nodded earnestly, then hurried away.

Tigerheart stared at Dovewing as another spasm gripped her. "Is she okay?"

Dovewing shot him a look. "Where's the stick?" she growled between gritted teeth.

He pushed it hurriedly into the nest and she clamped her jaws around it and groaned as another spasm made her stiffen. She shuddered, then jerked.

Spire broke into a purr as a small, wet sac slid into the nest behind her. Quickly he nipped the sac's membrane with his teeth and peeled the bundle of slick fur from inside. He placed it beside Dovewing's cheek. "Meet your firstborn."

Dovewing let go of the stick and, purring loudly, lapped at the tiny kit as it squirmed and mewled beside her.

"You have a daughter." Spire blinked at Tigerheart happily.

Tigerheart stared at the kit, hardly able to believe his eyes. This small scrap of fur was what all the heartache and worry of the past two moons had been about. His heart seemed to swell until joy burst from his throat in a purr. "She's beautiful." How could he have ever doubted that he should be here with Dovewing? He thrust his muzzle close to hers, nuzzling first the kit and then her cheek.

She purred too, their gaze meeting as she turned her head to press her nose against his. "She's so soft and—" A spasm cut her off. She nudged Tigerheart away, tucked the kit close to her chest, and clamped her teeth around the stick once more. Jerking, she groaned, and another kit dropped into the nest.

"A son," Spire mewed happily, placing the soggy bundle beside the first.

Tigerheart watched as Dovewing bit down once more on the stick.

"Another daughter." Spire placed a third kit beside the others. He ran his paw over Dovewing's belly. "That's the whole litter." He sat back on his haunches and looked at Peanut.

Peanut purred. "It's always good to help with kitting after taking care of so many sick and wounded cats." Her gaze wandered to Marigold's nest, which was empty.

Tigerheart looked at it. Boots, the one-eyed cat, was dragging the bundle of furless pelts apart and shaking them out with his teeth. "Where's Marigold?"

Spire nudged Tigerheart away and lowered his voice. "She died last night," he whispered. "She's free from her suffering now."

Tigerheart began to feel a felt a pang of sadness, but Peanut's mew distracted him.

"You did well." Peanut dipped her head to Dovewing. As Tigerheart hurried back to the nest side, the tortoiseshell padded away.

Spire followed her, and Tigerheart was suddenly very aware that he was alone with Dovewing and their three newborn kits. His fur prickled uneasily. What was he supposed to do now? Dovewing lapped the kits until their wet fur fluffed out; then she nosed them toward her belly, where they nuzzled until they found milk. Dovewing purred and curled around them. She seemed to know what to do instinctively. So did the kits. Tigerheart's belly tightened as the huge responsibility of taking care of them gripped him. The freedom he'd felt since leaving ShadowClan seemed to evaporate like morning mist. Suddenly all the ties that had once held him were binding him again. He had left his Clan, but it had traveled with him. These kits were his to protect and to raise. They were as much a part of him as ShadowClan, and he was part of them.

Dovewing looked at him, her eyes sleepy and filled with love. "Aren't they perfect?"

"Yes." Tigerheart crouched awkwardly beside the nest and stretched his muzzle in to sniff them. In the shadow beneath the ledge, he could see their colors now. One she-kit was gray, like Dovewing, the other tabby like him, and the tom-kit was a gray tabby, with wide dark stripes along his flanks. They smelled warm and sweet. The tom-kit mewled indignantly as Tigerheart lapped his rabbit-soft fur, and pressed closer to Dovewing's belly. "I don't think he likes me," Tigerheart murmured anxiously.

"Of course he does. You're his father." Dovewing touched a paw to Tigerheart's cheek, and the tenderness in her touch made him feel guilty all over again about their argument.

"I'm sorry," he murmured. "Perhaps I shouldn't have told you about Puddleshine's dream. But I couldn't lie to you. You have to believe that you are the most important thing in my life, but without my loyalty to my Clan, what would I be?"

She gazed at him softly. "I know. Your loyalty makes you who you are. And I know you will love our kits with the same fierce loyalty with which you love your Clan. I love you, Tigerheart. I would have loved you even if you hadn't followed me here. I will always love you." She paused, her green eyes shining. "Not just because you're the father of my kits, but because you're *you*. I'm sorry I made you choose between your Clan and me. No cat should ever have to make that choice. I was scared of facing this alone. I've been a coward."

"No!" He licked her cheek fiercely, his heart bursting with pride. "You've been brave. So very brave. And I would have loved you too, even if my Clan had kept me from you. Nothing could stop the way I feel about you."

She returned his gaze steadily. "We will always love each other. But we have a responsibility to our Clans and to our kits. We are warriors—"

Tigerheart cut in: "And our kits will be warriors too."

Dovewing nodded. "They will be raised in a Clan."

Tigerheart searched Dovewing's gaze, relieved to find agreement shining in their green depths. "Yes," he purred.

Dovewing purred too and then added, "But first they must

be weaned and grow strong enough to travel."

"They're not going into the belly of a Thundersnake," Tigerheart meowed firmly.

"No." Dovewing gave a *mrrow* of amusement. "Thunder-snakes can fill their bellies with Twolegs. Our kits will walk."

Tigerheart saw tiredness in her eyes. "You must be exhausted. Sleep now and I will keep watch."

Dovewing blinked at him gratefully, then cast her gaze across the cavern. The guardian cats sat in groups, sharing prey. Mittens was leading Pipsqueak and Blaze out through the entrance. Fierce dozed in a strip of sunshine. "There's no need to keep watch," she mewed sleepily. "They'll keep watch for us." She closed her eyes and let her chin rest on her paws. The kits had grown still and were purring softly.

Tigerheart rested his head on the side of the nest, con-tentment enfolding him like a warm breeze. As he watched Dovewing sleep, he heard paw steps behind him. He lifted his head and looked around.

Spire was padding toward him. The clear, bright gaze he'd had while he'd helped with Dovewing's kitting had given way to the glazed look Tigerheart had seen in the tom's yellow eyes when they first met. Was he having one of his visions?

Tigerheart sat up, blocking the way to his kits. "Spire? Are you okay?"

Spire peered past him, staring directly at the dark gray tom-kit. His fur ruffled along his spine. "This one will see into the shadows."

Tigerheart tensed. "What do you mean?"

Spire looked at him vacantly, then padded away.

Tigerheart shook out his fur, irritated by the uneasy feeling Spire had awoken beneath his pelt. *Don't be silly. He's not a medicine cat.* He stared after Spire. *But why did he speak of shadows again?* Did this tom have some strange connection with Shadow-Clan? Was StarClan speaking through him?

Tigerheart shifted his paws nervously. He glanced up at the flat white roof, wondering if StarClan could see them here. *We'll come home as soon as we can,* he promised. Turning to gaze once more at Dovewing and their kits, he leaned down and breathed in their scent. His heart ached with love, and he settled beside the nest and closed his eyes.

CHAPTER 19

☘

Hurry up. Tigerheart glanced down the alley to where Cobweb, Mittens, and Fierce had stopped to drink from a puddle. It was bad enough they had to scavenge for scraps even Two-legs didn't want; did they have to take so long? There were no mouthwatering prey scents carried on fresh forest breezes here. Tigerheart wanted to get the patrol over with.

The laid-back life of the guardian cats no longer felt like a relief. It had begun to irritate him. Scavenging was all they did now. In the two moons since Shadowkit, Pouncekit, and Lightkit had been born, leaf-fall had hardened into leaf-bare. Prey had become scarce, and the guardian cats relied on Two-leg scraps more and more. This morning, Tigerheart had woken to a hard frost, which had turned the clear walls of the gathering-place den into patterned ice. And yet when he'd followed the others out into the streets, the city lacked the stone-cold chill of the forest, holding a warmth of its own like a huge living creature.

Fierce had suggested they take a tour of their favorite scrap-cans, clustered in the alleys that ran behind the rows of dens. Tigerheart had offered to come, as he always did. He owed the guardian cats his loyalty. But he secretly hoped that he would find a mouse or bird to take home to Lightkit, Pouncekit, and Shadowkit. Weaned now, they were eager for food, and Tigerheart hated that they had only tasted Twoleg scraps. What if they didn't grow up to be strong? City strays were agile and wily, but none of them were as well-muscled as a forest cat. He'd hunted around the gathering place, but in the city there was always the sudden rumble of a monster or the thumping paws of a passing Twoleg to scare prey before he could finish stalking it. He hadn't caught anything for half a moon. He guessed that was why the guardian cats weren't even trying to hunt now. Besides, the scrapcans were overflowing, even as the weather grew harsher. He remembered with a pang the anxious days of leaf-bare in the forest, when catching a single rabbit brought joy to the whole Clan because it meant a warm night's sleep on a full belly.

These cats have no idea what it is to go hungry, Tigerheart thought as he watched Cobweb shake puddle water from his whiskers and Fierce lap a few more sour mouthfuls. He wondered if they had ever been truly cold. The gathering-place den had grown chilly, but it was sheltered from wind and free of the drafts that would be slicing through gaps in the walls and dens of the ShadowClan camp now. It was easy to warm up in the furless-pelt nests.

In the past two moons, he'd learned city words like *alley*, *street*, and *scrapcan*; he'd grown accustomed to monsters and had learned to dart between them with ease as they crawled between the dens. He hardly noticed the Twolegs now as he wove between their legs on patrol.

This was the only world his kits knew. They'd never seen forests and streams and real prey. He wondered how long it would be before Dovewing agreed that they were old enough to make the journey home. By the time they reached the lake, would they be able to adjust to warrior life?

His pelt ruffled uneasily at the thought and he pushed it away. There would be plenty of time for them to learn to become warriors. But what if this first glimpse of life stayed with them? What if they always found warrior ways strange?

"I'm going on hunting patrol," he'd told Pouncekit before he'd left.

She'd blinked at him. "Don't you mean scavenging?" she'd asked. "That's what the others call it."

"Scavenging is like hunting," Dovewing had answered quickly as Tigerheart's pelt ruffled, then added, "Tigerheart used to be the best hunter in ShadowClan."

Pouncekit didn't seem to hear. "Why don't warriors scavenge like city cats?"

Tigerheart stared at her. What could he say? That warriors had more pride and more skill? That they kept their distance from Twolegs, and definitely didn't eat their scraps? He didn't want to insult the guardian cats. But he wanted Pouncekit to understand what it meant to be a warrior.

Dovewing spoke for him again. "There aren't any scrapcans to scavenge from by the lake," she told Pouncekit diplomatically. She caught Tigerheart's eye. "Besides, hunting is much more fun than scavenging. You'll find out when you become a warrior."

Tigerheart had turned away heavily and followed Fierce,

Cobweb, Cinnamon, and Mittens out of the gathering place. He hoped that soon he'd be able to show Pouncekit what a warrior was. Now, as the sun lifted over the Twoleg dens, Tigerheart glanced at the bright blue sky showing between the rooftops. They'd scavenged all morning, but he hadn't once smelled prey, and his hope of finding fresh-kill for the kits was fading.

Fierce flicked her tail happily. "Cold weather like this makes Twolegs hungry," she meowed. "Which means more leftovers for us." She led the way to another cluster of scrapcans and jumped onto one. As she knocked it open with practiced ease, Tigerheart jumped onto the next and pushed away its cover while Cobweb and Mittens rummaged through litter at their base. Tigerheart dug deep into the trash, his paws feeling the softness of something edible. He hooked it out with his claws. A round lump of something that smelled a little like meat but he knew would taste sour.

Cobweb glanced at it, his eyes brightening. "Meat scraps!"

Mittens hooked out a soft white strip from among the litter. "Dotty will like this," he mewed. "It's easy to chew."

Fierce pulled a bone from her trash and flicked it triumphantly onto the ground below. "There's more in here." She delved deeper and hauled out another.

Tigerheart swallowed back distaste as she tossed it over the side. *Warriors leave bones for the crows.* Here they were a treat.

Fierce jumped down. "Let's take these scraps back to Cinnamon."

They'd left Cinnamon guarding their first haul—a collection of scraps they'd fished out of a scrapcan nearer the gathering place. Tigerheart had suggested a moon ago that the guardian patrols stash the scraps they'd gathered before taking them home. It was an old warrior trick that freed up their paws for more scavenging. But the city was full of cats and foxes, and they'd often return to find that their stash had been raided. It had been Cinnamon's idea to post a guard. Tigerheart had been pleased that one of the guardian cats had begun to think like a warrior.

He hurried back toward Cinnamon. The strange meat he'd scavenged dangled from his jaws and smeared grease on his chin. As he ducked from the alley and followed the street that led to their stash place, pigeons fluttered between the dens above him. If only he could reach one. Why hadn't the guardian cats come up with a plan to catch them? There must be some place in the city where the clumsy birds settled within reach. Hadn't the guardian cats worked out where it was?

As he turned in to the narrow alley between dens where they'd left Cinnamon, his fur bristled. Four strays surrounded her. They'd backed her against the wall where her stash was piled. Cinnamon spat at them, back arched and fur bushed. One of the strays reached for a scrap trailing from the pile behind her. Cinnamon lashed out with a hiss. The tom backed away, snarling. Fur sparking with alarm, Tigerheart dropped the meat he'd been carrying and leaped in front of Cinnamon.

He faced the strays and growled at them menacingly. "This is our stash," he snarled. "Go find your own."

As he spoke, Fierce padded into the alley. Cobweb and Mittens watched, wide-eyed, from the end. Tigerheart beckoned them closer. He might need backup. The strays were standing their ground. Greed shone in their eyes.

One of them—a lithe gray she-cat—narrowed her bright blue gaze. "Your friend *wanted* to share," she told Tigerheart.

"No, she didn't," Tigerheart snapped.

The gray cat glanced around at the guardian cats, food dangling from their jaws, then nodded to the scraps piled behind Cinnamon. "There's enough to share."

Tigerheart growled. "We have other mouths to feed."

"We might have other mouths to feed too." The gray she-cat tipped her head.

"That doesn't mean you can take our catch." Tigerheart glanced at Fierce. Was she going to speak up?

"Why shouldn't we?" the gray cat meowed.

"You didn't catch it," Tigerheart growled.

"Nor did you." The she-cat glanced dismissively at the scraps. "You found it. Now *we're* finding it too."

Shame scorched beneath Tigerheart's pelt. She was right. They'd picked these scraps out of cans. *I'm fighting over crow-food!* And yet this crow-food would feed the cats waiting at the gathering place. *It will feed my kits.* He lifted his chin. Even if it wasn't prey, it would keep them from starving. A new, protective anger surged in his chest. *It belongs to us!* Did this cat have no sense of honor at all? He looked around at the guardian cats, who were watching uneasily. "You're trying to steal from my friend," he hissed slowly.

"Steal!" The gray cat lifted her chin. "No cat owns anything until it's safely in her belly. Here it's every cat for herself. You're obviously not city-born, or you'd know that."

"I'm glad I'm not city-born." *But my kits are.* Tigerheart

pushed the thought away. "I was born in a place where we feed our Clan before we feed ourselves."

The gray cat shrugged. "But you'd let *us* go hungry?"

Tigerheart blinked. How was she making *him* out to be the bad cat? "You're not my Clanmate. Besides, there are plenty of scrapcans in the city. You won't go hungry."

"'Plenty of scrapcans,'" the she-cat mimicked. "But only if we can get to them before the foxes."

"Foxes only come out at night, when the Twolegs have gone," Tigerheart pointed out.

"What do you know, outsider?" For the first time, the she-cat's eyes rounded, betraying unease. Pelt ruffled, she nodded to her companions. "Come on. Let's try somewhere else." She shot Tigerheart a look. "Don't get too comfortable. You don't belong here. I can still smell the grass on your paws." Turning her tail on him, she padded away down the alley. The others followed, glancing reproachfully over their shoulders.

"Well done." Fierce blinked at Tigerheart warmly.

"You saved us a fight." Cinnamon looked relieved.

For now. Tigerheart watched the city cats disappear around the corner. *Don't get too comfortable.* The gray cat's parting threat made him feel this confrontation might just be the beginning.

Back at the gathering-place den, the guardian cats clustered around the patrol as they dropped the scraps they'd collected. Tigerheart eased himself away from the crowd and glanced toward his nest. He was relieved to see that Dovewing and the kits were sleeping.

"Those smell like good scraps."

Spire's mew took him by surprise.

The skinny black tom was sitting in the shadow of a wooden ledge, watching Blaze scramble for food with the others. Tigerheart had avoided Spire as much as possible since the strange healer cat had told him Shadowkit would be able to see into the shadows. He hadn't told Dovewing of Spire's prediction, even after she'd named the tom-kit. "Shadowkit, in honor of your Clan," she had explained. How could he have argued with her? The coincidence had unnerved him, though, and he'd kept clear of Spire in case the tom announced any more alarming visions.

Now Spire watched the guardian cats with a clear, even gaze. "How are your kits?"

"Fine," Tigerheart answered quickly. "I was thinking of catching some *real* food for them."

"Food is food," Spire mewed casually.

"Scraps aren't warrior food." *They're crow-food.* Tigerheart didn't meet the healer's gaze. "Warriors eat fresh-kill."

"And your kits will be warriors." The healer's tone was matter-of-fact.

Tigerheart felt Spire's gaze burning into his pelt. Unable to resist, he turned to meet it. Did this strange cat know for sure that his kits would be warriors? *Or am I just taking him seriously because he's saying something I want to hear?*

He gave the tom a questioning look.

"What else could they be with Dovewing and you as their parents?" Spire got to his paws and padded toward Blaze.

Blaze met him, greasy scraps hanging from his mouth. The

young tom's eyes shone brightly as he dropped them at Spire's paws. "Look what I got for us!"

Tigerheart looked up at the den entrance. Determination hardened his belly. He *would* catch fresh-kill for his kits. Was there time before they woke? Quickly he leaped onto the wooden ledge and up through the gap in the wall.

Outside, pigeons fluttered around the great spike sticking up from the thorn den. Hope pricked in Tigerheart's paws as one swooped low, but a passing monster sent it rushing upward once more, and his heart sank as it nestled beside its companions on the roof.

Pelt itching with frustration, he stalked between the stone slabs. The frost on the grass had melted, and icy water seeped into his paws. This grassy stretch around the gathering den was the only green he'd seen since arriving in the city. His heart ached for the crunch of pine needles beneath his paws. He longed for the scent of sap and the familiar smells of home. Had Rowanstar chased the shadows away yet? Was Shadow-Clan back to normal? Was it safe for him to return without blocking the sun? Even if it was, he knew the kits were too young for such a journey.

A loud chirrup sounded nearby. Tigerheart jerked his muzzle toward it. A thrush was hopping along the branch of a cherry tree. The colored walls of the gathering place glittered behind it.

Tigerheart sank into the grass. Dampness soaked his belly fur as he fixed his gaze on the thrush. Keeping as still as one of the stone slabs, he waited. The thrush chirped again. A warning cry? Had it spotted him? Tigerheart's chest tightened. He glanced at the trunk, wondering if he could climb without being seen. But the branches had been stripped bare by the cold. The thrush would see any movement.

Frustrated, Tigerheart flexed his claws, longing for the shadows of the pine forest. Feeling helpless, he watched the thrush flutter onto a higher branch. It pecked at the bark, then hopped to a spot of moss farther along and began pecking again.

Disappointment dropped in Tigerheart's belly like a stone. There was no way to reach the thrush without scaring it off. His kits would eat crow-food again today. Guilt tugged him toward his nest. If they woke, he wanted to be there to share crow-food with them at least. As they ate, he could reassure them that one day they'd eat real prey.

Movement jerked him from his thoughts. The thrush dived suddenly down and landed in front of one of the slabs. It began rummaging in the grass with its beak. Hope sparked beneath Tigerheart's pelt. Slowly, he drew himself to his paws and began to creep toward it. The stone slabs hid his approach. He quickened his pace. He had to reach the thrush before it fluttered away again. *Slow down,* he told himself. He couldn't let desperation make him mess this up.

Stopping behind the slab where the thrush was digging for worms, Tigerheart steadied his breath. He peered around the edge. The thrush hadn't noticed him. As he eased into the open, Tigerheart's belly fluttered with excitement. Whiskers twitching, he pounced and slapped his paws onto the thrush a moment before it could flap away in panic. Pinning it to the earth, he grabbed its neck between his jaws and killed it fast. *Thank you, StarClan.* Happiness surged through him at the taste of blood. He picked it up in his teeth, relishing its warm prey-scent as he hurried back to the den.

"Wake up!" He dropped his catch at the side of Dovewing's nest.

Dovewing lifted her head, her nose twitching. "Thrush!" Pleasure sparked in her green gaze as she sat up and looked from Tigerheart to the limp bird. She prodded the kits, still snuggling against her belly. "Wake up, Pouncekit! Lightkit, wake up." She lapped Shadowkit between the ears. "Tiger-heart's brought food."

Blinking in the sunshine, which flooded the den, Pouncekit peered over the side of the nest. Her shoulders drooped as she saw the thrush. "That's not food," she mewed sadly. "It's just a bird."

"It's prey!" Tigerheart bristled angrily. "And you're going to eat it."

Lightkit scrambled out of the den, her brown tabby kit fluff ruffled by sleep. She sniffed at the thrush. "It smells sweet."

Shadowkit balanced on the edge of the nest, his nose twitching suspiciously. "Weren't there any scraps?" He looked across the den to where the guardian cats were lounging, the scraps they'd gathered gone.

Pouncekit followed his gaze, sniffing. "I can smell meat." She scanned the den.

"*This* is meat." Tigerheart poked the thrush.

"It's all feathers." Pouncekit dismissed it with a flick of her muzzle.

Tigerheart's belly tightened. Why wasn't the scent of fresh-kill making them hungry?

Dovewing climbed out of the nest and began to tear the thrush into strips as the kits watched with a look of horrified fascination. Putting the feathery parts aside, she laid a small, meaty strip in front of each of them.

Irritation clawed Tigerheart's belly. "Tawnypelt never had to tear my food up when I was a kit."

Dovewing shot him a look. "Of course she did. They're only two moons old. You can't expect them to rip up their own prey."

Tigerheart sat back on his haunches. Perhaps she was right. He must be patient.

"Try it," Dovewing encouraged the kits gently.

Pouncekit sniffed uneasily at the strip of red meat before dabbing it with her tongue. She frowned and dabbed it again. Shadowkit touched his piece with his paw before sinking his teeth in. Lightkit grabbed one end of hers in her mouth and, hooking the strip with her claw, began tugging it with her teeth.

Dovewing blinked affectionately at Tigerheart. "It was good of you to catch fresh prey for us."

Tigerheart didn't answer. He was still staring anxiously at the kits. What if they never learned to love fresh-kill? What if he took them back to ShadowClan and they refused to eat?

"All kits are fussy about food at first," Dovewing murmured.

"Ivypool refused to eat rabbit until she was four moons old. And I hated shrews."

"Really?" Tigerheart looked hopefully at her.

She held his gaze for a moment, then nodded at the kits. All three were busy chewing on their strips of thrush. Shadowkit looked thoughtful. Pouncekit was still frowning. Lightkit's cheeks bulged with food where she'd bitten off too much.

"Chew it properly before you swallow," Dovewing warned. "Or you'll get a bellyache."

Tigerheart watched them eat, pride swelling in his chest. Even if they didn't like the thrush, they were trying to eat it. *Your kits will be warriors.* Spire's words rang in his mind. Of course they would be. Especially if he took them home soon.

CHAPTER 20

Tigerheart fluffed his fur against the cold. Outside the gathering place, wind whipped rain against the stone slabs. Fierce, Spire, and Ant were already heading across the grass. Beside him, Dovewing shivered.

"Are you sure you want to come?" Tigerheart glanced at her. It would be the first time she'd left the den since kitting.

"I need fresh air." She lifted her face into the breeze, half closing her eyes against the rain; then she stiffened and looked anxiously at Tigerheart. "Blaze and Peanut will take good care of the kits, won't they?"

"Of course," he reassured her. "Blaze will keep them busy, and Peanut will make sure they stay out of troub—" He paused as a familiar scent touched his nose.

He'd learned by now to untangle jumbled city scents and pick out prey, cat, fox, and food smells from the acrid stench of monsters. He could smell the gray she-cat they'd met the day before. His ears twitched uneasily. Ant, Fierce, and Spire had reached the Thunderpath and were waiting for a gap to cross. "Come back!"

Fierce looked back questioningly and turned back as

Tigerheart beckoned her with a flick of his tail. Ant and Spire followed. "What is it?"

Tigerheart sniffed the air again, smelling the she-cat once more. Other cat scents mingled with it. "The strays have been here." The smell strengthened with the wind. "They're still around." Tigerheart jerked his nose toward an unkempt patch of trees and bushes at the far end of the gathering place. Was that movement in the long grass beside it? His pelt prickled. "They've invaded our land!" Without waiting, he raced toward the cat scents. He stopped as he reached the trees and stared into the bushes crowding their trunks. "Come out!" he demanded.

The branches rustled, and the gray she-cat slid out and gazed at him impassively. "Hi again."

"What are you doing here?" Tigerheart demanded as Dovewing caught up to him. She was panting a little. It had clearly been a while since she'd run. Fierce, Ant, and Spire followed slowly.

The gray she-cat stared at Tigerheart, looking puzzled.

He glanced at the guardian cats. They didn't look concerned. "She's on our land!" he growled.

"This isn't our land." Fierce flicked her tail as she reached him.

Tigerheart could hardly believe his ears. "It's where you live and hunt."

Ant frowned. "We sleep in the gathering place and scavenge all over the city." He clearly didn't understand.

"But *this* is your home." Tigerheart glanced around the

stretch of grass surrounding the thorn den.

A tom emerged from the bushes, followed by three other strays. They lined up beside the gray she-cat, blinking at him curiously.

"What's the fuss about, Fog?" A brown tom looked at the gray she-cat.

"I'm not sure, Tuna." Fog stared at Tigerheart. "This cat's complaining again."

Tigerheart struggled to understand their indifference. Even Dovewing looked unconcerned. If this were the forest, pelts would be bristling and teeth bared by now. He blinked at Dovewing. "I know this is the city, but all cats have territory, right? Don't they want to defend it?"

She looked at him. "They obviously don't mind sharing." She looked at Fierce inquiringly.

Fierce shrugged. "What's the point of arguing over land?"

Tigerheart stared at her. "Don't you have borders?"

"No."

"Well, you should." He looked pointedly at Fog. "Then other cats would know not to trespass."

Rain dripped from Fierce's whiskers as she glanced past Fog. "Have you built dens here?"

"Not dens," Fog answered. "Just a few nests. Foxes invaded our old home. We needed a new place to sleep."

Tigerheart pricked his ears. "So you're planning to make a new home here?"

Fog shrugged. "Why not? We won't bother you."

Tigerheart narrowed his eyes accusingly. "What about

yesterday?" he challenged. "You tried to steal our food."

Tuna shifted his paws. "We were just scavenging, like you."

Tigerheart growled. "In the future, don't scavenge where we scavenge."

Fog stared back innocently. "We're still getting used to this part of the city. We didn't know you owned the scrapcans here." Her pelt ruffled into spikes as rain soaked her fur.

"Go easy on them." Fierce swished her tail at Tigerheart. "They've had fox trouble. We know what that's like."

Tigerheart didn't care. He was wondering how many more cats were hiding in the bushes. "Are you going to let them stay on your land?"

"I told you," Fierce meowed. "This isn't our land. We don't *own* land."

"How do you know where you can hunt?" Tigerheart couldn't understand how they could live in such a disorganized way. "You have sick cats to feed," he reminded her. "And kits. You need to know you have territory that can support them even in the coldest weather. You—"

Fog interrupted him. "What's the weather got to do with it? Do you think Twolegs stop leaving trash because it gets cold? Ice-chill is the best weather for scavenging. Food rots slower."

"Come on." Fierce began to head away. "This argument is pointless. These cats aren't harming anyone."

Ant and Spire followed her wordlessly. Tigerheart exchanged looks with Dovewing. Foreboding hollowed his belly. Hadn't Rowanstar let rogues live beside ShadowClan land because he thought they wouldn't do any harm?

Fog shook rain from her fur and headed back into the dripping bushes. Her companions followed.

Alone with Dovewing, Tigerheart's pelt prickled along his spine. "I can see trouble coming."

"I know it's different from how Clans live, but the cats here seem happy with it." Dovewing began to head after Fierce, Spire, and Ant.

Tigerheart wondered why Dovewing didn't see the danger in living so chaotically. "They may be happy now, but what if Fog and her friends decide they want a warmer den and invade the gathering place? There are sick cats there who can't defend themselves! Just because the guardian cats chased off a couple of foxes, it doesn't mean they're ready for a full battle over territory." He paused, his heart quickening. "They don't even understand what territory is!"

Fierce, Ant, and Spire were already crossing the puddled Thunderpath. Dovewing stopped at the edge and blinked at Tigerheart. "We can't tell them to change the way they live," she argued. "We're just visitors here."

"But don't you want to help them?" He trotted after her.

"Not if they don't want to be helped."

"But it's so obvious." As he reached her, Tigerheart felt exasperated. "All they need to do is mark some boundaries and organize some patrols, and everyone will sleep a lot safer in their nests."

Monsters sent up spray as they passed. Crouching against it, Dovewing waited for a gap and then splashed across the

Thunderpath. Tigerheart followed. "This isn't a Clan, Tiger-heart. These cats don't even have a leader. They're just a bunch of healers and scavengers who have been kind to us. Don't start bossing them around."

"I wasn't bossing." Tigerheart's paws pricked indignantly.

Dovewing went on. "I know you're used to being Clan dep-uty and believing that one day you'll be leader. But you're not in the forest now, and you won't be for a while. So you might as well get used to living like a city cat."

Ahead, Ant, Spire, and Fierce turned a corner. Dove-wing quickened her pace. Tigerheart hurried beside her, his thoughts churning. *And you won't be for a while.* He glanced at Dovewing, trying to read her gaze. The kits would be ready to travel soon, surely? They were weaned now and growing stronger each day. "How long are you planning to stay here?"

"Are you in a rush to get back to the lake?" She kept her gaze ahead, scanning the bustling Twolegs as they turned the corner.

"I want our kits to grow up in ShadowClan," Tigerheart told her.

"Why not ThunderClan?" Dovewing dodged between a Twoleg's paws. The guardian cats were waiting at the mouth of an alley.

Tigerheart stared at Dovewing. Was she planning to take their kits to ThunderClan? His belly tightened. "I'm Shadow-Clan's *deputy.* I can't just join another Clan."

"But *I* can?" Dovewing shot him a look. "Besides, are you sure there's a ShadowClan to go back to? Didn't you say it might disappear? Who knows what might have happened while we've been away?"

How could she say that so casually? Had Dovewing stopped caring about the Clans? Had she forgotten how much she'd loved her life before she came to the city? Didn't she remember what it was like to be a warrior? His pelt prickled uneasily. She had never complained about feeding scraps to the kits. And she didn't seem to worry about territory anymore. Was she *enjoying* this life? The thought struck him like a blow. He steered her to the side of the path, out of the way of Twolegs. "Don't you want to go back?"

"Of course I want to go back." Dovewing blinked at him, her green eyes sparking as the rain pattered around them. "But I want our kits to be safe. It's a long journey, and it might be dangerous."

"But they need to grow up in a Clan, among Clan cats, with the warrior code, or they may never truly understand what it is to be a warrior. We need to get them home as soon as possible."

"Even if that means endangering their lives?" Dovewing's hackles lifted.

"Of course not." Tigerheart's fur prickled uncomfortably. "I'd never let harm come to our kits."

"Then why are you in such a rush to leave? They're only two moons old." Dovewing didn't wait for an answer. She turned away and hurried toward the guardian cats.

Heart pounding with anxiety, Tigerheart followed her.

He didn't speak as Fierce led them on a tour of her favorite scrapcans. He waited while the others rummaged through the trash, and he gathered up the scraps they tossed down and hid them. As they headed down another wet alley, he glimpsed movement at the end. Something small was scuttling there. He opened his mouth, letting damp air bathe his tongue. *Prey.* Narrowing his eyes, he made out the slick pelts of several black rats. They were swarming at the end of the alley where a tall mesh fence blocked the end.

"Look!" Tigerheart nudged Dovewing and jerked his muzzle toward the rats.

Fierce, in a scrapcan above them, stopped delving. Ant and Spire paused. They followed Tigerheart's gaze.

"Let's catch them," Tigerheart flexed his claws eagerly.

"But this can is full." Fierce dropped a soggy scrap onto the ground.

"Fresh prey will be better for the sick cats," Tigerheart pointed out. "Littlecloud used to say that warm fresh-kill was the best medicine."

Spire nodded. "That scrawny tom we took in last quarter moon could do with some fresh meat."

Dovewing shifted her paws. "I guess the kits have to get used to fresh-kill eventually."

You guess? Tigerheart's belly tightened. "Come on." Without waiting, he hurried along the alley.

Dovewing and the guardian cats followed.

The rats were bunched against the mesh at the end. This would be an easy kill. Tigerheart swiped his tongue around his lips and dropped into a stalking crouch as he neared them.

The others fanned out beside him.

The rats saw them. Fear sparked in their small, black eyes. They scrabbled against the fence, squabbling as they fought to escape. One squeezed through a gap where the mesh was torn. It escaped into the alley beyond. A moment later, the other rats broke through and streamed after it.

"Quick!" Tigerheart leaped to the fence and, seeing where the mesh was torn, tugged a curled edge with his paws. Triumph sparked in his chest as it gave easily and opened into a gap big enough to push through. The swarm of rats was already at the end of the alley. They disappeared around the corner as he scraped through the gap and raced after them.

He heard the guardian cats splashing through the puddles behind him as he rounded the corner and spotted the rats fleeing downhill. They were following the edge of a Thunderpath as it disappeared into a tunnel.

Dovewing caught up to him. "Where are they?"

"In there." He nodded toward the tunnel and ran harder. Dovewing was at his tail as darkness swallowed him. Monsters roared through the tunnel, their blazing eyes illuminating the stone walls. Tigerheart glimpsed the rats in their eye beams. They were running for the light at the far end.

Tigerheart glanced over his shoulder. Fierce, Spire, and Ant were catching up, and as he neared the end, they spread out beside him. He charged out into the rain with them at his side. "There they go!"

The rats were streaming away from the Thunderpath, toward a vast field of trash piled high beside water. "We have to catch them before they reach the trash." There was no way they'd be able to follow them into the chaotic mess of discarded Twoleg litter. He pushed harder, leading the patrol close to the trash. If they could steer the rats away from it, they could catch them. He was close now, herding the rats toward a muddy ditch at the bottom of a slope. The ditch would crowd them together and slow their flight. Stragglers would fall behind, and it would be easy to pick them off.

Suddenly the rats veered sideways. Tigerheart blinked in surprise as the terrified prey cut across his path. He lunged for them, but he'd been caught off guard. They streamed around him, slipping around his paws. He stretched his claws, trying to get a grip on the wet stone as the rats fled out of reach. What had made them change course? He glanced up the slope. Fog and Tuna were pounding toward him, a white tom at their heels. Their eyes were fixed on the rats, which swarmed into the trash field, where they scattered. Fog, Tuna, and the white tom pulled up as the rats disappeared among the heaps of stinking litter.

"You scared them away!" Tigerheart faced the strays angrily.

"Why didn't you stop them?" Fog blinked at him. "They were right under your paws."

"Have you ever tried catching rats before? They're fast and they're slippery." Tigerheart jerked his nose toward the ditch. "*I* had a plan and you ruined it! You drove them straight into the trash field." These cats hunted like mouse-brains. As Fierce slewed to a halt beside him, Tigerheart glared at her.

"This is why you need borders!" he snapped. "If you knew where your land was, you could hunt there without other cats interfering with your catch."

Ant, Spire, and Dovewing reached them and stared at the strays.

Tuna stared back. He nodded to the white tom. "These are the cats we mentioned, Streak."

Streak looked at them through narrowed eyes. "Are they the ones who live inside that big, warm, dry den?"

Tigerheart glared at Fog. "You promised to keep out of our way."

She flicked her tail. "You told us not to scavenge. We're not scavenging; we're hunting."

Fierce shook rain from her pelt. "Let's go back to the scrap-cans. The rats are gone, and there's more shelter in the alleys."

"Don't you care that they frightened our prey away?" Tiger-heart didn't wait for an answer. "We must establish borders *now*. We need to know which land belongs to us and which belongs to them."

Fog looked toward the trash heaped over the field. "You can have this land," she offered.

Fierce wrinkled her nose. "The scraps here are rotten."

"But there are plenty of rats for you to hunt." Fog caught Tigerheart's eye scornfully. "Go ahead."

The stench wafting from the trash made Tigerheart feel sick. "No, thanks." If he'd known this was where the rats scavenged, he'd never have chased them.

Spire shivered. "I'm getting cold. Let's go back to the

scrapcans. It smelled like there were bones in them."

Streak's eyes lit up. "Which cans?"

Tuna licked his lips. "We could help you look."

"I told you not to scavenge where we scavenge." Tigerheart unsheathed his claws.

"And I told you, this is the city. We can scavenge where we like." Fog's eyes suddenly darkened.

Tigerheart glimpsed menace there. These cats meant trouble. "We need borders," he growled.

"Borders need patrolling. It sounds like a lot of effort." Fierce flicked raindrops from her ears.

"She's right," Fog sniffed. "It would be better to spend the time scavenging."

Tuna whisked his tail nonchalantly. "The city is full of cats. It's pointless making boundaries."

Spire agreed. "We'd just have more to fight over. I don't want to waste herbs treating battle wounds."

"Live and let live." Fierce headed toward the tunnel.

"Life's too short to bother with grudges." Fog headed up the slope, Tuna and Streak at her tail. Spire and Ant padded after Fierce.

Tigerheart watched them go. "I don't trust her," he told Dovewing.

"Who? Fog?" Dovewing blinked at him. "She's just another stray. You know what city cats are like. They like an easy life."

"An easy life." Tigerheart snorted. "There's no such thing."

"The guardian cats seem to have a pretty easy time."

"They need to learn to defend themselves."

"Why fight if you don't have to?" Dovewing touched her nose to Tigerheart's cheek. "I know you miss your Clan. But we're not going to change these cats. Why bother trying?"

She turned and followed Fierce, Ant, and Spire.

Why fight if you don't have to? Tigerheart stared after her. Of *course* they'd have to, one day. The city was crowded. There was little space to roam or scavenge undisturbed. Sooner or later, they'd find themselves competing for the same scrap-cans. With so many cats and no borders, eventually their lives would descend into an endless running battle.

Icy rain soaked deeper into his fur. Why did city cats have so little honor? They were hardly better than foxes. And Dovewing was starting to agree with them. His heart ached. He missed the warrior code. He missed feeling proud at the end of a hard day's patrolling. Was he the only cat here who saw himself as more than a scavenger?

CHAPTER 21

"Why are there more nests now?" Lightkit looked out from beneath
the ledge that sheltered their nest, while behind her, Shadowkit
chased Pouncekit around its wooden legs.

Tigerheart followed the kit's gaze to the two new heaps of
furless pelts, which Bracken, Boots, and Spire had assembled.
"Mittens and Rascal found two sick cats while they were out
scavenging yesterday. They brought them back so the medicine cats can look after them."

Lightkit blinked at him. "How come you call them medicine cats when everyone else calls them healers?"

"Because that's what we call healers back home," Tigerheart explained.

Pouncekit skidded to a halt beside them. Shadowkit bundled after her, his tiny paws slipping on the shiny floor.

"Dovewing says that home is such a long way away it would
take days and days to walk there," Pouncekit mewed.

"Will we ever go there?" Lightkit asked eagerly.

Shadowkit shifted his paws. "It's dark in the forest."

Tigerheart glanced at him sharply. How did he know what
the forest was like? Tigerheart had talked of trees and prey,

but not of light and shadow. And the kit had spoken solemnly, as though his words carried hidden meaning. *This one will see into the shadows.* Spire's words rang in his mind. Did Shadowkit know something? Had shadows swallowed his Clan? Tigerheart swallowed back fear. *Don't be dumb!* How could a kit know what was happening in ShadowClan? He'd never even been there. Dovewing had probably told the kits how dark the pine forest could be. It probably did seem dark to her. She was ThunderClan after all. "The woods *are* shadowy," he conceded. "But when you train to be warriors, you'll find the shadows are your friend. You can hide in shadows, or keep cool in them, or shelter there from bad weather."

"I don't want to hide in shadows." Lightkit gazed up at the clear stretches of wall. Blue sky showed beyond. "I like sunshine."

Pouncekit padded toward the middle of the den. "Can we go and look at the new cats?"

"No," Tigerheart told him. "They're sick. Leave them in peace."

"But Spire gets to look at them," Pouncekit argued. The healer was leaning over one of the new nests, where a black-and-white tom was wheezing.

"He's taking care of them," Tigerheart explained. His gaze drifted longingly toward Fierce. The tortoiseshell was padding between Cobweb, Ant, Rascal, Mittens, and Dotty. They were going on a special patrol.

Fierce and the other guardian cats had been talking excitedly about it for days. "We call it the outdoor gathering," Fierce had told him. "Every moon, Twolegs set up ledges in the biggest stone clearing in the city and pile food on them, right out in the open, even when it's raining or snowing. There's smoke and some fire. The smells are delicious. It's easy to scavenge. There are Twolegs everywhere, but no one looks at what happens under the ledges. Sometimes they drop food. Sometimes we can reach up and take it. Some of the ledges are covered with meat." Fierce had paused to lick her lips hungrily. "Meat like you've probably never seen or smelled before. We always feast well after the outdoor gathering."

Tigerheart wanted to join the patrol. *Hurry up, Dovewing!* He glanced at the den entrance. She'd gone out to make dirt. He couldn't leave the kits. Perhaps Blaze and Peanut would watch them again. His heart leaped as he saw a gray pelt beyond the clear stretch of glass beside the entrance. Dovewing slid through.

Tigerheart blinked at the kits. "Dovewing's back. Be good for her. I'm going out with Fierce."

"When can *we* go outside?" Pouncekit's mew echoed after him as he hurried across the floor. He passed Dovewing and paused, his head drooping. "I wish I could bring home real prey," he told her.

She nosed him playfully. "I don't care what you bring home, so long as it fills the kits' bellies." She hurried quickly away as Pouncekit, Lightkit, and Shadowkit raced to meet her.

Blaze charged from between the nests where Spire was tending to the sick cats. "Can I come?" he asked.

"There will be a lot of Twolegs there," Tigerheart warned.

The young tom had grown in the past two moons, but he was still a kit. Tigerheart didn't want to lose him in the crowd.

"Please?" Blaze trotted beside Tigerheart. "Spire's busy with the new cats. It's boring here. I want to see the outdoor gathering."

Fierce looked up as they reached her. "Are you coming?" she asked Tigerheart.

"Yes, please."

"I want to come too," Blaze mewed.

Fierce glanced at the young tom. She narrowed her eyes thoughtfully. "You'd make a good lookout," she meowed. "You could help Dotty guard the stash." She glanced at the pale white-and-ginger she-cat.

Dotty nodded. "Don't wander off," she warned Blaze. "It gets crowded. You have to stay near me, okay?"

"Okay." Blaze nodded eagerly.

Fierce headed for the den entrance and leaped onto the wooden ledge. Tigerheart waited for the rest of the patrol to follow and fell in at the rear. He jumped up onto the ledge and squeezed out of the entrance after Rascal and Mittens.

Fierce followed a new route away from the gathering place. Tigerheart had never been this way before. It led through quieter streets, where few monsters and even fewer Twolegs patrolled outdoors. Then she cut through a narrow alley, which opened onto a wide, open stretch of stone. The clearing was lined with ledges, just as Fierce had promised. The Twolegs had decorated them in bright colors; some had roofs. Tigerheart could see food piled high wherever he looked. The smell of smoke tinged the air. *Fire?* He scanned the clearing warily and saw plumes rising here and there among the ledges. But there was no sign of fire raging out of control. And the smoke carried mouthwatering scents. Countless Twolegs filed slowly between the ledges, picking at the food, lifting it to smell it, passing it to other Twolegs to wrap. Delicious scents filled Tigerheart's nose. His belly growled with longing. He hadn't smelled such tempting prey since he'd left the forest. No wonder the guardian cats came every moon and were willing to brave the crowds of Twolegs to scavenge here.

Fierce led the patrol quickly beneath a line of ledges. Twoleg paws padded around the edges, but in the shadows beneath, Tigerheart felt safe. A Twoleg would have to crawl on all fours to see them.

"We could keep the stash here." Dotty stopped beside two low stones jutting up from the ground. Dotty reached into the gap between. "This will be easy to guard."

"From what?" Tigerheart wondered out loud.

Rascal glanced around. "Some of the Twolegs bring dogs. They keep them tied to vines. But the dogs can still reach under the ledges."

"Don't worry." Dotty unsheathed her claws. "A few quick swipes will scare then away."

"Not *too* vicious, though," Fierce warned. "Remember. We mustn't attract the Twolegs' attention."

Mittens lifted his nose, his eyes sparkling. "I'm heading for the ledge where they pile the fish."

Cobweb purred. "I'll come with you."

Tigerheart blinked at the two cats. "You like fish?"

"*All* cats like fish," Ant meowed.

Tigerheart wrinkled his nose. "Where I come from, we only eat prey with legs. Except RiverClan."

The other cats stared at him as though he were crazy. His pelt prickled self-consciously.

Fierce whisked her tail. "I'll take Tigerheart and Cobweb to see what food the Twolegs have brought this moon." She nodded at Mittens, Rascal, and Ant. "You hunt for fish while Blaze and Dotty wait here."

The patrol split, and Tigerheart followed Fierce and Cobweb as they slid from the ledges and dodged between the Twolegs streaming past. With relief, Tigerheart saw another row of ledges and ducked under it with the others.

Fierce tasted the air. "This way." The ledges formed a tunnel, edged with Twoleg paws, and she led the way along it before dashing across another stream of Twolegs, and then another, until they reached a ledge where the scent of food was so strong, Tigerheart's mouth began to water. Fierce stopped beneath it and glanced up at a narrow gap. A grouse's head hung over the edge. Fierce lifted her forepaws off the ground and peered through the slit. "No one's watching," she whispered. Reaching up a paw, she tugged at the grouse's head. It shifted a little, then tumbled through the gap.

Tigerheart stared down at the fat piece of prey. He couldn't believe his eyes. A grouse in the middle of the city. Delight surged beneath his pelt. The kits were going to taste real prey today.

"Take it to Dotty, then come back here," Fierce told him.

Eagerly, Tigerheart lifted the grouse between his jaws. The weight of it reminded him of hunting trips with ShadowClan. None of the scraps they scavenged from scrapcans weighed so much or smelled so good. Musky prey-scent filled his nose as he carried the grouse along the ledge tunnel. Peering between the brightly pelted paws of the Twolegs, he scanned the far ledges, looking for Dotty. He spotted her, crouching with Blaze beside the jutting stones. Looking both ways, he waited patiently for a gap in the stream of Twolegs that filled the space between the ledges. As the crowd eased, he darted from one row to another until he reached the stash place.

"Wow." Blaze stared wide-eyed at the grouse as he dropped it between the stones. "I've never seen fresh-kill that big."

"Fierce and Cobweb are collecting more." As Tigerheart spoke, Rascal and Mittens dashed toward him, Ant on their tail. Each cat held a glittering fish between his jaws.

They dropped the fish between the stones.

"*They're* here," Rascal huffed.

"Who?" Alarm sparked in Tigerheart's chest.

"Fog and her gang," Ant told him. "They're scavenging."

Tigerheart peered through the maze of ledges, his fur spiking as he spotted Tuna slinking through the shadows on the far side of the clearing. Fog was with him, and an orange she-cat. Fog stopped and signaled to another group of cats nearby with a flick of her tail. How many cats did Fog have following her? Unease rippled beneath Tigerheart's pelt.

Dotty followed his gaze, her fur pricking nervously.

"There's enough food here for everyone to share, isn't there?" She sounded uncertain.

"*If* Fog wants to share it," Tigerheart meowed darkly. He didn't trust the smoky she-cat. She'd chased away the guardian cats' rats. What if she wasn't simply a mouse-brained hunter? What if she'd been *trying* to wreck the guardian cats' hunt? Perhaps depriving her rivals of prey was more important than hunting. Perhaps she was just here to cause trouble, like Darktail. He nodded to Ant, Rascal, and Mittens. "Keep collecting prey. I'll warn Fierce."

He headed back toward the meat ledge where he'd left Cobweb and Fierce. They greeted him, eyes shining. Fresh-kill was piled at their paws. "We'll have to make several trips back to the gathering place with a haul as big as this," Fierce meowed happily.

"Let's get this back to Dotty quickly." Tigerheart nodded anxiously at the prey.

Fierce narrowed her eyes. "Is something wrong?"

"Fog and her gang are here."

Fierce shrugged. "I guess they're looking for food. It's not a problem. They need to eat just like we do."

Tigerheart gazed at her. She'd clearly never had to deal with cats like Darktail. "Not all cats want to share."

"What do you mean?" Cobweb glanced around nervously.

"When Fog chased those rats into the trash field, did it look like she wanted to catch them?" Tigerheart stared at Fierce.

Fierce looked puzzled.

"Was she chasing them, or was she just trying to scatter

them so *we* couldn't catch them?" Tigerheart pressed.

Fierce frowned. "You think she wants to stop us scavenging. Why?"

"I'm not sure," Tigerheart admitted. "But she's camped outside your den, and we seem to trip over her wherever we go. I think she might be trying to take over your territory."

Fierce looked unconvinced. "But we don't *have* territory."

"So you keep saying." Exasperation tightened Tigerheart's belly. "But you have places where you live and places where you scavenge. Imagine if you couldn't live beneath the gathering place anymore. Imagine if you had to fight every time you wanted to rummage through your favorite scrapcans." He remembered the rot pile cats. They'd stopped Dash's scavenging. City cats weren't as easygoing as they liked to make out. "Imagine Fog sleeping in your nest."

"She couldn't!" Fierce looked alarmed for the first time.

"Why not?" Tigerheart pressed. "She has more cats with her every time we see her. Her gang is getting bigger, and she has no sick cats to care for, or kits. If she decides to drive you out of your home, she could probably do it."

As he spoke, he saw alarm flash in Cobweb's eyes. He followed the gray tom's gaze and saw Fog, Tuna, and a stout black-and-white tom padding toward them. "Take this catch to Dotty," Tigerheart ordered. "I'll speak to Fog."

Fierce and Cobweb snatched up what they could, leaving a rabbit beside Tigerheart as they hurried away.

Tigerheart turned to face Fog.

The gray she-cat padded toward him, her eyes glittering with satisfaction. "I've never seen this place before." She stopped in front of him and looked down at the rabbit. "Perhaps it's a good thing those foxes drove us out of our home. The scraps here are much better than anything we used to scavenge." She glanced at the black-and-white tom. "I bet you're glad you joined our little community, Growler."

The tom purred and reached a paw toward the rabbit.

Tigerheart slapped it away, keeping his claws sheathed. He wasn't going to fight unless he had to. "I thought you didn't want to invade our territory."

"I thought you didn't have any territory," Fog countered.

"Maybe the guardian cats don't, but I do." Tigerheart curled his lip.

Fog looked at Tuna and then Growler. "And you're going to defend it single-pawed?"

"I'm going to stop you stealing my catch." Tigerheart dragged the rabbit closer.

"I told you." Fog's eyes shimmered with menace. "In the city, it's every cat for herself." She darted forward and hooked the rabbit away.

Anger scorched through Tigerheart's fur. With a hiss, he swiped his claws across her cheek. Paws slammed into his flank as the black-and-white tom flew at him. Tigerheart fell onto his side. Kicking out his hind legs, he knocked Tuna away before he could join the fight. Then he rolled nimbly back onto his paws and reared. Growler glared at him, hissing. Fog lunged, her claws stretched as she raked his muzzle. Tigerheart ducked his head and rammed it into her belly. He lifted her off her paws and tossed her to one side, then spun and faced the black-and-white tom. Thrusting his muzzle forward, he snapped at Growler's leg. He sank his teeth in hard, tasting blood and feeling bone. The tom screeched and pulled away. Claws pierced Tigerheart's tail. He spun and saw Tuna clinging on. With a snarl he aimed a flurry of swipes at Tuna's muzzle. Yowling, Tuna ducked away. Gray fur flashed at the side of Tigerheart's vision. He turned in time to see Fog attacking once more. He reared to meet her as she dived at him, and he wrapped his forelegs around her. Knocking her off her paws, he rolled her onto her back and began churning her belly with his hind claws. She screeched, struggling in his grasp. Clinging on, Tigerheart rolled from under the ledge. Alarm shrilled beneath his pelt as he knocked against a pair of Twoleg paws. The Twoleg screeched.

Around him, the clearing exploded into chaos as Twolegs yelped and howled and waved their front paws. They crowded around him and glared, their white, sunken eyes stretched in surprise. Tigerheart let go of Fog and ran. Dodging between shrieking Twolegs, he hared along the small alley between ledges before ducking into shadow. He glimpsed Dotty ahead. Fierce and Cobweb were with her. Blaze stared at him with wide eyes. Ant, Mittens, and Rascal streaked toward them, fish between their jaws. "Grab what you can and get out of here!" Tigerheart yowled. They snatched prey in their teeth and headed for the alley. Tigerheart grabbed the grouse as he passed the jutting stones and followed them.

Twoleg shrieks followed Tigerheart and the others as they

skimmed the stone, veered away from the stone clearing, and ducked into the alley. They ran until the screaming faded. Then Fierce pulled up. Tigerheart slewed to a spot beside her. He dropped the grouse and gasped for breath as Ant, Cobweb, Dotty, and Blaze scrambled to a halt beside them. Rascal and Mittens turned and stared, still holding their fish.

"What happened?" Fierce demanded as she dropped the hunk of meat she'd been holding.

"Fog and her friends tried to steal the rabbit," Tigerheart panted.

"Why did you fight her?" Fierce looked indignant. "Now we can't go back! The Twolegs will be looking out for us."

"Do you think I should have let her take the rabbit?" Tigerheart stared at her.

"There was plenty for everyone!"

"Then why did she want *our* rabbit?" Frustration flared in Tigerheart's chest. When would Fierce understand that Fog wanted what the guardian cats owned and that she wouldn't stop until she had driven them away? Just like Darktail.

The guardian cats looked at one another uncertainly.

"It is strange that she didn't just find her own scraps," Cobweb murmured.

"Why did she have to take Tigerheart's catch?" Rascal agreed.

Fierce glared at the tabby tom. "Probably because Tigerheart's been trying to start a fight with her since he met her," she snapped. "Perhaps that's what warrior cats do."

Tigerheart met the tortoiseshell's angry gaze unflinchingly.

"Warriors believe that some things are worth fighting for."

Fierce turned away angrily. Suddenly she stiffened, her ear pricking. Tigerheart jerked his muzzle around to follow her gaze. Fog and her friends were padding down the alley toward them.

Tigerheart glanced at Fierce, resentment seething beneath his pelt. He stepped aside as Fog reached them and let Fierce face the smoky she-cat. "Fine. Why don't I let you handle this?"

CHAPTER 22

Fierce eyed Fog warily as the gray she-cat stopped a muzzle-length from her nose. Tuna and Growler flanked her. Streak watched from behind with six more strays.

"You realize we might never be able to go scavenging there again," Fierce snapped. "The Twolegs will be looking out for us next time."

"Of course we will," Fog sniffed. "Twolegs have memories like birds. They won't remember us now that we've left."

"You didn't have to try and steal Tigerheart's rabbit," Fierce told her. "If you'd scavenged for your own scraps, we'd *all* have scraps to take home."

Fog glanced at the prey piled at the guardian cats' paws. "We could still all have something to take home." She licked her lips.

Fierce's fur bristled. "We caught this prey, fair and square. It's for the cats at *our* camp."

Fog tipped her head as her gang fanned out around her. "But it looks so *tasty.*"

"We'd have more of it if you hadn't started a fight." Fierce unsheathed her claws.

Tigerheart's chest swelled with hope. Was Fierce finally realizing that even city cats had to fight for what belonged to them? He looked from Fog's ragged gang to the guardian cats. Fierce and her friends were outnumbered. Would they remember the battle moves he'd taught them? Doubt pricked in his pelt. If there was a fight, there would be wounds, and they might lose the food they'd stolen. Perhaps reason would sort this out. He padded between the two groups and looked from Fierce to Fog. "If Twolegs have such small memories," he meowed to Fog, "why don't you go back and get some scraps of your own? I'm sure you can find better prey than this. Besides"—he flicked his gaze to her companions—"this won't be enough to feed all your bellies."

Fog narrowed her eyes. "Why don't you give us your scraps and *you* can go and find more?"

"No." Fierce's mew surprised Tigerheart. The tortoiseshell bushed out her fur. "Why are you bullying us? What did we ever do to you?"

Fog looked amused. "Why do you need to have done anything to us? We're just a bunch of cold, hungry cats looking for food and somewhere warm to sleep."

"We said you could sleep near the gathering place," Fierce snapped. "Isn't that enough? Why don't you leave us in peace?"

Tigerheart pricked his ears. He wanted to hear Fog's answer.

"I told you," Fog meowed. "We were driven out of our home by foxes. It was a good home. A nice deserted stretch of scrub between some broken Twoleg dens. Lots of shelter, lots of prey. But now it belongs to foxes, and we need somewhere new to live."

Unease wormed though Tigerheart's fur. If this went on, would Fog want to take over the guardian cats' home as well as steal their food? He stared at her, fluffing out his fur to look bigger. "I'm a warrior," he growled, "so fighting us for this food won't be as easy as you think. I'm sorry you've lost your home, but this is a big city. Maybe you should look elsewhere for somewhere to live." He unsheathed his claws and stared at the scratches he'd left on her muzzle. "I fought three of you earlier and I don't have a single wound. And I've taught these cats how to fight like warriors too."

Fog exchanged a look with Tuna. Tigerheart was relieved to see worry pass between them. Pressing his advantage, he leaned closer. "If you want to start a fight, go ahead." He lashed his tail. "But it won't end here. Don't forget, you decided to make your home next to ours. I can promise that if you try to take this food from us, you won't ever sleep easily in your nests again." He showed his teeth and let his breath bathe Fog's muzzle.

She backed away. "Okay," she snarled. "We'll go and find better prey than this." Flicking her tail, she turned away.

Tuna glared at Tigerheart menacingly, then followed. Growler showed his teeth. One by one, her ragged crew padded after her.

Tigerheart turned on Fierce. "Do you see now why every cat needs borders?"

Fierce bristled. "We don't all dream of being a warrior.

We're healers, not fighters, and we managed to live in peace before you arrived. Not every argument needs to be settled with claws." She picked up her hunk of meat and headed away. Cobweb, Ant, Mittens, and Rascal avoided his gaze as they followed with their catch.

We managed to live in peace before you arrived. Tigerheart flexed his claws angrily. *You didn't have to deal with Fog before I arrived.* How could Fierce be so shortsighted? Didn't she realize that the more she appeased Fog, the bolder Fog would become?

"*I* want to be a warrior." Blaze's mew took Tigerheart by surprise.

He blinked at the young tom, who was puffing out his chest. "I'm glad it's not just me."

Dovewing leaned closer to Tigerheart as they lay beside their nest, their bellies full of grouse, while the kits chased one another around the legs of the wooden ledge. "Did something happen while you were out?"

"Only what I told you." Tigerheart had recounted their encounter with Fog's gang. He still hadn't told her about the worry nagging deep in his belly. City cats had no code at all. From what he'd seen, they were hardly better than rogues. He didn't want his kits to grow up thinking the way they did.

Outside the gathering-place den, the sky darkened as night drew in. The clear stretches of wall shimmered in the orange light from the Twoleg dens.

"Tigerheart." Shadowkit clawed his way onto his father's back. "Can you give me a bodger ride?"

"Me too!" Pouncekit jumped up beside her brother.

Lightkit scrambled on. "And me."

Tigerheart winced at the prick of their tiny claws. "It's not a *bodger* ride," he corrected. "It's a *badger* ride." He pushed himself to his paws, lurching a little to make them squeal, and began to stomp across the shiny floor.

"What *is* a badger?" Lightkit asked.

"I told you." Tigerheart paused to let them settle, then staggered forward suddenly. The kits squealed again and clung on harder. "A badger is a big black-and-white creature that lives near the forest. It has a huge muzzle and beady eyes, and it eats kits if it catches them."

"Why didn't a badger eat you?" Pouncekit demanded.

"I never got caught," Tigerheart told him.

"Did a badger ever chase you?" Pouncekit pressed.

"I fought one once," Tigerheart told her.

"You *fought* one?" Shadowkit's gasp ruffled his ear fur.

"I was with two Clanmates," Tigerheart meowed. "Three warriors against one badger, and it still nearly won."

"How did you beat it?" Lightkit mewed breathlessly.

Tigerheart turned sharply. The kits squeaked and scrabbled deeper into his fur. "I had to use all my best warrior moves," he told them. "And I had my Clanmates by my side. When it saw the three of us lined up in front of its muzzle, it wailed in terror and ran away."

"You scared a badger away!" Lightkit tugged at his pelt.

"You're the best warrior ever," Pouncekit squeaked.

Shadowkit slid off his back and hurried back to Dovewing.

"Will we have to fight badgers one day?" he asked her.

She nuzzled his ear affectionately. "Perhaps," she mewed. "But so long as you have Clanmates fighting at your side, you'll be safe."

Tigerheart tipped Lightkit and Pouncekit onto the floor with a shrug.

Pouncekit tried to cling on. "Don't stop!"

"It's getting late," he meowed firmly. "You should go to sleep."

"But I want to hear more about badgers!" Lightkit protested.

Dovewing got to her paws and nudged the brown tabby kit toward the nest. "If you go to sleep, we'll tell you about hawks tomorrow."

"What's a hawk?" Lightkit stopped at the edge of the nest as Shadowkit and Pouncekit scrambled in.

"It's a bird with a huge, sharp beak made of claws," Dovewing mewed.

Lightkit leaped down beside her littermates. "It sounds scary."

"It is." Dovewing nuzzled them down into the soft folds of the furless pelts, then padded back to Tigerheart. She settled beside him as he lay down on his belly and began to wash his paws. "It's so nice being together without the Clans judging us," she mewed absently.

Tigerheart stopped washing. Why had she said that? Did she prefer it here?

She nudged his shoulder with her nose. "It is, isn't it?"

He met her green gaze and tried to read it. Was she about to tell him that she'd changed her mind? Did she want to stay in the city? "I guess," he murmured.

"Sneaking around never felt right." She turned her gaze toward the guardian cats who were moving around the shadowy den. Spire padded between the nests of the two new sick cats. Fierce washed her chest. Ant and Cobweb were still gnawing on the meaty bone they'd stolen, while Rascal and Mittens picked fish bones from their teeth. Blaze was already sleeping in his nest, tired out from the day's adventure.

Tigerheart looked at Dovewing. Was she wondering what it would be like to live here forever? "When we go home," he meowed pointedly, "we won't have to sneak around. We can be honest. We just need to decide which Clan we want to raise our kits in."

"I guess it will have to be ShadowClan," Dovewing sighed. "I can't ask you to give up your chance to be the leader of your Clan."

"I might not have a chance anymore." For the first time, Tigerheart wondered with a sickening jolt if he'd been replaced as ShadowClan's deputy. He had, after all, deserted them.

Dovewing sniffed. "Who else could lead ShadowClan? You said that your Clanmates were begging you to lead them before you left. Of course you have a chance."

Tigerheart eyed her nervously. She was still gazing across the den. Was she testing him? Was he meant to say that he would give it up?

She turned and caught his eye. "I know how important it is

to you. I want you to be happy."

"So you'll join ShadowClan?" Hope flickered in his chest.

"I guess." She didn't sound convinced. "If there's still a ShadowClan to join."

He tensed. *It's dark in the forest.* He remembered Shadowkit's words and shivered. *Stop it!* He was seeing prophecies everywhere. Even in the words of a kit.

Dovewing went on. "But we don't have to worry about that now. We can worry about it when the kits are old enough to travel."

When will that be? He didn't dare ask, but he felt they should leave soon. She was so wrapped up in her love for their kits, perhaps going home wasn't important to her anymore. Perhaps their safety was the only thing she cared about. He glanced toward the nest, where the kits had settled into silence. They must be asleep already. Perhaps she was right. His heart ached with love for Dovewing, Lightkit, Pouncekit, and Shadowkit. He should put their interests first. But wasn't getting them back to the Clan so that they could grow up surrounded by warriors just as important as keeping them safe? If they didn't become warriors, what would they become?

Dovewing's breath deepened beside him, and he realized she had dozed off. He pressed closer against her. It would all be okay. He had Dovewing and his kits, and one day he'd have his Clan again.

He looked up at a clear stretch of wall, hoping to spy starlight piercing the harsh Twoleg light. A shadow moved beyond the stone. Tigerheart stiffened. A face was peering into the den. He recognized the wide ears and pointed muzzle. *Fog.* She was spying on the guardian cats. Fear quivered in his belly. Was she planning her next move? Did she have an eye on the cozy den the guardian cats had made for themselves beneath the gathering place?

I have to stop her. Tigerheart knew that, whether they left this place or not, he had to make sure these cats were safe from Fog and her gang.

His thoughts flitted as he watched Fog's silhouette move along the stretch of clear wall. How could he drive her away? An idea sparked in his mind. Perhaps there was no need to drive her away. She might be happy to return to her old home if he could figure out how to get rid of the foxes that had stolen it.

CHAPTER 23

❧

"*We'd need to find out how* many foxes live there before we make a move." Fierce paced the shiny floor of the gathering-place den.

"Of course," Tigerheart agreed. "But if we can get Fog and her gang to join us in the fight, I think we can drive them away."

He'd called a meeting the next morning, as soon as the guardian cats began to stir. Pouncekit, Lightkit, and Shadowkit watched from their nest. They stared with round, dark eyes, their ears pricked. Dovewing had given them strict instructions to keep quiet while the older cats talked. She stood beside Cobweb now, her gaze fixed on Fierce. Tigerheart had told her about his plan. He could sense Dovewing silently urging him on, but the guardian cats weren't enthusiastic. Although Blaze watched curiously, Peanut and Bracken listened anxiously, their pelts prickling. Ant frowned, shifting his paws uneasily. Dotty, Pipsqueak, and Boots glanced at one another as he went on. "Fog is only going to make our life difficult if she stays," he told them. "Last night, I saw her looking into our den." He nodded toward the clear stretch of wall. "Her cats are not going to sleep outside in this weather if they think they can sleep in here."

Dotty looked puzzled. "Why don't we invite them to join our group?"

Tigerheart's hackles lifted as he remembered Darktail. "Fog believes in every cat looking after himself. Her denmates probably feel the same. Do you want cats here who are only interested in filling their own bellies?" He flicked his muzzle toward the nests where Feather and Scowl, their newest patients, lay. Spire was stripping herbs from their stems beside them. "I've met cats like Fog before. In the forest, we call them rogues. They have no pity for sick cats. They see them as burdens. Inviting Fog to join this group would destroy everything you've built here!"

Fierce listened thoughtfully. "But you think, if we can drive the foxes away, Fog and her friends would go home?"

"Yes." Tigerheart ignored the doubt pricking in his belly. "They liked their old home. I think they'd choose it over this place if they could."

Pipsqueak's tail twitched. "Just because we chased a pair of foxes from the herb patch doesn't mean that we can fight a whole clan of them."

"We don't know that it is a whole clan," Tigerheart argued.

"It was enough to drive away Fog and her cats," Rascal commented darkly.

"But if we fought together . . ." He looked pleadingly around the guardian cats. "With Fog fighting *with* us instead of against us, we could do it. I could offer to show them the battle moves I taught you."

Fierce blinked at him. "First you tell us Fog's cats are a threat; then you offer to teach them how to fight?"

Dovewing padded forward and stood beside Tigerheart. "Tigerheart's only trying to help. He speaks from experience. Rogues drove his Clan from their home. He had to fight to get it back. His Clan still hasn't really recovered."

"Why is he here, then?" Dotty looked at him through narrowed eyes. "Doesn't his Clan need him?"

Guilt sparked in Tigerheart's chest. "I'm here because I think my Clan is better off without me for a while."

Dovewing shifted beside him. "And because he wants to be with me and our kits."

Dotty tipped her head toward Dovewing. "Why did *you* come?" she asked. "You talk about the Clans like they're better than strays. Why did you leave them?"

Tigerheart felt Dovewing's fur bristle self-consciously. He met Dotty's inquisitive stare. "She dreamed that her kits would be safer here."

Dotty rolled her eyes. "She sounds like Spire."

Spire lifted his head. Herb specks were caught in his whiskers. "Dreams sometimes reveal the truth." He nodded distractedly at Dovewing and Tigerheart. "I dreamed they would come, didn't I?"

"Dreams are nonsense," Dotty huffed. "What does it matter if Spire dreamed you were coming? It doesn't change anything."

As she spoke, Rascal and Mittens squeezed through the entrance and jumped to the floor. Mittens's eyes glittered with alarm. Rascal's pelt was ruffled.

"There are cat scents around the slabs," Mittens mewed breathlessly.

Fierce stiffened. "Fog's cats?"

Mittens nodded. "They've clearly been snooping around in the night."

"And there are Twoleg scents too," Rascal added. "Fresh ones. They must have come before dawn."

Tigerheart lifted his muzzle. "Fog's group is clearly attracting the attention of the Twolegs, just like they did at the outdoor gathering. We need to get rid of her before the Twolegs discover our den."

Fierce gazed at him thoughtfully for a moment and then nodded. "Let's practice those battle moves you taught us," she meowed decisively.

Pipsqueak's pelt bristled nervously. "Are we going to fight the foxes?"

"Not until we know how many there are and if Fog will help us," Fierce told him. "But it sounds as though we are going to have to defend our home one way or another, so we might as well be ready."

The guardian cats looked at one another. Tigerheart's paws pricked nervously as they leaned close and murmured. One by one, they met Fierce's gaze and nodded.

Hope swelled in Tigerheart's belly. He was doing what was best for the group. He couldn't let Fog drive them away. "We should train outside," he suggested. "We need to get used to fighting on uneven ground." He swept his tail over the shiny floor. "And I hope the battle never reaches this den."

He let Fierce lead the way out. Pipsqueak, Dotty, Rascal, and Mittens followed, Ant and Cobweb at their tails. As Bracken, Boots, and Peanut headed after them, Tigerheart called them back.

"You're healers," he meowed. "Perhaps you should be gathering herbs for the wounded rather than training how to fight." He searched their gazes. He didn't want to frighten them, but if there was a battle, they would need to be prepared.

Peanut nodded. "We'll go to the herb patch now," she mewed. "There may be some leaves left untouched by the frost."

As she led Boots and Bracken out, Dovewing glanced at Pouncekit, Lightkit, and Shadowkit. They were still watching, leaning forward eagerly. Dovewing purred. "They're desperate to help."

Tigerheart blinked fondly at them. "Perhaps they could watch the battle training." It would be almost like being among real warriors.

Dovewing's ears twitched anxiously. "You mean, take them outside?"

"Just as far as the stone slabs," Tigerheart encouraged. "Fresh air will do them good. And there won't be any Twolegs around. It's not a yowling day."

"What about the Twolegs Rascal smelled?"

"They must be gone. He didn't see them. He only caught their scent." Tigerheart felt a prick of guilt. Would Dovewing guess that he was eager to get the kits outside because he wanted them to taste the wind and feel soft grass beneath their paws? He wanted to know if the leaf-bare wind would pierce their kit fluff too easily. Would the cold earth freeze their pads? Were they ready to make the journey home?

She looked at him uncertainly, and then at the kits.

Pouncekit was already racing across the shiny floor. "Did Tigerheart say we could go out?"

Lightkit charged after her sister. "I want to go first."

"Won't it be cold outside?" Shadowkit trailed them doubtfully.

"That's what you've got fur for, silly!" Pouncekit called over her shoulder.

Dovewing's tail drooped. "I guess we can take them out," she conceded. "But only for a while."

Lightkit tried to haul herself up the leg of the wooden ledge. Dovewing scooped her up and carried her up to the entrance. "Don't go outside until I've got Shadowkit and Pouncekit," she warned. As she jumped down to fetch them, Tigerheart noticed Spire. The healer had wandered into a pool of sunshine at the far end of the den and was staring at the air, his eyes glazed. Was he having a vision?

"I'll join you in a moment," Tigerheart called to Dovewing as she dropped Shadowkit beside his littermates.

"Don't be long," Dovewing answered, nosing them through the gap in the wall.

Tigerheart padded toward the skinny black tom. Spire didn't shift his gaze from the shaft of light that seemed to have hypnotized him. Tigerheart wondered whether to disturb him, but as he neared, Spire spoke, his gaze still distant.

"Take care of Blaze."

For a moment, Tigerheart wondered who the healer was talking to, but there was no cat left in the den aside from Feather and Scowl, and they were hidden among the furless pelts of their nests. Was he talking to an imaginary cat?

"I will not live beside the widewater. But Blaze will."

Widewater? Instantly Tigerheart thought of the lake. Was he talking about their journey there? "Are you saying Blaze will travel home with us?"

Spire's yellow gaze flashed toward him, focusing suddenly. "Of course."

He's talking to me. Tigerheart leaned closer. "So *widewater* means the lake?"

"That's where the Clans live, isn't it?"

"Yes." Surprise set Tigerheart's fur prickling. "How do you know?" Had Dovewing mentioned the lake?

"I told you." Spire shook out his pelt. "I see things."

"Do you see our journey? Do we make it home safely?"

Spire looked away. "Go teach battle moves, like you promised."

Unease wormed in Tigerheart's belly. The healer was avoiding his question. "Do you know if we get home safely?" he pressed.

Spire padded past him, heading for the sick cats' nests. "I don't see everything," he meowed briskly.

Tigerheart hurried from the den, suddenly anxious to see

Dovewing and their kits. Did the black tom know something? Something he didn't dare tell?

Pouncekit, Lightkit, and Shadowkit were bouncing over the grass beside a stone slab. Dovewing watched them protectively, her gaze flitting beyond them, as though checking for danger. She caught sight of him and blinked at him, purring. "They like the grass."

"It's so soft," Lightkit squeaked.

"And tickly." Pouncekit rolled over in it, mewling with delight.

Shadowkit stayed in the shelter of the slab and watched anxiously.

"I want to explore," Pouncekit mewed.

"I want to play." Lightkit called to Tigerheart. "Are you going to play with us?"

Tigerheart looked to where the guardian cats were already practicing the battle moves he'd taught them to fight foxes. "I have to go and help Fierce," he told Lightkit. "We can play another time."

Lightkit wasn't listening. She was following Pouncekit as the gray kit sniffed her way to the next stone slab like a fox following scent.

Tigerheart purred. It was good to see the kits with grass beneath their paws and sky overhead. For the first time, he could imagine them as warriors. He turned toward the guardian cats. Cobweb and Ant were stalking around Rascal. Rascal eyed them sharply. As Cobweb dived for Rascal's forepaw and Ant lunged for his tail, Rascal ducked and rolled. Cobweb and

Ant landed clumsily as Rascal tumbled out of reach.

"Nice move, Rascal!" Tigerheart was pleased the guardian cats had remembered the skills he'd taught them.

Blaze bounded toward him. "I want to learn a new move!" he mewed. "I already know all the old ones."

"You do, do you?" Tigerheart purred at him proudly. "Show me one."

Blaze arched his back and flattened his ears. Hissing, he approached Tigerheart side-first, looking as big as he could. Tigerheart shot out a paw to tumble the kit onto his back, but his sheathed claws swiped thin air. Blaze had ducked beneath his chest and was clinging to his hind leg, churning his paws against it energetically.

"Very good!" Tigerheart purred. "You're a natural fighter."

"I am?" Blaze leaped to his paws and stared excitedly at Tigerheart.

Tigerheart cuffed his ear playfully. *You've a long way to go before you'd make a warrior.* But the kit definitely had talent. He was quick-thinking as well as fast.

Movement near the trees caught his eye. Fog and Tuna were stalking through the grass there. Streak and Growler were heading the other way. *They're still checking out our territory.* Tigerheart's pelt prickled. He wished the guardian cats would admit this was their land and mark some borders. It would make it easier to challenge Fog and her gang. And yet how could he confront her now? He needed her to help them fight the foxes. As Fog caught his eye, he looked away. *Focus on training the guardian cats.*

Fierce lifted her muzzle. "What do we do if we're attacked by two foxes at once?"

Tigerheart flicked his tail approvingly. She was thinking like a warrior. "If we fight the foxes, we'll stay in pairs. That way we can be more prepared for an attack on two sides." He beckoned Rascal and Mittens forward. "Stand tail to tail," he told them. As they shifted into position, he padded around the circle of watching cats and nudged Pipsqueak forward with his nose. "You can be one fox," he mewed, then moved on to Dotty. "You can be the other." He guided her past Rascal and Mittens, who were facing outward, their tails touching. "If two foxes attack from two sides, get straight into a tail-to-tail position. Foxes will instinctively go for your legs. Duck down and claw their muzzle as they come in for the attack. Aim for their eyes if you can. Then rear up fast, so your backs are touching, and use each other to push off. Leap clear of the fox's muzzle, onto its back. The foxes will crash into each other while you've got your claws around their spines. Try it." Tigerheart stepped back to watch. "Remember," he told Pipsqueak and Dotty, "you're foxes. Aim for their legs. Everybody, keep your claws sheathed. We don't want injuries."

He watched, concentrating, as Dotty and Pipsqueak circled Rascal and Mittens.

"Keep your faces toward the fox at all times," Tigerheart warned. "When you're fighting large enemies, your teeth and claws are more important than your strength."

Rascal and Mittens shifted to keep their muzzles pointed toward Pipsqueak and Dotty as they continued to circle. Then

Dotty caught Pipsqueak's eye and lunged forward. Pipsqueak followed. Rascal and Mittens threw a flurry of blows at their denmates' muzzles, then reared together and pushed away from each other. They sailed over their attackers, flattening them as they landed squarely on their backs.

Pipsqueak grunted as his paws collapsed beneath him. "Rascal, you're heavy!" He wriggled indignantly from under the tabby tom.

Dotty scrambled from under Mittens. "It seems like a good strategy."

"Let's all practice it." Fierce waved Ant, Cobweb, Blaze, and Rascal into group with a flick of her tail.

Cobweb hesitated, his gaze flicking toward Blaze. "He's too young to fight foxes," he pointed out.

"He won't be involved in any battles," Fierce promised. "But he might as well learn the moves. He might need them one day—"

The terrified squeal of a kit cut her off.

Tigerheart froze. *Pouncekit!* He recognized her cry. Heart bursting with terror, he raced for the patch of grass where he'd left them. The kits were gone. He saw Dovewing's pelt flash between the stone slabs and chased after her.

He caught up as she reached a shiny mesh cave, which sat in the grass behind a stone. Pouncekit was trapped inside, staring through the silver mesh, her eyes wide with horror.

"What happened?" Dovewing pressed her muzzle against the mesh.

Pouncekit pushed the tip of her nose through a gap and

mewled pitifully into her mother's cheek fur. "I smelled something tasty. And I crept inside to get it. But it banged shut behind me."

Shadowkit and Lightkit scrabbled at the outside with their paws.

"She's trapped!" Lightkit squealed.

"It's eaten her." Shadowkit looked at Tigerheart, his eyes dark and round. "She's trapped forever!"

CHAPTER 24

☘

Tigerheart sniffed the edges of the cave. "Which end was open?" he asked Pouncekit.

"The small end behind me," Pouncekit wailed.

"It's okay, dear," Dovewing crooned softly. "We'll get you out." She glanced at Tigerheart. Guilt glittered in her green eyes. "She was only away from me for a moment."

"She'll be okay." Tigerheart hoped Dovewing couldn't hear panic in his mew. His heartbeat pounded in his ears as he sniffed the small end and hooked a claw into the mesh. It was stuck firmly shut.

Fierce, Cobweb, and Dotty reached them.

"What is that?" Dotty stared in horror at the mesh cave.

"It must be some kind of Twoleg trap," Fierce growled. "I can smell their stench on it."

"That's what they were doing in the night," Cobweb gasped. "Setting this trap."

A monster rumbled nearby. Tigerheart looked up and saw it stop at the edge of the grass. A Twoleg got out, headed toward the smooth path that led to the gathering-place entrance. Tigerheart felt sick. Was it coming to claim its trap with

Pouncekit inside? Relief flickered in his chest as the Twoleg headed around the back of the gathering place. "We've got to hurry," he meowed. "That Twoleg might come back."

Dotty had pulled Lightkit and Shadowkit against her belly and was soothing them with gentle laps of her tongue, while Dovewing comforted Pouncekit through the mesh. Her eyes were still wide, but her breathing was slowing as Dovewing nuzzled her cheek.

Cobweb crouched beside Tigerheart and examined the trap. "There's a gap," he mewed. "Where the edges meet." He hooked a claw into it and tugged. It shifted, but not much. He strained harder. "It's stiff, but I think we can get it open if we can find something to wedge in."

"A stick," Fierce suggested. She darted away toward a tree.

Tigerheart glanced at Dovewing. Her gaze was fixed on Pouncekit as she whispered reassurance through the mesh. "Just hold still a bit longer. We're getting you out."

"We've got a plan," Tigerheart told her.

She met his gaze, fright flashing in her eyes, then turned back to Pouncekit.

Fierce raced back, a stick between her jaws. "This end is thin," she meowed as she dropped it beside Tigerheart. "But the other end is thick."

Cobweb sniffed it. "If we feed the thin end through, we can wedge it open."

Tigerheart understood, hope flaring beneath his fur. "If we push it all the way inside, up to the thick end, it might be strong enough to move the mesh."

Fierce picked up the stick again and threaded the thin end

through the gap while Tigerheart and Cobweb pulled at the mesh with their claws.

"Move out of the way, Pouncekit," Tigerheart warned as Fierce pushed the stick deeper into the trap.

Pouncekit squeezed against the side, trembling as Dovewing nuzzled her through the mesh. She stared, wide-eyed, as the stick nudged past her. "Will it work?"

"I hope so," Tigerheart muttered, straining at the trap. His claws burned with the effort. The stick was deep inside now, its thicker end holding the gap open wide enough to squeeze a paw through. "Pull on the stick," he told Fierce.

Digging her paws into the grass, Fierce tugged on the stick. The thin end caught in the mesh, and she began slowly to lever the small end open.

"It's working!" Dovewing pricked her ears as the gap widened. "Go on, Pouncekit, squeeze through. But be quick."

Pouncekit darted to the opening and wriggled through like a mouse squeezing beneath a root. As she bundled out, the stick snapped. Fierce fell backward and the trap slammed shut.

Tigerheart got his claws out of the way just in time. Cobweb hopped nimbly to one side.

"Pouncekit!" With a gasp, Dovewing leaped to the kit's side, her gaze flitting toward the gray kit's tail. Tigerheart stiffened. Had the trap bitten her as it closed? His shoulders sagged with relief as Pouncekit fluffed out her fur happily.

"I'm okay!" She flung herself against her mother's belly and nuzzled hard into her fur.

"I knew they were too young to be outside," Dovewing

fretted. "It's dangerous." She glared accusingly at Tigerheart. "How could you think of making them travel through a city when they're so young?"

"I never said—" Tigerheart stared at her, searching for words. He'd only *thought* about the journey home. He'd never mentioned it. He held his tongue now. Dovewing had been frightened. The trap had shocked them all. With cold certainty that sat like stone in his belly, he knew that it was far too soon to make the kits travel.

Just seeing them near the dens and Thunderpaths made him realize how small and vulnerable they were. And even if they made it out of the city, fields and forests might be more dangerous. In the Clans, didn't queens keep their kits in camp until they were six moons old to protect them from the owls and foxes that might carry them off? He returned Dovewing's gaze evenly. "You're right. They are too young to travel." He blinked at Fierce, his thoughts spinning. "Have you seen these traps before?"

"Never." Fierce poked it warily with her paw.

Lightkit looked out from below Dotty's belly. "Are the Twolegs trying to hurt us?"

"I don't know." Tigerheart frowned. Why had the Twolegs decided to leave such a dangerous thing now? He glanced toward the trees beyond the slabs where Fog and her gang had made their nests. Had too many cats caught the Twolegs' attention? "But I think they might be trying to catch us." He'd heard nursery tales about cats carried off by Twolegs and forced to live as kittypets. He shuddered.

A terrified wail sounded at the far end of the gathering den. The Twoleg had appeared from behind it and was carrying a mesh trap. White fur flashed inside. Paws scrabbled against the mesh as the trapped cat wailed again. Tigerheart recognized the anguished face of Streak.

"No!" Fog stared from beside the den wall, her face twisted with grief as she watched the Twoleg carry the trap to its monster and shut it inside.

"Quick." Tigerheart nudged Dovewing toward the den. "We need to hide. It might be coming for this trap. It mustn't find us here."

Dovewing scooped up Pouncekit by the scruff. Cobweb picked up Lightkit. Dotty grabbed Shadowkit. Keeping low, they scurried toward the den entrance. Fierce waved Mittens, Rascal, and the others toward the gathering place with a flick of her tail. As the cats streamed toward their home and began to file inside, Tigerheart watched Fog. The gray she-cat was staring desperately at the monster where Streak was trapped while the Twoleg headed toward Pouncekit's trap. It grunted angrily as it picked up the mesh cave. Tigerheart guessed it wasn't pleased to find the trap closed but empty.

As the last of the guardian cats followed Dovewing and Dotty inside, he slid into the shadow of the gathering-den wall and crept to where Fog stood as rigid as stone. "Don't let the Twoleg see you," he hissed. "It might take you too." He nudged her backward until a jutting wall blocked the Twoleg's view.

"It stole Streak!" Fog's eyes were wide with disbelief. "He's my brother. They can't take him!"

Tigerheart stared at her, his heart aching with pity.

"We've got to rescue him." She lurched forward, but he blocked her way.

"We can't," he meowed flatly. "There's nothing we can do."

Fog turned her stricken gaze on him. "You've traveled. You're a warrior. You must have seen this happen before. You must know where the Twolegs take the cats they steal!" Her pelt bristled with alarm. "Tell me where they're taking him!"

"I don't know." Tigerheart mewed helplessly.

"I can't lose Streak."

"He'll be okay."

"How do you know that?"

"They'll make him live like a kittypet. But eventually he'll escape. Twolegs can't stop a cat from leaving if he wants to leave. He'll find his way back."

"What if they don't make him a kittypet?" Fog's grief was quickly hardening into rage. "What if they kill him?"

The monster began to rumble. Fog darted from behind the wall and stared at it. Tigerheart padded after her and watched the monster pull away.

"No!"

Fog's wail tore his heart. As the monster disappeared around a corner, she turned on him. "This is your fault!"

"My fault?" Tigerheart blinked at her.

"Why didn't you tell us there were traps?"

"I didn't know."

Paw steps sounded beyond the wall. Tuna and Growler

raced around the corner. They stopped in front of Fog.

"Did it take him?" Tuna asked.

Fog stared at him bleakly. "There was nothing I could do."

Growler glanced around nervously. "We've found more traps."

"More?" Fierce's mew took Tigerheart by surprise. He turned to see the tortoiseshell padding toward them. Ant and Cobweb were following.

"Are the kits hidden?" Tigerheart asked.

Fierce nodded. "Even if the Twolegs found the den, they wouldn't find the kits. There's a lot of clutter to hide behind." She turned to Growler. "Show us where these other traps are."

Growler headed across the grass, leading Fierce around the end of the gathering place. Tigerheart followed, Cobweb and Ant at his heels.

He glanced back and saw Tuna weaving around Fog, trying to comfort her.

"Here." Growler led them to a mesh trap identical to the one that had caught Pouncekit. It sat behind a stone slab, one end wide open. The mouthwatering scent of fresh-kill wafted from inside. Tigerheart could see how Pouncekit had been tempted.

"There's another one over there." Growler nodded toward the slabs a few rows away. Then he turned his muzzle toward the patch of trees. "And one near our camp."

Cobweb was leaning close to the trap, sniffing at it.

"Don't go inside," Fierce warned.

"I'm not a mouse-brain," Cobweb answered. "I was just wondering how Pouncekit made her trap shut."

Tigerheart peered through the mesh. He could see the tasty fresh-kill wasn't fresh-kill at all, but just mush smeared beyond a shiny strip that stuck up in the middle of the trap. "It's not even real fresh-kill."

Cobweb's gaze paused as it reached the shiny strip. "That part of the trap wasn't sticking up in Pouncekit's trap."

Ant's ears pricked. "Do you think it went down when she stepped on it?"

"And shut the trap!" Growler's eyes shone.

"Let's find out." Cobweb hurried away toward a tree and returned carrying a stick.

Tigerheart's chest tightened as Cobweb poked the stick through the mesh and touched the end to the strip. The trap snapped shut. Tigerheart's pelt bushed with alarm.

Fierce blinked, her hackles lifting. "Twoleg fox-hearts!"

Cobweb lifted his muzzle triumphantly. "Now we know how to close them!"

Fierce padded away. "Come on. Let's close the others."

"Let's hurry!" Cobweb followed her, tail twitching anxiously. "The sound of the traps shutting seems to attract the Twolegs."

As they headed toward the next trap, Ant and Growler at their heels, Tigerheart paused. Fog had seen danger here. Now would be the best time to persuade her that they needed to do something about it. . . . He called after Fierce. "There's something I must do."

She waved her tail in reply. Cobweb was already fetching a stick to close the next trap. Tigerheart turned and padded around the end of the gathering den. Fog was still standing beside Tuna, staring at where the monster had disappeared as though she could still hardly believe her eyes.

Tigerheart dipped his head as he reached her. "I'm sorry for your loss," he meowed gently.

She turned on him. "You're probably glad to see one of us gone," she snapped.

Tigerheart shifted his paws. He had to handle this conversation carefully. "I'm never glad to see a cat fall into Twoleg paws," he meowed. "I'm a warrior. I believe all cats should live free." He caught Tuna's eye. "But now you see that this is a dangerous place to live." Tuna shifted his paws. "Perhaps you and your friends would be safer in your old home."

"How could we be?" Fog demanded. "It's full of foxes."

Tigerheart changed tack. "Did you see us training earlier?"

"Do you call jumping around on the grass 'training'?" Fog grunted.

"We wondered what you were doing." Tuna looked curious.

"We were practicing battle moves, so we could drive the foxes away from your old home," Tigerheart explained.

"Battle moves?" Tuna tipped his head.

"Where I come from, all cats learn how to fight," Tigerheart told him. "We have to fight badgers and foxes and sometimes hawks. It takes special training to learn to fight bigger creatures."

Fog glared at him. "There are five foxes living in our camp. Do you think that bunch of featherbrains will be able to fight them?"

Tigerheart felt his paws dig into the earth. Five foxes certainly sounded terrifying—but if he could convince Fog that *he* wasn't scared, then maybe she'd believe that her cats stood a chance. "We could if you and your friends fought beside us." He searched her gaze hopefully.

Tuna glanced at her. "We'd outnumber them," he meowed.

"They're *foxes!*" Fog snapped. "They could strip the fur off your muzzle and crush your spine in their jaws."

"Not if I taught you how to fight." Tigerheart's chest tightened with hope. "And once you learned, you'd always be able to defend your land. You'd be safe forever."

Tuna blinked encouragingly at Fog. "It would be nice not to have to sleep in grass nests anymore."

"It would be nice to keep my pelt," Fog growled. "I'm not risking it fighting foxes. Can't you see? He's trying to trick us." She flicked her nose dismissively toward Tigerheart. "He wants us gone, and he's willing to do anything to get rid of us, even if it means feeding us to foxes."

"It sounds like a good plan," Tuna persisted.

"It *is* a good plan," Tigerheart pressed. "Two groups of trained cats could fight a whole pack of foxes."

"Really?" Fog sneered at him. "In that case, train *your* friends. I'm not risking mine. If you manage to drive the foxes away, we'll go home."

Tigerheart's belly twisted with disappointment, but he squared his shoulders. He wasn't going to let this rogue-hearted stray think she'd won. "Do you promise?"

Fog looked at him warily. "Promise what?"

"That you'll leave here and go home if we drive away the foxes."

"Sure." Fog turned her tail on him. "I promise."

He watched her walk away, his heart sinking. The guardian cats could never fight five foxes alone. If only there were another way to get rid of them . . .

CHAPTER 25

♣

"Fierce!" Mittens's yowl woke Tigerheart. He jerked up his head as the tabby tom jumped down from the entrance.

Dovewing opened her eyes and blinked anxiously at Tigerheart. "What is it?"

"I'll find out." Tigerheart slid gently from beneath Shadowkit and Pouncekit, who were sleeping on his flank. They murmured but didn't wake as Dovewing scooped them close to her belly. He climbed quietly out of his nest, fluffing out his fur as he stepped into the chilly air. Most of the guardian cats were still sleeping. Soft dawn light filtered thought the clear stretches of wall. Fierce sat up sleepily in her nest as Mittens reached it.

The tabby glanced over his shoulder as Rascal squeezed through the entrance. "Did you find any more?" he called.

"Three." Rascal hurried to Fierce's nest.

"Find more what?" Fierce gazed blearily at the two toms.

"Traps," Rascal meowed.

Tigerheart hurried to join them.

"The Twolegs have been back," Mittens reported. "Their scent is so fresh they must have only just left."

"They've taken all the traps we closed." Rascal's pelt prickled nervously.

"They've left new ones," Mittens told her.

"Bigger ones this time," Rascal chimed.

"Big enough to trap a fox." Mittens's eyes were dark with worry.

Tigerheart reached Fierce's nest and glanced around the three cats. "Could we close them all again?"

Mittens flicked his tail. "What good would that do? They'd only bring more."

Fierce gazed anxiously around the den. "Perhaps it's time we moved on."

"Where to?" Mittens demanded. "This is the quietest part of the city."

Fierce's pelt was still ruffled by sleep. It prickled along her spine. "I don't know," she mewed irritably. "I thought this place was safe."

"It was, until Fog and her gang arrived," Rascal growled. "The Twolegs didn't know we were here."

"We need to get rid of her," Mittens grunted.

Fierce looked at Tigerheart. "What about your plan to get her cats to help us fight the foxes?"

Tigerheart shifted his paws. He hadn't told the guardian cats about his conversation with Fog yet. "I asked her," he confessed. "She said no. She said she'd go back to her old home if we drove off the foxes, but her cats won't help us."

"Did you find out how many foxes there are?" Fierce asked.

"Five," Tigerheart told her.

Mitten's tail twitched angrily. "We can't drive off five foxes alone!"

Rascal looked up at a clear stretch of wall, narrowing his eyes against the light outside. "Perhaps we *should* fight Fog and her friends," he grunted.

"We should shove them into those traps and let the Two-legs take them away," Mittens growled.

Tigerheart twitched as a thought sparked in his mind. He wouldn't drive any cat into the paws of Twolegs, but perhaps there was another way to use the traps. "We don't have to give cats to the Twolegs," he ventured. "But what if we gave them something else?"

Fierce's sleepy gaze sharpened suddenly. "Like what?"

Tigerheart hesitated. This would be a dangerous plan, but if it worked, it could solve all the guardian cats' problems.

Fierce stepped out her nest and pricked her ears. "Well?"

"If we can trick the foxes into the traps—"

Mittens cut him off with a snort. "How could we do that?"

Fierce flicked her tail at the tabby irritably. "Let him fin-ish." Her green eyes sparkled with interest.

Tigerheart's mind quickened as he traced out the plan. "We'd need to get Fog to show us where they are." He hesi-tated, remembering Fog's hostility yesterday. "Or Tuna. Yes. Tuna would show us." The brown tom had wanted to go back to his old home. "Then we'd just need a small patrol to get the foxes to chase it. It could lead them here, and the rest of us could lead them into the traps."

Mitten's pelt bristled. "They'd kill us."

"Cats are fast," Tigerheart argued. "And we'd know where we were running. We could choose a route that would be hard for a fox's clumsy paws."

Rascal looked unconvinced. "And what if we get them here and they don't go into the traps? We'd have led foxes right to our home for nothing!"

"We have enough cats here for two cats to take on each fox once they reach the gathering place." Tigerheart pictured the stretch of grass around the den. "There are plenty of stone slabs to dodge around. Cats are nimble; foxes aren't. We could easily confuse them until they don't know where to run. Then we'd guide them to the traps. Even if we can't drive them right inside, the scent of food might draw them in."

"That Twoleg mush does smell tempting," Mittens conceded.

"If my plan doesn't work," Tigerheart went on, "we could just hide in the den. The entrance is too small for the foxes, and they won't stay here. There's not much for them to scavenge. They'd probably go back to their den. But if it does work, we'll get rid of the foxes, *and* Fog's cats. And with Fog's cats gone, if we keep a low profile for a while, the Twolegs will think they've gotten rid of us and stop leaving traps."

Fierce looked from Rascal to Mittens. Her gaze was thoughtful. "There is a lot to gain."

"It's dangerous," Mittens murmured.

"I can lead the foxes here," Tigerheart offered. "But I'll need some help."

"I'm fast, even if I run a little wonkily," Fierce meowed,

stretching out the leg that was shorter than the others. "I'll help."

A mew sounded across the floor. Tigerheart turned. Ant was sitting up in his nest, his ears pricked. "I'll come."

Cobweb padded from the shadow of Twoleg clutter. "Me too."

Mittens and Rascal exchanged glances.

"Okay." Mittens sounded suddenly determined. "If you four lead the foxes here, Rascal and I will organize the rest of the group to lead them to the traps."

Excitement pricked in Tigerheart's paws. The guardian cats were talking like warriors! "We can do this." He whisked his tail encouragingly. All he had to do now was persuade Tuna to show them where his old camp was.

"Tuna." Tigerheart crouched in the long grass beside Fog's camp. He glanced up at the sky. Dark clouds were swallowing the blue, and he smelled rain as the cold wind pierced his fur. He pricked his ears, hoping Tuna would hear him before any of the other cats. "Tuna," he hissed again.

"What do you want?" Growler nosed his way from the bushes.

"I have a message for Tuna," Tigerheart mewed.

Growler narrowed his eyes. "You're up to something," he meowed. "I'm going to fetch Fog. You can talk to her."

Tigerheart's belly tightened. Fog might get in the way of his plan. "No," he meowed quickly. "I just came to tell Tuna about the new traps. I wanted to show him where they were."

"You can show me." As Growler glanced at the sky and shivered, Tuna peered from the bushes.

He blinked at Tigerheart. "I thought I smelled you."

Tigerheart tried to hide his eagerness at seeing the brown tom. "I wanted to show you where the new traps were."

Growler glanced at Tuna. "For some reason, you're the only cat who's allowed to know."

"You can come too if you like." Tigerheart forced his shoulders to loosen. He wanted to look relaxed. "You'd better hurry, though. It looks like rain."

Growler flicked his tail. "Let Tuna get wet. I've got scraps to finish."

As the black-and-white tom disappeared into the bushes, Tigerheart beckoned Tuna closer with a flick of his muzzle. "I have to talk to you," he whispered.

Tuna frowned but followed him to the closest slab. "Is something wrong?"

"You want to go back to your old camp, right?"

Tuna eyed Tigerheart warily. "If there are no foxes."

"I've got a plan to get rid of them," Tigerheart told him. "But I need you to show me where to go."

Tuna narrowed his eyes. "Why should I do that?"

"Because, surely, you can't be so mouse-brained as to not realize that this would be good for every cat?" Tigerheart stared at him pleadingly. "If you don't help, the Twolegs and their traps are going to drive us *all* away from here."

"Okay." Tuna hunched tighter against the cold wind. "Tell me your plan."

* * *

The next morning, before dawn, Tigerheart crept out of the guardian cats' den. The night sky was swathed in cloud. He narrowed his eyes against the rain that was gently misting the city. Fierce, Cobweb, and Ant followed as he padded across the grass. Shivering in the cold, he fluffed out his fur. Orange Twoleg light reflected eerily off the wet stone. The towering dens slept in shadow except for occasional patches of light, which showed in their walls where Twolegs were beginning to stir for the day. Tigerheart quickened his step. The foxes would have spent the night scavenging and would be heading back to their den before Twolegs took over the city. The walkways and Thunderpaths were empty now. There would be no better time to lead the foxes to the traps.

He smelled fear-scent on the guardian cats and wanted to reassure them. But he couldn't make any promises. They'd traced out two routes yesterday with the help of Tuna. With any luck, they could split the fox pack and lead them to the gathering place in two groups. The fewer foxes each patrol had to manage, the better.

"Tigerheart!" A whispered mew sounded through the rain. A dark shape bounded toward them. It was Tuna. "I'm coming with you."

Tigerheart felt a surge of gratitude. Not all city cats were rogues after all. "You don't have to risk your pelt."

"I want to help." Tuna stopped in front of him, his eyes shimmering in the strange Twoleg light.

Ant shrugged. "It can't do any harm."

Tigerheart saw doubt in Fierce's gaze.

"Can we trust him? What if he tries to confuse the foxes?" she demanded.

"Why would he do that?" Tigerheart countered. "We're going to get his old home back."

"And he knows the routes even better than we do," Cobweb pointed out.

Fierce stared at Tuna for a moment, then nodded. "Okay."

Tigerheart hesitated, unsure which cat should take the lead. It was his plan, and Fierce claimed that the guardian cats had no leader, but he knew the others respected her authority and he didn't want to challenge it. Suddenly he felt like a deputy again. With a pang he thought of Rowanstar. Had his father finally found his paws and taken firm leadership of Shadow-Clan?

"Come on." Tuna surprised him by heading first into the yellow light pooling beneath a pole at the side of the Thunderpath. As the brown tom passed through the light and into the shadow beyond, the others followed, glancing nervously at one another. Tigerheart fell in behind.

No cat pushed ahead of Tuna as he led the winding way through alleys and streets to the dilapidated part of the city where his camp had been. He picked his way along a crumbling wall, which edged an open space between two broken Twoleg dens. Twoleg clutter littered the site.

"My nest was in there." Tuna nodded to gap beneath a slab of wood. "There's a fox nest inside now."

Tigerheart padded softly along the wall, weaving past

Cobweb, Ant, and Fierce. He stopped beside Tuna and tasted the air. The fox scent was strong, but stale after the night's rain. "They're not back yet." He scanned the dark camp. No Twoleg light flickered here, and he strained to see through the gloom.

Overhead, the pale clouds were showing the first signs of dawn. "Let's stay out of sight until they come." Tigerheart hopped off the wall and crouched behind it. Silently, Cobweb, Ant, Fierce, and Tuna followed. "You remember the plan?" he whispered.

They nodded.

"Which group will Tuna be in?" Ant asked.

"He'll come with me and Cobweb." He glanced at Cobweb. The gray tom dipped his head in agreement. He looked small, his long fur slicked against his body by the rain.

They crouched in the shelter of the wall. Fear fluttered like a trapped bird in Tigerheart's belly. The stone beneath his pads was slippery. What if one of the cats lost their footing while leading the foxes through the twisting route they'd picked out? "Keep your eye on your partner," he warned Fierce, Ant, and Cobweb. "If you fall, call for help. Leave no cat behind to face the foxes alone." He blinked at Tuna. "Agreed?"

"Agreed." Tuna's tail twitched nervously.

Ant and Cobweb eyed each other doubtfully.

"What?" Tigerheart glared at them. This was no time to start questioning orders.

"Aren't you scared?" Cobweb ventured.

"Of course I'm scared," Tigerheart told him. "But this needs to be done."

"Maybe it would just be easier to find a new home after all," Ant murmured.

Tigerheart stiffened. "Not after—"

Fierce cut him off. "We're not leaving." She looked sternly from Cobweb to Ant. "A cat can spend her whole life running, or she can make a stand and defend her home."

Warmth washed Tigerheart's pelt. Fierce was sounding like a leader.

Ant blinked in surprise. "You're starting to sound like Tigerheart."

Fierce sniffed. "I like our den, that's all. Do you really think we could find a better place to spend the rest of ice-chill?"

"I guess not," Ant conceded.

Cobweb shifted his paws. "Is this what it's like to be a warrior?" he asked Tigerheart.

"Not all the time," Tigerheart told him. "But we're prepared to take risks to defend what's ours, when we have to."

Tuna's whiskers twitched wryly. "I'm guessing warriors aren't used to change."

Tigerheart frowned. "What do you mean?"

"In the city, it's rare to have anything long enough to need to defend it." He nodded toward his old camp. "This was swarming with Twolegs before I was born. Now it's swarming with foxes. Fog was raised beside the trash field. Then she lived under a bridge. Growler moved here when his Twolegs abandoned him."

Tigerheart felt a twinge of pity for these strays, but they didn't seem downhearted. They were watching him with interest, as though trying to make sense of him.

"Don't you get bored of fighting for the same territory?" Tuna asked. "Don't you ever just want to move on and find a new way to live?"

Fierce answered for him. "He's here, isn't he? He left one life to make a new life here."

"Then why does he act like he's still a warrior?" Tuna asked.

"Because I am!" Tigerheart bristled. Did these cats think he'd left the Clans because he was tired of Clan life? Did they think he wanted to be like them? To stay here forever?

Fierce tipped her head sympathetically. "You'll need to learn to be more flexible if you want to survive in the cit—"

The crunch of shifting rubble made her stop. Tigerheart pricked his ears.

Tuna opened his mouth to taste the air. "They're back."

Tigerheart listened to the brush of fur and scrabble of paws beyond the wall. "Do you remember your routes?"

Cobweb, Ant, and Fierce nodded.

"Tuna," Tigerheart blinked at the brown tabby. "Stay with me."

"Okay."

Tigerheart leaped onto the wall. His pelt prickled with fear as he saw five shapes moving in the half-light. Three of the foxes were large and well-muscled. The two smaller foxes looked lithe. The stench of them made Tigerheart's nose wrinkle. As Fierce, Cobweb, Ant, and Tuna jumped up beside him, he nodded toward the biggest fox. "Tuna and Cobweb will surround that one while Fierce and Ant try to corner the other." He pointed his muzzle toward the second largest fox. "If we can separate them now, hopefully the others will split up when they follow. Fierce, lead yours back the way we came. Cobweb, we'll lead ours through the big stone clearing."

The cats nodded.

"Let's go." Tigerheart jumped softly onto broken stone and picked his way down the pile. Tuna and Cobweb followed, while Fierce and Ant approached the sleek dog fox Tigerheart had directed them toward.

Tigerheart kept low as they moved through shadow to where the biggest fox was snuffling beside a heap of Twoleg clutter. The smaller foxes were snarling softy at each other, arguing over scraps they'd dropped at the edge of the camp. Tigerheart signaled to Cobweb and Tuna with a flick of his tail, ordering them to circle around the far side of their target. He paused and waited for them to get into position. As they surrounded the fox, Fierce's yowl wailed eerily through the dawn air. Tigerheart saw the foxes freeze. Their beady eyes flashed toward Fierce. The orange flecks in her tortoiseshell pelt glowed in the dawn light. A moment before they lunged for her, Tigerheart lifted his head and screeched. The large dog fox, which he'd been stalking, jerked its muzzle toward him. Tigerheart leaped for it, raked his claws across its muzzle, and ran.

Blood roared in his ears as fear shrilled through every hair on his pelt. He streaked from the camp onto the deserted

Thunderpath. Leaping scattered rubble, he glanced over his shoulder. Rain sprayed his face. Cobweb and Tuna were behind him. The dog fox followed, two vixens at its tail. Triumph surged in Tigerheart's chest. They'd split the pack as they'd planned. All they had to do now was keep ahead of it. "Take the lead!" he called to Tuna. The stray had traveled these streets more often than Tigerheart, and Tigerheart wanted to stay between the foxes and the city cats. His fighting skills were better. If they hit trouble, he wanted to face the foxes first.

A deserted white dwelling loomed ahead. An alley opened beside it. This would be the first of their turns. Tuna had picked the alley especially because it led to a maze of passageways that cut one way, then the other. The cats could negotiate the turns more nimbly than the foxes, which would let them put some distance between themselves and their pursuers. They had to pull ahead as far as they could here, because once they hit the stone clearing, the foxes would have the advantage of speed. Alarm gripped Tigerheart's belly. What if the foxes gave up chasing?

Tuna was almost at the head of the alley. Cobweb was at his heels. As Tigerheart reached the entrance, he stopped, twisted, and reared. The fox behind him bristled in surprise. Behind it, the two other foxes blinked in confusion as the lead fox slowed and showed its teeth.

"What are you doing?" Tuna's panicked screech faded behind Tigerheart as the brown tom hared onward.

Making sure these sly-hearted scroungers never want to stop chasing us.

Tigerheart threw himself, hissing, at the head of the lead fox. Lashing out with one paw, then another, he felt fur rip under his claws. He smelled the warm scent of blood and heard the fox screech. Jaws snapped beside his cheek. He saw white teeth flash. In an instant, he turned and ran again. Cobweb and Tuna had stopped, their pelts bushed, their backs arched. "Run!" Tigerheart shrieked, nudging them ahead of him.

Hot fox breath blasted his tail. He hared along the alley, picking up speed until he was pelting over the stone so fast, his pads burned.

Tuna signaled the upcoming turn with a flick of his tail so that Tigerheart would remember which way to run. Skidding around a sharp corner, he followed Cobweb and Tuna into a narrow passageway. It curved one way, then another, the dens towering high on each side. Shadow hid the end, but Tuna signaled again before they reached it, and Tigerheart was ready for the next turn. As he skidded around it, the thumping of fox paws receded behind them.

Tigerheart glanced back as the foxes scrambled around the corner in pursuit. They crashed clumsily into one another, bouncing off the wall of the passageway as they fought to keep their footing. Rage glittered in their eyes. The plan was working. With each turn, the patrol pulled farther ahead of the foxes, but each time he glanced back, Tigerheart could see determination in the eyes of their pursuers; the foxes weren't about to give up.

The stone clearing was near. It would be deserted now and easy to cross. But the foxes would cover the ground faster.

Tigerheart's lungs were burning. He could hear Tuna panting. Cobweb's breath was fast and rough. Fear flickered through his thoughts. What if Cobweb and Tuna lacked the stamina to keep up this pace as they crossed the wide stretch of open stone?

"Not far now!" Tigerheart yowled. He streaked past them as the passageway opened into the clearing, pushing harder against the ground, hardly seeing where he ran. But he knew where he was heading. The gap between the dens on the far side would lead though another short maze before it opened onto the green stretch of grass around the gathering place. Rascal, Mittens, and Pipsqueak would be waiting to take it from there. They would lead the foxes toward the traps, zigzagging around the slabs until each fox had stumbled into one of the mesh caves.

The clearing echoed with the screech of one of the foxes. Tigerheart glanced over his shoulder. The lead fox was yelping. Its eyes shone with excitement as it spotted the open ground. Cobweb was lagging. The foxes were closing the gap. *Hurry up!* Tigerheart pushed harder, willing Cobweb on. He felt Tuna's breath on his tail. "Is Cobweb going to make it?" the stray panted.

Tigerheart saved his breath for the final push. The opening between the dens was close now. The next turn was only a few paces beyond it. They would have a chance to put some distance between themselves and the foxes once more. He dived into the alley and made the turn. A shriek sounded behind him. Had a fox caught Cobweb? He slowed, panic searing beneath his pelt. Turning, he saw Tuna streak past him.

Cobweb swerved around the corner a moment later, surprise lighting his gaze as he saw Tigerheart lagging behind. "Keep running!" Cobweb wailed as he shot past Tigerheart.

Tigerheart smelled the hot stench of fox breath. He turned and ran as paws pounded around the corner. Ahead, Tuna and Cobweb had reached the opening where a passageway cut across the alley. They ducked down the passage out of sight. Tigerheart chased after them. He heard the panting of the foxes behind him and unsheathed his claws. Hooking them against the rough stone, he propelled himself forward, running faster than he had in his whole life. He struggled for breath, his chest screaming for air as he reached the corner and veered along the passageway. Cobweb and Tuna raced ahead of him. Fox paws slithered behind on the wet stone.

He smelled the familiar scents of the gathering place ahead and hared after Cobweb and Tuna. One turn, then another. The final alley. He burst from between the dens and raced across the Thunderpath, onto the grass. Then a paw hooked him from behind a stone slab and he fell sprawling on the ground. He smelled Dovewing's scent and saw gray fur as strong paws dragged him behind the shelter of the stone. "Hush!" Dovewing whispered in his ear. "Rascal, Mittens, and Pipsqueak will handle this."

He glimpsed Cobweb and Tuna. They were safe behind the next slab, crouching in the grass as they struggled for breath. As the sound of fox paws rang on the Thunderpath, Mittens, Rascal, and Pipsqueak leaped from behind a slab a few rows away and yowled at the foxes. Red fur streaked past Tigerheart, not even slowing. With a snarl of frustration, the foxes raced toward Mittens. The tabby zigzagged around the stones in one direction, drawing the lead fox away. Mittens doubled back around a slab, raked his claws across the vixen's snout, and led her another way. Pipsqueak stopped in front of the third fox and, as it stumbled in surprise, veered toward the far side of the gathering place.

As the fox raced after him, Tigerheart saw Fierce and Ant explode from a passageway beyond the gathering place. Two foxes followed them onto the swath of grass as Dotty, Cinnamon, and Peanut ducked out from behind stone slabs. Deftly, they separated the pair. Peanut and Cinnamon led the larger fox one way; Dotty led the smaller fox another.

Tigerheart felt the world blur around him.

"Breathe," Dovewing murmured into his ear. Like a half-drowned cat coming up for air, Tigerheart drew in a long, shuddering breath. Yowls and screeches filled the air around the gathering place. "Have they reached the traps?" he panted to Dovewing.

Dovewing was straining to see through the drizzle. "I don't know yet."

Paw steps sounded on the grass nearby. Fog appeared around the side of the stone slab. "What going on?" She looked from Tigerheart to Cobweb, her eyes widening as she saw Tuna. "Where have you been?"

Tuna sat up. "Catching foxes," he panted.

As Fog stared at him wordlessly, Fierce crossed the grass to join them. Ant padded at her side, his paws trembling.

"I hope Pipsqueak and the others get them into the traps," she puffed. "I don't ever want to do that again." She flicked her tail around to show Tigerheart. A tuft of fur was missing from the end. "One of the foxes got closer than I'd planned."

Tigerheart blinked at her proudly. "But you made it."

As he spoke, Pipsqueak bounded across the grass to meet them. "We got them!" he meowed triumphantly. "Every one of them. Blaze, Boots, Bracken, and Spire were waiting beside the traps. The foxes were so confused to see more cats, they practically fell inside!"

"What about the fifth fox?" Tigerheart asked anxiously.

"Mittens and Rascal rounded it up and chased it into the big trap over there." He pointed across the grass with his muzzle. Red fur flashed inside the mesh cage. Angry screeches rose around the gathering place as the foxes howled in frustration.

Dovewing purred. "If they keep up that noise, it won't be long before the Twolegs come to take them away."

Tigerheart looked at Fog. The stray's eyes were wide with amazement. "You led the foxes here?" she breathed. "Into the traps?"

Tuna purred breathlessly. "It was Tigerheart's plan."

Fog blinked at Tigerheart. "You're even crazier than I thought."

Tigerheart's fur tingled with joy. "Now you have to keep your side of the agreement," he meowed firmly. "You and your cats have to leave."

Fog stared at him for a moment, then dipped her head. "Okay."

"We can move back home," Tuna meowed happily.

"It'll smell of fox stench," Fog grunted.

"Not for long," Tuna promised. "It's hardly changed apart from the smell. In fact I think the foxes have dug a few new nests in the rubble."

"You have to go *now*," Tigerheart told Fog. "Before the Twolegs come to get their traps." He wanted the Twolegs to find the land around gathering place deserted. They'd probably believe the foxes had chased the cats away before being trapped.

Fierce stared at the Fog, her gaze hard. "Don't come back," she growled. "From now on, this is guardian-cat territory, and we're ready to defend our borders."

Fog blinked at her, surprise showing in her blue gaze. "Okay." She dipped her head. She clearly didn't want to argue with cats who could trap foxes.

Dovewing nuzzled Tigerheart's ear. "Come on," she murmured. "Let's go and tell the kits."

As he followed Dovewing across the grass, Fierce's words rang in his mind: *From now on, this is guardian-cat territory, and we're ready to defend our borders.* At last she was beginning to think like a warrior. Tigerheart's chest swelled with pride. He suddenly felt hopeful that the guardian cats could survive anything. Maybe this wasn't such a bad place to raise kits after all.

CHAPTER 26

The kits!

Dovewing's alarmed cry jerked Tigerheart from his doze. He opened his eyes and saw her, pelt still ruffled from sleep, scanning the gathering-place den frantically. "Pouncekit! Shadowkit! Lightkit! Where are you?"

"They're too small to reach the entrance by themselves." Tigerheart lifted his head, irritated at being woken unnecessarily. "They're probably just playing hide-and-seek again."

Tigerheart and Dovewing had drifted to sleep in a pool of afternoon sunshine, their bellies full after a meal of Twoleg scraps. Now the sky outside had turned pink as afternoon slid into twilight.

Dovewing stared at him, round-eyed. "No, they can reach the ledge now! I caught them sniffing the entrance yesterday."

Tigerheart scrambled to his paw. Had they grown so much? Only a few days had passed since the Twolegs had carried away the traps. With the foxes gone and Fog and her friends back at their old camp, life had returned to its easy routine.

"Blaze!" Dovewing crossed the den to where the ginger-and-white kit was nipping herbs from a twig. "Have you seen the kits?"

Blaze looked up. "Sorry," he mewed, spitting out leaf flecks. "I've been busy. I didn't notice."

"Fierce? Mittens?" They were lounging at the far end of the den. "Have you seen my kits?"

Fierce jumped to her paws. "Are they missing?"

"I can't see them anywhere."

Mittens glanced at the entrance. "Have you looked outside?"

Tigerheart saw Dovewing's pelt bush. He hurried to her side. "Let's go and look."

"Do you want help?" Cinnamon ducked out from her nest beneath a pile of Twoleg clutter.

"I'll come too." Pipsqueak left a half-chewed bone and padded to join them.

"What if they've wandered onto a Thunderpath?" Dovewing fretted.

"They're too smart." Pipsqueak jumped up to the entrance.

Cinnamon hopped after the brown-and-white tom. "I can smell their scent here," she mewed. "I'm surprised no cat saw them leave."

Pipsqueak nosed through the gap. "They probably waited until no cat was looking."

"No, I saw them go." Feather, the sick white she-cat, looked over the side of her nest. "But I didn't know they weren't allowed out."

Tigerheart paused. He'd never told the kits not to go outside. He'd assumed they were too small to reach the entrance. He looked at Dovewing. "Did you tell them not to go out without us?"

Dovewing blinked at him. "Did *you*?"

Tigerheart's pelt prickled guiltily. "I should have." He was angry with himself for not thinking of it, and angry at being stuck in the city. He shouldn't need to explain such simple rules to kits. In the Clan, no kit was allowed out of camp. Every cat knew the rule. Few kits dared to break it. They knew their apprenticeship might be held back for a moon as punishment.

"We have to find them." Dovewing brushed past him and jumped up to the entrance. He scrambled after her.

They won't have strayed beyond the hedge, surely? Tigerheart reassured himself as he slid outside. A heavy dew had already settled on the grass. The clear sky promised a chilly night. The dew would soon turn to frost. Dovewing was already nosing around the stone slabs. Pipsqueak and Cinnamon were ranging farther, sniffing the stone boundary that edged the stretch of grass on this side of the gathering place.

Tigerheart pricked his ears as he heard Twolegs murmuring. He jerked his nose around. A small group was clustered around one of the slabs at the end of the gathering place. They meowed quietly to each other. Tigerheart scanned the grass. Had the kits been mouse-brained enough to stray near them?

"I see them!" Dovewing's relieved mew rang through the air. Tigerheart followed her gaze and saw Pouncekit, Lightkit, and Shadowkit sitting like starlings in the branch of a tree at the edge of the grass. Dovewing bounded toward them.

Tigerheart chased after her. "Thanks," he called to Cinnamon and Pipsqueak who had turned to look. "We can get them down."

Cinnamon turned anxiously toward the cluster of Twolegs. "Do you want us to distract them?"

"No." Tigerheart slowed. "It's probably best if you and Pipsqueak go back inside. If the Twolegs see too many cats, they might bring their traps back."

Cinnamon dipped her head and beckoned to Pipsqueak with a flick of her tail. Skirting the Twolegs, they headed back toward the den entrance.

"What are you doing up there?" Dovewing called.

Pouncekit looked down, breaking into a purr as Tigerheart reached Dovewing. "Look at us!" she squeaked. "We climbed up all by ourselves."

Tigerheart frowned at the excited kit. "Have you planned how you're going to get down?"

Pouncekit's face fell as she looked toward the ground. She nudged Lightkit. "Look!" Her sister wobbled on the branch. She was straining to see the Twolegs. Pouncekit nudged her again. "Dovewing and Tigerheart are here."

Lightkit looked down, her eyes lighting up as she saw them. "We're watching the Twolegs."

Shadowkit peered over the edge. Guilt flashed in his eyes as he met Tigerheart's stern gaze. "We weren't going to be long. But Pouncekit said that the Twolegs were being weird."

"They've dug a hole in the ground and they've put something in it," Pouncekit mewed excitedly. "What do you think they're hiding? It looks big. Perhaps it's something special they want to keep safe during ice-chill."

"*Leaf-bare*," Tigerheart corrected tetchily. She sounded like a stray.

Lightkit's fur was spiked with excitement. "They've gathered flowers and put them all around the hole. It looks pretty."

As she spoke, Shadowkit's eyes widened in alarm. A Twoleg kit had broken away from the cluster and was running toward them.

"Quick!" Tigerheart ordered. "Come down from there. We have to go inside."

"But we're safe here." Pouncekit watched the Twoleg kit running closer. "Why don't you jump up?"

Tigerheart turned toward the Twoleg kit and arched his back. He hissed loudly, flattening his ears.

The kit stopped, alarm sparking in its tiny eyes.

A big Twoleg hurried after it, holding out a paw and mewling. It pulled the kit away.

Tigerheart jerked his gaze back toward Pouncekit. "We have to get back inside right now," he meowed sternly. "Do you want the Twolegs to start leaving traps for us again?"

Pouncekit frowned crossly. "It's not fair. All we ever see is the inside of the den, and we've explored all the Twoleg clutter in there. We want to see something new."

Dovewing reached up the tree with her forepaws, her gaze sparking with worry as Pouncekit padded toward the trunk and began to slither down, tail first.

"Dig your claws in!" Dovewing gasped as Pouncekit slipped suddenly and her hindquarters thumped against the bark.

"I'm digging!" Pouncekit puffed as she clung to the trunk like a squirrel and eased herself down, a muzzle-length at a time.

Dovewing grabbed her scruff as soon as it was within reach

and plopped her on the ground. "Stay there," she meowed firmly, and looked up toward Lightkit. "Your turn."

While Dovewing watched Lightkit, Tigerheart frowned crossly at Pouncekit. "You're not meant to leave the den without us."

Pouncekit stared back at him, her dark amber eyes wide. "But why? The traps are gone."

"What if the Twolegs put them back?" Tigerheart challenged.

Pouncekit narrowed her eyes petulantly. "It's not fair," she mewed. "You're only yelling at me because I was the first one to come down. But being the first to come down was good, wasn't it?" She looked up at Shadowkit, who was waiting while Lightkit slid clumsily down the trunk. "He's still there, and you're not yowling at him."

"I'm not yowling at any of you." Tigerheart swallowed back frustration. "I'm just telling you that you're not allowed outside without Dovewing or me."

"*Ever?*" Pouncekit frowned. Lightkit squeaked as Dovewing grabbed her scruff and dropped her on the grass. Pouncekit turned her head and stared indignantly at her sister. "Tigerheart says we're never allowed to leave the den *ever.*"

"Ever?" Horror sparked in Lightkit's gaze. "That's not fair! The other cats go out all the time."

"I didn't say ever." Tigerheart's pelt prickled irritably. He wondered if the kits would be so argumentative if they'd been raised in a Clan. He felt sure that he'd never argued with Rowanstar like this when he was a kit.

Dovewing was staring into the tree, where Shadowkit was teetering nervously in the crook of a branch. "You're going to have to go up and get him," she meowed.

Pouncekit looked at her brother disdainfully. "Poor Shadowkit. He's such a scaredy-mouse."

Tigerheart padded to the foot of the tree. Hooking his claws into the bark, he hauled himself up until he was level with Shadowkit. Then he grabbed the kit's scruff and let himself slide carefully down, balancing Shadowkit on his chest.

As he reached the ground, Shadowkit leaped onto the grass. "I didn't need help." He shook out his pelt. "I was just planning my route so I didn't look as clumsy as Pouncekit and Lightkit." He glared at his sisters.

Dovewing whisked her tail. "Come on," she ordered. "Let's go inside."

"Can't we explore some more first?" Lightkit pleaded.

Dovewing pointed her muzzle toward the cluster of black-pelted Twolegs. "Not while they're here."

Lightkit huffed and began to march toward the den. Pouncekit followed, and Shadowkit hurried at their heels.

Dovewing caught Tigerheart's eye. "At least they're adventurous." Her whiskers twitched suddenly with amusement.

Relieved they were safe, Tigerheart touched his muzzle to hers. "They're going to be fine warriors one day."

"Yes." Dovewing purred and followed the kits.

Tigerheart glanced across the grass, wondering how long he would have to wait before they could take the kits back to the Clans. The den was clearly no longer enough to keep them occupied. But outside, the city was full of danger. They should be in the forest, learning the difference between a mouse and a shrew, and which birds woke them in the morning and sang them to sleep at night.

As his mind wandered, he noticed Spire. The healer was sitting a few slabs away, gazing at the Twolegs. As Dovewing guided the kits through the gap beside the clear stretch of wall, Tigerheart headed toward the skinny tom. Ducking behind slabs, he reached Spire without being spotted by the Twolegs.

"What are you doing here?" he whispered.

Spire looked at him blankly. *He's having a vision.* The healer's gaze barely focused on Tigerheart before drifting lazily back to the Twolegs.

Tigerheart shifted his paws. Should he leave Spire in peace? But what if that Twoleg kit started to nose around again? The tom probably wouldn't notice until too late. *I'll stay and guard him.*

Spire closed his eyes. He swayed, murmuring to himself. "Kits or no kits."

Tigerheart's belly tightened. "Spire?" What was the strange cat dreaming about?

Spire opened his eyes and stared at Tigerheart, as though expecting to see him. "You came."

Tigerheart twitched his tail nervously. "What did you dream?"

"Dream?" Spire tipped his head. He looked confused. "I heard a voice. A voice . . . from the stars . . . meant for you."

"Stars? For me . . . ?" Tigerheart's pelt prickled. Spire had never mentioned stars before. Did this mean StarClan *was* trying to reach him through this strange cat? Should Tigerheart have gone back to ShadowClan after Spire's first dream?

But how could I have done that? The kits . . . Anxiety began to churn in his belly. Suddenly all the worries that had suffocated him while he was in the forest seemed to swirl around him once more. "What did it say?"

Spire's yellow gaze seemed to clear as he stared at Tigerheart. His eyes flashed as though he'd remembered something long forgotten. "I had to tell you that he needs you."

"Who needs me?" Tigerheart leaned closer, his breath catching in his throat.

Spire didn't seem to hear him. "The shadows are fading. He can't keep them together."

Alarm flared beneath Tigerheart's pelt. *Rowanstar!* His father needed him. He knew it as certainly as he'd known he should be with Dovewing. There was no doubt now that StarClan was trying to reach him here in the city. . . .

They want me to go back!

CHAPTER 27

♣

Tigerheart hardly slept. He stared into the darkness while Dovewing and the kits snored gently beside him, anxiety swirling through his thoughts. How would he tell Dovewing? There was no time to wait. The kits were so young. But he had to go back now.

As dawn lifted the darkness, he gazed at Dovewing, still sleeping beside him. The kits were too big now to curl at her belly, and they snuggled around her instead. Pouncekit's tail trailed over her cheek. Lightkit's forepaws rested on her flank, while Shadowkit stretched along her spine. Were they old enough to make the journey? Would Dovewing agree? Tigerheart's throat tightened. Would he have to leave without them?

He crept from the nest and scanned the den. The guardian cats were stirring as gray dawn light filtered through the walls.

Fierce climbed from her nest and stretched. "Who wants to come scavenging with me?"

"I will." Ant slid from beneath a pile of Twoleg clutter.

Cinnamon crossed the floor. "So will I."

Mittens stretched beneath the den entrance. "I'll come."

Tigerheart hurried forward. Fresh air would help him

think. He had to find the words to tell Dovewing that he needed to leave. "I'll join you."

Fierce was already leaping onto the wooden ledge that led to the entrance. Cinnamon, Ant, and Mittens followed her out of the den.

"Wait." Dovewing's soft mew sounded behind Tigerheart.

He glanced over his shoulder. She was stepping softly from the nest. The kits had rolled into the space she'd left, still asleep.

"I'm coming with you." Dovewing's green gaze was soft in the dawn light. She hurried past him, stopping at Blaze's nest. As he lifted his head sleepily, she blinked at him. "Can you keep an eye on the kits? We're going scavenging with Fierce."

"Okay." He yawned, climbed from his nest, and headed toward the kits.

"Thanks, Blaze." Dovewing turned to Tigerheart and flicked her tail. "Do you mind if I come?"

"Of course not." His heart sank. There would be no time to think of the right words to tell her. He couldn't keep this to himself. He'd have to tell her now. What would she say? Sadness swamped him. If she thought the kits were too young to travel, he would be abandoning her a second time.

Dovewing followed him from the den. Outside, the streets were quiet. Monsters were beginning to prowl, and here and there a Twoleg scuttled along the walkways, head bent against the cold wind. She shifted beside him as he waited for a Twoleg light to turn green. "What are we waiting for?" She looked along the deserted Thunderpath, then bounded across the stone. "I haven't been out this early since before the kits were born," she mewed as he followed her to the other side. "I forgot how quiet the city could be."

Fierce's scent drifted on the breeze here. Tigerheart guessed that the tortoiseshell was heading for her favorite scrapcans. He headed in the opposite direction. If he was going to talk to Dovewing, he didn't want to bump into the guardian cats.

"Fierce and the others went that way." Dovewing gestured away from herself, glancing at him curiously.

"I need to talk to you." Tigerheart kept his gaze straight ahead. His heart quickened as he spoke. There was no avoiding the conversation now.

"Okay." Dovewing didn't look at him, but moved closer, guiding him toward the wall as a Twoleg turned the corner and began hurrying toward them.

Tigerheart didn't speak until the Twoleg had passed. Ahead, a narrow gap opened between the dens. Tigerheart knew that it led to a small opening where Twolegs left scrapcans. They rarely contained food, but it would be a sheltered spot to talk. He turned in to the gap as they reached it and led the way to the small clearing.

Dovewing followed wordlessly. "So?" She searched his gaze anxiously as he stopped beside the scrapcans and faced her. "What did you want to tell me?"

Tigerheart gazed into the green depths of her eyes. *Please understand that I love you.* "Spire had another vision."

Dovewing's gaze didn't flicker. She stared at him, stiller than stone.

"He heard a voice," Tigerheart went on. "A voice Spire said was for me. It gave him a message about Rowanstar."

Still, Dovewing did not speak. Anxiety glittered in her eyes.

"The voice said he needs me. It said he can't keep the shadows together." Tigerheart saw Dovewing's flanks move as her breath quickened. She held his gaze mutely. *Say something.* He had to know what she was thinking. When she didn't speak, he stumbled on, trying to explain. "I can't ignore this sign," he meowed desperately. "Rowanstar can't keep the Clan together. I have to go back. Please don't think I don't love you. You and the kits are the most important things in my life. But if I abandon my Clan now, when they need me, I will never forgive myself." Grief pressed in his chest. *Will I ever be able to forgive myself for abandoning Dovewing and our kits?*

Dovewing's eyes shimmered with pain. She stared at him, the wind ruffling her pale gray fur. "I once told you that I would love you whatever choice you made," she mewed thickly. Tigerheart could hardly breathe as she went on. "I won't make you choose between your Clan and me this time."

Was she telling him to go? Tigerheart's thoughts seemed to freeze. He could only stare into Dovewing's eyes, trying to read what she was feeling. Was she angry? Was his leaving all she and the kits would remember of him? "I'm sorry," he murmured, his heart splitting with pain. "Please forgive me."

Dovewing blinked. "Forgive you for what? We'll leave together."

Really? As he stared at her dumbly, hardly able to believe his ears, dawn sunshine found a crack between the nests and cut a strip across the clearing.

"You saw the kits yesterday," Dovewing went on. "They climbed a tree by themselves. No one taught them how to climb. They wanted to see more of the world than we have shown them. They are eager for adventure." She paused, fear darkening her gaze. "I think they are ready to make the journey home."

Tigerheart could hardly believe his ears. "Do you mean it?"

"Yes." Dovewing whisked her tail. "It's a dangerous journey. I'm not letting you make it alone."

"But the kits." If it was dangerous for him, then for young kits it could be deadly. "They're not old enough to—"

Dovewing cut him off. "As long as they are with us, they will be safe." She glanced the way they'd come. Monsters moved beyond the gap. "Come sunup, the city will be crowded with Twolegs and monsters. Foxes roam the streets at night. Cats with no more honor than rogues scavenge in every alley. This is no place for kits to live. Besides . . ." She looked away, her pelt prickling. "Spire isn't the only cat who's had dreams."

Tigerheart leaned forward anxiously. "Did you have another dream? Like the one that led us here?"

She shook her head. "Shadowkit told me he dreamed about a silver-and-white tabby."

Tigerheart stiffened. Had Spire been right about the kit? Had Shadowkit seen this tabby "in the shadows"?

Sadness misted Dovewing's gaze. "It sounded like Ivypool. And the cat in the dream had kits. What if Ivypool's really had kits? I want to meet them. I want them to meet Pouncekit, Lightkit, and Shadowkit. I don't want them to be strangers. They need to be with the Clans. We have to get them home before they're old enough to become 'paws. They have so much to learn about Clan life."

Become 'paws. Tigerheart could imagine Pouncekit clinging to the trunk of a pine, arguing with her mentor about how far up she should climb. He purred suddenly. "I feel sorry for the warrior who has Pouncekit as an apprentice."

Dovewing's whiskers twitched with amusement. "She'll question every order."

"She'll probably try to give her mentor hunting tips." Tigerheart's heart warmed as though sunshine poured through it.

"The guardian cats have been good to us," Dovewing meowed. "But I don't want our kits to think that healing the sick and avoiding Twolegs is all there is to life."

Tigerheart purred louder. "Our kits aren't even very good at avoiding Twolegs. Did you see them in that tree?"

Dovewing purred too. "The only way they could have attracted more attention would have been to yowl at them."

"I'm glad we found them in time." Tigerheart stopped purring as he pictured the Twoleg kit running toward the tree. What would have happened if he hadn't been there to scare it away? The kits had been trapped and hadn't even realized it.

Dovewing's gaze darkened. "We did find them, though. But they need to be back in the forest. For the first time, I realized how little they understand about what it means to be a warrior. No Clan cat would have let curiosity cloud their judgment. The kits should have known the risk they were taking."

They need to be back in the forest. Tigerheart's belly twisted with worry at Dovewing's words. "Which forest?" he asked bluntly.

Dovewing hesitated.

"You said that Pouncekit, Lightkit, and Shadowkit mustn't be strangers to Ivypool's kits," he pressed. "Do you plan to raise them in ThunderClan?"

Dovewing shifted her paws self-consciously.

"You know I have to go back to ShadowClan," he breathed.

"I know." She dropped her gaze. "My heart tells me to be with you. My head tells me to raise my kits among my kin."

"They're my kits too," Tigerheart pointed out.

Alarm sparked in her eyes. "Would you try to take them from me if I don't join ShadowClan?"

The pain in her mew sliced his heart. Now he was making *her* choose, and trying to use their kits to pressure her. "I'm sorry," he blurted guiltily. "Of course I wouldn't. If you want to be with ThunderClan, the kits must stay with you until they are old enough to make their own decision."

Her fur smoothed. She lifted her chin. "We don't need to think about that yet," she mewed decisively. "It's a long way to the lake, and we don't know what we'll find when we get there. Let's get home first, then worry about what to do next."

Tigerheart padded forward, guessing that, despite her words, Dovewing must be feeling as anxious as he was. Could they really make such a journey with kits? He tried not to think of all the dangers that lay between the city and the lake.

Even the thought of Pouncekit beside the Silverpath made his belly clench. The wind from a Thundersnake was strong enough to sweep her beneath its paws. He closed his eyes, trying not to tremble as he pressed his cheek against Dovewing's. "Everything will be okay," he murmured softly, trying to reassure himself as much as Dovewing.

Fierce blinked slowly at Tigerheart. He wondered for a moment if she'd heard him. "We have to leave," he meowed again. "My Clan needs me."

Fierce got to her paws and dipped her head to Tigerheart. "We will miss you."

Dovewing sat behind him. He could hear Pouncekit, Lightkit, and Shadowkit fidgeting beside her. The kits had been fizzing with excitement since Tigerheart and Dovewing had told them that they were going back to the lake.

"We're going to be warriors!" Lightkit had squeaked.

"Can we ride real badgers when we get to the forest?" Pouncekit had asked eagerly.

Shadowkit's gray pelt had rippled nervously. "Will we see a Thundersnake?"

Tigerheart and Dovewing had answered as many questions as they could, but as the kits grew noisier, Tigerheart knew he'd have to break the news to Fierce before the guardian cats overheard them. Telling Pouncekit, Shadowkit, and Lightkit to sit quietly, he'd crossed the floor to share their news with Fierce.

The tortoiseshell beckoned the other guardian cats closer

now with a flick of her tail. Cobweb and Rascal left the scraps they were sharing. Mittens, Ant, and Cinnamon padded from the strip of sunshine they had been bathing in. Spire and Blaze left Feather and Scowl watching from their nests. Dotty, Pipsqueak, Peanut, and Bracken fanned out around Tigerheart and Dovewing, while Boots watched from beneath the wooden ledge near the entrance.

Fierce lifted her chin. "Tigerheart and Dovewing have to leave us," she announced.

Dotty frowned. "Where are you going?"

"Have you found a new den?" Mittens asked.

"We're going back to the lake," Tigerheart told them. "My Clan needs me."

Cinnamon padded closer, her eyes sharp with interest. "How do you know?"

"I think a StarClan cat spoke to me through Spire." Tigerheart decided that it was easier to be honest, even if the cats didn't believe him. "ShadowClan is in trouble."

Blaze glanced at Spire in surprise. "How did it talk through you? Did it come to visit?"

Spire met the young tom's gaze. "I heard a voice in a vision."

"And that's why you're leaving?" Mittens's eyes widened.

"That's crazy!" Rascal spluttered. "Spire's always having visions. We don't act on them."

Cinnamon had narrowed her eyes. "You forget that where Tigerheart and Dovewing come from, cats take dreams seriously." Her gaze drifted toward Dovewing. "Isn't that what brought you here in the first place?"

"Yes." Dovewing wrapped her tail around Shadowkit, who huddled closer as the guardian cats stared. "And now a dream is taking us home. Our hearts tell us it's the right thing to do."

Mittens sniffed. "It seems like a weird way to make decisions."

Spire blinked slowly at the tabby tom. "You listen to your belly when it's hungry and your throat when it's thirsty. Why not be guided by your heart when it speaks to you?"

Fierce padded forward and touched her muzzle to Tigerheart's cheek, then to Dovewing's. "We are glad you came. You have taught us a lot, and we'll miss you when you're gone. But I guessed you wouldn't stay forever." She looked fondly at Pouncekit and Lightkit. "The call of home is strongest when you have kits." She purred at Shadowkit. "I'm glad they will be raised among their own kind as warriors."

"*I* want to be a warrior!" Blaze's mew took Tigerheart by surprise. The kit was beginning to lose his kit fluff, but he still wasn't old enough to become a 'paw.

"You're too young," he answered.

"*They're* not!" Blaze pointed his nose as Pouncekit and Lightkit.

"They'll have to train for many moons," Tigerheart explained.

"I could train too." Blaze stared at him boldly. "Let me come. I can help you scavenge and take care of the kits."

Dovewing shifted her paws uneasily. "You're still a kit yourself."

Spire padded to Blaze's side. "Let him join you," he mewed

softly. "It would make my decision easier."

Dovewing tipped her head. Tigerheart blinked at the skinny tom in surprise. "What decision?" he asked.

"I'm traveling with you," Spire told him.

I will not live beside the widewater. Tigerheart remembered their conversation. Spire had wanted Blaze to go, but he hadn't wanted to come with them. "I'll take Blaze. If he's prepared to train hard, then he might make a great warrior one day. But you said you didn't belong beside the lake."

"It is not important that I belong," Spire mewed softly. "It is only important that I make the journey."

Cinnamon swished her tail. "I want to come too."

"So do I." Ant hurried to the she-cat's side.

They stared hopefully at Tigerheart.

Taken aback, Tigerheart looked at Dovewing. Suddenly their small party had become a patrol. He guided Dovewing to the side of the den. "What do you think?" he whispered.

"I think that we are traveling with young kits." Dovewing looked past him to where Cinnamon and Ant were watching hopefully. "They would be safer if we had company."

"But what will ShadowClan say if I return with strangers?" Would they turn them away? Tigerheart wouldn't blame them. "They will remember what happened when they took in rogues."

"These cats aren't rogues," Dovewing reminded him. "We have seen them fight to protect their denmates, and scavenge for others. They take care of their sick like Clan cats." She looked at Tigerheart defiantly. "If ShadowClan won't take them in, then ThunderClan will."

He saw a flash of pride in her green gaze. Unease prickled beneath his pelt. Here, among the guardian cats, it had been easy to forget she was a ThunderClan cat. She was clearly still fiercely proud of her Clan and shared their values. Could she ever learn to live as a ShadowClan cat? He pushed the thought away. They were both warriors. That was enough for now. "Okay." He turned to Cinnamon and Ant. "You can come."

Cinnamon's eyes shone.

Ant looked at Fierce. "We're sorry to leave."

"Others will come," Fierce reassured him. "Ice-chill is here. Your nests won't be wasted."

"When are we leaving?" Blaze asked excitedly.

Tigerheart glanced through a clear stretch of wall. It was sunhigh and the weather was fine. The cold would be hard on the kits, but rain would be worse. "We leave now."

Cinnamon hurried quickly toward Mittens and Rascal, touching them each on the cheek with her muzzle. Tigerheart pressed against Dovewing as they watched the guardian cats say good-bye to their denmates. Then Ant jumped toward the den entrance. Cinnamon, Spire, and Blaze followed and waited on the wooden ledge for Tigerheart, Dovewing, and the kits.

Pouncekit rushed ahead, leaping nimbly onto the ledge. Lightkit jumped after her and turned as Shadowkit leaped up. His forepaws reached the ledge and clung on, his hind legs dangling. Tigerheart felt Dovewing stiffen beside him. He guessed what she was thinking. If Shadowkit couldn't make such an easy jump, how would he manage the long journey to the lake? Then Lightkit ducked down and nipped Shadowkit's scruff between her teeth. Pouncekit reached a paw under his tail and helped heave him up. Hope flickered in Tigerheart's belly. *That's how. We'll take care of one another.*

Blaze glanced down at him. "How do we get out of the city?"

Tigerheart returned the young tom's gaze. He'd thought about this night after night. There was only one way he could be sure that they'd find their way home. "We head for the station. We have to find the Silverpath that led me here."

CHAPTER 28

❧

Cinnamon helped Tigerheart retrace the path he'd followed from the station, on his way here, a few moons ago. She'd lived in this part of the city before she joined the guardian cats, so she knew it very well. Tigerheart hadn't walked this way since he'd first found the thorn den. But as soon as he followed her around the final corner, he recognized the tall, wide Thundersnake camp.

He glanced over his shoulder at Dovewing and the kits. The walk here had been slow. Crossing the Thunderpaths had been easier than he'd expected. They'd used the green Twoleg lights to find gaps in the traffic, and carried the kits over by their scruffs. But the bustling walkways had been harder to negotiate. Dovewing and Ant had flanked Pouncekit, Lightkit, and Shadowkit; Blaze had walked behind with Spire as Tigerheart and Cinnamon led the way. Twolegs hardly ever seemed to look where they were walking, so steering the kits between their legs had proved tricky. In the end, Dovewing, Spire, and Ant had scooped them up, ducking into alleys whenever Twolegs seemed to take an interest in the strange patrol.

Crowds of Twolegs flocked at the entrance to the station. Monsters crawled outside, stopping to let out or pick up Twolegs. Tigerheart took the lead. He knew where he was going now. He skirted the thickest part of the crowd, heading toward the alley that led to the rot piles Dash had shown him.

Relief washed his pelt as he ducked clear of the thronging Twolegs and into the quiet of the deserted alley. He waited while Dovewing, Cinnamon, Ant, Blaze, and Spire caught up. "You can put the kits down now," he told them. "There aren't any Twolegs here."

Dovewing placed Pouncekit on the stone path as Ant and Spire put Lightkit and Shadowkit down. Her gaze darted around warily as she gathered Shadowkit and Lightkit closer to Pouncekit with a swish of her tail. "Where now?" she asked Tigerheart.

"We need to get inside." Tigerheart nodded down the alley. "There's an entrance along here."

He knew Dovewing hadn't been here before. She'd found her own way into the city, avoiding the long tunnel that had swallowed the Thundersnake at its outskirts. Instead she'd padded along countless streets, wandering for days before she'd found the thorn den. What would she think when she saw inside the Thundersnake nest? Tigerheart shuddered, remembering the terrifying Thundersnakes, each with its own Silverpath. They needed to find the right one. If they chose the wrong track, only StarClan knew where it might lead.

Tigerheart pushed back the fear pressing in his chest and

headed down the alley. The three-pawed monster was still sleeping at the side. He tasted the air as he approached the rot piles, pleased to find only Dash's scent lingering there. Mae, Floyd, and Scrap had clearly found new territory to scavenge. Past the rot piles, he found the loose mesh where he and Dash had squeezed out. Lifting it with a paw, he let the others inside. "Keep going until you reach the next mesh," he called, his mew echoing along the narrow tunnel. He followed them in, his belly tightening as the rush of scents washed over him. For a moment, terror gripped him as he remembered arriving. The shock of the sounds and scents had overwhelmed him. They threatened to overwhelm him now. But he had to be brave. Dovewing and the kits were depending on him. "Have you found the mesh?" he called as he saw her shape silhouetted against the harsh light streaming in at the far end.

"I think so." Dovewing's ear flicked nervously.

He hurried toward her, squeezing past Ant, Spire, Cinnamon, Blaze, and the kits. Their fear-scent filled the space. He pushed against the mesh at the far end and let them into the big bright tunnel beyond.

A pair of Twolegs clip-clopped past them, heading toward the wider space. Tigerheart faced the group. "We have to stay bunched tight," he warned them. "There are a lot of Twolegs here. And the lights and scents and movement will be disorienting. Don't lose sight of one another. I'm going to lead us to Dash. He helped me when I first arrived. He can help us find the right Silverpath out of here."

"I'm not scared." Pouncekit puffed her chest out. But her

pelt was bushed. So was Lightkit's. Shadowkit cowered against Dovewing's legs, his eyes wide with alarm.

"Let's carry the kits." He scooped up Shadowkit, worried at how cold his pelt felt. Tucking in his chin to hold the kit close, Tigerheart headed along the tunnel.

He retraced the steps he'd followed with Dash, eventually leading the cats into the great arching space where he'd first scented the station cat. Glancing past the Twolegs hurrying in every direction, he recognized the brightly lit Twoleg den at the side of Dash's nest and hurried toward it, hoping that Dash would be there.

The station cat's scent touched his nose. Hope flashed beneath Tigerheart's pelt. Picking up his pace, he headed for the gap in the wall where he'd first met Dash. He dropped Shadowkit inside as soon as he reached it. "Dash," he called into the darkness.

Yellow eyes blinked ahead of him, and Dash's scent filled Tigerheart's nose as the black-and-white tom scrambled to his paws.

"Tigerheart?" Dash looked alarmed as his gaze slid past Tigerheart and rested on Dovewing and the others crowding behind him. "What are you doing here?"

"I found my friend," Tigerheart told him quickly. He didn't want to scare the station cat. "We need your help."

Dash slunk from the shadow and squeezed out past Tigerheart. He stared in surprise at Shadowkit, Pouncekit, and Shadowkit. His ears twitched. "Are these yours?"

"Yes." He nodded to Dovewing. "This is Dovewing, my

mate. We're taking them home."

"To the forest?" Dash narrowed his eyes as he looked at Spire, Blaze, Ant, and Cinnamon. "Are they going with you?"

"Yes."

Dash tipped his head. "City cats in the forest?" He sounded unconvinced.

Cinnamon flattened her ears. "We just need your help, okay? We don't need your opinion."

Ant glanced at the Twolegs swarming her. "Let's be polite," he warned Cinnamon.

Dash was looking at the kits. "Do you want me to show you which train to get on?"

Dovewing bristled. "We're not taking our kits into the belly of a Thundersnake."

"Then how will you get home?" Dash looked confused.

"We'll walk," Dovewing told him firmly.

"There's nowhere to walk," Dash argued.

Tigerheart shifted his paws. He didn't like lingering here. A strange Twoleg yowl was echoing around the den. "We'll walk on the paths the Thundersnakes use."

Dash's eyes widened. "You want to go into the *tunnels*?"

"They lead out of the city, don't they?" Tigerheart blinked at him.

"It's dangerous!"

"I've been in tunnels before," Tigerheart meowed breezily. "When Thundersnakes came, I just crouched at the edge. Thundersnakes never leave their path. It's easy to keep out of their way." *Please, StarClan. Protect us.* His heart seemed to beat in his throat. He hoped no one guessed how scared he was.

Dash narrowed his eyes doubtfully.

"I just need you to help me find the Silverpath that brought me here," Tigerheart told him firmly.

Dash looked thoughtful. "I didn't see which train you came out of, but if you lead me to the ledge where you got out, I can take you into its tunnel."

Tigerheart frowned. "Have you been in the tunnels before?"

"I hunt for rats there," Dash told him.

Dovewing's ears twitched suspiciously. "You told us the tunnels were dangerous."

"*I'm* used to them," Dash told her. "I'd never take kits or strays in there!"

Cinnamon flattened her ears. "Who are you calling a stray?"

Ant shifted his paws. "He's just worried about us," he reassured Cinnamon.

Cinnamon huffed. "Well he doesn't have to be rude about it."

Dash dipped his head to the orange she-cat. "I'm sorry. But there's a difference between a loner hunting the tunnels when the trains are sleeping and a group of cats and kits trying to find their way out of the city. It's a long way." He looked at Tigerheart. "Are you sure you want to walk? Hiding in the belly of a train would be quicker."

Tigerheart looked at the kits, remembering the flurry of Twoleg paws as they crowded in and out of the Thundersnake. It would be too easy to lose them. He shuddered. "We want to walk."

"Okay." Dash padded into the Twoleg bustle. Tigerheart caught Dovewing's eye questioningly. "Ready?" Dovewing nodded.

Tigerheart picked up Shadowkit while Cinnamon and Dovewing grabbed Lightkit and Pouncekit. Then they hurried after Dash.

The skinny black-and-white tom led them to the large cavern where Thundersnakes dozed between ledges.

Tigerheart scanned them, trying to remember which direction he had run after leaving the Thundersnake that had brought him here. He recognized the gaudy Twoleg clutter—Twoleg shells and furs—lining the middle of one ledge. That was the one. He hurried ahead of Dash and led him toward the gap where the Thundersnake had stopped. It was empty now. Tigerheart peered over the edge and saw the Silverpath a few tail-lengths below. It led away between the ledges and disappeared into a tunnel at the end.

"Is this the one?" Dash asked, following his gaze.

Tigerheart nodded, Shadowkit swinging from his jaws.

"Follow me." Dash looked around at the cats. "Follow me *exactly*. Only put your paws where mine have been. I've seen rats get burned on the tracks here if they touch the wrong one."

Twolegs began to gather along the ledge. Were they waiting for a Thundersnake to arrive? Tigerheart's breath quickened with fear. He had to trust Dash. Dash would keep them safe. He followed the black-and-white tom as he led them along the ledge to where the tunnel opened.

Dash jumped down, landing neatly between the tracks of the Silverpath. He waited, looking up. "Follow me," he ordered. "One at a time."

Cinnamon jumped down first, Lightkit swinging in her jaws. Lightkit squealed as they fell, whimpering as Cinnamon landed with a thump and staggered to find her footing. Ant followed. Dash waved them quickly toward the wall of the tunnel. "Remember, don't touch the tracks," he warned.

Blaze peered over the edge. "It's a long way down." His voice was small, frightened—the young tom was not much bigger than Tigerheart's own kits, after all.

"Jump toward me," Dash called. "I'll help break your fall."

Tigerheart saw Blaze swallow as he crouched at the edge, his tail trembling. Then he launched himself toward Dash.

The station cat reared and wrapped his paws around Blaze as he fell. Deftly he swung him down between the tracks, then nudged him toward Ant and Cinnamon. Spire followed while Dovewing teetered at the edge.

"Don't drop me," Pouncekit wailed as Dovewing leaped down. As she landed, Tigerheart tightened his grip on Shadowkit's scruff and jumped down beside her.

He followed Dash and Dovewing into the darkness of the tunnel. Cold wind streamed through his fur. It filled his nose. Through the stench of Thundersnake, he could smell the perfume of meadows and woods. The city seemed to be drawing in fresh air, like a breathing animal.

Dash slid into the lead. "Follow me."

Tigerheart put Shadowkit down. "You don't have to come

any farther, Dash," he said. "We can follow the tunnel to the end."

The station cat's eyes flashed in the darkness. "Do you think I'd have a moment's peace knowing you and your kits were wandering down here alone?" he asked. "I'm staying with you until you reach daylight."

Tigerheart felt a wave of gratitude toward the black-and-white tom, and realized that he was surprised at how willing Dash had been to help. He'd expected a city cat to only care about himself. But then he remembered Fog. She might have behaved like a rogue, but she'd stayed loyal to her group, hadn't she? And he could still remember her wail of grief as she'd watched the Twoleg carry her brother away. Perhaps all cats were warriors at heart. He glanced at Cinnamon and Ant. He hoped so, at least.

Stones littered the track, sharp on Tigerheart's pads. His belly tightened as Dovewing placed Pouncekit gently on the ground. Her paws had known nothing but the shiny floor of the gathering-place den and the softness of grass outside.

"I want to walk too." Lightkit wriggled beneath Cinnamon's chin.

Cinnamon put her down, and Lightkit shook out her pelt.

"I bet no kits as young as us have ever walked along a Thundersnake tunnel before," Lightkit meowed proudly.

Tigerheart's chest swelled as she lifted her tail high and began to follow Dash along the Silverpath. Pouncekit and Shadowkit clustered beside her, pelts fluffed out against the icy draft. He fell in beside Dovewing, staying close at their heels. Spire, Blaze, Cinnamon, and Ant followed.

Before long, the dazzling lights of the station had disappeared behind them. Darkness stretched ahead. Dim, round lights flickered from the roof every now and then. Twolegs must have fixed them there to guide the Thundersnake to its den.

"We begin in darkness and end in darkness." Spire's mew took Tigerheart by surprise. He glanced back at the tom, wondering what had made him speak now. In the dull glow of a Twoleg light, he could see that Spire's eyes had a faraway look.

Blaze caught Tigerheart's eye. "Don't disturb him," he whispered. "He's dreaming."

Tigerheart's pelt prickled uneasily. *End in darkness.* This journey was already daunting. Spire's grim words didn't help. He whisked his tail enthusiastically. "We'll be out of the city soon. Pouncekit, have I told you about rabbits?"

Pouncekit glanced back at him. "Are they like weasels?"

Dovewing purred. "Weasels are like stoats. Rabbits are like hares."

Lightkit's ears twitched. "It's so confusing. How will we ever learn it all?"

"Don't worry. It'll be easier than you think." Tigerheart's spirits lifted as he imagined showing the pine forest to his kits.

Shadowkit gasped, stopping in his tracks. His pelt bristled. "What are they?"

Tigerheart followed his gaze. Rats were darting across the Silverpath ahead. In the dim light, they looked slippery and fast. "That's prey," he meowed breezily. He didn't want to betray the fear in his belly. Some of the rats looked as big as the kits. What if there were more? A swarm could overrun them, and a bite from their sour teeth could be deadly. "We can catch some if we get hungry. For now, stay close to us. We don't want rat stench on our fur."

Dovewing glanced at him. Fear tinged her gaze. He pressed closer against her, hoping his warmth would reassure her.

Pouncekit halted suddenly. "I can't walk any farther. My paws are too sore." She lifted one of her forepaws and lapped her pad gingerly.

"The stones are rather sharp," Dovewing sympathized. "But we have to keep going. There'll be grass once we get to the end. And your pads will toughen up as we travel."

Ant mewed from behind. "I could give her a—what do you call it?—a badger ride?"

Pouncekit turned around eagerly. "Can I?" she looked hopefully at Dovewing.

Tigerheart answered. "A warrior walks."

Dovewing blinked at Tigerheart. "She's not a warrior yet. And the stones are sharp."

"This will be a long journey." Tigerheart pressed back guilt. This wasn't a time for softness. He had to be strong. They all had to be strong. "The kits need to learn how to be tough if we're going to reach the lake."

Pouncekit sniffed. "Okay. I can be tough."

Lightkit nudged her sister. "Try to imagine what the grass will feel like when we get to the end. It will take your mind off the soreness."

Shadowkit flicked his tail. "Will the grass outside the city be like the grass near the gathering place?"

"Grass is the same everywhere—" Tigerheart stopped. The breeze had stiffened. He heard a familiar hum from the track. His heart lurched. A Thundersnake was coming.

Dash must have heard it too. He stopped and turned to face the group. "We have to crouch down at the edge of the tunnel," he warned.

Tigerheart could see the bright eye of a Thundersnake in the distance.

Shadowkit blinked at it. "Is that the end of the tunnel?" he mewed hopefully.

"No." Tigerheart guided him toward the wall. "A Thundersnake is coming. We have to duck."

"Will it squash us?" Pouncekit's mew was shrill with fear.

"No." Dash sounded calm. "There's plenty of space. But it will be loud and windy."

"Flatten your ears as much as you can." Tigerheart's throat tightened as he remembered the Thundersnake that had screamed past him in the tunnel on his way to the city. What if the wind of this snake's passing whisked the kits away? "Hold on to the kits!" he called as the roar of the Thundersnake rose around them. The Silverpath was singing now as it vibrated harder. Wind tugged at Tigerheart's pelt. He grabbed Shadowkit's scruff and tucked him under his chest as he flattened himself into the corner where the wall met the ground. He looked back and saw the others pressing themselves hard against the stone. Dovewing had Pouncekit's scruff in her jaws and had wrapped her paws around the kit. Lightkit's tail showed from beneath Cinnamon's belly as the she-cat sheltered her against the wind. Blaze huddled between Spire and the wall. Tigerheart flattened his ears. The air throbbed around him as the Thundersnake pounded closer. He screwed his eyes shut. Shadowkit trembled beneath him. The ground shuddered and the walls rang with the howling of the Thundersnake. Its foul stench scorched his lungs. As it screeched past, the tunnel seemed to explode around him. Every hair on his pelt shrilled with the clattering roar as the earth shook. Stiff with terror, Tigerheart waited for it to pass.

In a few moments, the Thundersnake was charging away. The wind swirled, then eased into a soft breeze once more. The tracks trembled and then grew still. Tigerheart pushed himself to his paws and forced his fur to flatten. Shadowkit shifted beneath him. Tigerheart saw him trembling, his eyes wide with terror. He grabbed the kit's scruff and lifted him gently to his paws. "It's gone now. You're safe."

Shadowkit blinked at him. "I thought the tunnel had fallen in."

Dash shook out his pelt. "Tunnels are used to trains. They never fall in," he promised.

Lightkit wriggled from beneath Cinnamon. "That was exciting!" Her eyes shone.

Pouncekit whisked her tail. "Can we wait for another one? I want to do it again!"

Dovewing blinked at Tigerheart. "Are you okay?" Her fur was bristling with fear.

316 WARRIORS SUPER EDITION: TIGERHEART'S SHADOW

"I'm fine. How are you?"

"I don't think I'll be able to hear properly for days." Dovewing twitched her ears.

Cinnamon stared after the Thundersnake, her flanks heaving. "That was horrible."

"I'm putting my paws in my ears next time." Ant mewed.

"That was bigger than all the monsters I've ever seen," Blaze breathed. He looked at Spire. The skinny tom was still lying on his belly. "Are you hurt?"

Spire lifted his nose from between his paws. "Was it real?"

Blaze stared at him. "Of course it was real. Can't you smell it?"

The air was thick with acrid Thundersnake stench.

"Come on." Tigerheart began walking. He wanted to reach fresh air as soon as he could. Air that made his lungs burn couldn't be good for the kits. He heard the stones crunch as the others hurried after him. Fixing his gaze on the shadows ahead, Tigerheart strained to see daylight.

He lost track of time as he pushed on. The kits stopped talking. Occasionally Ant and Cinnamon murmured something to each other. Dash hurried ahead from time to time, scouting for rats or some sign of the end. Two more Thundersnakes howled past. Shadowkit trembled harder each time, as though each passing reached deeper into his fur. Lightkit and Pouncekit seemed energized by them, their weariness evaporating for a few moments after the roar had subsided.

Spire trailed behind, and Blaze fell back to urge him on. "Come on. We'll be in the open soon." The young tom's mew echoed off the stone walls.

"It feels like we've been walking for *moons,*" Ant mewed grimly. "Are you sure there *is* an end to this tunnel?"

"It can't be far now," Tigerheart told him, trying to sound convincing. Then his eyes blinked as he saw pale light far ahead. Another Thundersnake? He pricked his ears. There was no distant growl. The earth felt still beneath his paws. He tasted the air. Fresher scents than he'd smelled in moons touched his tongue. "We're nearly there!" His heart soared. He quickened his pace.

Pouncekit hurried ahead, Lightkit at her heels. "I want to see outside."

"Will we be able to see the lake?" Lightkit asked.

"Not yet." Tigerheart wondered if he should warn them that the lake was days away.

Shadowkit trotted after his sisters.

Blaze left Spire's side for the first time and caught up with them. His ginger-and-white pelt was ruffled with excitement. "I've never seen outside the city."

"Nor have I." Ant sounded excited.

Tigerheart purred, wondering what Ant expected to find.

Cinnamon and Spire padded after them, stumbling a little as the stones shifted beneath their paws.

Dovewing looked at Tigerheart, her eyes shining. There was enough real light now to see the green of her gaze. "We've made it out of the city." She looked at the kits as they hurried ahead, Dash trotting protectively alongside them. She purred loudly. "We're going to make it back to the lake, aren't we?"

She spoke as though this was the first time she'd believed it.

Tigerheart purred back. "Yes."

Behind them, Spire was muttering, but Tigerheart couldn't make out the words. He didn't care about the strange tom. He just wanted to see the sky. Hurrying, he caught up with the kits, and before long they were padding out of the stinking tunnel into fresh air. A few moments later, Spire followed.

Stars glittered above. A sliver of moon hung between them. The dark sky reached to the horizon, so wide, Tigerheart's chest seemed to burst with joy. He breathed in the scents of trees and grass. Dew-scented, the landscape stretched before them like a dream.

Shadowkit blinked at it. "Where are the big Twoleg dens?"

Small Twoleg nests crowded the Silverpath. But they nestled low against the ground like prey. The only shapes that tried to reach the stars here were the distant hills.

Lightkit moved closer to Tigerheart as Dovewing, Cinnamon, Spire, and Ant caught up to them. "It's so big." She sounded frightened.

"And quiet." Pouncekit pricked her ears. Only the cry of a distant owl disturbed the peace. "I don't like it." She blinked at Tigerheart with wide, frightened eyes.

He leaned down and licked her head. "You'll get used to it," he promised.

Dovewing smoothed her tail along Lightkit's spine. "When you've been out of the city for a few days, you'll realize it's not so big. And there are plenty of noises. The sound of the wind in the trees is like the rumbling of distant monsters, and the birds chatter like Twolegs."

"Really?" Lightkit looked hopefully.

"What's that funny smell?" Pouncekit twitched her nose.

Tigerheart breathed deep the familiar scents of wind and grass. "That's what fresh air smells like."

Shadowkit padded along the Silverpath for a few paces, then stopped. He looked up at the stars twinkling overhead. "There are more stars here!" His tail twitched excitedly.

"Wait until we're far away from the Twoleg nests," Tigerheart told him. "You'll see more stars than you could ever dream of."

Shadowkit blinked at him. "Are those our ancestors?"

Tigerheart nodded solemnly.

Lightkit looked up and frowned. "We have a *lot* of ancestors."

Dash shifted beside them. "I'd better head back," he meowed.

Dovewing met his gaze. "Will you be okay on your own?"

"Yeah." Dash shook out his fur. "I've never been this far, but I'm glad I came."

"You can come with us," Dovewing offered suddenly.

Tigerheart looked at her in surprise. Was that a good idea? They would already be bringing four strange cats back to the Clans.

"Thanks," Dash purred. "But I like city life."

Tigerheart blinked at him gratefully. "Thank you, Dash. You have the heart of a warrior."

"I don't know about that," Dash twitched his tail, clearly

pleased. "But I've been glad to help." He dipped his head. "Good luck to you all." Pausing to glance at each cat for a moment, he turned and headed into the tunnel.

Tigerheart stretched. It was good to feel the moonlight on his pelt once more. It seemed to wash the stench of the city from his fur. "Let's find somewhere to make camp for the night." He looked toward the grassy bank beside the track. Twoleg nests clustered at the top. But a stretch of ground lay beside them, dotted with trees. The bushes around their roots would provide shelter until dawn. They could hunt then and fill their bellies with warm, clean prey before they set off for the lake. He blinked at Dovewing. "We'll start early tomorrow."

She stretched her muzzle forward and touched her nose to his cheek. "Yes," she breathed happily. "Tomorrow we can head home."

CHAPTER 29

❧

The moon showed in the late afternoon, pale against a paler sky. It had grown fat in the days they'd been walking. A half-moon had passed, and each dawn brought colder weather. Tiger-heart fluffed his fur out against it and looked at Pouncekit, Lightkit, and Shadowkit. They were quiet today, walking close to Dovewing.

"Don't forget," she told them softy. "If you get a piece of grit in your paw, lick it out straight away or it'll work its way into your pad and hurt."

Lightkit's tail drooped. "My pads already hurt."

"They're tougher, though," Pouncekit encouraged. "You stuck one in my muzzle while you were sleeping last night, and it felt as hard as stone."

Shadowkit looked thoughtful. "If our pads are tougher, will it be harder for grit to get in?"

"Yes." Dovewing leaned down as she walked and licked him gently between the ears.

"How far is there to go?" Lightkit asked.

Dovewing turned her anxious gaze on Tigerheart.

He glanced at the landscape stretching around the

Silverpath. The Twoleg dens were fewer, dotted now. Yesterday they had passed the ledge where he'd been pushed into the belly of the Thundersnake. He tried to remember how many days he'd walked to get here. "We just need to keep going," he meowed. "If we make good time, we'll be there for full moon."

"Full moon!" Pouncekit flicked her tail crossly. "Yesterday you said we'd be there *before* full moon."

Traveling with kits was slower than Tigerheart had imagined. "We *might* make it home earlier if we don't dawdle," he told her.

Cinnamon hurried to catch up to the kits. "Why don't we play a game to make the time pass?"

Lightkit looked at her, brightening. "What game?"

"Let's make up names for the trees and plants and creatures we see, and Tigerheart and Dovewing can tell us if we're right." Cinnamon looked hopefully at Tigerheart.

He blinked at her gratefully. He'd been surprised at how hard she and Ant worked to distract the kits. Yesterday, Ant had persuaded Pouncekit, Lightkit, and Shadowkit to race him as they traveled; he had pointed out trees along the way and challenged them to reach them before he did. The guardian cats had also turned out to be useful hunters. Tigerheart had wondered how they'd manage without scrapcans to scavenge from, but they'd adapted easily to chasing prey, and their pelts grew glossier, their eyes brighter, and their muscles tighter each day.

Blaze was shaping up to be the best hunter. Two days ago he'd caught his first rabbit. He'd outwitted it by cutting across its path, and his killing bite was so accurate that it had hardly mattered that the rabbit was almost as big as him. Hunting was when the young tom seemed happiest. During the day, as they walked, he kept quiet and stayed close to Spire, shadowing the healer protectively. Spire hardly spoke, but watched the passing fields and hills as though looking for something. Tigerheart had the feeling that he was making this journey for a reason he had left unspoken. He was uneasy that the strange tom never shared the dreams and visions that seemed so often to cloud his gaze.

"Thorn-thistle!"

Shadowkit's mew jerked Tigerheart back to the present. He blinked at the kit, wondering why he was staring at him so eagerly.

Pouncekit bounced to Tigerheart's side. "He's guessing a plant name," she explained. She pointed her muzzle to a large bush dotted with red hips.

"That's sweetbriar," Tigerheart told them. "But thorn-thistle was a good guess."

Shadowkit puffed his chest out proudly. Lightkit wandered across the track and climbed the bank to where the shrub sprouted from among the browning bracken. She sniffed one of the red buds that weighted down a stem. "Can we eat these?" she asked.

"I don't think so." Dovewing hurried to her side. "Jayfeather might use them to make medicine, though."

"Who's Jayfeather?" Lightkit blinked at her.

Pouncekit lifted her tail." Don't you remember? Dovewing

told us about him. He's the blind healer cat."

Spire's gaze sharpened suddenly. "Healers!" he meowed. "I remember now. You said each Clan has healers like me."

"Kind of," Tigerheart told him. "Except medicine cats have been trained since they were 'paws."

"Will *we* be 'paws when we get to the lake?" Pouncekit asked eagerly.

"Not straight away," Tigerheart told her. "You have to be six moons old before you can become an apprentice."

"But you said we've walked farther than any kits have ever walked." Lightkit padded back down to the track and fell in beside her sister. "Doesn't that mean we can start training sooner?"

Dovewing joined her. "No." As she looked sternly at the kits, Spire suddenly stopped.

Tigerheart glanced back at the skinny tom. "Are you tired? We can stop soon and hunt. But we need to keep going a while longer."

Spire's eyes had misted once more. He was staring into the far distance, beyond the trees that lined the track to the softly rolling hills beyond.

"We need to leave the track." His meow suddenly rose into a panicked wail. "Here! We must leave it here. This is where we must find the orange sun."

Tigerheart stared at him warily. The crazy cat was staring *away* from the sun, which was dipping toward the horizon, a red fiery ball. There was no time for this. They needed to head home. But he didn't want to argue with the healer. "It will be safer if we keep following the track."

Spire bounded up the bank. "This way," he mewed urgently. "The orange sun is this way. We have to find it. They need us."

Unease prickled through Tigerheart's pelt. *What if this vision is important?*

Cinnamon hurried to the healer's side. "Come on, Spire. Let's stay on the track. We don't want to get lost."

Blaze's pelt lifted along his spine. "You have to believe him." He looked pleadingly at the others. "When he's like this, you have to believe him."

"But he seems confused to me," Dovewing meowed. "The orange sun's over there." She pointed to the sunset with her muzzle. "Who could possibly need us out here? We don't know any cat."

"And we're needed at home." There wasn't time to chase *more* visions. And Cinnamon was right. What if they left the track and couldn't find their way back? How would they ever find their way home?

Blaze squared his shoulders. "We have to listen to him."

Ant padded forward. "We're all tired and hungry," he meowed. "Why don't we find a place to spend the night? We can hunt and fill our bellies." He glanced at Tigerheart, lowering his voice. "Spire's always had crazy visions. In the morning he'll have forgotten about it."

Tigerheart's head felt like it was filled with rushing water. He didn't believe that Spire was crazy, but he was beginning to wonder if, without proper medicine-cat training, the skinny black tom really *understood* his own visions.

Spire might not be crazy . . . but what if he's wrong?

Ant was still staring at him. Tigerheart dipped his head to the small brown-and-black tom. "We should rest." As the sun set, the air chilled. The kits would be cold, although he knew they wouldn't complain. He could taste ice in the wind. The ground would freeze tonight, and they would wake to a heavy frost. They needed food and a warm nest. And maybe it would give Spire enough time to think about his latest vision—figure out what it meant before they decided to go off in search of an orange sun.

He followed Spire up the bank, overtaking him as they reached the top. A meadow stretched toward the hills. Hedgerows bounded it. He saw a patch where rowan trees sheltered bushes. "We'll make camp over there." He nodded toward the rowans as the others climbed the bank.

Spire's eyes glittered with alarm. "What about the orange sun?"

"We can worry about that in the morning," Tigerheart told him. "The sun will rise over there." He nodded toward the hills where Spire had wanted to go. "We can head toward it then."

Spire shifted his paws distractedly. "Not the dawn sun!" he snapped. "The *orange* sun!"

Tigerheart curled his tail around Spire. "We'll find it tomorrow," he soothed, tugging the skinny tom toward the meadow.

When they reached it, Spire settled in the roots of a rowan. Blaze walked up to Tigerheart, frowning. "He won't relax until he finds it," he warned.

"A belly full of food and a warm nest will calm him down," Tigerheart promised, staring at Spire. His eyes were closed, yet he still seemed to be *looking* at something.

It's just because he's never had any cat to help him, Tigerheart told himself. *Without a mentor, of course he can't figure out what his visions mean. We are going the right way.*

We have *to be. . . .*

As Tigerheart drifted wearily toward sleep, the kits snuggled tighter around him. He could hear Dovewing's tail flicking uneasily against the side of their makeshift nest. They'd hunted and swept leaves into piles to sleep on. Now the kits were asleep. Cinnamon and Ant were snoring gently, and Spire had stopped murmuring to himself at last.

Dovewing's tail carried on flicking.

"What's wrong?" he whispered.

"How do you know this isn't another vision about Shadow-Clan?"

He lifted his head and blinked at Dovewing. Her green eyes were shining in the moonlight. "There were no shadows in his vision," he mewed.

"So you think only *some* of his visions are true?" Dovewing looked worried.

"I think StarClan used him to send me a message," Tigerheart told her. "But you've heard him. Even he doesn't always know which parts of his visions are useful."

Dovewing's gaze hardened.

"Then how do you know we're right to be heading back to the lake? What if Spire doesn't have a connection to StarClan after all?"

"He does!" Tigerheart belly knotted with frustration. "Or he *did*."

Dovewing stood up, her tail straight and her eyes blazing with worry. "Tigerheart, what if we're risking our kits' lives for no reason—"

"Tigerheart!" Blaze's anxious whisper sounded beside his ear. He turned to see the young tom staring over the side of the nest. "He's gone!"

"Who?"

"Spire!" Blaze sounded frantic. "Spire's gone! I left the camp to make dirt, and when I got back, his nest was empty. I think he's gone to find the orange sun."

"But it's nighttime." Tigerheart slid from among the kits. "How does he think he'll find the sun?"

Blaze blinked at him, starlight shimmering on his pelt. "I told you we should have listened to him."

"Did you know he'd go running off?" Tigerheart fluffed out his fur against the icy chill.

"If I'd known, I wouldn't have left him alone." Blaze stared past the rowans and across the meadow. "I followed his scent. He headed that way."

Tigerheart flexed his claws. He ached from the day's walk. He didn't want to spend the night hunting for a lost cat.

"We have to find him before he freezes." Blaze's breath billowed around his muzzle.

"Okay." Tigerheart wasn't going to let the skinny tom come to harm. He blinked at Dovewing. "Stay here with the kits. We're going to look for Spire."

Dovewing got to her paws, her fur rippling indignantly. "I'm coming too," she growled. "You're not the only warrior in camp."

"What about the kits?"

"Cinnamon and Ant can take care of them." Dovewing leaned into the nest and plucked Shadowkit by his scruff.

The dark gray kit murmured sleepily as she carried him to Ant and Cinnamon's nest. "What's happening?"

Dovewing placed him between the guardian cats. "You and your littermates are spending the night in Cinnamon's nest," she told him briskly.

Ant opened his eyes.

"Can you and Cinnamon take care of the kits?" Dovewing asked him. "Spire's wandered off and we have to go and find him."

Ant blinked at her sleepily. "Okay."

Cinnamon lifted her head. "What's going on?"

"We've got the kits tonight." Ant yawned. "Spire's wandered off."

Cinnamon sat up, her eyes sparkling with worry.

Dovewing fetched Pouncekit and dropped her in the nest. "It's okay," she reassured Cinnamon. "We'll find him and bring him back."

Pouncekit looked around blearily. "What's happening?"

Cinnamon wrapped her tail around the kit while Dovewing

fetched Lightkit. "Don't worry, little ones. Tigerheart and Dovewing are going to look for Spire. Go back to sleep." She drew Lightkit close to her belly as Dovewing placed her beside Pouncekit.

"We'll be back soon." Dovewing blinked at the kits, who stared back like anxious owls. "Be good and go to sleep. And try not to fidget."

"We'll take care of them," Cinnamon promised.

Ant stared across the meadow. "Spire can't have gone far, and on a cold night like this, his scent should be easy to follow."

"We'll bring him back." Dovewing turned her tail and joined Tigerheart.

Tigerheart could smell Blaze's fear-scent. The young tom was pacing impatiently around him. "Come on." He headed away from camp. "Show me where you picked up Spire's scent."

Blaze hurried ahead, sniffing at the ground. "It's fresh, but he was running. Look how he's scuffed the grass."

Tigerheart saw the paw marks. Spire's claws had kicked lumps from the frozen ground. He must have been moving fast. "He won't be able to keep that pace up for long." He broke into a trot. He was annoyed with the skinny tom. Spire had made him and Dovewing argue. Now he'd gotten him out of his warm nest in the middle of the night. It would do the dumb cat good to freeze a little.

Dovewing padded beside him as they crossed the moon-drenched meadow. Blaze kept a little way ahead, trying to push the pace but slowing each time he looked back and saw

Tigerheart lagging. Tigerheart felt a prick of guilt as Blaze reached the foot of the hill. The young cat was worried. It wasn't fair to let him suffer just because Spire was being difficult.

He picked up his pace, Dovewing trailing him as he caught up to Blaze. The slope grew quickly steeper. Heather sprouted among rocks as the grass grew rougher beneath his paws. Soon they were following a gritty trail between wind-hewn stones. "Can you still smell his scent?" he asked Blaze.

"Can't you?" Blaze flashed him a look.

Tigerheart didn't want to admit that the guardian cats smelled so much like the Twoleg tang that had infused their den, he'd never really been able to tell their scents apart. Only now that wind and rain had washed the city smell from them was he beginning to recognize Cinnamon's and Ant's smells when they were out of sight. He wondered, with a spark of alarm, if he'd have the same problem with his Clanmates when he got home. Would the pungent smell of pinesap overwhelm him now?

"Look!" Dovewing nudged his flank as she caught up to him. She was staring along the trail. The stones opened onto a rocky rise. Above it, an owl circled. "Maybe we shouldn't have left the kits." The owl was huge, its wingspan as long as a branch.

"They're hidden beneath the rowans, and Cinnamon and Ant are with them," Tigerheart told her, anxiety pricking in his pelt. "Besides, the owl's here, not back there."

Blaze fell in beside them, his gaze following theirs. "Why

is it circling? Do you think it's spotted prey?" He glanced at Tigerheart with round, frightened eyes, and Tigerheart guessed what he was thinking. A small, skinny tom like Spire would be easy for an owl that big to carry off.

"Let's hurry." He avoided Blaze's question and scrambled to the top of the slope. He crossed the summit quickly and gazed into the valley below. A Thunderpath ran along the bottom. It was wide where the ground flattened between the hills. A lone monster was heading into the distance, its blazing eyes the only Twoleg light in the landscape.

He scanned the grass on the slope below, searching for movement. "Can you see him?" he asked Blaze.

"No." Blaze's fur ruffled in the breeze.

"What's that?" Dovewing's mew made Tigerheart stiffen. Had she spotted the tom on the hillside? He followed her gaze to a shape looming beside the Thunderpath. It looked small from up here, but he guessed that it was as big as the side of a Twoleg nest—a tall, flat, solitary wall, facing the Thunderpath. Dovewing narrowed her eyes. "Why did Twolegs build a wall there? Is it a signal for the monsters?"

Blaze was staring at it. "It has shapes on it, like the shapes Spire used to draw in dirt sometimes to show me what his visions looked like."

Tigerheart strained to see. The flat surface of the wall was shaded with color that he couldn't make out in the moonlight.

Blaze hurried suddenly forward. "Spire's scent!"

Tigerheart followed the young tom as he raced down the hill. The coarse grass felt slippery beneath his paws as Blaze led him zigzagging between rocks and heather. He was out of breath by the time they reached the side of the Thunderpath.

Dovewing pulled up behind him, panting. She scanned the valley. "Did he follow the Thunderpath or cross it?"

Blaze ducked and sniffed the grass, following a trail over the grass. He stopped and lifted his tail. "He crossed here." The young tom stood opposite the Twoleg wall, which loomed on the other side.

Tigerheart blinked at the colors that stained the wall, frowning as he tried to make out a picture. In the moonlight, the stains looked gray, but he realized, with a jolt, that the shapes were familiar. The great Twoleg wall had been stained to look like a city skyline, and above the jagged roofs Tigerheart saw the shape of a big, round sun. He stared at it, surprise bristling through his fur. Could this be the orange sun Spire had meant?

Blaze was already crossing the deserted Thunderpath. The young tom stopped beneath the wall and gazed up at it. "This must be his vision!" He spun around, searching. "Spire's scent is here."

Dovewing blinked at Tigerheart. "I guess he's been right all along." Was that relief in her gaze?

"Come on." Tigerheart led the way across the Thunderpath. It sparkled where frost was beginning to creep over the smooth stone. He stopped below the stained wall. Blaze was sniffing the bottom eagerly.

Tigerheart pricked his ears. He could hear cats talking nearby. He stiffened, alarm sparking in his belly. "There are cats behind the wall," he hissed to Blaze.

Blaze lifted his muzzle, pausing as he listened. "It's Spire," he mewed. "He's talking to some cat."

"Who would be out here?" Dovewing stared at the young tom.

As she spoke, Tigerheart's pelt prickled. An unexpected jab of longing made him stiffen as scents that he hadn't smelled in moons touched his nose. His heart quickened as he followed Blaze around the wall. On the moonlit grass behind, he saw Spire with two cats. Blaze stopped and stared at his friend. The healer seemed to be trying to beckon the strange cats away from a dip in the grass where they'd made a nest.

"You don't have to stay here," Spire called. "I can take you to my friends."

Tigerheart looked past Spire and saw a familiar pelt. "Rippletail?" The tom's white pelt looked nearly blue in the moonlight.

Rippletail jerked his gaze toward Tigerheart, his eyes widening with shock. "Tigerheart?"

"You're alive!" Tigerheart hadn't seen Rippletail since the battle with Darktail. Rippletail had stayed in ShadowClan when Darktail's rogues had taken over. After the battle, he'd disappeared along with several other members of Shadow-Clan. Tigerheart had assumed they must be dead. What else would have kept a warrior from his Clan? *What else?* Tigerheart stiffened, fear hollowing his belly.

Dovewing stopped beside Tigerheart, her pelt bristling. "Is that Rippletail?" She paused as her gaze flicked to a second figure in the shadowy dip behind Rippletail—his sister, Berry-heart.

Tigerheart couldn't believe his eyes. He padded closer until he could make out the she-cat's black-and-white pelt. His former Clanmate was clearly thriving, because she'd grown fat since leaving ShadowClan. He froze. *She isn't fat—she's expecting kits!* Which meant maybe Sparrowtail was with them too!

He narrowed his eyes as a thought crept into his mind. Why hadn't these cats returned to their Clan? He fixed Rippletail with an icy stare. "Are you . . . rogues now?"

CHAPTER 30

Rippletail stared back. "Rogues? No!" Shock edged his mew. "Is that what ShadowClan thinks?"

"Our Clanmates think you're dead." Anger hardened Tigerheart's mew. "Why have you let them grieve for so long?" His gaze flitted from Rippletail to Berryheart. "You are Snowbird and Scorchfur's kits. Can you imagine their pain?"

Berryheart pressed close to her brother, her gaze shimmering with hope. "They still have Yarrowleaf, don't they?"

"We think she went with the rogues after the battle with Darktail." A bone-chilling wind swept down the hillside and bit through Tigerheart's pelt.

Berryheart blinked in disbelief. "We thought she'd returned to the Clan!"

"Like *you* did?" Tigerheart curled his lip.

Rippletail stepped forward, shielding his sister. Alarm glittered in his eyes. "We meant to, eventually, but—"

"You *betrayed* your Clan!"

As Tigerheart bristled, Dovewing brushed against him. "Be gentle," she murmured. "We don't know what they've suffered."

Guilt jabbed Tigerheart's belly. Dovewing was right. Moons had passed since these warriors had left their Clan. And hadn't he left ShadowClan too? Perhaps they had their reasons for staying away, like he had. He dipped his head to Berryheart and Rippletail. "I'm sorry. You're not responsible for your littermate's decision. But ShadowClan has lost so many. Mistcloud, Lioneye and Spikefur . . ." Berryheart's eyes widened with horror as Tigerheart went on. "Please tell me Sparrowtail's with you, at least."

Rippletail pricked his ears. "Sparrowtail and Cloverfoot are with us!"

"They are?" Tigerheart breath caught in his throat.

Rippletail nodded toward a shadow on the hillside. "We've been living up there. In an abandoned Twoleg nest."

"Are Sparrowtail and Cloverfoot there now?" Tigerheart could hardly believe his ears. He'd found four of Shadow-Clan's missing warriors.

"They're hunting," Rippletail told him. "We were getting ready to go out ourselves when this cat found us." He nodded to Spire. The healer was gazing blankly toward the abandoned Twoleg den.

Blaze stood beside him, staring at Rippletail and Berry-heart with wide moonlit eyes. "Are these warriors too?"

"They were Clanmates once," Tigerheart told him. Were they Clanmates now?

Rippletail went on. "Sparrowtail is the father of Berry-heart's kits."

Dovewing padded forward and blinked kindly at the

queen. "When are they due?"

"Soon." Berryheart shifted her paws nervously.

Rippletail narrowed his eyes as he stared at Tigerheart. "What are you doing here? Why are you traveling with *them*?" He looked suspiciously at Dovewing, Blaze, and Spire.

Blaze puffed out his chest. "I'm going to be a warrior. And Spire is going to be a medicine cat."

If only it were that simple. Tigerheart glanced at the young tom, imagining all the questions and recriminations that might be waiting at the end of their journey. "It's a long story," he told Rippletail. He felt suddenly tired. What would Ripple-tail think when he discovered that he and Dovewing had kits waiting for them on the other side of the hill? "Too long to tell here."

As he spoke, paw steps thrummed across the frozen hill-side. Tigerheart recognized the shapes of Cloverfoot and Sparrowtail at once. Lit by the moon, their pelts gleamed as they raced closer.

Cloverfoot called out anxiously from the darkness. "Ripple-tail? Berryheart? Who's with you?" The gray tabby she-cat pulled up, blinking in surprise at Tigerheart.

Sparrowtail scrambled to a halt beside her. A fat rabbit dangled from his jaws. He dropped it as he saw Tigerheart. "What are you doing here?" His surprised gaze flitted to Spire and Blaze. "Who are you?"

Rippletail fluffed out his pelt. "Let's have this conversation somewhere warmer."

Berryheart's eyes were clouding with tiredness. She

blinked gratefully at her brother.

"Let's go back to our den." Cloverfoot nodded toward the abandoned Twoleg nest as Sparrowtail hurried to Berryheart and pressed his muzzle against her cheek.

Dovewing glanced anxiously at Tigerheart. "The kits," she whispered. "They'll be worried about us."

Blaze whisked his tail. "Ant and Cinnamon will want to know that Spire's okay."

"Ant and Cinnamon?" Cloverfoot frowned.

Berryheart pricked her ears. "Kits?"

Rippletail padded between the cats, his tail flicking. "I guess you *do* have quite a story to tell."

Spire flicked his tail impatiently. "The past is irrelevant. Now that we've found you, you must come with us."

"Where to?" Rippletail looked alarmed.

"To the Clans, of course," Spire meowed.

Rippletail and Sparrowtail exchanged anxious looks.

"We've been worried about going home," Cloverfoot explained. "We joined the rogues. We fought the Clans. We weren't sure ShadowClan would have us back. That's why we've stayed away."

Tigerheart returned the gray tabby's gaze. After such disloyalty, any cat would find it hard to return to the Clan they'd betrayed. But ShadowClan was in trouble. Doubt fluttered in his belly. Could he trust them? He met Cloverfoot's eye. "Would you join the rogues again?" he asked.

Her eyes flashed in alarm. Sparrowtail and Berryheart pressed together.

Rippletail lifted his chin. "Never." His meow was unflinching. "We made a terrible decision. We didn't realize that Darktail was a liar and a bully. We truly thought he could make ShadowClan stronger and safer. We were wrong. And we will spend our lives making it up to ShadowClan, if they agree to take us back."

"They may not have much choice," Tigerheart meowed grimly. "We lost so many warriors to the rogues that we didn't have enough to patrol our territory. We gave some of it to Sky-Clan. The remaining cats lost faith in Rowanstar, and I . . . I left the Clan to give him a chance to be leader."

Rippletail looked confused. "But you're his son! You were always Rowanstar's strongest ally."

"I was causing trouble for the Clan just by being there," Tigerheart told him bluntly. "My Clanmates were looking to me for orders. It undermined Rowanstar's leadership. I thought Rowanstar had more chance of keeping the Clan together without me. And Dovewing . . . was expecting my kits. We traveled far, to a territory with many, many Twolegs, so she could give birth in a place where no cats could judge us." He looked around the ShadowClan cats, daring them to criticize him. After all, he'd not only left his Clan, but he'd had kits with a warrior from ThunderClan. But there was truth in his curt explanation—and none of them were in a position to criticize the choices he'd made. And Tigerheart felt sure that he would make the same choice all over again, if he had to.

Sparrowtail glanced past Tigerheart. "Where is your camp?" Clearly he didn't want to dwell on the past. "If you have kits, we should go to them."

Blaze blinked at him. "Are they coming back to the Clans with us?"

Tigerheart looked at them. "Are you?"

Cloverfoot, Sparrowtail, Berryheart, and Rippletail exchanged glances, then nodded. "We're ready to go home," Rippletail meowed.

Dovewing padded anxiously around Berryheart. "Are you well enough to travel?" Her gaze flicked over the queen's swollen flanks.

Spire answered for her. "It'll be easier for her to travel with the kits inside her belly than outside," he meowed matter-of-factly.

Berryheart's eyes flashed with amusement. "Your friend is right." She padded forward heavily. "I'm afraid I may slow you down. But if I wait until the kits are born, it may be moons before we can travel back to the lake."

Tigerheart huffed in reluctant agreement. "Let's go back to our camp," he meowed. "We can rest for the night." He glanced at Cloverfoot's rabbit. Its warm prey-scent was bathing his tongue. "You can eat and rest there, and we can start the journey home in the morning."

Spire glanced up. Tigerheart followed his gaze, his eyes resting on the stained wall looming above them. He dipped his head to the skinny tom. "The orange sun," he said. "You were right."

Two days of rain were followed by a crisp, bright day. Blue sky stretched toward the horizon. White clouds whisked across the sky, driven by a brisk, chilly wind. Tigerheart followed the

Silverpath around a wide, curving valley, Dovewing padding at his side. There were only a few Twoleg nests dotted among the frosty meadows here. Spire kept his distance from the track, eyeing it warily from time to time. Blaze stayed close to him, glancing back at Rippletail and Berryheart.

The queen had slowed down their pace as she'd predicted. Her swollen belly made her breathless, and she tired easily. Pouncekit, Lightkit, and Shadowkit scampered ahead with Rippletail and Cloverfoot. They'd been excited to meet ShadowClan warriors and seemed eager to impress them. Ant and Cinnamon seemed pleased too, and asked their new traveling companions almost as many questions about Clan life as the kits did. Tigerheart hadn't told any of them that the last time he'd seen these warriors, they were fighting *alongside* rogue cats who had threatened to destroy all the Clans. He eyed Rippletail now, his pelt pricking with an unease that hadn't left him since they'd found their former Clanmates.

Dovewing brushed against him as they walked. She followed his gaze toward Rippletail. "You've forgiven them, haven't you?" She sounded uncertain.

"We all make mistakes," Tigerheart murmured. "But I keep thinking of the moment when the rogues came, and our *Clanmates*"—the word felt bitter on his tongue—"didn't lift a paw to stop Rowanstar, Tawnypelt, and me from leaving the camp. They *wanted* us to go. They chose Darktail instead."

Dovewing turned her soft green gaze on him. "That must have felt terrible. But things have changed. They know they were wrong."

Tigerheart shook out his pelt. He knew he must get rid of the resentment worming beneath his fur. If ShadowClan was to survive, past grievances must be forgotten. "When I left ShadowClan, there was so little trust in the Clan. I'm worried that bringing traitors back will only make it worse."

Dovewing flicked her tail. "For a start, you have to stop thinking of them as traitors." She watched Pouncekit duck beneath Cloverfoot's belly and pop out the other side. Lightkit ducked after her, purring. "They are clearly sorry for the choices they made. You're helping to reunite your Clan. You need to show by example that old wounds can heal and old arguments can be forgiven."

Tigerheart's thoughts flitted back to the city cats. He remembered Fierce's reluctance to hold grudges. Her easy acceptance of other strays. He remembered Tuna's words. *In the city, it's rare to have anything long enough to defend it.* Perhaps the Clans had been trying too hard to hold on to the past. "I thought I had nothing to learn from the guardian cats," he meowed thoughtfully. "But they've learned to live with change. It might be easier to live life the way it is now than to try to keep it the way it was."

Dovewing nudged her shoulder softly against his. "You're starting to sound like a leader," she murmured teasingly.

He met her gaze. "Am I?" He remembered Rowanstar's offer to step aside and make him leader of ShadowClan. He hadn't felt ready then. Did he feel ready now? He pushed the thought away. It had brought swirling with it memories of Spire's dark vision. *The shadows are fading. He can't keep them together.* Was there a ShadowClan left to lead?

"Tigerheart!" Shadowkit's mew distracted him. The gray kit had stopped and was waiting for Tigerheart and Dovewing to catch up to him. Lightkit and Pouncekit had rushed ahead, batting an acorn between the tracks. "Rippletail wanted to know if we are going to be ThunderClan cats or ShadowClan cats." He gazed inquisitively from Tigerheart to Dovewing.

Dovewing answered. "We don't know yet," she told him. "We'll decide when we reach the lake."

There may be no ShadowClan to join. Tigerheart was relieved that Dovewing hadn't mentioned this possibility. Why worry the kits about something that might not be true?

"Can *we* choose?" Shadowkit fell in beside his father. "Because I think I'd choose ShadowClan."

"Why?" Tigerheart looked at his son.

"I don't know." Shadowkit shrugged. "I just feel like ShadowClan needs me. And I *am* called Shadowkit."

Tigerheart smoothed his tail along the kit's spine. "When we reach the lake and see the Clans again, we'll decide where you and your sisters should live. And when you're old enough to start your training, you can decide for yourself which Clan you prefer."

"Is that what all Clan kits do?" Shadowkit asked.

Tigerheart thought of Violetpaw and Twigpaw. "No," he answered. "But it happens from time to time. Especially when kits are born outside the Clans."

Shadowkit frowned. "Will the other cats think we're strange?"

Before Tigerheart could answer, a yowl split the air. Tigerheart jerked his muzzle toward the bank. Spire was staring at the Silverpath, his eyes lit with panic. "It's coming! Too fast! Quick! It's coming! It's too fast!"

Tigerheart pricked his ears. He heard the distant rumble of a Thundersnake. The tracks began to hum. Why was the healer making such a fuss? Thundersnakes passed them several times a day. "Every cat get off the tracks," he called.

As Sparrowtail guided Berryheart to the safety of the grassy bank, Ant, Cinnamon, Cloverfoot, and Rippletail hopped from the tracks. Dovewing grabbed Shadowkit's scruff and hurried to join the others. Like a fox darting from the shadows, a Thundersnake appeared from behind a rise. It was moving fast.

Tigerheart's belly tightened as he saw Lightkit and Pouncekit chasing their acorn toward it. Hadn't they heard him? "Get off the tracks!" The Thundersnake's roar drowned his cry. Heart lurching, he raced toward the kits. "Run!" They turned as he yowled again, blinking first at him and then at the Thundersnake.

Pouncekit's eyes widened in terror. She scrambled away from the acorn, tripping over the track. Tigerheart reached her and scooped her up, racing to the bank to drop her. He turned back for Lightkit. She was frozen between the tracks. The Thundersnake pounded toward her, moving faster than any Tigerheart had ever seen.

"Lightkit!" He hared toward her, but black fur flashed past him. Spire pelted onto the Silverpath as the Thundersnake howled closer. With a yowl drowned by its roar, the healer dragged Lightkit from the track. The Thundersnake screeched past. Its wind hit Tigerheart like a wall of water. As he staggered, he saw Lightkit tumble toward its flashing paws. Spire, pelt plastered against his thin frame, grabbed her scruff between his teeth. She clung to the ground, the Thundersnake tearing at her pelt as Spire gripped her, ears flat, belly pressed against the earth.

Horror surged beneath Tigerheart's pelt as he watched, and then, as suddenly as it had appeared, the Thundersnake passed and roared away into the distance. Lightkit scrambled to her paws, her pelt bushed. "Tigerheart!" She raced toward him, her eyes wide with terror, and huddled against his belly as he wrapped his tail around her.

Dovewing rushed to their side. She was trembling almost as hard as Lightkit. "It nearly killed her." Her mew was breathless. She hauled Lightkit toward her, pressed her close, and licked her head fiercely.

"Didn't you hear it coming?" Tigerheart stared at the kit, his heart pounding.

"We were playing with the acorn." Lightkit's eyes glittered with shock.

"It was going so fast." Pouncekit hurried toward them, Shadowkit at her heels. "We didn't have time."

As Dovewing pulled the kits close to her and purred quick, desperate purrs to reassure them, Tigerheart hurried toward Spire. The healer was pushing himself stiffly to his paws.

Blaze was already at his side. "Are you hurt?"

"I'm fine." Spire shook out his pelt and gazed along the Silverpath.

"You saved my kit." Gratitude swelled in Tigerheart's throat.

Spire met his gaze. His eyes were dark with foreboding. "Next time, I might not be able to."

"Next time?" Tigerheart bristled.

"If we stay on the Silverpath, there will be death." He held Tigerheart's gaze. "Death too quickly. Death without meaning."

The cold wind seemed to reach Tigerheart's bones. He shivered.

"We have to leave the Silverpath." Spire stared at him unblinking.

Ant reached them, Cinnamon at his side. "What did he say?"

Berryheart, Sparrowtail, Rippletail, and Cloverfoot crowded around Tigerheart, Blaze, and the healer.

Death without meaning. Fear tightened Tigerheart's belly as Spire's words burrowed deeper.

"That was close," Rippletail murmured.

"Is Spire okay?" Berryheart's pelt pricked anxiously.

"Why was the Thundersnake running so fast?" Cloverfoot asked.

Blaze glanced around them. He ignored their questions. "Spire says we have to leave the Silverpath."

Cloverfoot blinked. "But Tigerheart said it leads to the lake."

"We'll have to find another way," Blaze told her.

Should we follow Spire's advice? Tigerheart's mouth grew dry.

Rippletail shifted his paws. "That was scary," he mewed. "But all it means is that we have to be more careful. There's no need to leave the Silverpath."

"We'll get lost if we leave it," Berryheart agreed.

Sparrowtail moved closer to his mate. "We need to get back to the lake before Berryheart starts kitting. We can't risk losing our way."

Spire's gaze was still fixed on Tigerheart. "We have to leave the Silverpath," he repeated. "If we don't, cats will die."

Tigerheart avoided the anxious looks of the others. "But we don't know how to get to the lake without the Silverpath to guide us," he told Spire.

"I know." Spire didn't move.

Tigerheart blinked. "But you've never even left the city before. How can you know?"

"My dreams will show me the way."

Berryheart stiffened. "I know he's some kind of medicine cat—somehow—but . . . are we sure he knows what he's talking about?"

Blaze glared at the black-and-white queen. "His dreams found *you*, didn't they?"

Tigerheart's thoughts quickened. Leaving the Silverpath was risky. They could follow the sunset. But what if the Silverpath changed direction and headed away from the sunset? *Why didn't I pay more attention to which way I was heading when I left the lake?* He should have watched the sunsets and made sure to remember the changing landscapes. But he'd followed the Silverpath blindly, like a squirrel chasing a trail of beechnuts.

He searched Spire's gaze. He'd listened to this cat's dreams before: the falling tree, Rowanstar's voice. And his vision of the orange sun *had* led them to the ShadowClan cats. "Do you really think your dreams can lead us home?"

"I know they can," Spire answered firmly.

Fear trickled along Tigerheart's spine. *I have to trust him.*

Rippletail grunted. "I hope you're right."

"He is." Tigerheart held Spire's gaze. "He dreams with StarClan."

Blaze lifted his tail. "Are we going to let Spire lead us?"

"Yes." Tigerheart dipped his head. He thought of Light-kit, so close to the paws of the Thundersnake. His heart quickened. He wasn't risking her life again by staying on the Silverpath. "We'll follow Spire."

CHAPTER 31

Tigerheart tracked Spire's and Blaze's scents under the hedge that bordered the sheep meadow. His paws were mucky from crossing. The sheep were crowded at the far end of the field, but the ground here had been churned to mud by their paws. Dovewing was guiding Pouncekit, Lightkit, and Shadowkit around the stickiest patch, helped by Ant and Cinnamon, but Tigerheart had hurried ahead, anxious not to lose sight of Spire and Blaze as they headed through the beech wood beyond.

Rippletail, Cloverfoot, Berryheart, and Sparrowtail were already following them between the trees. The bare branches filtered sunshine, which dappled the golden forest floor. Tigerheart glimpsed Blaze and Spire beyond them, padding between the trees, and looked back to make sure Dovewing and the kits were okay. Dovewing was nosing Pouncekit beneath the hedge. Ant followed the kit through and turned to help Lightkit and Shadowkit over the roots while Dovewing and Cinnamon squeezed through on either side.

Pouncekit raced into the woods, her tail high. "It's so crunchy!" she squeaked, padding happily over the near-frozen layer of dry leaves. Lightkit and Shadowkit hurried after her, their paws clogged with mud. Tigerheart caught Dovewing's eye. She looked weary. "Do you want me to stay close to you and the kits for a while?" he asked.

"No." She peered between the trees. "Keep your eye on Blaze and Spire. They're moving so fast."

Spire had been pushing ahead relentlessly, and the other cats always seemed to be trailing behind. Tigerheart wondered if the healer had forgotten that he had a queen and kits with him. The days of walking had been hard for them all. But at least the rain, which had started to fall soon after they left the Silverpath, had stopped now. It had rained for two days, and as the fields and meadows had become muddier underpaw, Tigerheart had increasingly wondered whether they'd been wise to leave the Silverpath. The stones there had been hard on every cat's pads, but trudging over sucking earth was exhausting.

Cloverfoot had stopped and was sitting at the foot of a tree while Berryheart caught her breath. "Can you ask him to slow down again?" Cloverfoot asked Tigerheart as he neared. "Berryheart can't keep up this pace."

"I will." Tigerheart looked back at the kits. Lightkit scooped up a pawful of dust and flicked it over Shadowkit. As it fluttered around him, the gray tom lifted his muzzle to the sky and sneezed. Pouncekit ran and skidded through a pile of dry grass. "There's no time to play!" Tigerheart called.

Pouncekit looked up from the grass and blinked at him sadly. "But it's so nice here. Can't we stop for a bit?"

"Not today." Tigerheart could see Spire and Blaze

disappearing over a rise. Why was Spire hurrying? Did ShadowClan need them so badly? Or was Spire just eager to get Berryheart home before she kitted? He left Berryheart and Cloverfoot with Dovewing, Cinnamon, Ant, and the kits and quickened his pace. He'd catch up with Spire and ask him to slow down. The woods thickened, and shadows striped the forest floor. As Tigerheart rounded a juniper bush growing between the trunks, he heard Rippletail and Sparrowtail. He could see their pelts through the branches. They had stopped and were talking in hushed tones. Tigerheart paused and pricked his ears.

"What if that weird tom has got it all wrong?" Sparrowtail snorted.

"I don't like the way he talks to himself," Rippletail mewed. "He stares into space and mumbles as though someone's listening. I've never seen a medicine cat act that . . . crazy."

"I don't think Spire's crazy," Sparrowtail sounded worried. "But I don't think he knows where he's going, either. That stream he made us cross yesterday was dangerous. Berryheart nearly fell off the log. The water would have swept her into rocks."

"He could be leading us anywhere," Rippletail murmured, her voice weary.

"What if we never find our way back to ShadowClan? The kits are due soon. What if Berryheart kits before we get home?"

Tigerheart backed away. He didn't want them to know

he'd been listening. He wish he could reassure them, but as they trekked farther and farther from the Silverpath, he too had begun to doubt whether Spire truly knew where he was headed.

He climbed the rise where Spire and Blaze had disappeared and saw them halfway down the slope below. Breaking into a run, he bounded after them, breathless by the time he caught up with them.

"Hi, Tigerheart." Blaze greeted him with a flick of his tail. "Is everyone okay?"

"Berryheart and the kits are struggling to keep up," Tigerheart told him.

Spire stopped and blinked at him, his gaze vacant.

"Did you hear me?" Irritation flickered through Tigerheart's fur. "You need to slow down."

"I can't," Spire answered distractedly. "There's no time to waste."

Anxiety pressed Tigerheart's belly. "Is ShadowClan in trouble, or are you worried about Berryheart kitting before we reach the lake?"

Spire frowned without focusing. "I don't know. I only know that something is tugging me forward, and we mustn't delay."

"Are you sure you know where you're going?" Tigerheart asked Spire. He saw worry flash briefly in Blaze's eyes. It alarmed him. If Blaze had doubts, then something must be very wrong.

Spire lashed his tail. "Of course I know," he snapped. "I told you."

"But *how* do you know?" Tigerheart pressed. "Do you dream tomorrow's route every night?"

"No," Spire meowed curtly. "But I can feel when we're on the right path."

"So we're going wherever you *feel* is best?" Tigerheart's paws pricked with alarm. They might be wandering around the hills for moons.

Spire began walking. "We must hurry. There's a river ahead. Crossing will be dangerous. But we must keep going."

Tigerheart saw brightness beyond the trees where the beech woods ended. He strained to see between them. Could Spire see water? Land stretched beyond, rising toward hills. His worry deepened. "Are you sure there's a river?"

Spire flashed him a look, then headed on.

"Blaze." Tigerheart held the tom back with a paw. "Do you think we're making a mistake, letting Spire lead?"

Blaze avoided his gaze for a moment, as though he was thinking. Then he blinked at Tigerheart. "I trust him."

Tigerheart dipped his head. They had come this far because of Spire's vision. They might as well keep going. What else could they do?

He followed Blaze and Spire to the edge of the wood and waited there while they carried on, crossing the wide field beyond. Spire veered to one corner of the field, heading for a dip that curved around the foot of the hill. Sparrowtail and Rippletail caught up with Tigerheart and paused beside him. They stared across the field at Spire.

"Where's he heading now?" Rippletail asked.

"He says there's a river ahead," Tigerheart told him.

"I don't see any river." Rippletail grunted.

Sparrowtail glanced back into the woods. "Let's wait for the others."

As Berryheart padded heavily from between the trunks, Sparrowtail hurried to meet her and fell in beside her. Dovewing, Ant, Spire, and the kits followed, Cloverfoot close behind.

"Can we rest soon?" Dovewing asked as she saw Tigerheart.

Tigerheart glanced at the sky. The sun was sliding toward the horizon, but there was still a way to go until sunset. "There's still plenty of traveling time left before dark."

"The kits are tired." Dovewing glanced across the field toward Spire and Blaze. "They need to rest."

"I'm not tired!" Pouncekit lifted her chin, but Tigerheart could see weariness in her face.

"Do you want a badger ride?" he asked.

Her eyes shone. "Yes, please!"

"I'll carry Lightkit," Cloverfoot offered.

Dovewing looked gratefully at the she-cat.

Ant stooped beside Shadowkit. "Do you want to ride on my back?" he asked.

Shadowkit scrambled onto the tom's shoulders and snuggled against his fur.

Tigerheart crouched so that Pouncekit could climb onto his back.

"How many more days do you think we'll be traveling?" Dovewing mewed softly to Tigerheart.

"I don't know." Tigerheart shifted his weight as he walked so that Pouncekit was balanced comfortably between his shoulder blades. "I lost track of where we were as soon as we left the Silverpath. But Spire seems to be in a hurry to get to the lake."

"Do you think he really knows the way?" Dovewing asked.

"I hope so." Tigerheart gazed at the horizon, hoping to recognize the shape of a distant hill. But nothing seemed familiar. He had to believe Spire would find the way.

They trekked on, and as they rounded the curve of the hill, Tigerheart saw a river meandering along a wide valley floor. Relief washed his pelt. "Spire said a river lay ahead," he told Dovewing. "He *must* know where we're going." *Crossing will be dangerous.* He didn't dwell on the healer's words.

The river was almost as wide as a lake. It flowed smoothly between tree-lined banks, brown and muddy. The water swirled, streams and eddies betraying the powerful currents that churned beneath the surface.

"Look!" Pouncekit squeaked from his shoulders. "A floating monster!" A large, pawless monster chugged upstream, sending wide ripples in its wake. Twolegs moved around near the top.

Dovewing looked at the river. "Is Spire planning to find a way around it?" The healer was heading downstream along the bank.

Tigerheart glanced at her. "He said we had to cross it." He didn't tell her the healer's warning.

"Can we cross it in a floating monster?" Pouncekit asked excitedly.

"No." Tigerheart never wanted to be in the belly of another Twoleg monster. He glanced beyond Spire and saw a large Twoleg bridge spanning the river. Monsters prowled over it. "I think he's planning to use that." It must be a Thunderpath, like the one that arced over the herb patch in the city.

Spire was already climbing the slope that reached toward the end of the bridge. At the top, the healer stopped and turned to watch the rest of the party. His tail flicked impatiently as he saw them trailing behind.

Dovewing's gaze was fixed on the bridge. "How will we get past all those monsters?"

Tigerheart let his flank brush hers. "We survived monsters in the city," he meowed encouragingly. "We can survive these."

Rippletail, Berryheart, Sparrowtail, and Cloverfoot were already beside Spire when Tigerheart and Dovewing reached them. Ant and Cinnamon caught up a few moments later.

The healer was sitting on the grass that edged the Thunderpath. As Tigerheart eased Pouncekit from his shoulders, he glanced along the line of monsters flowing across the bridge in both directions. They lurched, growling as they sped up; fumes billowed from their tails as they slowed down. Tigerheart slid in front of Pouncekit protectively. He could see that a narrow walkway edged the Thunderpath as it crossed the bridge, but a high fence hemmed it in. His pelt prickled nervously at the thought of being trapped between monsters and a wall. "We should wait till sundown," he suggested. "There may be fewer monsters then."

Spire narrowed his eyes as he followed Tigerheart's gaze

along the bridge. "We can't wait. We're already behind. We have to keep going."

Rippletail and Sparrowtail exchanged glances.

Ant put Shadowkit down and padded a few steps closer to the bridge. "It's a bit cramped," he mused. "But no worse than a Thundersnake tunnel."

As he spoke, clanging filled the air. Tigerheart's pelt bushed as Twoleg lights began to flash above him. The cats bunched protectively around Berryheart and the kits as the monsters halted beside them and, with a clatter, two long fences began to descend like slow-falling trees across both ends of the bridge.

"What's happening?" Cloverfoot jerked her muzzle around, eyes wide with alarm.

Dovewing pulled Pouncekit, Lightkit, and Shadowkit close to her chest as monster fumes rolled over them.

Cinnamon peered between the thin slats of the fallen fence. The stretch beyond was clear right up to the fence at the far end. "We should cross it now."

"Before the monsters clog it up again." Rippletail hurried toward the fallen fence and squeezed between the slats. He beckoned the others toward him with a flick of his tail.

Tigerheart hesitated. "Is it safe?" He looked at Spire, remembering his words. *Crossing will be dangerous.*

"We have to get across. There's no time to lose." Spire followed Rippletail and slid between the slats, Blaze at his tail.

Dovewing glanced questioningly at Tigerheart, the kits sheltering beside her flank.

"Come on." Tigerheart led her to the fence. "There are no monsters."

Berryheart was already heaving her wide belly between the slats after Sparrowtail. Ant and Cinnamon slid through either side. As they followed Rippletail, Spire, and Blaze across the bridge, the monsters behind them began to honk like geese.

Tigerheart's chest tightened. "Quick." He glanced back and saw Twoleg faces staring in horror. "I think they're angry." He nudged Pouncekit through the fence while Shadowkit, Lightkit, and Dovewing squeezed through the slats on either side. Relief washed his pelt as he led Dovewing and the kits across the clear stretch of Thunderpath. Behind them, the monsters honked harder. Why were they so furious?

A hard silver strip spanned the stone halfway across. Tigerheart hopped over it, worried it might be a trap. Berryheart, Sparrowtail, Ant, and Cinnamon were almost at the far side. Rippletail and Cloverfoot were already squeezing through the fence.

"Hurry!" As Tigerheart called over his shoulder to Dovewing and the kits, the stone jerked beneath his paws. Alarm sparked through his fur as the Thunderpath began to lift. It tipped beneath his paws, turning the flat stone into a slope slanting down toward the flat stretch of Thunderpath where Rippletail and Cloverfoot watched, pelts bristling.

What's happening! Tigerheart's thoughts whirled as he struggled to keep his balance. He looked back to where the silver strip had marked the halfway point of the bridge. There, the bridge had cracked and opened like a stick snapping in half.

Dovewing yelped beside him and gripped the rapidly slanting Thunderpath. Lightkit and Shadowkit squealed in panic. Below them Berryheart, Sparrowtail, Ant, and Cinnamon leaped clumsily down onto the stretch of flat stone where Blaze and Spire had already landed.

Tigerheart gasped as Lightkit and Shadowkit plummeted past him. Cinnamon reared and caught Shadowkit. Rippletail reached out and wrapped his paws around Lightkit.

Tigerheart flattened himself against the stone, clinging with his claw-tips as he watched Dovewing desperately trying to scrabble up the slope. "Where are you going?" he yowled. "We need to get off the bridge now!"

"Pouncekit!" Terror filled in Dovewing's cry.

Tigerheart looked up. Pouncekit was teetering at the top of the slope where the bridge had cracked in the middle. Her ears flat, she wailed with terror.

Fear-scent pulsed from Dovewing. "She's going to fall through the gap!"

"Pouncekit!" Tigerheart's breath caught in his throat as Pouncekit tumbled out of sight. His belly lurched. *She's gone!* He tore at the stone, trying vainly to haul himself closer. *Pouncekit!* Horror shrilled beneath his pelt as he scanned the top.

Two small paws showed against the silver strip. Hope flashed in his chest. Pouncekit was clinging on. He tried again to heave himself toward her, but his claws couldn't dig into the stone. Dovewing wailed desperately as she slipped farther away from her kit.

Suddenly, claws scraped the stone beside him. Spire's black pelt flashed past. Scrambling higher, the healer leaped for the top of the raised bridge. He must have pushed off from the flat stretch of stone with such power that momentum carried him forward. The healer hooked his paws over the end of the bridge. He churned the stone with his hind paws and managed to pull himself up so that he was balancing at the top. Hindquarters trembling, he leaned over and hauled Pouncekit up, then let her drop toward Dovewing. With a squeal, Pouncekit tumbled past.

Tigerheart watched the kit fall, his heart in his throat. As Ant stretched to catch her, relief flooded his pelt. The tom grabbed Pouncekit and swung her safely onto the Thunderpath.

"Spire!" Dovewing's anguished cry made Tigerheart look up again. The bridge was still rising, so steep now that Tigerheart couldn't keep his grip. As he began to slide, he saw Spire wobble at the top. The skinny black tom opened his mouth in a wail that never came. As he swayed backward and fell, silence filled the space where he'd been.

CHAPTER 32

"Spire!" Disbelief swept Tigerheart. He can't be gone! The stone of the Thunderpath scoured his belly as he slid down the bridge. Landing with a thump, he stared blindly at the top.

Dovewing dropped beside him, grunting as she landed. "Pouncekit." She rushed to her kit and began washing her frantically.

Tigerheart couldn't move. "Spire." His mew came as a helpless whisper.

"We have to get off the bridge." Ant nudged his shoulder.

Tigerheart blinked at him. "What about Spire?"

"He's in the river!" Blaze had already dashed to the edge of the Thunderpath and was scrambling down the steep grass bank to the water's edge.

Rippletail, Cloverfoot, and Cinnamon streamed after him while Sparrowtail steered Berryheart, Dovewing, and the kits to the side of the Thunderpath.

Tigerheart's mouth was dry. "He can't swim." The river was so huge. How could any cat survive?

"Come on." Ant nosed him forward. "He might have made it to the bank."

Tigerheart could hardly believe what was happening. He ran numbly after Ant, his paws slipping on the grass as he followed the others down the bank.

Blaze was leaning out over the swirling water, scanning the surface desperately.

Cinnamon and Cloverfoot scurried beneath the bridge, their gazes fixed on the river. Tigerheart stared blankly at the floating monster, which was gliding through the gap the raised bridge had made. Water whirled at its flanks and churned at its tail. Dread hollowed Tigerheart's belly. Even if Spire had survived the drop and managed to swim to the surface, the monster would have chewed him up.

"I can't see him!" Panic edged Blaze's mew. He paced up and down, straining harder to glimpse the black tom.

Had Spire foreseen this? Had he known when he suggested the crossing? *Why didn't he find another way?* Tigerheart swallowed back the grief threatening to overwhelm him. He couldn't give up. Blaze would need him. The whole patrol would need him. He had to be strong. There was no sign of Spire. No black pelt showed on either bank. The river had taken him.

He padded to Blaze's side and waited until the young tom stopped pacing. Pain glittered in the young tom's amber eyes as he gazed over the muddy water. The floating monster was gone. Above them, the bridge was slowly lowering its legs. Tigerheart heard the clatter of the fences lifting and the rumble of monsters moving once more. "He saved Pouncekit," he murmured.

Blaze turned on him, helpless grief twisting his young face.

"Why didn't he find another way to cross the river?"

Tigerheart held his gaze. "There was no other way." The river stretched wide on either side for as far as the eye could see. He touched his nose to Blaze's ear. "We will remember him. StarClan will remember him." Tigerheart glanced at the darkening sky where the first stars were beginning to show. "His visions helped me and Dovewing, and they led him to Clanmates I thought were lost forever."

Rippletail padded to his side. "How are we going to find our way now that Spire is gone?" Worry darkened the white tom's gaze.

Blaze bristled. "Oh, *now* you believe him?" He glared at Rippletail. "Spire died trying to *help* you. Are you only bothered that we don't have a guide anymore?"

Rippletail dropped his gaze. "Of course not, but how will we find where we . . ."

As his mew trailed away, Sparrowtail padded forward. "Rippletail meant no disrespect." He glanced toward Berryheart, who had climbed down the slope with Dovewing and the kits and waited now beside the others. "But we need to get home before Berryheart starts kitting."

"Especially now that we've lost Spire." Cinnamon stood at Blaze's side. "He was the only healer with us."

"We should go back to the Silverpath." Cloverfoot's tail twitched anxiously. "We know it leads to the lake."

"It would take too much time to retrace our steps," Ant argued.

"But we might be wandering forever without a guide."

Cinnamon gazed across the river. "Surely it's better to travel longer and be sure of getting where we're going."

"I think we should keep going this way." Blaze pointed his muzzle toward the side of the valley where the Thunderpath cut between hills. "Spire said a Twolegplace lies that way and we must travel around it."

"But where do we head after that?" Tigerheart searched the young tom's gaze.

Blaze looked at the ground. "Spire didn't say."

Tigerheart paused, willing his heart to feel less heavy. "I came past a Twolegplace when I left ShadowClan," he mewed hopefully. "Maybe this Twolegplace is the same one. . . ."

"I guess we could keep going," Cinnamon conceded. "If we get lost, we can still retrace our steps to the Silverpath later."

Cloverfoot's pelt prickled along her spine. "We could be walking for moons."

"We've traveled so far already." Dovewing's green eyes shone in the dying light. "We must be getting closer to the lake. Surely we'll see it soon."

Tigerheart glanced around at the patrol. Doubt darkened every gaze. "We'll follow the route that Spire began," he meowed firmly. "He would not have set us on this path if he thought we couldn't reach the end."

Ant shifted his paws. "Spire would have known we'd find our way."

Cinnamon and Blaze nodded. Cloverfoot, Berryheart, Sparrowtail, and Rippletail mumbled in reluctant agreement.

Lightkit glanced nervously to where the Thunderpath cut

between the hills. "Are we going to follow the monsters to the Twolegplace?"

"No." Tigerheart nodded to the hill rising beside it. Trees and bushes covered the slope. The ground would be soft underpaw and provide shelter.

Rippletail followed his gaze. "It looks like a good place for prey."

Tigerheart glanced at Dovewing. "Are the kits okay?" Pouncekit, Lightkit, and Shadowkit were clustered beside her. They looked at him with wide, worried eyes.

"They're fine, but it's been a long day," Dovewing mewed. "We should make camp soon."

"Once we're away from the river." Blaze glanced at the flowing water, fresh pain in his eyes.

"Let's travel until sunset and then hunt and rest for the night," Ant suggested.

"Okay." Stiffening his shoulders, Tigerheart led the party away from the river. With each paw step, his grief at losing Spire deepened, and his regret at ever having doubted him stuck in his belly like a claw trying to rip its way through.

Spire might not have grown up among the Clans, he thought, *but if we make it back to the lake, if ShadowClan is restored, then he'll have done more for our Clan than some of our own warriors.*

He pushed on as the slope grew harder, and ducked between swaths of bracken. No cat spoke as they walked. The wind stirred the trees and bushes around them as they headed into thicker vegetation. Soon they were climbing through a stretch of forest. Birds began their evening song, calling from the branches above their heads. The moon rose, burning a patch in the darkening sky, and as they reached a clearing in the trees, Tigerheart stopped.

"Are we going to make camp?" Rippletail stopped beside him.

Tigerheart gazed between the trees. Far below, the wide river reflected moonlight. The image that had burned in his mind since they'd left its banks burned stronger still—Spire lifting Pouncekit to safety, then swaying and disappearing... giving his life for cats he hadn't known very long, and for a way of life he had never known at all. "We should honor him."

Rippletail blinked at him in surprise. "What?"

Blaze hurried closer. "Are you talking about Spire?"

"Yes." Tigerheart watched his kits pad to a halt. They looked tired, but they were safe. "Spire saved Lightkit from the Thundersnake and Pouncekit from the river," he meowed. "He was as brave as any warrior, and we should honor him as a warrior."

"How?" Cloverfoot frowned.

Sparrowtail tipped his head. "Should we sit vigil for him tonight?"

"A vigil is not enough to thank him for what he has done." Tigerheart glanced at his Clanmates. "He was loyal and brave. He should become one of us."

Rippletail glanced at the stars. "How?"

"Let's have a warrior naming ceremony for him now and give him a warrior name."

Blaze pricked his ears. For the first time, grief cleared

from his gaze. "A warrior name?"

"But he's dead," Cloverfoot pointed out. "It's too late."

Tigerheart stepped from the shadow of the trees and let moonlight wash his pelt. "StarClan knew him. They will be watching. They will know, and once he has his warrior name, he'll be able to walk among them as the warrior he has always been, even though he never had the chance to live as one."

"But you're not a leader," Sparrowtail meowed. "How can you give a cat their warrior name?"

Dovewing padded forward. "Tigerheart is leader of this patrol."

Berryheart sat down wearily. "How can a cat who's never known ShadowClan be a ShadowClan warrior?"

Blaze blinked at her. "He's known you, and Tigerheart and Ripple—"

Cloverfoot cut in. "It's true. He has known our Clan through us. And by finding us and protecting Tigerheart's kits, he's done more for ShadowClan these past moons than we have." *Exactly,* Tigerheart thought. Guilt sparked in Cloverfoot's gaze as she looked from Berryheart to Rippletail and Sparrowtail. Then she blinked expectantly at Tigerheart. "I think he deserves a warrior name."

Rippletail dipped his head. "Okay."

Sparrowtail and Berryheart nodded in agreement. Tigerheart lifted his muzzle to the stars. "I, Tigerheart, deputy of ShadowClan and leader of this patrol, call upon my warrior ancestors to honor Spire. He never knew the warrior code, and yet he lived by it. He healed the sick and protected the weak. He gave his life to save another. I commend him to you as a warrior of ShadowClan, and from this moment forward, he will be known as Spiresight, for his visions and his wisdom."

"Spiresight." Blaze breathed his friend's new name.

"Spiresight!" Dovewing called out, her gaze sparkling as she looked at Pouncekit.

"Spiresight! Spiresight!" The cries of the patrol drowned out the evensong of the birds as they celebrated Spiresight's warrior name.

Tigerheart looked once more toward the river. As the cries of the others died away, he prayed silently to StarClan. *I hope he is safe among you now. Honor him. One day I hope to walk beside him.*

He opened his eyes and looked at the gathered cats, all of their eyes alight with excitement—it felt good to be enacting a Clan custom after so long.

Ant shifted his paws self-consciously. "Should we hunt now?" The brown-and-black tom furtively scanned the undergrowth around the clearing.

Tigerheart could hear the rustle of prey. Squirrel scent touched his nose. The kits would be hungry. "Yes."

"I'm staying here." Blaze fixed Tigerheart with a solemn stare. "Sparrowtail said you honor fallen warriors by sitting vigil. I want to sit vigil for Spiresight."

Tigerheart dipped his head. "Once the kits have eaten and have warm nests to sleep in, I will sit vigil with you."

As Blaze blinked at him gratefully, Berryheart grunted with pain.

Dovewing hurried to the queen's side as Berryheart sank to her belly. "What's wrong?"

Berryheart gave an anguished moan. "The kits! I think they're coming."

Tigerheart kept out of the way while Berryheart wailed and grunted through the night. He sat with Blaze a little way from the nest Sparrowtail and Cloverfoot quickly made for the queen and watched Rippletail and Ant hurry back and forth, soaking moss in a nearby stream, fetching sticks, pacing anxiously while Dovewing and Cinnamon crouched around Berryheart, trying to help with her kitting. Cinnamon looked a little nervous.

Blaze did not speak as the moon moved above the trees. The young tom seemed lost in thought, making his silent vigil for his friend while the others bustled nearby.

Tigerheart's thoughts wandered between grief for Spiresight and worry for Berryheart. How could the kits come now? They were not even close to ShadowClan's borders; the landscape was unfamiliar, the journey ahead uncertain without Spiresight to guide them. He waited for worry to deepen into fear. And yet, as the night wore on, his anxieties unraveled into relief. Spiresight was in StarClan now, safer than he'd ever been in life. Berryheart's kits would be with them by morning.

There was no use in worrying. He knew what must be done. Newborn kits could not travel. The patrol would stay here until Berryheart's young were strong enough to finish the journey their mother had begun. This wooded hillside was not a bad place to wait; the stream Ant had found ran nearby, bubbling down from the hilltop, fresh and clear. The forest had the clean crisp smell of wildness, untainted by the Thunderpath, which was too far away even to hear. Prey would be fresh, and the trees would provide shelter even if the weather hardened from frost to snow.

When he heard the mewl of Berryheart's first kit, a sense of peace enfolded Tigerheart for the first time in a moon. He remembered the first happy days with Pouncekit, Lightkit, and Shadowkit. Since there was nothing to do but wait, he might as well relish the comforts of their temporary home. As dawn began to lighten the sky beyond the hill, he climbed higher to see the rising sun. A rabbit strayed across his path, and he tracked and hunted it with a simple relish he'd not felt since he'd been an apprentice. He laid the rabbit at his paws and lifted his gaze to watch the orange crown of the sun lift above the distant hills.

"Tigerheart?" Dovewing's mew sounded between the trees.

He didn't move, but shifted to make room as she joined him. "How is Berryheart?"

"She's well. The kitting was hard, but she was brave." Dovewing sat down. "She had three kits. She's suckling them already."

"Has she named them?"

She leaned against Tigerheart, her flank warm against his. "Hollowkit, Sunkit . . . and Spirekit."

"Spirekit?" Tigerheart stared at her.

Dovewing stretched her forelegs. "Berryheart insisted; no other name would do."

Tigerheart pondered this. It was not very common for kits to be named after dead cats, but when he thought of bringing another Spire back to ShadowClan, he purred happily. "I think that's a perfect name. Have you told Blaze?"

"Yes," Dovewing murmured. "He went straight to Berryheart's nest to see them."

Tigerheart looked anxiously into Dovewing green eyes. "Do you think Blaze will be okay? Spiresight cared for him ever since he was born."

"He will grieve," Dovewing told him gently.

"Do you think he regrets coming with us to ShadowClan?"

"Not for a moment." Dovewing turned her gaze toward the rising sun. "Spiresight wanted him to come, remember? I think Blaze will feel he is honoring his best friend's wishes as well as his own."

Tigerheart touched his nose to Dovewing's cheek. She was gentle in her wisdom.

Dovewing purred for a moment, then paused. "It's strange how Spiresight found Berryheart and the others."

"I suppose he was guided by StarClan," Tigerheart murmured.

"I wonder if StarClan guides many cats beyond the lake. . . ." Dovewing met his gaze. "Or do they just touch cats lost warriors will encounter?" As she paused again, Tigerheart wondered what she was trying to say. "Do you think we were *meant* to travel to the city?" She blinked at him, sunlight flaming in her green gaze.

Tigerheart had never wondered if StarClan had sent Dovewing's dreams. He'd assumed they were the anxieties of an expectant mother, and he'd followed because he'd trusted Dovewing's instinct. But she could be right. He remembered, with a shiver, Spiresight's strange greeting when they'd first met in the gathering-place den. *Now they're both finally here.* He blinked at Dovewing. "I think you may be right." His pelt prickled. "I was alone when I left ShadowClan, but I will return with Clanmates, both new and old. And ShadowClan needs warriors more than ever." He felt the tug of home like a claw in his belly. *I am coming, Rowanstar.* His father needed him.

Can I wait while Berryheart's kits find their traveling paws? Tigerheart flicked his tail. *I'll have to.* He'd found old Clanmates, and he wasn't going to risk losing them again by leaving them here. When he returned to ShadowClan, he would bring with him enough cats to make the Clan strong once more. He lifted his face to the rising sun. *You'll be proud of me, Rowanstar, I promise. Just hold on until I reach you.*

CHAPTER 33

🍀

Tigerheart pricked his ears. Ahead the bracken—still stiff from the morning's frost—crackled. He dropped into a hunting crouch.

"We don't need more prey." Behind him Cloverfoot stood over the squirrel they'd already caught. Blaze held a fat pigeon between his jaws.

"Hush." Tigerheart flicked his tail impatiently to quiet the tabby she-cat. "Berryheart needs as much food as we can catch until the kits are fully weaned."

A moon old now, Hollowkit, Sunkit, and Spirekit had tasted their first prey. But although they were growing fast and exploring farther from their nest each day, they still suckled at night.

The bracken crackled again. Pelt prickling excitedly, Tigerheart leaped. He dived between the fronds and clamped his paws over a mouse. It twitched in panic as he hooked it toward him and gave it a killing bite. Its musky scent made his mouth water. Even now, nearly two moons after leaving the city, the taste of forest prey still filled him with pleasure. He wondered if he'd ever get the taste of scrapcan trash off his tongue. He lifted the mouse and carried it back to Cloverfoot.

She purred. "Are you enjoying hunting for your Clan again?"

"I never really stopped." Tigerheart dropped the mouse beside the squirrel. "The guardian cats were like a Clan to me. But there's no honor in scavenging. When I bring my Clanmates forest prey, I feel I am feeding them prey worthy of them."

He picked up the mouse and headed toward the temporary camp they'd built between two swaths of bramble. They had dug nests among the roots and dragged bracken to make a low camp wall where the brambles didn't reach. Berryheart's nest was deepest inside the bush, safe from nosy predators. This stretch of hillside had sheltered them peacefully. Owls called where the forest deepened into oak and birch, and foxes screeched in the valley below, but Tigerheart had never scented predators on the territory he'd marked around the camp.

He hadn't declared himself leader of their tiny Clan, but no one questioned his orders, and it was to Tigerheart they looked to organize the daily hunting and border patrols. Cinnamon had managed to build a small store of herbs, remembering, with the help of Blaze, the sight and scent of the leaves Spiresight and the other healers had used. Luckily, no cat had fallen ill, despite the cold weather. Cinnamon had treated an occasional bellyache and sore throat, but her skills hadn't been stretched beyond mild ailments.

The cats were rested by the enforced break in their journey, and Tigerheart sensed relief in Dovewing's gaze as she watched Pouncekit, Lightkit, and Shadowkit play in the shelter of the camp. He'd felt relief too. The long days of walking had been hard on the kits. But as the moon had worn on, impatience had begun to itch beneath his pelt. Rowanstar's message rang in his mind. *Tell Rowanstar I'm sorry it's taking so long.* Had StarClan known the journey would be this long when they'd sent Rowanstar's words to Spiresight? Would Tigerheart arrive too late to help his Clan? The tug of home grew stronger each day, and he realized that once more he was beginning to feel trapped, worrying more about ShadowClan with each passing sunset.

As Tigerheart reached the camp now, he heard the kits squeaking. His whiskers twitched with pleasure as he glimpsed them over the bracken. Hollowkit and Spirekit were stalking Pouncekit and Lightkit while Sunkit nestled at Berryheart's belly. Were they old enough to travel yet?

"Watch out!" Pouncekit mewed a warning to Lightkit as Spirekit sprang. Lightkit pretended to struggle to escape as the tiny kit began tugging at her tail. Hollowkit squealed with delight and flung himself at Pouncekit. He reared and hooked his claws into her shoulder, and she wailed dramatically and fell to the ground.

"You got me!" Pouncekit groaned as he clambered onto her flank and stood there triumphantly.

"Tigerheart!" Lightkit's eyes lit up as she saw her father pad into camp. She pulled free of Spirekit and raced to meet him, sniffing eagerly at the prey he was carrying. "You caught a mouse!" She bounced around him. "Can I have it? I love mouse. It's my favorite."

Tigerheart dropped the prey at the edge of the small clearing. "It's Shadowkit's favorite too," he told her. "You'll have to share." He glanced around the camp. Ant and Cinnamon were resting in a patch of sunshine that filtered between the branches. Rippletail was mending a hole in the bracken wall, threading brambles through, which Sparrowtail passed over the top. "Where is Shadowkit?" He couldn't see the gray tom-kit.

"He and Dovewing went out of camp to talk." Lightkit was sniffing the mouse distractedly.

Hollowkit and Spirekit hurried to sniff it with her.

"It's all furry." Spirekit frowned.

Pouncekit padded to join them. "I like the fur," she mewed. "It's chewy."

As Hollowkit wrinkled his nose, Tigerheart peered over the top of the low camp wall. He could see Dovewing and Shadowkit a little way away, their heads bent together as they talked. He nodded to Lightkit. "Why don't you show Spirekit how to strip out the meat?" he suggested. "But remember to leave some for Shadowkit."

"Okay." She dragged the mouse away from the fresh-kill pile and began to nibble through the fur. Spirekit watched her eagerly.

Tigerheart leaped the camp wall and padded toward Dovewing and Shadowkit. What were they talking about so intently?

Dovewing looked up as he neared. She blinked as though she was relieved to see him. "You're back." There was worry in her mew.

"Is everything okay?" Tigerheart glanced from Dovewing to Shadowkit. The gray tom's eyes were round and anxious.

"Shadowkit had a dream," Dovewing told him.

"A bad one?" Had the kit had a nightmare?

"No." Dovewing smoothed her tail along Shadowkit's spine. "Tell Tigerheart what you told me."

"I know how to get to the lake," Shadowkit mewed earnestly.

Tigerheart frowned. "Really?" Had the kit been exploring?

"I dreamed it," Shadowkit explained. "I dreamed about the Twolegplace Spiresight said was at the end of the Thunderpath, and then I saw beyond. There was a valley with birch trees edging a small stretch of water and then a hill rising to moorland."

Moorland? Tigerheart stiffened. Was Shadowkit talking about WindClan territory? "Did you see beyond the moor?" He leaned closer to Shadowkit.

"The moor stretched over a hilltop, then down to a lake."

Tigerheart's throat tightened with excitement. Were they that close to home? "What did the lake look like?"

"There was pine forest on one side, and oak forest, and near a marshy stretch of reeds at the far end, there was an island."

Tigerheart lifted his gaze to stare at Dovewing. "Our lake," he breathed. "He saw our lake in a dream."

This one will see into the shadows. Tigerheart remembered Spiresight staring at Shadowkit on the day he was born. This dream must be a vision. How else could Shadowkit describe the lake so exactly? Pelt prickling along his spine, he stared at

Dovewing. "Have you ever described the lake to him?"

"Not in that much detail," she told him. "I said that there was forest beside it, but I don't think I said what kind, and I didn't mention the reed marshes or the island."

Tigerheart's gaze flitted eagerly back to Shadowkit. "Do you think you could lead us there?"

"I dreamed the whole route," Shadowkit told him. "As though I were a hawk flying over it."

"But could you recognize it from the ground?" Tigerheart pressed. Asking such a young cat to lead the patrol home was a big responsibility to place on small shoulders. He wanted to make sure Shadowkit could do it. "Could you tell us which paths to follow?"

"Yes." Shadowkit nodded eagerly. "That's why I had the dream. I knew it while I was dreaming. It was to show you the way home."

Tigerheart's belly tightened. Shadowkit's bond with StarClan must be strong. He wondered whether it would last, or if their ancestors were just using the kit to guide their paws now. He blinked fondly at his son. "Thank you, Shadowkit. We'll discuss what you've told us with the others."

Shadowkit's pelt prickled uneasily. "We will go, won't we?"

"Of course," Tigerheart promised. "We just need to decide when."

"Soon." Urgency shone in Shadowkit's eyes.

"As soon as we can." As Shadowkit searched his gaze, Tigerheart waved him away with a flick of his tail. He had to talk about it with Dovewing and then the other cats. "Lightkit's stripping a mouse for Spirekit. She promised to save you some. Go and eat. You must be hungry."

Shadowkit gazed at him for another moment, then turned toward the camp. As he padded away, Tigerheart looked at Dovewing. "Do you think StarClan is really sharing dreams with him?"

"I don't see how else he could have described the lake so precisely."

"It seems too good to be true."

"You saw him," Dovewing mewed. "How sincere he was. He believes his dream is true, and so do I. Perhaps he *is* connected to StarClan. Perhaps I dreamed I should travel to the city because I was carrying him in my belly."

Tigerheart shifted his paws. Spiresight had said that Shadowkit would be special. "Do you think he'll be a medicine cat?"

"Let's worry about that when we get home." Happiness suddenly sparked in Dovewing's green gaze. "I never imagined we were so close."

Tigerheart could see over the camp wall from here. Spirekit had wandered away from Lightkit as she pulled the mouse apart and was watching his father's tail twitch as Sparrowtail worked on the camp wall. Excitement sparked in the tiny kit's gaze as the tail flashed back and forth in front of him. With a squeak, he pounced and fell onto his side. Wrapping his paws around the tail, he began churning it with his hind claws. Sparrowtail hardly seemed to notice.

Tigerheart turned back to Dovewing. "Do you think

Berryheart's kits are ready to travel?"

"They're still very small," Dovewing murmured. "Even walking for two days would be hard on them. Especially in cold weather. They only have kit fur."

"Let's ask the others." Tigerheart headed back to the camp, Dovewing at his heels. When he reached the small clearing, he lifted his chin. "I must speak with you." He looked around the camp, meeting the gazes of Ant, Cinnamon, Cloverfoot, and Blaze as they turned to look. "Shadowkit has had a dream."

Rippletail left his work at the camp wall.

Sparrowtail shook Spirekit from his tail and licked him between the ears. "Go and play with the other kits," he mewed.

"You too." Berryheart got to her paws, nudging Sunkit away.

Dovewing nodded at Pouncekit. "Will you keep the young kits busy while we talk?"

"Can't we listen too?" Pouncekit asked as Sunkit, Hollowkit, and Spirekit hurried toward her.

"You can listen," Dovewing meowed. "But you can't interrupt."

As the kits clustered together, Berryheart padded closer. Ant and Cinnamon sat beside Cloverfoot and blinked at Tigerheart.

"Shadowkit dreamed of the lake," Tigerheart began.

Rippletail pricked his ears. "Are you sure it was the lake?"

"He described it exactly," Tigerheart told him. "He saw the route we must take to get there and says he can lead us to it."

Shadowkit huddled closer to his sisters as the warriors turned to look at him.

"Does he have visions like Spire?" Ant asked.

"I guess he does." Tigerheart felt a rush of pride.

Cloverfoot tipped her head questioningly. "Do you really think a *kit* can lead us home?"

"I think StarClan has chosen to share with us through him," Tigerheart meowed. "We need to know how to get home. Now we have been shown a way. It isn't far. Only a day or two." He looked at Berryheart. "Do you think your kits are ready to make the journey?" Hope rose in his chest as Berryheart's gaze flicked toward her kits. *I'm coming, ShadowClan. I'll be there soon.*

Berryheart shifted her paws uneasily. "Not yet," she meowed. "They're barely weaned."

Shadowkit stiffened, his pelt pricking. "But—"

Tigerheart spoke over him. "The journey is not long." His Clan was so near, and in need of his help. The tug of home felt like a thorn in his heart. "We can carry them most of the way."

"If you must go now, you can leave without us," Berryheart offered.

"No," Tigerheart meowed firmly. "We leave together or not at all."

Dovewing blinked softly at Berryheart. "Will they be ready in a quarter moon?"

Shadowkit flicked his tail. "We must leave before that!"

Dovewing silenced him with a look. "I said no interrupting."

"But it was *my* dream—"

Dovewing cut him off. "You are too young to be telling warriors what to do."

Shadowkit tucked his tail around his paws and stared at the ground.

Dovewing turned back to Berryheart. "A quarter moon?"

"Yes." Berryheart gazed anxiously at her kits. "But only if the weather is fine."

Tigerheart flicked his tail eagerly. "Then it's settled. In a quarter moon, we'll go home."

Dusk turned the thin clouds above the forest pink. A fresh wind stirred the branches. Tigerheart gazed at the moon as the sky darkened around it. The quarter moon had passed. They would leave at dawn. Anxiety fluttered in his belly. What would he find when he reached the lake? *The shadows are fading. He can't keep them together.* He couldn't believe Rowanstar had let ShadowClan fall apart. They must be waiting for him. A forest without ShadowClan would be like a forest without trees.

Dovewing gazed across the camp wall, scanning the woods. "The hunting patrol will be back soon," she meowed. Cloverfoot and Sparrowtail had gone to find prey with Rippletail and Ant. Tigerheart had told them to catch as much as they could; he wanted the party to start their journey with full bellies.

Blaze had left the camp with Cinnamon to hunt for herbs to give them strength. Berryheart was purring as she played moss-ball with Spirekit. Hollowkit and Sunkit were exploring beyond the camp wall. Dovewing could see them now, sniffing at the roots of a beech while Pouncekit and Lightkit bounced around them, trying to catch the moths flitting around the bracken.

"Why don't you go and play with the other kits?" Tigerheart glanced at Shadowkit. The young tom was crouching in the shadow of the brambles, his eyes dark with worry.

Shadowkit ignored his question. "We should leave tonight." His gaze flashed toward the sky. "Tomorrow will be too late."

Tigerheart's belly tightened. "Has StarClan shared something with you?"

Shadowkit looked away. "I wish they had," he murmured. "Then I could explain."

"Explain what?"

"This feeling." Shadowkit shifted his paws beneath him. "We shouldn't be here."

"We leave in the morning," Tigerheart soothed. Sharing a dream world with StarClan must be hard for a kit who was too young to understand even the real world. And yet he couldn't resist probing. "In your vision," he mewed softly, "have you seen a ginger tom?"

Shadowkit glanced at him sharply. "No? Was I meant to?"

"No." Tigerheart shook out his pelt. He was putting too much pressure on the young tom. It wasn't fair to ask him if StarClan had shared any news about Rowanstar. *Shadowkit would have told me if he knew anything.* Why would there be news of his father? Rowanstar had probably solved ShadowClan's problems by now.

"Tigerheart!" Dovewing's mew was taut. He looked at her. She was still watching the kits. Had she spotted the hunting patrol?

"What is it?" He followed her gaze as she raised her eyes to the canopy.

A dark shadow flitted between the branches. Tigerheart's pelt spiked with alarm.

Owl.

It was gliding silently above the kits. His heart lurched as he saw it swoop. With a gasp, he leaped the camp wall and pelted toward Pouncekit. "Hide!" Lightkit and Pouncekit scattered into the bracken. Sunkit stared at him, her eyes wide. Hollowkit seemed rooted to the spot. Tigerheart looked up as he felt the wind from the owl's wings. The owl was so huge it blocked out the sky. Pelt bushing, he saw its talons reach for Hollowkit. He lunged forward and pushed the kit clear, then reared to beat away the owl.

Gray fur flashed at the corner of his eye. Dovewing leaped for the owl, her claws outstretched. With a screech, she tore at its wing as it began to lift. Tigerheart glimpsed its beady eye. It flapped its giant wing, knocking Dovewing away. Tigerheart slashed at its chest, blinded by a flurry of feathers. Then pain pierced his flanks. Talons clutched him as hard as stone. Shock pulsed in his chest as he felt himself lifted. The owl had caught him. He thrashed helplessly in its grip as the earth fell away from his paws. Wind rushed around him as the owl rose among the trees and glided between the branches. A moment later the trees were below him. Tigerheart struggled for breath as air rushed around him. Dizzy with terror, he stared as the ground disappeared into shadow.

Dovewing and Berryheart were screeching. Their cries echoed far below. The kits mewled in terror. Panic shrilled beneath his pelt. Numb with fear, Tigerheart twisted between the owl's talons and swung his paws around. Claws stretched out, he sliced at the owl's belly. The owl screeched in pain and loosened its grip.

Tigerheart felt himself slipping from its talons. His heart leaped to his throat. Wind battered his pelt as he fell, his thoughts reeling. He flailed, grasping at nothing. Then branches whipped his face and battered his flanks as he dropped through the canopy. He saw tree trunks blur around him, and then he hit the ground.

The thump of earth against his chest knocked the breath from him.

Then everything went dark.

CHAPTER 34

❧

Blazing pain dragged Tigerheart into consciousness. Agony seared in his chest and seemed to reach through his body to the tip of each hair on his pelt. He wanted to hide in sleep, but pain forced him awake. Reluctantly, he opened his eyes. He was lying on his side, paws stretched in front of him. Around him, night had swallowed the forest.

"Tigerheart." Relief throbbed in Dovewing's mew. He felt her muzzle sink into his neck fur, and he groaned at the weight of it. She jerked away. "Can you move?"

Fighting pain, Tigerheart rolled onto his paws and forced himself up. The world spun as he fought for breath. Stone seemed to grip his chest, while rats gnawed inside his belly. He collapsed.

"Are his legs broken?" Rippletail thrust his muzzle close. He sounded scared.

"Let me see." Cinnamon ducked closer and began to run her trembling paws over his pelt.

Their voices sounded distant. Through the fog of pain, Tigerheart became aware of cats around him. Cloverfoot, Rippletail, and Sparrowtail clustered beside Ant and Blaze.

Hollowkit, Sunkit, and Spirekit hid behind Berryheart. The queen stared at Tigerheart, rigid with shock. Lightkit, Pouncekit, and Shadowkit stood beside Dovewing, fear glittering in their eyes.

Cinnamon sat back on her haunches. "I can't feel any broken bones." She lowered her voice so that Tigerheart had to strain to hear. "But there's swelling in his belly."

"What does that mean?" Dovewing whispered in panic.

"Something is broken inside." Cinnamon's gaze darkened.

"Can you do anything?" Dovewing was trembling.

"I can give him thyme for the shock," Cinnamon murmured.

Dovewing stared at her. "Didn't you learn anything else while you were with the guardian cats?"

Cinnamon stared back helplessly. Dovewing's eyes flashed with frustration. She turned to Blaze. "What about you? You worked with Spiresight. Did he teach you anything?"

Blaze blinked at her nervously. "We never had to treat injuries like this."

Cloverfoot caught Tigerheart's eye. "He's probably just badly shaken. Let him rest."

He heard the lie in her mew. *I'm going to die.* He tried to focus on Dovewing, fear flickering beyond the pain. *Don't let the kits see.*

Dovewing nudged Shadowkit forward. "Can you treat him?" She stared desperately at the young tom. "You share dreams with StarClan. They can tell you what to do."

Shadowkit blinked at her, then looked in panic at

Tigerheart. "I don't know," he whimpered.

Cinnamon eyed Dovewing sternly and wrapped her tail around Shadowkit. "How could a kit so young know how to fix him?"

Dovewing's eyes misted with grief. "Someone has to help him!" She looked at the stars. "This can't be happening."

Tigerheart struggled to speak. So little breath! *I'm sorry.* For a moment, grief clouded the pain that scorched from his belly to his chest. He was breaking Dovewing's heart. And the kits'. They watched, their eyes round with fear. He tried to meet their gaze.

"You saved Hollowkit." Berryheart's breath bathed his muzzle. She was leaning close. "How can I ever thank you?"

For a moment, the memory flashed in Tigerheart's mind. Hollowkit had weighed so little when he'd pushed him clear of the owl's talons. Terror flooded him as he remembered the claws curling around his flanks and the ground falling away. He closed his eyes, trying to block out the thoughts, wishing he could block out the pain, seeking the refuge of sleep.

"No!" Paws shook him. Dovewing was glaring into his eyes. "You mustn't sleep!" Determination hardened her gaze. Grief was gone. Her green eyes were clear with purpose. "We're going to get you to a medicine cat."

"How?" Rippletail gasped in shock.

Dovewing ignored the tabby tom. She was glaring at Shadowkit. "How far is it to the lake?"

"I d-don't know." Shadowkit flinched from her. "There's the Twolegplace and the water and the moor."

"Tigerheart said no more than two days' walk," Cloverfoot reminded her.

Dovewing was still glaring at Shadowkit. "Is that what it looked like in your dream?" she snapped.

Pouncekit darted to her brother's side. "Don't scare him." She stared defiantly at her mother. "He'll help if he can."

Dovewing shifted her paws, taking a deep, slow breath. "You're right. I'm sorry, Shadowkit."

Tigerheart could hear that she was forcing herself to be calm. She blurred in front of him. The frozen forest seemed to whisper around him. He could smell frost and imagined it creeping across the grass toward him. He pictured it stealing over his body and drawing the last drop of warmth from his pelt. Tiredness pulled him deeper into the earth.

"Stay awake, Tigerheart." Dovewing's muzzle was beside his. Her voice was soft. "We're going to save you. I can't lose you. Not after all we've been through. There's so much left for us to do together. Our future is beside the lake. We always knew that. I won't let that future be snatched away from us now." Her gaze fixed on his. "Do you want to live?"

"Yes." He shuddered as he breathed.

"Then you have to get to your paws." She straightened and swished her tail. "We have to leave now. We're going to the lake."

"He can't walk that far!" Sparrowtail's eyes widened.

Cloverfoot stepped forward. "He can if we help him."

"It's his only chance." Dovewing looked around the cats, her eyes glittering as though half pleading, half demanding.

Tigerheart felt a rush of love for her and pushed himself to his paws. He swallowed back the agonized wail that wanted to escape from his throat. He wasn't going to let his kits know how much he hurt.

Rippletail leaned against one flank. Sparrowtail pressed against the other. Together they lifted him so that his paws barely skimmed the grass as they began to walk forward. Blind with pain as they moved him, he tried to focus. Trapped in a tunnel of agony, he kept his gaze ahead. The tunnel would end with the lake. He had to make it.

He lost sense of time. Earth passing beneath his paws. Flashes of starlight. Staggering pain. The brush of fresh pelts against his flanks as the other cats took turns to support him. And then dawn. Light seeped across the land. He half expected the rising sun to lift the white-hot agony from his limbs. But the pain stayed, obscuring his thoughts, blocking his gaze.

How long could he bear it? Sometimes he closed his eyes and let his campmates carry him, but each time, Dovewing thrust her muzzle against his and hissed, "You can't sleep, Tigerheart. Wake up!"

There was such power in her mew. He fed off it like a starving kit, sucking strength from her, holding it deep inside. For a few wonderful moments, it even blocked the pain.

And then he could smell water. "The lake?" He grunted as his campmates lowered him gently to the ground. He gazed across the grass. Birch trees lined a small stretch of water. Hope flickered in his chest.

"We're not there yet." Dovewing was beside him. "But look." She lifted his chin toward the horizon. A hill rose from the valley, and he recognized WindClan's moor, bending its back toward the sky like the spine of a cat. Through the stabbing in his chest, he felt joy flood his heart. "Home," he whispered.

He felt Dovewing's cheek warm against his. "Home," she breathed.

"Why have we stopped?" Tigerheart tried to make out the others. They were padding away, into the long grass that surrounded the water.

"They've gone to hunt," Dovewing told him. "We need to eat."

"The kits?" He looked around, searching for Pouncekit, Lightkit, and Shadowkit. They were crouching in the grass a few tail-lengths away. "Come here," he called hoarsely.

They looked up and stared at him with wide, frightened eyes.

"It's all right." Dovewing reassured them softly. "You can come near."

Tigerheart saw reluctance in their movements as they padded toward him. "There's nothing to be scared of."

"Are you dying?" Pouncekit asked tremulously as she reached him.

He reached a paw out to touch hers. "I can't die now." He fought for air. "Home is so near."

"You'll get well, won't you?" Lightkit's eyes misted with fear.

Shadowkit pressed against his flank. "You promised to show us the pine forest."

"I still will," Tigerheart promised, focusing through a fresh wave of pain.

Berryheart hovered nearby, her kits clustering around her. "I can try to find some poppy seeds," she meowed hopefully. "They'll be hard to find in leafbare, but they'd help his pain."

"No," Dovewing meowed sharply. "Poppy seeds would make him sleep. He mustn't sleep."

As she spoke, Blaze bounded toward her, a mouse dangling from his jaws. He dropped it in front of her. "For Tigerheart," he meowed. "To give him strength." He headed back into the long grass.

Dovewing settled beside Tigerheart and began carefully to strip flesh from the mouse's carcass.

Tigerheart smelled the warm scent of fresh-kill. "Share it with the kits," he murmured. "They like mouse."

Dovewing was chewing a lump of meat. She took it from between her teeth with her paw and pressed it to Tigerheart's mouth as though he were a kit. "Eat it," she ordered.

He took the morsel and let it sit on his tongue. He closed his eyes as he struggled to swallow. Pain seared his flanks at the effort. He turned his face away as Dovewing tried to give him more. "Give it to the kits."

Exhausted, he closed his eyes.

"Don't sleep!" Dovewing pulled his muzzle toward her. She searched his gaze desperately, as though reaching for something she could not see. "Remember before the cats of the

Dark Forest came, when we used to meet on the ShadowClan border?"

He struggled to recall the memory as she went on.

"You were so cocky and sure of yourself." She purred.

"You were such a goody-four-paws," he teased, his words hardly more than a breath.

"And the time in the Dark Forest when . . ."

Her mew faded as he drifted into dream. Darkness swirled around him. Stars sparkled, and he opened his eyes and saw sunlit meadows, lush with the richness of greenleaf. His paws pressed into soft grass. Pain faded, distant now, as though pushed beyond the bright green horizon.

A tom padded over the rolling slope, his orange pelt like flame against the grass.

Tigerheart recognized him at once. His heart leaped. "Rowanstar!" His father looked so sleek and strong. He was once more the noble warrior Tigerheart remembered from his kithood. He hurried to meet him. "Is ShadowClan safe?"

Rowanstar stopped and met his gaze, his green eyes flashing. "I'm Rowanclaw now."

Tigerheart frowned, confused. "Why?" How could a Clan leader lose his name?

"I forgive you for leaving." Rowanclaw's gaze fixed unwaveringly on Tigerheart.

Shame flashed hot beneath Tigerheart's pelt. *I left my Clan.* He'd forgotten. The pain of the fall had blotted out memory. "I had to," he blurted. "I was blocking the sun. I needed to give you space to make the shadows strong again."

"There's no need to explain." Rowanclaw's gaze was gentle now. No recrimination flickered there. "Now that I'm with StarClan, I understand. I see it all, and everything makes sense."

Tigerheart's thoughts jumbled. "You're . . . dead?" He felt sunshine on his pelt. A warm breeze tugged at his fur. "Is this StarClan?" Grief swamped Tigerheart, but he wasn't sure whether it was pain at the loss of his father or at being here, separated from Dovewing and his kits. "Am I dead too?"

The ground shifted beneath him. Like night rushing in, darkness swallowed the green fields, and Tigerheart found himself engulfed by water. It pulled him down into depths that pressed against his pelt and filled his ears and nose. He twisted, trying to haul himself to the surface. Orange fur moved beside him. *Rowanstar?*

No. The face that floated before him in the cloudy water belonged to Flametail. His brother's eyes were wild with panic. Bubbles drifted from his mouth and nose as he thrashed in desperation, falling ever deeper into the murky gloom.

Tigerheart's lungs burned. As panic lit every hair on fire, he opened his eyes. He was beside the pond once more. Darkness was creeping across the grass, swallowing the meadows around him. Gulping for air, he tried to draw in a shuddering breath. Pain clamped his chest. "I can't breathe," he gasped.

Dovewing crouched beside him, fear sharpening her green gaze. Ant and Cinnamon stared in horror. Cloverfoot, Rippletail, and Sparrowtail watched with dark, round eyes while Berryheart tried to shield her kits.

"ShadowClan." Tigerheart felt darkness pressing at the edges of his thoughts. Rowanstar was dead. So much was left undone. "ShadowClan must survive." He stared desperately at Rippletail. "You have to save it."

Dovewing trembled, pressing her flank against his. "Don't die," she whimpered. "Please don't die."

Shadowkit buried his nose in Tigerheart's fur. Pouncekit and Lightkit clung to his neck.

"Take the kits to ThunderClan." Tigerheart breathed the words and could not draw in air for more. *I always loved you.* Peace flooded him. Pain melted. *Dovewing.* He regretted nothing except that he would never see his kits grow into warriors. *I'll watch them from StarClan.* Like a warrior releasing prey, he let go his grip and allowed darkness to swallow him.

CHAPTER 35

❧

Tigerheart shifted on his side. He felt the familiar crunch of pine needles beneath his flank. The scent of sap filled his nose, and he was suddenly aware that he felt no pain. Relief flooded him. He opened his eyes. Pines stretched around him. Fresh brambles sprawled around their trunks. Ferns, green and bright, sprouted where the sun reached through the dark branches. *I'm home.*

And yet the forest was warm. The biting chill of leaf-bare had lifted. Prey-scent hung in the warm air. Confused, Tigerheart clambered to his paws. He'd closed his eyes in cold and pain.

His heart lurched as he understood. *This is StarClan.* He was dead. Before had been a dream, but this was real. He spun, scanning the trees. *Dovewing! Pouncekit, Lightkit, and Shadowkit!* Grief hollowed his heart. This wasn't supposed to happen. He'd promised to take them home.

He ran, skimming the forest floor, racing for sunlight filtering in at the edge of the forest. He reached it, blinking against the brightness as he broke from the trees. In meadows stretching ahead, he saw cats moving over the grass. Panic spiraled in his thoughts. *Take me back!*

He forced his breathing to slow. Drawing in deep breaths, he stopped himself trembling. This was the will of StarClan. He must accept it. He remembered the agony of his final moments. Did he really want to go back to that?

"Tigerheart?" A surprised mew sounded behind him.

He glanced over his shoulder and saw, with a rush of delight, Spiresight padding from the ferns. "You made it to StarClan!" He hurried to greet the black tom, touching his nose to his cheek. "The warrior ceremony worked."

"Yes." Spiresight stopped in front of him. "Thank you."

"Where are the others?" Tigerheart peered past the healer, scanning the forest behind him for more Clanmates. Euphoria suddenly welled in his chest. Why had he been so scared? He would be among old friends here. Dovewing would join him one day, and there would be no pain to endure, no cold to shiver through, no hunger, no responsibility. Here there was no need for leaders or warriors or medicine cats. There would be peace. "Where's Rowanstar—I mean Rowanclaw—and Flametail? They're here, right?"

Spiresight's gaze was troubled. "You mustn't meet them."

Tigerheart blinked at him. "Why?"

"You shouldn't be here."

"But I died."

"Look." Spiresight brushed his paw through the pine needles coating the forest floor. As they stirred, Tigerheart saw an image shimmering below him.

He could see WindClan's moor, crouched like a black cat

against the stone cold of leaf-bare. And beyond it, the lake sparked beneath a chilly sun. *This must be how birds see the land.* "Why are you showing me this?"

"Look closely." Spiresight gazed at the image.

Tigerheart peered harder and glimpsed pelts moving across the moor, trailing like ants through the faded heather. As he focused, the image grew and sharpened, closer now. He recognized the pelts. *Dovewing!* She staggered beside Ant while Rippletail and Sparrowtail flanked them. A shape was draped across their backs. With a jolt, Tigerheart recognized his own pelt. "They're carrying my body!"

Behind the patrol, Berryheart carried her kits on her back, huddled deep into her fur. Pouncekit, Lightkit, and Shadowkit trailed behind, hollow-eyed, while Cinnamon and Cloverfoot shielded them against the biting wind.

Pouncekit stared after Dovewing, her gaze fixed on the body across her mother's back. Tigerheart's chest tightened as he saw pain in the kit's gaze. She'd never looked sad before. Shadowkit stared at his paws. Lightkit's eyes were misted with grief. No cat spoke as they trudged slowly toward the lake.

Tigerheart blinked at Spiresight. "Why are they carrying me home?" It made no sense to make their journey harder. "They should have buried me where I died."

Spiresight gazed back unwavering. "They are not as willing to let go of you as you are to let go of them."

"That's not true!" Tigerheart bridled. "I had no choice."

Spiresight blinked at him. "You have a choice now. It's not your time yet, Tigerheart."

"But my body is broken. I can't go back. It hurt so much. Don't make me go back." Fear sparked beneath his pelt. He couldn't face more pain.

"What about your kits?"

Tigerheart looked down at Pouncekit, Lightkit, and Shadowkit once more. Their shoulders sagged with sorrow only a grown cat should know. Grief crushed his heart. "Dovewing is strong," he told Spiresight. "She's a great mother. She can raise them in ThunderClan, and they will never feel the pull between Clans that we did."

Spiresight stared back bleakly. "Without ShadowClan, there can be no ThunderClan, no WindClan, no RiverClan, no SkyClan. Five Clans or none. ShadowClan needs you, Tigerheart. It's not your time to die. You have to go back."

Tigerheart stared at the healer, his thoughts whirling. Below there was pain and struggle and responsibility. Everything that had weighed his paws while he was alive still waited for him. But so did Dovewing and their kits. Was a life with them worth the hardship of living? Tigerheart pushed away the beguiling murmur that whispered of the prey-rich forest behind him and the sun-drenched meadows ahead. Comfort was for kits. Pouncekit, Lightkit, and Shadowkit deserved to be safe, warm, and well fed. *I am a warrior. It is my duty to suffer for them.* He dipped his head. "You're right," he breathed. "It is not my time. I want to go back."

As he spoke, the forest shifted and blurred. Shadows engulfed him, lifting him up until he was spinning among the stars. He closed his eyes, bracing himself for pain and cold, and drifted down onto chilly stone.

He opened his eyes. The exposed rock beneath his paws stretched toward a night sky on every side. He blinked in surprise as he saw starry cats moving around him. "StarClan?" Their pelts glittered like fire and ice, and they carried the scent of the seasons, stone-cold snow mingled with sweet blossom, leaf musk tinged with sharp sap tang.

"Tigerheart." Rowanclaw stepped forward.

Countless eyes reflected starlight, watching as Rowanclaw padded toward Tigerheart.

"My son." He stopped in front of Tigerheart and gazed with eyes brimming with love. "We knew this day would come."

Tigerheart frowned, puzzled. "You knew I was going to die?"

Rowanclaw tipped his head, blinking gently. "Do you know what happens now?"

Tigerheart shifted his paws, self-conscious under the gaze of so many cats. "I'm . . . I'm being sent back. But how?"

"There is only one way a cat may receive another life." Rowanclaw paused as Tigerheart struggled to understand.

A leadership ceremony! His pelt prickled with anxiety. "I'm not ready!" he blurted. "I'm not strong enough to lead a Clan."

"Really?" Rowanclaw gazed deep into Tigerheart's eyes. Memories shifted as though woken by his father's gaze. He'd persuaded Scorchfur and Juniperclaw to stay with Shadow-Clan. He'd journeyed to the city to find Dovewing and his kits. He'd helped the guardian cats learn how to defend what was theirs. And he'd led his family and his friends home.

Rowanclaw broke their gaze with a blink. "You will never be more ready than you are now." He leaned forward and touched his nose to Tigerheart's head.

Fierce heat seared through Tigerheart's pelt. Flame seemed to burn away his fur like grass in a prairie fire, but he could not flee. His paws were weighted like stones.

"With this life I give you strength. Don't let softness sway you from what must be done for your Clan." Rowanclaw broke away, and the fire subsided, leaving determination burning in Tigerheart's belly.

He opened his eyes, trembling. StarClan watched in stillness, and Tigerheart began to recognize some of their faces. Pinenose, Kinkfur, Flametail. His brother looked so young and strong, his broad shoulders squared as he gazed proudly at Tigerheart.

As Rowanclaw turned away, Kinkfur padded forward.

The ShadowClan elder looked sleek and young. He hardly recognized her. Only the knowing flash in her eyes betrayed her long life. She pressed her nose to his head. "With this life I give you courage. Fear will always pull at your tail, but the courage I give you now will always draw you on."

His body was seized by a hard, fierce agony that stiffened his muscles and left him shaking with shock.

Pinenose was beside him now, touching her nose to his head. "With this life I give you compassion. Love your Clan as you love your kits. Forgive them their flaws and love them even when they fail you."

Warmth flooded his heart and reached deep into his belly.

It snatched his breath with its intensity, and as Pinenose pulled away, he met her gaze and saw the deep affection he'd seen in Dovewing's eyes on the night Pouncekit, Lightkit, and Shadowkit were born. He returned her gaze, hoping she could read the promise in his. *I will.*

Another cat padded from the ranks of starry cats, a familiar face he hadn't spotted yet. A familiar face he had hoped to one day see again—just not in StarClan

Dawnpelt! His sister's eyes shone like stars. Tigerheart wanted to greet her, but he couldn't move or speak. *You really are dead.* He'd suspected, but hadn't been sure until now. Joy and grief seemed to fight within his heart as she touched her nose to his head. "With this life I give you hope. As long as hope burns in your heart, it will burn in the hearts of your Clanmates."

Energy fired through Tigerheart. In his mind he was running, skimming the earth, pines blurring beside him. His heart beat so fast that the breath caught in his throat. As his body shivered in spasm, Dawnpelt padded away, and a ragged she-cat took her place.

"I am Yellowfang, once of ShadowClan."

Tigerheart stared at her, breathless. He'd heard nursery tales of this cat. Exiled by her Clan, betrayed by her son, she'd found sanctuary with ThunderClan before she died. What blessing could she give him?

She leaned close, her breath meaty, and touched her nose to his head. "With this life, I give you forgiveness." Ice seemed to grip Tigerheart's body, freezing him rigid until he could hardly breathe. Pain streaked through him, like stone cracking. And then suddenly it eased, and warmth bathed him once more as Yellowfang went on. "Forgiveness will give you more power than vengeance will ever bring."

As Yellowfang stepped away, a snowy white she-cat padded from the ranks of star-pelted warriors. She nodded to Yellowfang before looking at Tigerheart. "I am Sagewhisker." Her blue eyes sparkled as she leaned close and touched her nose to his head. "With this life, I give you persistence." A bolt of energy, as fierce as lightning, seared through Tigerheart. He stiffened against the pain, but it melted into a soft warmth through which he could feel the strong steady beat of his heart. "Don't let failure sap your determination or rejection change your mind. A true leader tries as many times as it takes to succeed."

"Tigerheart." Littlecloud's mew took Tigerheart by surprise. His heart swelled with joy at seeing the old medicine cat. The familiarity in his bright eyes warmed him. For a moment he remembered what it was like to live in a Clan that was united and strong. "Fear of failure has kept you too long from leadership. But leadership is your destiny, and one that you must embrace if you are to save your Clan. So with this life I give you acceptance. Accept with all your heart what you cannot change, and fear will vanish." As he touched his nose to Tigerheart's head, Tigerheart felt engulfed by peace. The worry that seemed to have pressed on him for moons melted like snow in sunshine. So what if he failed to save his Clan? The only failure was not to try. And all that truly mattered was that, for a while, they had felt cool forest shade on their pelts.

A dark tabby tom stepped into Littlecloud's place. His pelt was patchy, and there were scars on his nose. "I, Raggedstar, give you this life for loyalty." As the tom's nose touched his head, Tigerheart was suddenly aware of the depth of rock beneath his paws. His pads drew in its burning chill until ice seemed to freeze his bones. He twitched as Raggedstar went on. "A leader's loyalty belongs only to his Clan. Let loyalty be your heartbeat, for when it stops, so will you."

Loyalty? Tigerheart's throat tightened. What about Dovewing? She was ThunderClan. What about his kits? Did leadership mean that he would be separated from them? Before he could think any more, Flametail stepped forward.

"I wish I could still walk at your side," Flametail whispered. "I wish I could help you reunite our Clan." Tigerheart felt his brother's breath stir his fur as he touched his head and went on. "With this life I give you love. You have known so much, but still have much to give. Leadership without love will never be enough to draw your Clan from the shadows. Let your heart lead when your head does not know the way." Tenderness surged in Tigerheart's chest, strong and yet fragile, and so fierce that he thought his heart would shatter. He closed his eyes and let the sensation overwhelm him. As he did, grief unfurled inside him. To have found so much and lost so much felt more than he could bear.

Nine lives. The thought burned in his mind as Flametail pulled away. Tigerheart staggered, limp from the intensity of his Clanmates' gifts. He gazed around at the cats he'd known and cats he'd only know once his lives had been used up.

Rowanclaw padded forward once more. He stared gravely at Tigerheart. "This has never been done before. You have already used up one life, but there are eight remaining. Use them as you used the first—with courage and for the good of others."

Raggedstar whisked his tail. "Reunite ShadowClan."

"There must always be five Clans," Dawnpelt meowed. "Where there is sky, thunder, wind, and river, there must also be shadow."

Flametail fixed him with his starlit gaze. "You are the only one who can bring ShadowClan back."

Bring it back? Tigerheart stared at him. "Where has Shadow-Clan gone?"

No cat answered. Instead they lifted their muzzles to the crow-black sky. "Tigerstar! Tigerstar!" The cold night rang with the voices of StarClan as they chanted his new name. The stars in their pelts shimmered and began to shift before his eyes. The cats lost their shape and merged into a great swath of stars. They swirled upward, like leaves caught in a sudden wind and scattered across the wide black sky.

Bring it back? Tigerstar's legs buckled beneath him. As he collapsed onto the cold stone, he saw what must be the Moon-pool shining beside him.

Puddleshine stood next to him, his eyes lighting with joy as Tigerstar looked up at it him. "It worked!"

Tigerstar hesitated, expecting to feel pain. But his body felt stronger than ever. He scrambled to his paws and stared at the medicine cat. "How did I get here?"

Puddleshine nodded toward the lip of the hollow. "Rippletail, Cloverfoot, and the others carried you home. They're waiting for you now."

Tigerstar's belly tightened. "Are Dovewing and the kits with them?" Had she taken them to ThunderClan as he'd told her?

"Every cat is waiting for you." Puddleshine blinked at him, moonlight shimmering in his eyes.

The medicine cat led him along a smooth path that spiraled away from the Moonpool, up to the stone ledge, where the encircling cliffs opened to the glittering night sky. Tigerstar blinked at the stars as he padded over stone dimpled by the paw steps of cats over countless moons. Was StarClan watching his first moments as leader of ShadowClan? *Rowanclaw! Spiresight!* He paused, gazing at the sky. *Are you there?*

"Hurry!" Puddleshine was already waiting at the top of the hollow. "They're anxious to see you." He looked over the edge as Tigerstar reached him.

Tigerstar followed his gaze. A steep jumble of rocks plunged toward a stream below. At the edge of the starlit water, which wound away between moor and forest like a glittering snail track, cats were crowding, their faces lifted toward the hollow. Their wide eyes glittered with wonder as they saw him.

Tigerstar spotted Ant and Cinnamon at the front. Blaze, Rippletail, and Cloverfoot clustered beside them with Berryheart, Sparrowtail and their kits, while the rest of ShadowClan gathered behind. His chest seemed to burst with joy at the sight of so many familiar faces. Scrambling past Puddleshine, he half leaped, half slithered down the rocks and landed lightly on the rough grass beside Ant.

He scanned the crowd, his breath catching in his throat. There was one face he wanted to see above all. "Dovewing!"

She pushed between Rippletail and Cloverfoot. "You're alive!" Her words were little more than a gasp, as though she hardly believed them.

Tigerstar wanted to press his cheek against hers and feel the warmth of her fur, but Cloverfoot wove excitedly between them. "It was Puddleshine's idea to bring you to the Moon-pool and let your nose touch the water so you could share dreams with StarClan."

"But I was dead." Tigerstar stared at them, gratitude swelling in his chest. He could feel the eyes of his Clanmates on him. Was he supposed to address them? What should he say? As he blinked at them, overwhelmed, Shadowkit padded from behind Dovewing. Pouncekit and Lightkit followed, their eyes as wide as moons.

Tigerstar rushed to meet them, pressing his nose to each one in turn, purring loudly. As Pouncekit and Lightkit crowded around him, Shadowkit touched his nose. "Spiresight says this is right."

Tigerstar lapped the tom-kit fiercely between the ears. "I saw him," he mewed. "He's with StarClan."

Shadowkit broke into a purr.

Tigerstar felt fur brush his side. Dovewing's scent billowed around him. Joy flared in his heart. He pressed his cheek against hers. "You've been so brave and strong."

"No more than you," she murmured.

A leader's loyalty belongs only to his Clan. Raggedstar's words suddenly rang in his mind. *I must choose my Clan over Dovewing and the kits.* He pulled away and stared at her, grief stabbing his heart. "Will you go to ThunderClan now?"

Dovewing gazed at him wonderingly. "Why?"

"Your head told you to raise our kits among your Clan, remember?"

"But my heart told me to stay with you." Her gaze clouded with love. "How could I leave, after all we've been through?" She glanced at the kits, who were weaving happily around them. "And how could I deprive our kits of such a wonderful father?" Purring, she thrust her muzzle against his.

Tigerstar closed his eyes and relished her warmth. Paws scuffed the grass around him. He pulled away and saw his Clanmates staring. There was uncertainty in their gazes.

Tawnypelt stepped forward. She flicked her tail toward Cinnamon, Ant, and Blaze. "You've brought back new warriors as well as old."

Tigerstar tried to read her gaze. Was she angry with him?

Tawnypelt looked at Dovewing and the kits. "And it seems we're getting ThunderClan cats too."

He hesitated, conscious of the unease rippling through the pelts of his Clanmates. Then he remembered his leadership ceremony. Strength, courage, compassion, hope, forgiveness, persistence, acceptance, loyalty, and love. These were gifts he carried with him now. He lifted his chin and swung his gaze around the watching cats. Stonewing, Strikestone, and Juniperclaw eyed him warily. "I left you," he meowed evenly. "But now I've returned. I bring with me cats who will make our Clan strong again. Accept them as I accept you. Give them your loyalty as I give you mine. I am ready to lead you."

Silence gripped the hollow. Tigerstar held his breath as he watched his Clanmates.

"Tigerstar!" Juniperclaw's mew was the first to ring through the night air. Snowbird's rose to join it. Stonewing and Scorchfur blinked at Tigerstar, then lifted their muzzles to chant their new leader's name. Within moments the hillside echoed to the call of every cat.

Tawnypelt's muzzle brushed Tigerstar's ear. "There is so much you have missed." Her mew was filled with grief. "The days since you left have been dark. And there are darker days ahead."

Tigerstar's pelt prickled along his spine as he drew back and met her gaze. "Let them come." He lifted his tail. "We will be ready to face them."

READ ON FOR AN

EXCLUSIVE MANGA ADVENTURE . . .

CREATED BY
ERIN HUNTER

WRITTEN BY
DAN JOLLEY

ART BY
JAMES L. BARRY

NEEDLETAIL FOUGHT SO FIERCELY AGAINST RIVERCLAN YESTERDAY.

WHAT IF SHE ACTUALLY IS LOYAL TO DARKTAIL, AND HIS KIN? LOYAL IN HER HEART?

IT'S TOO LATE FOR QUESTIONS NOW.

I'M ALIVE, AND I NEED TO STAY THAT WAY.

JUST... DELIVER MY MESSAGE? PLEASE? AND THEN GET OUT.

IF YOU CAN.

I'LL MAKE SURE TO TELL THEM, BERRYHEART. GOOD LUCK.

HOW MANY TIMES HAS THE SUN RISEN AND SET SINCE I LEFT THE CAMP? SINCE I LEFT MY MATE AND OUR DAUGHTER?

MOST OF A MOON. THE GROWLING IN MY BELLY MAKES IT FEEL LONGER THAN THAT.

BUT IF SPARROWTAIL AND NEEDLETAIL MAKE IT OUT...

I HAVE NO CHOICE. I'VE GOT TO WAIT FOR THEM.

WAIT--IS THAT...?

IS THAT PAWSTEPS?

CAN'T TAKE ANY CHANCES--

CAN'T LET A ROGUE FIND ME OUT HERE ALONE.

COULD BE ANY CAT, COMING ALONG THE PATH. COULD BE--

SPARROWTAIL!

BERRYHEART! THANK STARCLAN I FOUND YOU!

COME DOWN. I, UH... A LOT HAS HAPPENED SINCE YOU LEFT.

SO NOW DARKTAIL HAS NEEDLETAIL HELD PRISONER. THERE'S NO WAY TO GET TO HER. THERE ARE TOO MANY ROGUES.

BERRYHEART, WE NEED TO GET AWAY. FAR AWAY. THE CAMP'S GOING TO PIECES. IT'S NOT SAFE TO BE THIS CLOSE.

SO MANY TWOLEGS! WHAT ARE THEY DOING?

I DON'T KNOW! I'VE NEVER SEEN ANYTHING LIKE THIS!

IT MUST BE SOME KIND OF...OF HUNTING PATROL!

COME ON! COME ON!

WHATEVER IT IS, WE DON'T WANT TO HAVE ANYTHING TO DO WITH IT!

RIGHT. RIGHT.

"WE'D BETTER STEER CLEAR OF THE TWOLEG PATH, AT LEAST FOR A WHILE. LET'S JUST KEEP HEADING NORTH."

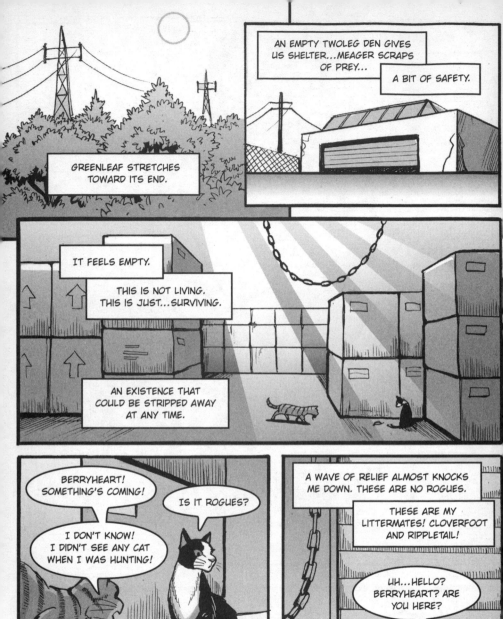

AN EMPTY TWOLEG DEN GIVES US SHELTER...MEAGER SCRAPS OF PREY...

A BIT OF SAFETY.

GREENLEAF STRETCHES TOWARD ITS END.

IT FEELS EMPTY.

THIS IS NOT LIVING. THIS IS JUST...SURVIVING.

AN EXISTENCE THAT COULD BE STRIPPED AWAY AT ANY TIME.

BERRYHEART! SOMETHING'S COMING!

IS IT ROGUES?

I DON'T KNOW! I DIDN'T SEE ANY CAT WHEN I WAS HUNTING!

THE SOFT SCUFF OF PAWSTEPS DRAWS CLOSER...

CLOSER... UNTIL--

A WAVE OF RELIEF ALMOST KNOCKS ME DOWN. THESE ARE NO ROGUES.

THESE ARE MY LITTERMATES! CLOVERFOOT AND RIPPLETAIL!

UH...HELLO? BERRYHEART? ARE YOU HERE?

CHAPTER ONE

Swiftcub pounced after the vulture's shadow, but it flitted away too quickly to follow. Breathing hard, he pranced back to his pride. *I saw that bird off our territory,* he thought, delighted. *No rot-eater's going to come near Gallantpride while I'm around!*

The pride needed him to defend it, Swiftcub thought, picking up his paws and strutting around his family. Why, right now they were all half asleep, dozing and basking in the shade of the acacia trees. The most energetic thing the other lions were doing was lifting their heads to groom their nearest neighbors, or their own paws. They had no *idea* of the threat Swiftcub had just banished.

I might be only a few moons old, but my father is the strongest, bravest lion in Bravelands. And I'm going to be just like him!

"Swiftcub!"

The gentle but commanding voice snapped him out of his

dreams of glory. He came to a halt, turning and flicking his ears at the regal lioness who stood over him.

"Mother," he said, shifting on his paws.

"Why are you shouting at vultures?" Swift scolded him fondly, licking at his ears. "They're nothing but scavengers. Come on, you and your sister can play later. Right now you're supposed to be practicing hunting. And if you're going to catch anything, you'll need to keep your eyes on the prey, not on the sky!"

"Sorry, Mother." Guiltily he padded after her as she led him through the dry grass, her tail swishing. The ground rose gently, and Swiftcub had to trot to keep up. The grasses tickled his nose, and he was so focused on trying not to sneeze, he almost bumped into his mother's haunches as she crouched.

"Oops," he growled.

Valor shot him a glare. His older sister was hunched a little to the left of their mother, fully focused on their hunting practice. Valor's sleek body was low to the ground, her muscles tense; as she moved one paw forward with the utmost caution, Swiftcub tried to copy her, though it was hard to keep up on his much shorter legs. One creeping pace, then two. Then another.

I'm being very quiet, just like Valor. I'm going to be a great hunter. He slunk up alongside his mother, who remained quite still.

"There, Swiftcub," she murmured. "Do you see the burrows?"

He did, now. Ahead of the three lions, the ground rose up even higher, into a bare, sandy mound dotted with small shadowy holes. As Swiftcub watched, a small nose and whiskers poked out, testing the air. The meerkat emerged completely, stood up on its hind legs, and stared around. Satisfied, it stuck out a pink tongue and began to groom its chest, as more meerkats appeared beyond it. Growing in confidence, they scurried farther away from their burrows.

"Careful now," rumbled Swift. "They're very quick. Go!"

Swiftcub sprang forward, his little paws bounding over the ground. Still, he wasn't fast enough to outpace Valor, who was far ahead of him already. A stab of disappointment spoiled his excitement, and suddenly it was even harder to run fast, but he ran grimly after his sister.

The startled meerkats were already doubling back into their holes. Stubby tails flicked and vanished; the bigger leader, his round dark eyes glaring at the oncoming lions, was last to twist and dash underground. Valor's jaws snapped at his tail, just missing.

"Sky and stone!" the bigger cub swore, coming to a halt in a cloud of dust. She shook her head furiously and licked her jaws. "I nearly had it!"

A rumble of laughter made Swiftcub turn. His father, Gallant, stood watching them. Swiftcub couldn't help but feel the usual twinge of awe mixed in with his delight. Black-maned and huge, his sleek fur glowing golden in the sun, Gallant would have been intimidating if Swiftcub hadn't known and loved him so well. Swift rose to her paws and greeted the great lion affectionately, rubbing his maned neck with her head.

"It was a good attempt, Valor," Gallant reassured his

daughter. "What Swift said is true: meerkats are *very* hard to catch. You were so close—one day you'll be as fine a hunter as your mother." He nuzzled Swift and licked her neck.

"*I* wasn't anywhere near it," grumbled Swiftcub. "I'll never be as fast as Valor."

"Oh, you will," said Gallant. "Don't forget, Valor's a whole year older than you, my son. You're getting bigger and faster every day. Be patient!" He stepped closer, leaning in so his great tawny muzzle brushed Swiftcub's own. "That's the secret to stalking, too. Learn patience, and one day you too will be a *very* fine hunter."

"I hope so," said Swiftcub meekly.

Gallant nuzzled him. "Don't doubt yourself, my cub. You're going to be a great lion and the best kind of leader: one who keeps his own pride safe and content, but puts fear into the heart of his strongest enemy!"

That does sound good! Feeling much better, Swiftcub nodded. Gallant nipped affectionately at the tufty fur on top of his head and padded toward Valor.

Swiftcub watched him proudly. *He's right, of course. Father knows everything! And I will be a great hunter, I will. And a brave, strong leader—*

A tiny movement caught his eye, a scuttling shadow in his father's path.

A scorpion!

Barely pausing to think, Swiftcub sprang, bowling between his father's paws and almost tripping him. He skidded to a halt right in front of Gallant, snarling at the small sand-yellow scorpion. It paused, curling up its barbed tail and raising its pincers in threat.

"No, Swiftcub!" cried his father.

Swiftcub swiped his paw sideways at the creature, catching its plated shell and sending it flying into the long grass.

All four lions watched the grass, holding their breath, waiting for a furious scorpion to reemerge. But there was no stir of movement. It must have fled. Swiftcub sat back, his heart suddenly banging against his ribs.

"Skies above!" Gallant laughed. Valor gaped, and Swift dragged her cub into her paws and began to lick him roughly.

"Mother . . ." he protested.

"Honestly, Swiftcub!" she scolded him as her tongue swept across his face. "Your father might have gotten a nasty sting from that creature—but *you* could have been killed!"

"You're such an idiot, little brother," sighed Valor, but there was admiration in her eyes.

Gallant and Swift exchanged proud looks. "Swift," growled Gallant, "I do believe the time has come to give our cub his true name."

Swift nodded, her eyes shining. "Now that we know what kind of lion he is, I think you're right."

Gallant turned toward the acacia trees, his tail lashing, and gave a resounding roar.

It always amazed Swiftcub that the pride could be lying half asleep one moment and alert the very next. Almost before Gallant had finished roaring his summons, there was a rustle of grass, a crunch of paws on dry earth, and the rest of Gallantpride appeared, ears pricked and eyes bright with curiosity. Gallant huffed in greeting, and the twenty lionesses and young lions of his pride spread out in a circle around him, watching and listening intently.

Gallant looked down again at Swiftcub, who blinked and glanced away, suddenly rather shy. "Crouch down," murmured the great lion.

When he obeyed, Swiftcub felt his father's huge paw rest on his head.

"Henceforth," declared Gallant, "this cub of mine will no longer be known as Swiftcub. He faced a dangerous foe without hesitation and protected his pride. His name, now and forever, is Fearless Gallantpride."

It was done so quickly, Swiftcub felt dizzy with astonishment. *I have my name! I'm Fearless. Fearless Gallantpride!*

All around him, his whole family echoed his name, roaring their approval. Their deep cries resonated across the grasslands.

"Fearless Gallantpride!"

"Welcome, Fearless, son of Gallant!"

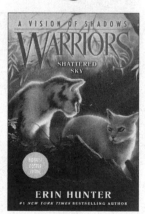
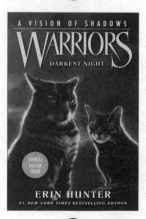

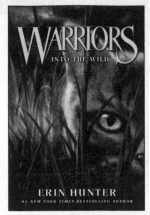
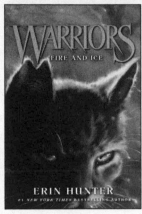

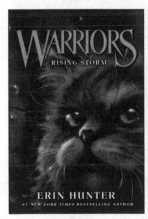

WARRIORS: THE NEW PROPHECY

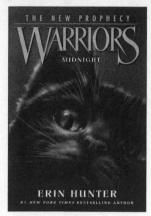

1

2

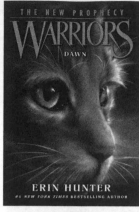

3

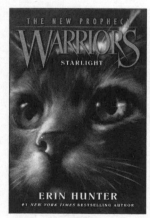

4

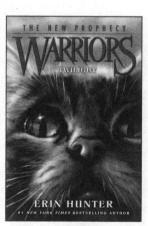

5

6

In the second series, follow the next generation of heroic cats as they set off on a quest to save the Clans from destruction.

HARPER
An Imprint of HarperCollinsPublishers

www.warriorcats.com

WARRIORS : POWER OF THREE

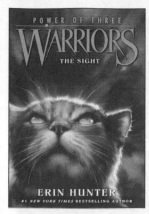

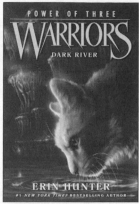

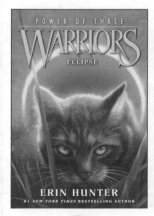

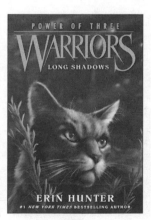

In the third series, Firestar's grandchildren begin their training as warrior cats. Prophecy foretells that they will hold more power than any cats before them.

An Imprint of HarperCollinsPublishers

www.warriorcats.com

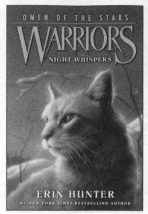

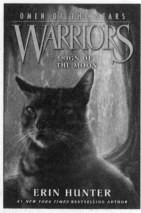

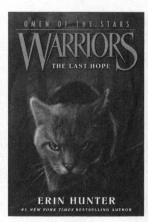

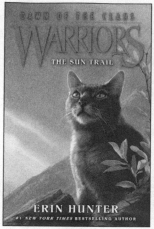

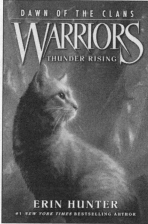

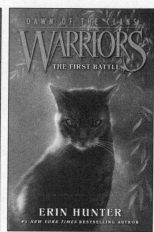

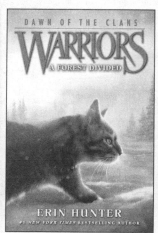

WARRIORS : SUPER EDITIONS

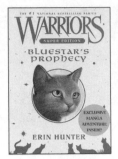

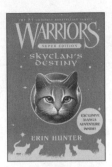

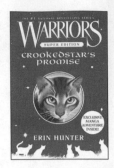

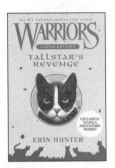

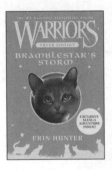

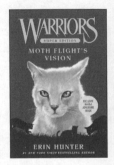

These extra-long, stand-alone adventures will take
you deep inside each of the Clans with thrilling tales
featuring the most legendary warrior cats.

WARRIORS: BONUS STORIES

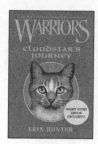

Discover the untold stories of the warrior cats and Clans
when you download the separate ebook novellas—or read
them in four paperback bind-ups!

HARPER
An Imprint of HarperCollinsPublishers

www.warriorcats.com

WARRIORS: FIELD GUIDES

FOR THE ULTIMATE FAN!

Delve deeper into the Clans with these Warriors field guides.

HARPER
An Imprint of HarperCollins*Publishers*

www.warriorcats.com

ALSO BY ERIN HUNTER:
SURVIVORS

Survivors: The Original Series

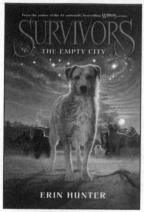
1

2

3

4

5

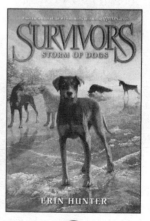
6

The time has come for dogs to rule the wild.

SURVIVORS: THE GATHERING DARKNESS

1

2

3

4

In the **second series**, tensions are rising within the pack.

SURVIVORS: BONUS STORIES

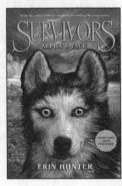

Download the three separate ebook novellas or
read them in one paperback bind-up!

HARPER
An Imprint of HarperCollinsPublishers

www.survivorsdogs.com